HUNGRY HEARTS

There was a severed head in the stainless steel kitchen sink. What looked like viscera sat in a lumpy mess on the draining board – looking closely, Rick thought he could make out a lung, a heart, lengths of looped intestine. He tried to look away but was unable to unlock his gaze from the nightmare. He stared at the head. Its eyes were gone, the sockets smooth and empty. There were teeth marks in one cheek – they couldn't be anything else – and the nose was gone.

"Cannibals," said D.I. Harper, his voice thin and reedy, the exact opposite of his build. "*Cannibals.*" He began to repeat the word, not even aware that he was doing so. Two other officers stood against the wall. One of them was covering his mouth with his hand and staring down at his feet. His shoes were covered in vomit.

The fridge door hung open, its hinges broken. The shelves were sparsely stocked: a few pieces of cling-filmed meat, half a pineapple, an opened can of baked beans. At the bottom, where the salad shelves should be, there was an open space occupied by several human hands.

"Sir... this isn't terrorism. What's going on?"

An Abaddon Books™ Publication
www.abaddonbooks.com
abaddon@rebellion.co.uk

First published in 2009 by Abaddon Books™, Rebellion Intellectual
Property Limited, Riverside House, Osney Mead, Oxford, OX2 0ES, UK.

10 9 8 7 6 5 4 3 2 1

Editor: Jonathan Oliver
Cover: Greg Staples
Design: Simon Parr & Luke Preece
Marketing and PR: Keith Richardson
Creative Director and CEO: Jason Kingsley
Chief Technical Officer: Chris Kingsley

Distributed in the US by National Book Network, 4501 Forbes
Boulevard, Lanham, MD 20706, USA

ISBN: 978-1-906735-26-5

Printed in Denmark by Norhaven A/S

TOMES OF THE DEAD

Hungry Hearts

GARY McMAHON

Abaddon
Books

WWW.ABADDONBOOKS.COM

For John Worley
The best man in any company...

Thanks must go to the following good souls:
My wife for putting up with my insanity during
the writing of this book.
My mother-in-law for not getting angry when
I told her I'd killed her.
Stephen Bacon, Simon Bestwick and Gary Fry for help,
support, encouragement and invaluable friendship.

"I will knock down the Gates of the Netherworld, I will smash the door posts, and leave the doors flat down, And will let the dead go up to eat the living! And the dead will outnumber the living!"

-The Epic of Gilgamesh

PART ONE

The End Of It All

"Truly, we are living in apocalyptic times."

-Unnamed presidential advisor, the Bush administration, 2008

CHAPTER ONE

Rick Nutman tried hard to breathe. It was something that should have been easy, a natural function of his highly trained body, yet he was currently unable to carry out the technique without feeling as if he were submerged in ten feet of dark water. The riot gear was heavy, constricting, and he was not used to being so trussed up.

Come on, he thought. *Get through this, get a grip. It's the real thing, not a training exercise, and if you don't act fast you might not see daylight. Or Sally... you might never see Sally again.*

This final thought galvanised him and suddenly he remembered how to breathe: his lungs sucked in the cold air, filled up, and then pushed the whole lot out again. He saw pinpoint stars, but when he looked up into the sky, at the real stars suspended in the black night, his vision began to clear.

"You okay, mate?" Trevor Hutchinson, the man at his side, narrowed his blue eyes in concern. He cocked his head, adjusted the grip on his Glock 17, and smiled.

"Yeah," said Rick. "Just... had a moment – you know?"

Hutch nodded once and switched his gaze back to the stocky grey tower block they were supposed to be watching. Nothing moved in the darkness, but several lights were on inside the building, bleeding patches of sickly yellow onto the ruined lawn outside the main entrance. Rick thought they looked like pools of urine.

The air was charged with a strange combination of fear and excitement. Everyone was tense; they just wanted to get into it, to start the action. A lone aeroplane flew overhead, its wide contrail glowing white against the dark and star-flecked sky. Rick watched as it traced a line across the flat black heavens, wondering where it was headed. Then, abruptly, the plane began to descend. He knew there were no airports in the immediate area – Leeds/Bradford was a few miles away, and certainly too far for the plane to be dipping in so suddenly to land. Puzzled, he began to stand. Hutch placed a firm hand on his shoulder. His grip was like steel pincers.

Rick glanced at the other man. Hutch shook his head, eyes narrow slits in the dark smudge of his face. "Best sit tight. It's all going off very soon." He held Rick's gaze until Rick relaxed. They knew each other about as well as any two men could, had trained together, fought together and become disillusioned with army life together. It was Hutch who'd convinced him to try for the police after his medical discharge from the Parachute Regiment.

The plane's unusual descent forgotten, Rick stared at the building they were here to raid. It was a squat concrete structure; a block of forty-odd flats spread over three floors. Their targets were ensconced on the first floor – they knew that from several intelligence reports gathered over the past few months – and the rest of the building was occupied by various low-level drug dealers and long-term benefit claimants who did illegal Black Market work on the side. This was a rough area; no one who lived here was totally clean. That's what DI Harper always said: in places like this, even the innocent are guilty. It was a harsh doctrine, but one that had apparently saved the DI's skin on more than one occasion.

A radio belched static. Someone coughed softly. The sound of hardcore dance music drifted in from somewhere nearby. There must be a party going on somewhere in the neighbourhood.

Hutch's hand still clutched Rick's arm. His friend had forgotten to take it away. Rick felt comforted by the proximity. Tonight was his first time out with the Armed Response Unit, but not his first time in the thick of the action. In the army, he'd served in places like Afghanistan and Iraq, so knew a lot about the tension and pressure of warfare. But this was different: it was at home, in England, not some far-flung war zone where the enemy wore black turbans and spoke in another language. These home-grown enemies were much harder to identify.

Distant sirens wailed like neutered choirboys, the emergency vehicles they heralded heading towards another fight in another part of Leeds. These were tough times: global economic slowdown, crime figures up through the roof, domestic violence on the increase, drugs and teen gangs ruling the streets. Rick was no mug; he knew what it was like out here, in the midst of it all, but to actually confront it was another matter entirely. He hoped he was up to the challenge.

He thought again of Sally, his wife of less than a year, and then pushed her pretty face as far as he could from his mind. She didn't belong here, with this shit. She represented what little good there was left in the world.

Someone whispered impatiently behind him, urging things to progress, and quickly. Rick knew how the man felt: the anticipation was almost unbearable. A woman's voice yelled through an open window, her words slurred and difficult to understand: something about spilling beer on the carpet. Someone sniggered. Hutch turned his head and glared at the offending officer.

They were crouched behind cars in the parking bays out front of the building. Another smaller team of men was hidden at the back of the block of flats. The plan was that their unit would storm the front of the building and enter through the main doors, then rush up to the second floor. The secondary unit would storm the rear and cordon off the ground floor, stopping anyone from exiting. It was a technique they'd carried out countless times in training, but only the superior officers had ever used it in the field. Both units were made up of a fair number of rookies, their first time out after months of training. Despite this being a suspected terrorist raid, intelligence led them to believe that there were only three suspects hiding out in the building.

In at the deep end, thought Rick, smiling despite the tension. It had been the same in the army. All the training in the world could not add up to the single thrilling-terrifying experience of a real-life operation. It set apart the men from the boys, the tough guys from the pretenders. Rick had proved himself several times in action, yet still he was afraid. He'd learned to use that fear, to focus it and direct it inward, where it became a vital strength rather than a debilitating weakness.

"Just waiting for the order," muttered Hutch, almost to himself. He'd taken his hand away. Rick almost missed the human contact.

He took a deep breath, held it... held it... then finally let it out. Swallowing the fear felt good. His hands were no longer shaking. He was ready.

As he watched, a small, thin cat walked coolly across the grass verge a few yards in front of him. The cat paused, glanced over at the crouching men, and then moved away, unconcerned.

Off to Rick's left, he caught sight of movement. A lone Constable ran, bent at the waist, from his hiding place to the corner of an adjacent building, where the command centre had been set up in an unmarked van. The van doors squealed open, the sound too loud in all that silence. Then, softer, they clunked shut.

Not long now. We're almost there.

A strange calmness descended upon him, coating him in a cool, dry layer. He was used to this from his time in the field. Once, during Operation Mountain Thrust, just before the convoy he was travelling in was bombed and came under fire from a small group of Afghan Taliban forces, he'd taken the weird sensation to be a warning, an indication that trouble was coming. The American forces leading them into the foothills to root out insurgents had sustained severe casualties, but because of Rick's sudden intuition his unit had come away relatively unscathed.

That moment of insight had saved his life. Now, in this grubby Yorkshire suburb, he took it to be a sense of calm before the storm.

When the order came he did not even hear it. Just a burst of rapid-fire static from his radio as everyone around him began to move in a rehearsed formation. Boots made little sound on the concrete footpath; voices were silent. Rick drew his Glock and remembered the choreography he'd been taught. He slipped into place alongside Hutch, who glanced at him and grinned.

The man at the head of the formation – Rick thought he might be called Tennant – ran silently towards at the unlocked double doors. He was a big bloke, and when he hit the glass barriers they flew open. Tennant was moving so fast that he almost fell but managed to keep his footing. He ducked in under the stairs, pistol up, and scanned the perimeter. All clear. The men who'd followed him in fanned out from the doors and began to climb the stairs, moving from half landing to half landing and checking the area before overlapping each other in a quick ascent.

A door opened on the first floor. A black face peered out, eyes white as two dabs of flour, and then the door quickly closed. The sound of locks being shot echoed along the landing, louder than the silent assault. Pre-agreed hand signals were used to direct team members to their positions on the second floor. Rick, being the newest and least experienced member, hung back with Hutch at the head of the stairs. A door to his left opened and a small boy stood there in his pyjamas, clutching a grubby teddy bear by one ear. The boy's face was so dirty that Rick cold not even guess at his ethnicity. The interior of the flat behind him was dark. The hallway was clotted with what looked like building rubble – bricks and random lengths of timber.

Rick smiled.

The boy stared, his eyes wide but not afraid, barely even curious. He went to take a step forward but Rick shook his head and moved quickly towards the boy, pushing him back into the flat. The boy stuck out his tongue and slammed the door in Rick's face. Then, from the safety of the flat, he screamed a single word, louder than he looked able: "Pigs!" And he kept screaming it, over and over again.

That was the moment when everything began to go wrong.

Someone screamed "*Go-go-go!*" and a large man – not Tennant this time, but someone else, someone even bigger – ran at the door of number twenty-four, using a battering ram. It took three hits close to the door handle for the door to buckle, and when it did the sound was like an explosive charge. The man stepped aside, allowing three officers armed with Heckler and Koch G3 machine guns to run into the flat past the flopping door, weapons held at chest height, faces white, mouths mere slits under the strengthened glass visors of their black riot helmets.

Suddenly, a series of doors opened along the landing, and the space began to fill with smoke.

The other tenants, now aware of the police presence, were throwing burning rags and plastic bags soaked with petrol into the hallway in an attempt to confuse matters and allow their neighbours time to escape. Thick, acrid smoke rose, stole the oxygen and invaded the lungs. It was difficult to see. Shouting filled the air. The stench of burning petrol clogged Rick's throat. It was chaos, like a battlefield, and he felt his instincts kick in and take control. Keeping low, he moved along the landing, reaching up and dragging the doors shut to prevent any further missiles being thrown.

He was shocked to see that most of the perpetrators were kids, not much more than thirteen or fourteen years old. Behind one of them, standing in a darkened hallway, a fat woman with unruly hair laughed, holding her stomach and stamping her foot as if to the rhythm of madness.

The confined space of the landing was soon filled with the jagged, nerve-bashing sounds of coughing, slamming doors, running feet, and war-like screams. Rick struggled to see, but his eyes were streaming. As he turned back to where Hutch was still waiting, he caught a stray kick to the head. Vision blurred, he reeled back onto his haunches; everything pushed in on him, pressing him down. He remembered the hot desert, a scouring diesel-tinged heat, the dull boom of explosions, and the cries of fallen comrades.

Then some damn fool started shooting.

CHAPTER TWO

Daryl was fascinated by the changes in Mother. In the space of three short months she'd gone from a spritely, if domineering, woman in her early sixties to a wasted, bed-ridden monster. Her body was rail-thin, the flesh hanging like wrapping paper from the gifts of her bones. Her small, nimble hands had lengthened into spiny claws. Her ribs protruded like the bars of a cage beneath the flattened expanse of her chest.

Mother's (never Mum or Mam or Mummy: such casual abuses of her title were simply not allowed) body was usually covered by sweaty sheets, so Daryl was spared the horror of looking at it every day, but her face remained above the covers, peeking out at him like a monstrous, wide-eyed baby.

Apart from these more apparent ravages, there had also been other, more subtle alterations to her physiognomy: the way her eyes looked glassy, like those of a doll; the waxen feel of her skin; the yellowish pallor of her sunken cheeks. Daryl stood over her now, staring into those black doll's eyes, wondering if she could still see him, or if she just sensed that he was there, as always, at her side.

"Mother."

The head stirred, twitching. The eyes widened impossibly – yellow gunk hung in strings from the thin lashes.

"I hate you, Mother." He smiled, rolling the words around on his tongue. Before her illness, Daryl would never have dared say such things. But now everything was different. Now, for once, he was in charge.

Mother let out a gurgling-rasping sound, as if she were trying to speak. She was in her last days now, which was why she'd been allowed home from hospital to die in her own home. Daryl had fought long and hard with the doctors to send her home, stating mock-sincere arguments for human rights, dignity; the fact that she should be given the choice where she would end her days. In reality, he just wanted her back so that he could torture her, just as she'd done to him his entire life.

Daryl knew that he was a pathetic specimen, a sad excuse for a man – Mother had told him this enough times that it had sunk in deep. But who was the more pathetic, a sick old woman or the son who cared for her?

"Sleep tight, Mother," he whispered, before turning away and leaving her alone, in the dark. She had always hated the dark, and insisted upon sleeping her entire life with a lamp by the bed. Upon her return from the cancer ward, Daryl had carefully, and in plain sight, removed the light bulbs from every light-fitting in her room. She winced as he smashed them on the floor, fearing both his wanton act of destruction and the darkness it promised. He had replaced the bulbs later, of course, but the act had been wonderfully symbolic.

He crossed the landing and entered his own room, glancing up at the print of one of John Wayne Gacy's prison paintings that hung on the wall by the door. He'd paid a small fortune for the framed print on eBay; it was one of his prized possessions.

His bookshelves bent under the weight of books on serial killers. The walls were plastered with newspaper cuttings, snips and snaps of unsolved murder cases and abductions. He was surrounded by his heroes, and each night before bed he would slowly leaf through the pages of one of his many scrapbooks, touching the glued-in faces of men like Ted Bundy, Fred West, Dennis Neilson and Albert Fish.

Daryl was intelligent and self-educated enough to realise that a lot of serial killers were mother fixated and possessed limited social skills. He knew that most of them started when they were very young, torturing small animals. What he could not understand was the secret element these killers seemed to have, the factor that made them step forward and live out the fantasy. Although he had been planning his first murder for several years now, Daryl was yet to take that step, to thrust his head above the parapet of normality and seize the moment.

He ran a hand across the spines of his books, closing his eyes and sensing the company of murderers. He longed to join their ranks, to accept membership into an elite band of men (they were always men, at least the ones he admired) who had actually taken a human life – more than one; scores of victims. It was his dearest dream to be like them, his heroes, his fathers. His first experience was so close that he could almost feel it brushing against his skin. Someday soon he would act, and the line would finally be crossed.

His attention was drawn by a sound from Mother's room. He stood and listened, waiting for it to come again. A slow, lazy thumping, like someone banging on a distant door. He knew that she was trying to move, shifting her wireframe body in an attempt to sit up in bed. Maybe she was thirsty, or simply craving his company.

Daryl left his room and went downstairs, ignoring her feeble movements. Let the bitch suffer, just as he had suffered for so many years, unable to cut the leash and get a girlfriend, not allowed beyond the doors of the big old house he'd been born in.

His heroes had all tasted the fruits that he desired – sex, death, adventure. Daryl was yet to glimpse such fascinations: his scope was limited, the level of his life experience pitiful.

In the living room he turned on the television. A news broadcast flashed onto the screen, something about a series of unprovoked attacks in Leeds city centre. The newsreader was pretty, blonde, and aching to be slashed. He imagined cutting her, peeling off her insincere skin to reveal the truth of the musculature beneath.

"... police are advising Leeds residents to stay indoors and lock themselves in. Episodes of civil unrest are increasing throughout the night, and an official spokesman has said that these events seem entirely random and unorganised. When asked about the possibility of terrorist activity, he stated again that the events are not linked. In other news..."

Daryl muted the set and went to the stereo, glancing out of the window as he did so. The curtains were open; he could see the stretched sheet of the sky, a shooting star crossing it like an animated image. *Wow*, he thought, *that's the first time I've ever seen a comet.*

He watched the fiery nova until it flared briefly and then faded, feeling an obscure sense of loneliness deep within his core. Was this an echo of what everyone else experienced when they fell in love, had babies, made a home together? Had he just been offered a glimpse into the world they inhabited, like a shooting star himself, coming close enough to see but not quite touch?

He forced his attention back to the stereo, disturbed by such maudlin thoughts.

Mother hated any music other than old time jazz, the kind played by big bands with busty female singers, and her beloved hymns. Daryl had smashed all her jazz records in front of her the day after she'd come home from hospital, and urinated on the remains. They were collectors items – most of them – and it had felt good to rob the world of their worth.

Selecting a Madonna CD from the stack, he slid it into the player and cranked the volume up way beyond what Mother thought of as acceptable.

Madonna: there was another slut who wanted killing. He failed to understand why no one had ever tried.

Daryl danced around the large room, his movements almost comically uncoordinated. He would never dance in public; the shame would be too heavy to bear. Anyway, Mother had not once agreed to him going anywhere that he *could* dance, even at the age when all his schoolyard acquaintances (never friends; Daryl had no idea how to form and maintain conventional relationships) had gone to the pubs and clubs in town. But here, alone, he was happy to kick off his shoes and boogie on down to the murder bop.

He knew this was no way for a twenty-three year-old man to act, but he was celebrating his newfound sense of freedom. Before Mother had fallen ill, when she had ruled over his world with a sharp tongue and a hard fist, he would never have dreamed of doing anything to upset her. Now that she was unable to fight back, he was prepared to do whatever the hell he wanted. No: whatever the *fuck* he wanted.

Yes, that felt good. Profanity, even in the privacy of his mind, was forbidden. He never understood exactly how Mother knew when he was thinking bad words, but she always picked up on it.

"Fuck you, Mother." He giggled and spun, spun and giggled. Madonna sang about a holiday, and Daryl realised with no little irony that he was currently embarking on a permanent vacation from all that had gone before. A further irony was that he didn't even like Madonna's music.

When the song ended he sat down on the couch, sweating and panting for breath. He picked up the remote control and flicked off the stereo, preferring silence for a little while. Too much freedom was making him giddy. He needed to regain some composure.

He reached under the floral print cushion and brought out a small, worn hardback book, a volume of poetry he'd never read. Mother had given it to him as a gift when he was a boy, expecting him to respond to culture. Unfortunately, his idea of culture was something that grew in a Petri dish, and would ooze foul-smelling liquor if you stabbed it with the nib of a pen.

He opened the book to the middle pages and took out the single photograph which lay inside. He handled it carefully, like a religious artefact, touching it only with the tips of his fingers. He would never forgive himself if he smudged the image, defaced the immaculate face in the photograph.

There she was. His proposed first victim. The woman he'd been thinking about killing for six months. He'd first seen her at a petrol station forecourt on Kirkstall Road, filling up the tank of her green Mini Cooper. Something about her had attracted him, but not in a sexual way. Like most of the men he sought to emulate, Daryl did not have a conventional sexual drive. His needs were much more esoteric than those of the average citizen.

He remembered following her home that first day, trailing her to the nice city centre flat where she lived with her husband. They had not been married long, and still seemed flushed by the excitement of simply being together. Daryl could not understand such things. Emotions like love and compassion were off his radar.

He'd kept a close eye on her after that; then, coming to a decision, he'd upped the surveillance and begun to stalk her. For the past three months he had charted her every move, keeping a dossier on her. He knew her husband's shifts, her routines, her patterns. Monday, Tuesday and Friday mornings she went to the gym. Every week-day afternoon she worked part-time at an Accountants office, walking the short distance from the flat. Weekends were changeable, but still followed a basic routine: a brisk morning walk down by the canal, breakfast muffins bought at Greggs bakery, then back to bed for a mid-morning nap – or, if her husband was not at work, a long work-out session between the sheets. Such creatures of habit, these people; they were so much more like him than they might like to think.

He'd taken the photograph early one morning when she was heading off for her usual visit to the gym. It was a full body shot, catching her just as she stepped out of the door, turning on her heel to close it behind her. Her almost shoulder-length blonde hair caught gems from the morning sun and her face glowed with what he could only describe as a supernatural radiance. There was magic in the picture. The sort of commonplace mysticism other people – normal people – might notice at sunset, or perhaps as twilight fell upon the land like a fine mist. Daryl loved the photo, and he loved the image it contained. As far as he was concerned, that also meant he loved the woman it represented. But it was not a natural kind of affection; no, it was something only he could understand, and to speak it out loud would end only in disaster.

Love, for Daryl, was a twisted thing, a malicious shadow tugging at his heels. Not for him the hearts and flowers of the rest of the world. He preferred knives and spleens, or skulls and hammers. Smiling, he brought the photograph up to his lips, kissed the air in front of it, and felt what passed for emotion in his dark world flood his senses like a short burst of bitter juice.

Daryl wanted to kill this woman so much that it manifested as an ache inside his gut, a low pulse that he could not deny. Lately the pulse had grown stronger, more difficult to ignore. The time was rapidly approaching when he must either shit or get off the pot. It was a crude metaphor – one he'd heard in a film – but a very apt one.

It was getting late. He knew he should be thinking about sleep, but these days he felt energised at night, as if he drew inspiration from the darkness. He thought he might torture Mother for a while before retiring to bed. Perhaps the flame of a lit match applied to the soles of her feet, or small slices from a razor blade directly under her armpits. There were so many methods to cause another human being pain. He'd researched them all, in books and on the Internet. The information was out there, in a variety of forms, if you looked hard enough, and wanted to find it badly enough.

He climbed the stairs and went to the bathroom, where he brushed his teeth and washed his face in the sink. The bowl of the sink was greasy with dirt; since Mother's illness took hold, he'd not bothered to clean the house. He considered using the toilet, but did not need to. He stared at his face in the mirror, reaching back behind him and to the left to turn out the light. His round, bespectacled face darkened, becoming something more sinister: a mask, with blackness peering out from the eye, nose and mouth holes. It was a wonderful illusion, and he marvelled at the fact that such hard truths nearly always presented themselves when one was least expecting them.

The truth, Daryl knew, rarely ventured out of its hiding place. But when it did... oh, when it did, huge changes were bound to follow.

CHAPTER THREE

Rick was shocked into immobility for a fraction of a second – certainly no more than that, but possibly even less – before his training kicked in. Hitting the floor, he rolled smoothly across the landing and kept close to the wall. If you stayed low you made a more difficult target, and moving in a straight line was out of the question. Confuse the enemy: do what is least expected.

Screaming and gunshots tore the air. Bodies tumbled by him, guns swinging up into active positions. Rick made his way back to the stairs, where Hutch was trying to aim at something through the dissipating smoke. "Good job," he yelled, his pistol twitching, shifting, eyes scanning the area for someone or something to target. He took off his helmet to scratch his head, sweat glistening in his hair and on his forehead.

Rick tucked himself in behind the thick concrete newel post, ensuring that he created as small a target as possible. He reached out to grab Hutch's arm, to tell his friend what he'd seen – the kids throwing smoking missiles, the laughing mad woman urging them on – but Hutch pulled sharply away, his movement violent and final. Rick felt a warm, moist sensation against the side of his face. His lips were pasted with hot fluid.

Hutch's body sagged. His gun fell to the floor; he began to inch backwards, down the stairs, his empty hands grasping at the air. When what remained of his face swung lazily into view, Rick saw that half the man's head had been obliterated. Bone was caught in a frozen spray; blood still spurted like strawberry syrup pumped through an air hose. Hutch's mouth was agape, but there wasn't enough of it left to describe a silent scream... his remaining eye had already rolled back into his shattered skull, and the other socket was filled with red.

Rick watched his friend fall, not even attempting to catch him. Hutch's slack body tumbled down the short flight, slamming into the wall on the half landing below, leaving bloody smears on the whitewashed plaster. Rick closed his eyes, pictured the scene, and started planning his next move.

Somehow finding a point of calm in the chaos around him, Rick rose and edged towards the mass of bodies around the door of the flat that was the subject of the raid – number twenty-four. Several police officers of various ranks formed a semi circle around the shattered entryway, most of them coughing; others ran along the landing, grabbing bystanders and pushing them back into their flats. Rick's emergency measures had not lasted: the doors inside certain buildings never remained closed for long.

"– fuck off me!" screamed a man who was backing out of number twenty-four. It was Tennant, the big man who'd been first inside the block. A woman hung from his chest by her hands; her feet dragged along behind her. She was spitting and snarling like a wild dog.

"Careful! HIV risk!" Rick did not recognise this second voice, but everyone seemed to take an unconscious step backwards, away from the woman who was trying her best to attack Tennant.

"Bitch!" said Tennant, swatting her away as if she were a small animal nagging him for food. The woman shot sideways, her head making contact with the door frame. Her eyes rolled back into her head and her tongue pushed between her swollen lips. She was tiny – almost a midget. Her hair was large and bushy, either completely unkempt or teased into some fashionable retro style.

Another officer emerged from the flat, his eyes streaming. Vomit speckled his lips and chin. "Oh, God," he said. "Oh, Jesus. Don't go in there."

The shooting had stopped. The hot stench of battle stung Rick's nostrils, but it was a smell he was used to, and even enjoyed in a twisted way. "What is it?" he said, stepping forward, taking the initiative.

The newcomer stared at him. His face was pale, bloodless, and his expression was one of utter despair. "I can't even tell you... it's a mess in there. A real fucking mess." The man stumbled off, heading for the stairs. Rick wondered if he'd puke again when he saw Hutch's body.

Hutch. The last of the guys he'd met all those years ago in basic training. They'd served their first tour of Iraq together, helping each other through, and left the forces at roughly the same time, but for different reasons.

How the hell was he going to break it to Hutch's wife, Jenny? It would have to be him; he'd known the woman for years, and liked her a lot. The baby was due in a month. The baby Hutch had left the army to be near.

Tensing his jaw, Rick moved into the doorway. No one else seemed willing to enter, and the superior officers were already inside. Without receiving further orders, Rick guessed that he was on his own. Maybe this was his chance to shine.

Someone pushed him forward, eager for another rookie to be thrust into the mix. Rick allowed his forward momentum to carry him across the threshold, and he was immediately struck by the sight of bloodstains on the floor and walls. So much blood. As if the short entrance hallway had been decorated with it. Smears and stripes and spatters – a Jackson Pollack configuration leading right up the wall to the tobacco-yellowed Artex ceiling.

The body of a man lay half in and half out of what he supposed must be the living room. He could only see the legs and buttocks.

The upper half was inside the other room. The white slacks on the skinny legs were covered with blood. One shoe and its corresponding sock were missing (blown off in the fire-fight, or not put on in the first place?) The left buttock was a mess of raw meat where he'd taken a hit in the arse.

Glancing across the felled victim, Rick saw that the television was playing in the darkened room. It was tuned to a news station, and a series of images showing mobs attacking police vehicles filled the screen. Words scrolled beneath the footage: LIVE FROM MILLENIUM SQUARE, LEEDS.

The volume was turned down low and some sort of dance music was playing on a sound system he could not locate. He resisted the urge to step over the corpse to closer investigate the news report.

Rick eased around the lower extremities of the corpse. He tried hard not to look, but when he drew level he was unable to keep his eyes from straying back into the room. Cheap wallpaper. Thrift shop furniture. Clothing scattered on the filthy wooden floor. The top half of the body had been almost severed at the hip. The man had taken several rounds before going down. A tiny bleb of creased intestine poked out from his side, just above the beltline. His dark shaven head was turned to one side, the cheek squashed against the laminated floor and one eye frozen open to stare into infinity.

Keep going. Let it all wash over you like a river over pebbles.

It was a mantra he'd heard during his final tour of Afghanistan, from a mate who'd been heavily into martial arts. The mate was dead now, like the rest of them, but his voice hung around like so many others inside Rick's head. Sometimes he thought those voices might never shut up; only fade into the background, a constant choral hum.

The voices of the dead; the voices of the dead men he had called friends; the voices of the dead friends whose lives had been wasted while his had been saved.

An open bedroom door further along and to the left offered him another glimpse of horror. Two members of his unit were kneeling beside the corpse of a young Asian man, this one with designer tram lines shaved into his close-cropped hair. Their victim was still twitching, gasping out his last breaths. The officers were silent, almost respectful, as they watched the man die. Blood on the floor; gasps in the air.

Moving on, he approached the kitchen. That was when things got bad.

"Nutman... that you, Nutman?"

"Yes, sir. It's Nutman, D.I. Harper, sir." Rick stopped outside the room, the familiar aroma of recent death in his nostrils. He removed his helmet and placed it on a shelf by the door, next to a long-dead prayer plant in a grubby plastic pot.

"Get in here, Nutman. You're not going to believe this, but try to keep your dinner down, yeah?" A large bulky frame hovered in the doorway. Behind him, a light began to flicker.

"Shit," said another voice. "All we need."

Rick stepped forward, his hands clenching into fists. His stomach was calm but his heart was beating double-time. He was sweating under the heavy riot gear; the stab vest stuck to his T-shirt; the T-shirt adhered to his chest.

The first thing Rick saw was D.I. Harper's ashen face. The huge man was leaning against a kitchen work bench, his head down but turned towards Rick. His eyes were hollow, lifeless, and his mouth was a grim slit. "Fuckin' animals," he muttered, shaking that large head in disbelief.

There was a severed head in the stainless steel kitchen sink. What looked like viscera sat in a lumpy mess on the draining board – looking closely, Rick thought he could make out a lung, a heart, lengths of looped intestine. He tried to look away but was unable to unlock his gaze from the nightmare. He stared at the head. Its eyes were gone, the sockets smooth and empty. There were teeth marks in one cheek – they couldn't be anything else – and the nose was gone.

"Cannibals," said D.I. Harper, his voice thin and reedy, the exact opposite of his build. "*Cannibals.*" He began to repeat the word, not even aware that he was doing so. Two other officers stood against the wall. One of them was covering his mouth with his hand and staring down at his feet. His shoes were covered in vomit.

The fridge door hung open, its hinges broken. The shelves were sparsely stocked: a few pieces of cling-filmed meat, half a pineapple, an opened can of baked beans. At the bottom, where the salad shelves should be, there was an open space occupied by several human hands.

"Sir... this isn't terrorism. What's going on?" Rick felt like the floor was rushing up to meet him, but he composed himself by thinking of Hutch, his wife, their unborn baby. "What is this?"

D.I. Harper straightened, his head almost touching the low ceiling. The dim light flickered again, lending his features an unearthly tint. "I don't know, son. I really don't know. We have four suspects dead inside this place, and every room contains what seem to be partially consumed human remains. We've either stumbled on a gang of serial killers here, or some sort of weird cult. I've never seen anything like it..." he finished lamely, shaking his head and rubbing his neck with a big square hand.

Time stood still for Rick. He was trapped in someone else's nightmare. The blood hardly bothered him now; there was so much of it that he stopped noticing it. What hit him hardest was not the wet pile of guts on the draining board, nor was it the head in the sink that almost broke him... no, it was those hands. Clean dainty human hands. Six of them: three pairs all lined up like crab claws in a neat row along the bottom of the fridge. What kind of insanity did it take to cut off those hands and then store them for later?

What stopped him vomiting was the piercing sound of screams erupting suddenly from the other room. At first he thought it was a woman, but then remembered that their particular unit was famously made up of all male officers. The only woman in the vicinity was the fuzzy-haired maniac he'd seen earlier, but Tennant had silenced her.

"What now?" D.I. Harper looked wasted, as if he could face no more of this night. The other two officers glanced at each other, then at Rick.

"I'll go," he said, turning away and walking back along the hallway. After three or four steps he saw where the screaming was coming from. Another rookie – someone whose name he had not been told – was shuffling backwards towards him, his backside scraping the floor and his hands clutching at the skirting boards. He was moving fast for a man on his arse, mainly due to what was pursuing him.

The designer-skinhead gunshot victim who'd been dying only moments earlier – the young man almost surely slain during the initial shoot-out – was slowly making his way along the hallway, lying on his belly and dragging himself forward with bloody hands, the bullet-addled lower half of his body spilling intestines onto the scuffed floor boards.

There was no way on earth the man could be doing this. He was dead, gunned down. But here he was, moving clumsily, inch by inch, and gaining ground on the screaming rookie.

"Shut up," said Rick, reaching down to grab the guy's shoulder. The rookie twitched, then managed to climb to his feet, using Rick's legs and torso as leverage.

The man – the dead man – moved relentlessly forward. His eyes were flat, dull, like old pennies, and his upturned face hung loose on his skull. He was grinding his teeth, just like Sally used to whenever she was nervous, before the dentist had fitted her with a bespoke gum shield to help her kick the habit.

But the dead man had no gum shield – he barely had any teeth. Those remaining in his head were shattered and projected from his lips like snapped pieces of wood.

"Shoot it!" Yelled the rookie. "For God's sake, just shoot it!"

Rick raised his pistol, aimed carefully, and put a shot in the dead man's shoulder. The dead man jerked like he was pulled by strings, but kept on coming. Rick put another round in his opposite shoulder. That didn't stop him either.

"*Oh-my-God-oh-my-God-oh-my-God-oh-my-God...*" The man at his side chanted like a Buddhist monk, fading from the scene, turning in on himself.

Rick aimed again, this time at the dead man's back, right above the heart. He pulled the trigger, feeling the gun buck in his hands. A chunk of flesh flew out of the dead man, blood tracing an arc in the air. He did not stop. His hands reached out; they were inches from Rick's boots. He shuffled backward, shoving the rookie out of the way. Then he aimed his Glock at the top of dead man's carefully crafted haircut, right between two of his carefully shaved tramlines.

Why doesn't he die? Rick thought, his mind focused, nerves strung as tightly as guitar strings.

The dead man looked up at him, nothing in his gaze.

This time when Rick squeezed the trigger blood and thick clotted matter sprayed in an elegant parabola, turning the wall and floor behind the dead man dark red. The dead man raised his eyes, and then lifted himself almost to his feet before toppling forward onto his face. The top of his skull was level with Rick's feet. He stared at the wound, at the grey-purple brains bulging out of the hole. They looked like those disgusting meat things Sally's granny used to eat – what where they called, faggots? Yeah, that was it: braised faggots.

The rookie started to cry. Rick turned just in time to see a dead woman emerge from the bedroom and grab the rookie's arm. She was Afro-Caribbean, with big eyes and thick lips, but her skin was curiously pale. Her teeth were shockingly white when she opened her mouth and bit down on the rookie's neck, scraping easily through the flesh to puncture his carotid artery. The spray of blood was majestic: a bright geyser. The rookie tried to slap her away but already his strength was failing; his arms flapped uselessly, his hands sliding off the dead woman's face.

Always a fast learner, Rick reacted instantly and shot her through the right eye. This time the blood misted, forming an ethereal pattern in the musty air – crimson dust motes caught in the meagre illumination. Rick watched it, enraptured by its slow-moving dance, the way the flickering kitchen light caught like rubies in its diaphanous mass.

He stared at the Glock, hypnotised by the sluggish movement of smoke as it poured from the muzzle and traced a grey puzzle in the air directly ahead of him. Then he looked back at the woman, tilting his head to one side in an odd unconscious mannerism that, unbeknownst to him, he'd last done as an inquisitive child of seven. She was laying face-up on the ground, her eye socket enlarged and red matter hanging in strings from the damaged orbit. Blood pooled around her pasty features even as he watched, shining dully on the floor.

He shot her again, just to make sure she stayed down, and the top of her head was vaporised in a bright shock of blood, brain and bone. Rick felt something in his head click, as if a switch had been thrown – he was not sure what it was, but it felt like some old, long-neglected mechanism was once more becoming operational.

He thought of the desert. The screams. The friends he had lost. Somehow, the memories did not hurt even half as much as they had fifteen minutes before.

CHAPTER FOUR

Sally had the feeling that something was terribly wrong.

It wasn't the sirens, or the fact that the electricity kept threatening to cut out for minutes at a time, or even the intermittent shouting she kept hearing somewhere out in the city streets as the lights inside flickered nervously. No, some internal barometer was telling her that Rick was in some kind of trouble. Ever since they'd first met, Sally had felt some inner *tugging* whenever he was in jeopardy. During Rick's army days, she'd known about it when things got tough; when he was seriously injured during a Taliban attack in Afghanistan, she'd felt a terrible pain in her guts.

The television was on but Sally was barely watching it. The show was sub prime-time filler: some kind of imported American talent contest between people whose only proximity to talent was by watching other performers on better TV shows. Sally wished that they'd all just demonstrate the good taste to take a running jump through the fuck off door, but sadly that didn't seem like it would happen any time soon.

She grabbed the remote control and switched channels to an old film. Robert Mitchum. Gregory Peck. Good stuff, but she wasn't quite in the mood for film noir. Sighing, she took a sip of wine, closing her eyes as the wonderfully cool liquid traced a pathway down her throat.

She glanced around the small seventh floor flat, her gaze restless, moving from object to object like a butterfly in a garden. Despite all the familiar things around her, this place had never quite felt like home. A photograph on the mantle, showing Rick and several buddies just before the attack in Helmand Province. The odd-shaped stone he'd brought her back from the desert – a rock shaped like a heart. The framed pictures hanging on the walls. The books and ornaments on the shelves. None of this stuff actually meant anything if Rick wasn't here with her, close enough to touch, to hold, to kiss...

The wine was making her maudlin, and along with the noise coming from outside it was also putting her on edge. She drained the glass but did not refill it.

When the telephone rang at first she thought it might be Rick, or worse still, someone calling on Rick's behalf to tell her that he'd been hurt, perhaps shot during whatever operation he was involved in. She rushed to the table by the door and picked up the receiver. "Hello."

"Oh, thank God. I've been trying to get you for ages. The lines have been busy."

"Mum? What's wrong, Mum?" Sally felt the tone of her own voice rise to match that of her mother's.

"Don't worry, I'm fine. Just a bit... well, to be honest I'm a bit unnerved." Her mother's voice sounded strange, strained.

"Tell me, Mum. What's up?" Sally's hand gripped the receiver, making her fingers ache.

"There's something going on. The lights keep flickering and going out; the TV won't come back on. The radio is reporting riots in London and Luton." Her mother was close to tears. Since Dad died, she'd been on her own and it didn't suit her.

"Calm down, Mum. I'm sure it's okay."

"I know, I'm probably being silly. But I'm sure someone was outside earlier, creeping around in the back garden."

Sally suddenly pictured her mother's house, located back from the road in a very quiet area just outside Bedford. The nearest main road was miles away; the surrounding countryside was beautiful during the day but at night could hide a hundred assailants. "Listen, Mum, please call the police and lock the doors and windows."

"I did all that ages ago." Sally held her breath, suddenly afraid. "The police said they'd get here as soon as they could, but they're busy on other calls."

"Call Derek, then. Right now. He'll drive out to get you." Derek was the nearest neighbour, another widower who had a soft spot for Sally's mother that everyone but her could see.

"You know I don't like to be a bother... it's late; he's probably in bed."

"Call him, Mum. Promise me you will. You know he'll be happy to drop by and sit with you until the police arrive. I'll feel better if he does, too."

There was a lengthy silence, and then her mother reached a decision. "You're right, darling. I *will* call Derek. He'll know what to do. He always does."

Calmer now, Sally made her mother promise again that she would call her suitor, and then she reluctantly hung up. It was horrible being miles away from her family at times like these. On the rare occasions that her mother needed her, Sally was never close enough to do much about it. The best she could offer was a promise to visit the following weekend.

During the phone call the TV had gone off. The lights began to flicker again, but more slowly, dipping the room into darkness for brief periods that seemed longer each time it happened. Sally felt her chest tighten. She knew, just knew, that one of these times the lights would go out for good. She picked up the phone again and called Rick's mobile. As expected, a recorded voice told her that it was switched off.

"It's me. I'm scared. Mum just rang, and there's something going on outside. Come home soon?" She pressed the button to end her message, then returned to her chair.

Sally was used to fear. It was almost an old friend. When she had been younger, her life had been made a misery by local bullies – her weight and her unusual looks had led to her being called names like 'Fat Cat' and 'Slit-eyed Slut.' The name-calling had progressed to physical abuse, and she'd sported scrapes and bruises for most of her school years. As an adult, once she'd grown into her looks, things had changed and she became popular with the opposite sex. Those early days, however, left deep scars, and she found it difficult to form relationships, hard to trust anyone.

Rick had been different. They'd clicked immediately. But he had come with his own fears, and his tours of duty with the army had brought terrors like none she'd ever experienced.

She recalled vividly the call from a corporal to inform her that Rick had been shot in Helmand Province, in a region whose name she could not even pronounce. *He's alive*, they'd told her, *but more than that we cannot say.* It was a week before she knew for certain that he would survive, and by then she'd been allowed to visit him in the military hospital.

It all made her childhood fears seem so trite, so pathetic, but when she saw him lying in that hospital bed, his body thin and bandaged, it opened the old scars and made them into fresh wounds.

Rick's body had healed but his mind remained damaged, a flawed tool of his trade. There was the depression, of course – the constant night terrors and the way his eyes narrowed at the slightest sound outside – but worse than that was the fact that he could never settle. That was why he joined the police force – to focus all the nervous energy he gave off like a damaged battery. She also suspected that he missed the action.

Headlights splashed the walls, turning the net curtains white. She glanced over, caught off guard, and listened intently to the sound of squealing breaks. Whatever the vehicle was, its driver had lost control. The brakes continued to scream and the sound was followed by a huge, rending crash of metal and a low, hollow explosion.

Sally ran to the window and peered through the partially opened blinds. Two hundred yards along the street, by the glow of firelight, she saw that a car had crashed into the concrete bollards along the side of the canal. Black water flared with reflected fire; yellow flames clawed at the dark sky. Someone was crawling from the wreckage. It was a woman, and she was moving slowly, clumsily, as she dragged herself through the shattered rear window. Another figure was slumped behind the wheel, but it was too obscured by smoke for Sally to make out if it was male or female.

The passenger squeezed out of the car and slumped heavily to the ground. She raised her head, staring at the night sky, and clutched at her cheeks, scraping them with her nails.

Sally stepped back, just half a step, and shot a glance at the phone. She knew that she ought to ring the police, an ambulance, but something about this scene struck her as all wrong. She looked back at the woman, and then it registered. Instead of screaming in pain, the woman was simply sitting there, on the ground by the canal, tearing at her own face. It was a weirdly compelling sight, and one that was unnatural in so many ways. After such an accident, the woman should surely be as dead as her driver – but there she was, out of the car and mutilating herself.

Sally held her breath, barely even realising that she was doing so.

The woman, as if sensing Sally's scrutiny, looked up and stared along the length of the canal, directly into the flat. Glimmers of firelight brightened her narrow face, and Sally could clearly see that the woman was smiling. But it was not a smile that held any trace of humour; instead, it was the slack-jawed idiot grin of someone whose mind was simply no longer operating as it should. An alien smile: a smile that should never be seen by human eyes.

The woman then began to drag herself back towards the car. The flames were dying, burning themselves out. No fuel had ignited, just the paint on the bodywork. Small bright tongues licked at the smoke-blackened wings and wheel rims, the tyres were thick molten rubber bands. The woman slumped round to the driver's side, pulling her weight up by the door handle. Then, settling against the door, she reached in and pulled a fist-sized chunk of still smoking flesh from the side of the driver's neck. Her hand went to her mouth; the cooked meat slipped between her lips, her reddened teeth. The woman began to chew, slowly and methodically, as if she were sampling nothing more exotic than a handful of *foie gras.*

Sally wished that she could look away, but her eyes were glued to the scene. There was still enough of the guttering fire left alive to allow her to witness exactly what was going on, but she could barely believe it.

"Oh my God," she said, shocking herself by speaking out loud. "What the hell...?" She walked quickly to the phone, remembering Rick's oft repeated advice about keeping your head in a crisis. When she picked up the receiver, the line was dead. Not even the dull hiss of white noise on the line.

She fished her mobile out of her jeans pocket and pressed the button to, once again, call Rick – she had him on speed dial, in case of an emergency. If this wasn't an emergency, then she didn't know what possible situation might qualify for the title.

Now she did hear white noise, followed by a series of clicks and fractured bleeping sounds. Then a recorded message told her in a smooth female voice that the number was unavailable. Either Rick's mobile was still switched off or the networks were all busy.

"Shit. Shit." She crossed again to the window. The car was no longer alight; it was now a smoking shell. The body behind the wheel looked misshapen and... well, *incomplete.* Sally peered along the canal in both directions trying to catch sight of the woman, but could see no one lurking in the vicinity. That was unusual in itself, as the canal at night was usually a regular hangout for drug dealers and homosexual pick-ups. She and Rick often stood at the window to watch the show, using it as a substitute for bad TV. She'd lost count of exactly how many times they'd seen what were probably illicit trysts and illegal transactions. Like most big cities, Leeds was packed with what

Rick for some reason always called the 'Scum of the Hearth.' He always found that funny, but Sally had never really understood what it meant. Nor had she ever felt like asking. Sometimes Rick could be almost wilfully obscure and in a way that scared her, and she preferred to ignore those occasional glimpses of a somehow complex darkness making itself known to her.

Sirens wailed far off in the night, either approaching or moving away at speed – it was impossible to tell. As she watched, a fire started in the east of the city, its wan glow reflected in the cloudless sky, shimmering against the heavens like a misdirected spotlight. Shouts and blunt screams were carried to her on the light breeze, as if they'd been waiting for her to act as an audience to their grim proclamations.

Sally checked the window and shut the curtains. Then she went round the entire flat, ensuring that all the door and window locks were secure, wishing that there were sturdy shutters instead of thin curtains across the window glass.

When she was finished she sat on the floor in the middle of the living room. The TV was showing a pre-recorded interview with some MP she'd never heard of, and he was talking about riots across the city, lootings, rapes and murders. Sally had the telephone clasped between her knees. Intermittently, she checked it for a signal, but all she got was a dead line. She tried to ignore the sounds coming from outside, knowing that on the seventh floor she was too far up for any passing psycho to bother with, and the main doors to the apartment block were time-locked anyway.

The night stretched ahead of her, unfurling like a ribbon quilted with myriad atrocities. She wished that Rick was here, at her side, and wept because she could not reach out to him for comfort. Her old fears returned, mutated into something much worse: demons that leered from the corners of the room. She wondered, briefly, if she would ever see her husband again, and then hated herself for such a display of weakness. Rick would expect her to be strong, to hold things together until he got back.

And he *would* get back to her – of this single fact she was absolutely certain.

That was the last thought she had before the lights in the flat flickered a final time and then went out for good.

CHAPTER FIVE

Rick stood in silence and surveyed the damage. There were bodies everywhere – the gunned down remains of the people who'd been in the Dead Rooms (that was what everyone was now calling this place) and several of his fellow officers. It wasn't good. In fact, it was appalling. A deep, heavy silence had drifted in to replace the chaos of screams and gunshots; that silence was all wrong, as if he'd gone deaf after being caught in a bomb blast. Then, bit by bit, it was punctuated by the occasional stifled sob.

A grown man was crying. More than one, actually, but he couldn't see who or how many. Smoke hung in small drifting clouds, dissipating gradually. Voices became clearer; other tenants were being herded either back into their own domiciles or down the stairs into the parking area outside the block. Rick was clutching his gun so tightly that his fingers had begun to ache. It felt like he might be unable to break the grip when the time came to put the weapon down.

"Sally," he whispered, unsure why. Her name held an almost mythical resonance, a calming influence. He said it again: "Sally."

"You men," said D.I. Harper, his eyes still glazed, his face too pale beneath the dark riot helmet. He'd unbuttoned his stab vest, probably to help him breathe, to allow him to fill his lungs with the putrid air. "Start getting this place cleared up."

The remaining on-site Constables moved efficiently considering the circumstances, checking bodies, searching the Dead Rooms, pulling plastic bags filled with drugs, body parts and all kinds of street weapons from various drawers and cupboards. Rick watched a young, fresh-faced lad heft a bread bag containing at least a hundred grams of cocaine from under the living room sofa. The body Rick had seen earlier – the first one he'd encountered, not the somehow reanimated madman – was still wedged in the doorway, its ruined buttocks standing proud.

Rick looked away. Blinked. The dead woman in the hallway – the one he'd shot through the eye – was being moved by two other officers who'd come in from outside. Their faces were grim; they worked in silence. Taking a leg each, they hauled her out through the front door and then disappeared into the haze of smoke.

It was such a mess, the whole damn situation. Even D.I. Harper, a seasoned veteran of countless operations, looked haggard and ineffectual. All they could do was mop up the mess. The inquest would come later, when everyone was out of there and out of trouble. For now, the main objective was to control the situation, to resist any attempt by civilians to encroach on the crime scene, and to effectively calm everyone down.

He glanced back into the living room, wondering what the fresh-faced Constable was doing now. Had he found something else in there?

The dead man was no longer in the doorway.

Somehow he'd managed to pull himself to his feet and stagger across the floor, where he was now closing in on the otherwise occupied officer.

Rick tried to remember where his gun was – in his hand? Yes, that was it. He raised the Glock, took aim, and shot the dead man in the back of the head, near the base of his skull. The air turned red. The dead man faltered, then froze. Finally, he dropped heavily, his face slamming bluntly into the floor.

The fresh-faced Constable turned around, shock twisting his face into a weird white mask. "Thanks," he mouthed silently, unable to drag real words from his stunned mind.

The silence had lifted. Sound rushed back into Rick's ears, filling his head.

D.I. Harper had obviously regained some of his composure, but he still sounded like a bad impression of himself as he barked orders in the other rooms. "Come on, let's get this sorted. Fire and ambulance crews are on their way – we need to minimise any shock value here, troops."

Rick was still staring at the Constable. The young man calmly lifted his hand and placed the barrel of his pistol between his teeth. He smiled around the dull metal, his eyes looking far beyond the scene, perhaps seeing some other landscape where he felt more at home: a land of the living and not the walking dead.

Rick turned his back on the officer just before the sound of detonation tore the air apart.

Things got a lot worse from that point on.

Out in the hallway a dead police officer was rising from the floor. It was the one who'd been attacked by the Afro-Caribbean woman what seemed like hours ago but in reality had only been about thirty minutes before.

The dead officer moved in twitchy slow motion, like something from an old German vampire film Rick had once seen on TV – was it *Nosferatau*? He thought it might be, but he always got these things mixed up. Sally would know; she always remembered information about books and films. The accuracy of her memory was one of her many strengths.

Rick watched calmly as the dead man began to stand. His gun was ready; he had plenty of time to take a bead on the fucker and put him back down. So he watched with the casual interest of an impartial observer, not feeling part of the scene but nonetheless fascinated by what was happening.

The dead officer jerked once, an oval chunk of flesh flying out of his shoulder and hitting the wall, where it stuck like a thrown turd. Rick had not even heard the gunshot. He raised his eyes, peering over the dead officer's head, and saw Tennant standing there in the doorway, sweat on his broad face and killing in his eyes.

Tennant stared back at Rick.

Nodded.

"The head," Rick heard himself say. "I think you need to shoot them in the head. Just like in the movies." *Dawn of the Dead*, *Zombie Creeping Flesh*. Rick had watched them all on video as a teenager, laughing and screaming in equal measures at the absurdly bloody onscreen spectacle. Not once had he ever entertained the thought that something similar might occur in real life. It was madness. The whole damn world had gone insane.

This time he heard the gunshot.

He closed his eyes and felt blood kiss his face, warm and wet and sticky. He heard the sound of a body slumping to the floor.

"Thanks," said Tennant, and when Rick opened his eyes again the other man was no longer there; the doorway was an empty frame with thin fingers of smoke billowing through it.

More acrid smoke drifted in through the doorway; people yelled out on the landing. Someone had set another fire in one of the flats, perhaps in an attempt to confuse them. It was working: officers ran like headless chickens across his line of view, guns cocked and ready, fingers like coiled springs on the triggers.

More gunshots. Someone screaming, their voice rising in pitch... going on and on and on, as if it might never end. It rung in his ears like the bells of hell.

Smoke curled around his legs like oily grey serpents, and he backed away, as if recoiling from their touch.

The Dead Rooms. He didn't know who'd said it first – it might even have been Rick himself – but the name was perfect. These rooms, this building – they all contained the dead. The dead that refused to lie down.

Then, a voice: "This way, man. Get the fuck out of there." He stepped forward, towards the voice, and Tennant's meaty arm shot out of the flat slab of smoke-filled doorway to grab him. Rick let himself be hauled out of the flat and onto the smoky landing. Figures barged past, pushing him aside; screams filled the air. The stench was unfathomable: a combination of burning tyres and cooking flesh.

"There's more!" Tennant was screaming into his ear, trying to make himself heard above the cacophonous roar that now filled the upper storeys of the building. "In the other flats... rooms filled with dead bodies. Some of 'em are rotting, others are fresh... but they're all standing up and attacking people."

"What? Are you insane?" He felt his mouth moving, the shape of the words caressing his lips, but it didn't feel like he was speaking. Rick once again felt detached, apart from it all. There was an inner core of calmness, a small, bright place he'd always retreated to during battle. His own private Dead Room.

"The fuckers," said Tennant, his eyes wide, almost popping out of his large bull-like head. "They've been hiding their dead relatives, keeping them holed up in more Dead Rooms. Keeping them safe and sound and away from prying eyes." He began to laugh, but it was a hideous sound, even worse than the constant screaming Rick could still hear coming from somewhere off to their left.

Another gunshot. The screaming stopped.

Rick pulled away from Tennant and watched as the other man waded into the churning wall of smoke, aiming his gun at something Rick could not make out – just a bulky shape, crouching low to the ground. Tennant was still laughing; his massive shoulders were hitching and he even threw back his head like a bad actor in a shitty melodrama.

Rick picked his way slowly along the landing, remaining calm, cool and collected. He glanced through each of the open doorways he passed, looking into other rooms – other Dead Rooms. In one, a young woman was wrestling with a small child. The child was covered in blood that clearly wasn't his own. In another, a man he didn't recognise but who was wearing riot gear sat on an old man's chest, dipping his hands into his abdomen to scoop out what was inside.

Rick made it across the landing without further incident. He had a sudden mental flash of when he had been about twelve years old, a bad time in his youth. His best friend had lived in a block of grotty council flats a lot like this one. The boy, Murray Smith, had been a budding artist. He drew pictures that made Rick believe in something beyond the grimy streets, the rotten neighbourhood, and the borderline poverty.

Murray Smith had been killed by another local youth, a drug dealing maggot aged thirteen; his throat had been slashed with a broken bottle on a narrow stairway just like this one. Murray had died slowly, and in agony. Not one of the neighbours had come out to investigate the sounds of his dying.

Rick failed to understand at first why he was recalling the awful memory. It was something he'd put behind him, a trauma he'd purposefully not thought of for years.

When he saw Trevor Hutchinson's body, he suddenly realised why Murray Smith had come lurching back into his mind.

Hutch had fallen face down, onto his front, but now he sat leaning against the concrete wall, blood down the front of his stab vest. The left half of Hutch's head was missing from the nose up. Rick could see Hutch's pulped brain through the gap in his skull.

"Oh, no," he said, pointlessly. "Oh God, mate. No."

He'd served in the Paratroopers with this man, had even followed him out of the army and into the police. His friend; his comrade; his fucking *blood brother.*

Hutch moved slowly, awkwardly, like a man suffering from severe brain damage. He was pulling at the rim of his wound with a twitching hand, stringy matter stretching like pizza cheese between the long, white fingers. His one good eye blinked mechanically. He reminded Rick of one of those Disney World animals, the robot bears and raccoons playing banjos and pianos during matinee performances. It was creepy – even creepier than those terrible severed hands in the bottom of the fridge – and for a moment Rick could think of nothing to do but watch.

Then he knelt down by his friend. His dead-but-alive friend.

No, not his friend... something else. Something *unnatural.*

His friend had in fact vacated this shell.

Reaching out with a tenderness that he felt was entirely appropriate to the moment, he slammed the dead man's head into the wall, mashing what was left of Hutch's brain. The body slipped down the wall, the limbs limp as spaghetti. Red pasta-sauce smears on the chipped plaster rendering. That single eye locked into a cold stare.

Unlike the things on the floor above, Hutch had not returned fully from his early death; like some idiot inbred offspring, he'd been only partially there, a fragment of a being. Rick was aware enough of his actions to consider this second death a mercy killing.

"Regroup! Retreat and regroup!" D.I. Harper's voice boomed down the stairwell, echoing like the voice of an angry god. He was back in control now, getting things sorted, just like he was paid to do. "Down to the ground floor, and then we fucking regroup outside the main doors! Now! Move! Move! *Move!"*

Rick did not need to hear the order again: he took the stairs two at a time. His boots thundered against the concrete but the sound they made was lost amid the deafening uproar of the approaching apocalypse.

CHAPTER SIX

This time Daryl knew he'd gone too far. He hadn't meant to cause that much damage, but there was something in the air tonight that made him feel reckless. He stared down at Mother, at her blank face and spit-frothed mouth, and felt a strange blooming sensation in his chest. If he had possessed any kind of normal human emotions, he supposed he might have recognised the complex reactions he was experiencing, but as it stood he was simply puzzled.

Mother's feet looked terrible.

Staring at the cigarette lighter in his hand, he wondered again how he'd managed to lose control so easily. Perhaps it was those earlier thoughts of Sally Nutman, or the fact that the city seemed to be exploding in waves of violence – the radio on Mother's bureau was reporting yet more riots breaking out to the south and west of the city.

Mother's feet were weeping blood and some sort of clear fluid that might easily become infected if he left them untended.

The voice on the radio said that police resources were at full stretch and the emergency services were unable to contain the outbreaks of civil unrest; that they were in danger of being overrun.

Those feet... the wounds were terrible, blackened around the outside and moist and meaty at the centre.

All other crimes, said the not-so-calm voice on the radio, were being left unattended. The violence and looting on the streets of Leeds were taking up all police time and effort. The fire service was struggling to cope with the blazes starting up across the skyline. The ambulance crews were at breaking point.

Daryl turned away from Mother's bed. He caught sight of fire in the sky outside; a pale yellow glimmer lightly painted the horizon. If he slowed his breathing and listened intently, he could just about make out the dull roar of an undisciplined crowd some miles away, like the sound of a football match being played at Elland Road Stadium.

Mother's room suddenly seemed so desperately small: the ugly patterned wallpaper pressed in on him, the badly plastered ceiling bowed towards his head, the hideous brown carpet bulged as if the floorboards beneath were buckling. The bibles and religious pamphlets on the shelves twitched forward, threatening to fall, and the posters of Catholic saints slipped from the walls, tumbling through the air like fragments of all the Christ-dreams Mother had ever forced upon him.

"Bitch," he said, enjoying the way the word filled the small space. "You. Bitch."

The world was changing. Not just *his* world, with Mother gradually but stubbornly leaving it. No: the whole world – the *real* world. His inner existence changed a little every day; the closer Mother edged towards death, the nearer he got to his dream of killing. He lacked the courage to take that final step, but Mother's eventual passing might see him transformed into another being, a man who could reach out and take what he wanted because the ties that bound him to banality were finally gone.

On the window sill there was an old framed photograph. It showed Mother with the man she had always told Daryl was his father. The couple stood smiling on a narrow promenade at some northern seaside resort, maybe Whitby. He reached out and picked up the photo, caressing it. As a child, he'd never been allowed to touch Mother's things – specifically her photographs – but when she started ailing, the first of his many tiny rebellions was to go through all of her stuff.

But he'd realised the lie years before, as soon as he was old enough to think for himself; and instead of making him angry it had made him laugh.

The photograph in the frame was a mock-up. Upon close inspection, it became obvious that the man had been cut out of a magazine and pasted next to Mother. She'd done a careful job that held up to distant inspection, but when you looked closer the colours didn't match; the man's image was slightly less faded than hers.

Daryl had seen the man on television when he was young, and at school, and then in newspapers, in retrospective documentaries and articles about American politics. Yet somehow he had not made the connection until long after he should have done. The man's name was Richard Nixon; he had been the President of the United States before Daryl was even born.

Shaking his head, he smiled at the fact that he'd believed Mother's story for more years than he liked to admit. What else had she lied about? What other stories had she fabricated to cover up the signs of her own madness?

He put the photo frame back in its rightful place, adjusting it to the same angle it always occupied, with Nixon smiling towards Mother's bed, hands held up in his famous victory salute. When Daryl raised his eyes he saw movement outside, on next door's lawn. He moved closer to the window and craned his neck, staring down into the neighbour's garden.

Two figures were tussling on the lawn. Initially, Daryl suspected they were intruders, but soon realised that one of the figures was Mr. Willows. He'd never particularly liked the old man, but nor did he have any real reason to hate him. He was just some nosey old geezer who lived on the same street.

Daryl watched with interest. Mr. Willows was caught up in some kind of wrestling match with a woman dressed in a white smock. The woman was very thin, her arms and legs like tinder sticks. Her hair was patchy, showing pink flashes of scalp, and her mouth was open wide in a ferocious snarl.

The woman was Mrs. Willows.

She had been dead for eight weeks. Mother had been upset because she was too ill to make it to the funeral.

"Help!" Mr. Willows was shouting, straight-arming Mrs. Willows, one hand planted firmly on her flattened chest to keep her at bay. "Please... *help!*" he looked up, directly at Daryl, and when their eyes met Mr. Willows began to shake his head and shout even louder. "Daryl! For God's sake... help me... Daryl!"

Daryl cocked his head to one side. He was fascinated. Was this some sort of delirium vision, a hallucination brought on by excessive stress? It had happened before, on several occasions, and he knew enough about his mental condition to be certain that it was associated with his repressed urges to commit murder.

"Hello, Mr. Willows," he said softly, and smiled.

Mr. Willows' eyes widened when he realised that Daryl would offer no help. The strength seemed to go out of him then, and his face deflated like a popped balloon. His cheeks sunk, hugging bone, his eyes receded into his skull, and his arm slackened, bending at the elbow.

Mrs. Willows lunged forward, her teeth bared, and latched onto her husband's throat. Mr. Willows sunk to his knees, his legs buckling beneath the weight of his dead wife.

Daryl continued to watch with interest as Mrs. Willows tore out the old man's throat, greedily gulping down pieces of his wrinkled flesh. When she started on the wizened face, Daryl looked away.

Mother moaned. It was a small sound, tiny really, but enough to announce her returning consciousness. Daryl looked back to the window, at the scene outside, and saw Mrs. Willows shambling clumsily across the lawn towards her house. She was carrying Mr. Willows' severed right arm; it dangled from her hand like a toy. The old man's remains lay unmoving on the grass near a tall rose bush – the same rose bush Mrs. Willows had tended lovingly every day when she'd been alive.

"Is this it, Mother?"

Mother did not reply.

"Is this the End of Days you were always rattling on about? The Book of Revelations, the Great Beast, the Reckoning? Is this what your Bible warned you about, the hour when we will all be judged as unworthy?"

There was nothing – not even the slightest movement – from where Mother lay, dying and withering on her sick bed.

"Despite your lies and your myth-making, it looks like you were right all along. And the best thing is, you're too fucking ill to see it. Your beloved apocalypse, the time you've prayed for, begged for, believed in for so long."

Breaking glass. A distant explosion. Was that a series of gunshots?

"It's here. It's happening. Your best, most hoped-for dream. This is the end of it all."

Mother did not say a word, but he imagined her cold, hard, brittle laughter, could almost hear it echoing through the empty rooms and hallways of the house. He was surprised and shaken to find that the sound comforted him.

He left Mother's room and went downstairs, shrugging on his coat at the front door. He opened the door a fraction, peering outside. Something was calling him, a sense of death, the essence of murder. He could smell, taste, hear it; death was so strong, so heavy, that it was like a giant striding through the night.

He could not possibly stay indoors when there was so much to be seen out there, so many fantasies to be acted out on the vast canvas of darkness.

He stepped outside into the chilly air, fastening his jacket. He'd neglected to bring a weapon – perhaps a knife for self-protection – but something told him that he would not need it... something old and weighty: a terrible presence long hidden beneath the weight of his life that was only now stirring, lifting its shaggy head up into the meagre light to taste the potential for mayhem.

He walked along the street, glancing at the houses on either side. Shadows danced beyond the windows, people embracing or rushing to shore up their homes against whatever was abroad in the night. Daryl did not fear this; he was rejoicing in the chaos he could sense around him.

A young woman in a nurse's uniform approached him at speed. She was running, one shoe missing and her stockings torn, her short chestnut hair in disarray. "Oh, thank God," she said, clutching at him. Her fingernails were painted bright red. Her hands were tiny, but the fingers were long. Daryl took in every detail, breathed in each vapour. She was wearing a fruity scent, something fresh and modern, not at all like the stale, cloying floral perfumes Mother always used to mask her unhealthy body odour.

"They're chasing me. Three of them. In rags. Blood... covered in blood. Something going on. Riots. Killing." The girl was breathless, her words coming out like garbled haiku. She had barely even noticed Daryl; he was just a body to cling to in her terror. "They came out of the hospital. The morgue."

Terror.

"I've been knocking on doors but no one would answer. Everybody ignored me..."

This was exactly what he sought: pure, undiluted terror. It tasted sweet, like honey, but possessed a wonderfully bitter aftertaste.

"Oh, yes," he muttered, reaching out a hand to stroke the girl's hair. Her boyish fringe had fallen across her lovely green eyes, obscuring them. Daryl thought of a quote often attributed to the famous American killer Ed Gein, something about whenever he saw a pretty girl part of him would imagine taking her out to dinner, sitting with her eating a nice meal. Another part of him always wondered what her head would look like mounted on a stick. "I see it," he said. "The fear. The potential."

For the first time since approaching Daryl, the young girl looked at him. She stared into his face, his eyes. Whatever she saw there, it scared her even more than her pursuers. She took a quick step back, almost turning the ankle of her shoed foot, and twisted into a shoulder-high privet hedge that ran along the front of someone's property.

Daryl stepped towards her, his skin tingling, fingertips on fire. Everything he'd planned and dreamed of was right here for the taking. The girl's features blurred, becoming indistinct, and another face overlaid hers like a fine line tracing. It was a familiar face, but one he'd only ever seen from a distance. A face he had coveted, along with the body it crowned, for too long.

The streetlights went out. An unholy roaring erupted from somewhere along the street. More rapid gunshots.

The girl screamed, breaking the moment and bringing Daryl out of his trance. She turned and ran back in the direction she'd come from, kicking off her shoe, her arms waving in the air. It seemed that she'd rather face whatever she'd been fleeing than remain with Daryl, the man she'd mistaken as a saviour.

Veering out into the road, the girl ran directly into the path of a speeding car. It took her down instantly, dragging her beneath the wheels and swerving, careering into a low stone wall at the street corner. The driver shot out through the windscreen, trailing a skirt of shattered glass. His body fell heavily, limbs loose and broken.

Daryl walked away, feeling more alive than he had in years. More alive than he had in his entire life until this moment, this glorious moment where he stood directly in the gaze of something majestic and so much larger than himself. His calling had come at last. After decades of dissecting stolen house pets, masturbating over pictures of corpses clipped from medical textbooks and pushing, pushing, towards some dimly realised goal, his time had come.

Daryl's head was filled with another image of Sally Nutman. He pictured her standing before him, unravelled, her skin punctured by his blades and the holes overflowing with his seed, babies of corruption being born through the wounds they had created together. She smiled; her teeth were eyes, her lips were the fingers of Mother's fist opening, parting, taking him in hand...

When he got back to the house he went to the kitchen and

drank a glass of water. He put his head under the tap, washing away the stinking sweat of lust, the filth of transformation, and then climbed the stairs to his room.

He stared at the photograph of Sally Nutman, licked it, and pressed it against his face, his chest, his aching erection – the first one he'd had in months. Then he placed it on the bed and bowed down before it, paying homage to the woman who had stepped forward from the crowd to offer herself up as his first victim, taking his cherry and allowing him into a select brotherhood.

Faces stared down from his walls, their lips moving in silence: praying to a new young god in the making. Ed Gein. Jeffrey Dahmer. Dennis Nilsen. Peter Sutcliffe. Countless others; his chosen audience.

Daryl dragged an old, battered cardboard suitcase from under his bed, threw it down on the divan. Then, moving slowly and with much reverence, he popped the clasps and laid out the contents on the mattress. He looked at them with an almost religious awe, the same expression Mother had on her face whenever she saw the Pope on television.

Daryl had bought most of these things on the Internet. They'd been delivered right to his door. It was funny how the methods of murder were so easily obtainable, like an order of groceries or a print run of self-help books.

He giggled, and then stopped himself, aware of the stern and disapproving eyes that stared down from his walls. This, he knew, was serious business.

Twines of good grade fishing line. Two rolls of duct tape. Several short lengths of industrial strength bungee. A long hunting knife with a serrated blade, a tool generally used for gutting wildlife. A thin-bladed flensing knife.

These were Daryl's chosen tools of his wished-for trade, the artefacts of his dark religion. His ritual would be carried out using these perfect objects, each ideally suited to its particular task. He had practised often on Mother as she lay there dying, trussing her up and sealing her mouth, and only drawing back moments before the kill. Yes, a real victim would struggle more, but that would only add to the power of the moment, the intensity of the event.

Soon the act would be over; he could take off the mask and become his true self, the being which had been growing inside him for so long. The butterfly could emerge from the pupa. The hatchling would come scrabbling out to dine for the first time on the manna of the world.

No more pretending. No more faking it. Soon, and for the first time since childhood, Daryl would know what it was like to *feel*.

CHAPTER SEVEN

"What the hell's going on, sir?" Rick was standing on the grass verge, bathed in flashing blue light. The sirens were off but the warning lights pulsed, pulsed, forcing an unwanted rhythm inside his brain. He stared at D.I. Harper, meeting the man's gaze, and refused to budge an inch.

"I dunno, son. This whole thing is a fucking mess." The big man shook his head, a sad look in his eyes. He was losing his grip, approaching an edge that he had previously skirted with ease.

"But... but what we saw in there, what we did. That wasn't normal. Any of it. There were people... *dead* people... fuck me, sir, you know what I'm talking about." Rick tensed his jaw, maintaining his gaze, flexing his fingers over the handle of the holstered Glock. It was a nervous habit, one he'd only just acquired. He wondered if it would be a keeper.

"Dead folk?" said D.I. Harper, his face a weird colour in the glow of the emergency lights. "Is that what you mean? Dead folk getting up and attacking us? Even our own men."

Men and women in uniform – police, ambulance, fire crew – were busying themselves at the scene, moving in well choreographed routines to secret music that Rick was unable to hear. His waltz was done, for now; but he was certain that it was too early to put away his dance shoes.

"Like I said, it's a mess." D.I. Harper had softened. His voice was low, slightly menacing, as if he were sharing a grim secret.

"What do you think caused all this?" Rick finally broke his gaze, glancing around at the activity. From the outside it no doubt looked frenetic, unfocused, but in reality everyone had a job to do and knew exactly what was expected of them.

D.I. Harper lit up a short fat cigar with a battered tin lighter. He rolled the lighter in his beefy hand, rubbing its well-worn surface with his fingers, as if it meant something to him – a gift, a memento. "My guess is that I have no guess. We could be looking at a new virus, or chemical warfare, even some sort of mass hallucination. But this is happening all over the city – all over the country. I suspect tonight is the culmination of events that have gone on for days, maybe even weeks."

Rick blinked, his eyes stinging from the smoke they'd run through inside the building. He was still focused, still in fighting mode, but some of his reflexes had slackened. "What are you saying, sir?"

D.I. Harper shook his massive head. His eyes were like those of a wise old dog, one that's seen just about everything the world has to offer yet is still capable of registering surprise. "Call me a conspiracy freak if you like, but this is too damn strange for my liking. It could have been anything, really. Bugs. Space aliens. That experiment over in France, the one they rigged up to re-enact the Big Bang. Fucking hell, it could even be some kind of Internet super-virus aimed at Bill Gates for all we know!"

Rick knew that he should think his superior officer's wild theories funny, but he couldn't find it in himself to laugh. The things he'd seen, the bloodshed he'd been part of... none of it made sense, not in a sane world. Maybe this *was* the result of something being passed through the world's computers, or a mutated virus let loose during illegal genetic experimentation. Who knew? Not him; not them. Nor was it their job to know, or to even think. Their job was to clear up the mess. To always, always just keep the hell quiet and clear up other people's messes.

Dark clouds passed overhead, their shapes writhing in the sky like stricken behemoths. The air turned damp, edgy. It would rain soon, possibly even snow. Rick thought of Sally, sitting there at home worrying, watching the news reports of all this madness and checking all the doors and windows.

He excused himself and walked to the edge of the building. Two men were loading a body onto a gurney, strangely silent as they worked. The body was covered in a white sheet with red stains. Near the top of the body, the sheet was a lot flatter than it should be. Rick wondered if the corpse was that of his friend Hutch.

He leaned against the wall and retrieved his mobile phone from a zippered pocket in his trouser leg. He took off his glove using his teeth, and then switched on the handset. The screen glowed, faintly at first but then brighter as the battery warmed up. When he was asked for his password he typed in the appropriate digits and waited for the handset to allow him to access the phone's memory.

The light grew brighter, stuttered, and then began to fade. He had two new messages, each of them from Sally. He listened to them both and smiled at the sound of her voice. She seemed wary but not terrified; worried but nowhere near to panic.

He dialled his home number.

A message appeared on the screen:

No network coverage.

He tried again and got the same result. Either everyone was clogging up the satellite relays and ringing their loved ones, or there was a problem with the signal. Of the two options, he preferred the former. It was easier to remain calm and focused if he thought that the reason he was unable to contact his wife was because the networks were busy – just like they got on the big holidays like New Year's Eve and Christmas Day – rather than imagining that the entire satellite grid had gone down.

Rick returned the handset to his pocket, forcing himself to remain in control. It was crucial that he was in charge of his emotions. He'd seen too many good men go down because they lost their heads in a crisis.

Like Hutch. He'd certainly lost *his* head in this crisis.

Not funny. Not fucking funny at all.

He stepped away from the building and joined a group of men he knew from his unit. They were jogging round to the back, checking that the perimeter was still secure. This was what he needed: routine, training; the ability to focus on his job, no matter how insane the situation. It had kept him alive in Afghanistan, and saved his skin in Iraq. Now it would keep him going long enough to get to Sally, and he'd work the rest out then, once she was in his arms, the warmth of her breath against his neck.

D.I. Harper nodded at him as he passed by, speaking into a two-way radio. He sounded stressed again, like he was hanging on by his fingertips. They all were. There was no other way to hang, not here, not now, amid this insanity.

A crowd had gathered to watch the clean-up. Most of the onlookers were on edge too, just like D.I. Harper, but their edginess was different: it promised yet more violence. Faces peered at him, their eyes huge and bright and perched on the precipice of panic. Sirens wailed across the rooftops; the fires still burned in the sky; distant gunshots punctuated the music of the city, an off-tempo rhythm section.

"Get back! Just get back! We have this under control. Please return to your homes and go about your business." A suited man Rick did not recognise was screaming into a bullhorn, his cheeks puffing out like those of a crazed cartoon character. "Return to your homes. Clear the area!"

Nobody moved. They just stood and stared, violence brewing. This was their turf; these were their streets. Nothing was allowed to happen here without them knowing, or even granting permission.

"This is going to kick off. Big style." The man next to Rick had a high-pitched voice, but he was broad as an ox. "They're just about to blow."

Rick said nothing. He simply watched and waited.

More bodies were being brought out of the building. There were no survivors. The terrorists had all been killed – most of them twice – and those officers who'd fallen under fire had been taken care of. The other corpses were those which had been discovered in some of the other flats, the departed loved ones of drugged-up tenants who'd been confused by the sudden death and resurrection of their friends and family members.

It had become obvious almost immediately that anyone who died would rise again within minutes, and they would attack whoever was nearest. The only way to prevent this was a headshot.

Rick had witnessed D.I. Harper shooting an unmoving corpse through the temple. Just to be sure, to be safe.

"God," he muttered. "Holy God..."

"What's that?" said the man next to him, the one with the high voice. He had beautiful clear blue eyes – young eyes in a baby face.

Before Rick had the chance to answer somebody started yelling.

The crowd began to surge, just a small movement but one that was building slowly, a ripple from the back that became a wave when it reached the front row of the massed onlookers. A barrier fell forward. There was no one to pick it up; everyone's attention was focused back at the building, where that yelling was still going on. The crowd shifted forward, forcing their way close to the action.

"Oh, shit!" Babyface ran towards two more men and another sheet-covered gurney, his gun drawn in an instant. The man on the stretcher had pulled himself upright by clawing his way along the ambulance man's arm. The other ambulance man was backing away: it was him who was doing all that yelling. He was crying for his God, his wife, his mother. For anyone who might listen.

Babyface ran at the corpse on the gurney, clearly unaware of the information those inside the building had been party to – not knowing that you had to shoot them in the head.

The dead man was already biting into the ambulance man's arm. The victim pulled away, stumbled, and fell beneath the gurney, stopping it dead. The dead man rolled off onto the ground, hands clawing, his arms flapping. He was still trying to reach the felled ambulance man.

Babyface arrived at speed and kicked the dead man full in the face. Unfortunately, the dead man had his mouth open and Babyface's foot smashed into the top row of teeth as it entered the gaping maw. The dead man bit down, a quick reflexive action. Blood spurted from Babyface's boot, and then as the dead man jerked his head to the side, the end of the boot came away. Along with a few of Babyface's toes.

Rapid bursts of gunfire. The dead man was blown to pieces.

Babyface screamed. And screamed. And screamed.

Rick turned away, making a decision that would eventually dictate the course of the rest of his life. *Fuck this*, he thought. *I'm out of here.*

"Nutman!" It was D.I. Harper. "Don't even think about it."

Rick was too stunned to speak. How had the D.I. known what he was about to do?

He watched as the big man approached, striding towards him with a cigar clenched between his teeth. "I know that look. I saw what you were about to do. I need every good man to remain at his post – particularly men like you: men with combat experience."

"Sir." Rick was unsure how to react.

"This is turning into a war, Officer Nutman. A fucking war. I've just spoken to the boys at the station, and they're under attack. Running battles all over the fucking city. Reports of walking dead are coming in thick and fast. We have a combat situation on our hands here, and we don't even know who the enemy is." He grabbed Rick by the lapel, pulled him up onto his tiptoes. "So *you're* staying put. Just like everyone else." The benevolent father-figure had vanished; now, in his place, stood a warrior, a leader of men.

"Yes, sir." Rick gently took hold of D.I. Harper's big-knuckled hands, tried to prise them from his clothing, but the man's grip was like iron. "I'm with you, sir. I'm with you."

D.I. Harper relaxed then, as if realising that he was stepping over the line. He let go of Rick's collar, stood back, and glanced around at the mayhem. "This is all so strange. So very strange." He had a faraway look in his eye. "I've seen some awful things in my life, son, some truly awful things, but never anything like this." His shoulders slumped, the energy spent. Then he looked up, directly into Rick's eyes. "Just stay with me, son. We all need to stick together, to act as a team. If we're going to get through tonight, we need to stand together like brothers, all of us pulling in the same direction."

The man's platitudes sounded vaguely ridiculous, as if they'd been scripted, but Rick nodded in agreement. He felt obliged to obey his superior officer, no matter how much the man seemed to be losing his grip. Obeying orders – both those of his unit and his own body – had helped keep him alive. But he couldn't remain here for long, whatever he was told. Sally needed him. He'd give it another hour for things to settle down, then leave quietly, without causing a fuss.

Mere seconds after this decisive thought, Rick's attention was drawn by the sound of many running feet. The watching crowd had finally been stirred into motion, and even now they were pushing a line of uniforms out of the way to get at the building and see for themselves what was going on.

Officers moved in, weapons aloft, and Rick closed his eyes and took a long, deep breath before joining his colleagues in their positions at the front line.

Rick knew what was coming. He knew it intimately.

CHAPTER EIGHT

Daryl felt oddly safe out on the streets. Despite the lawlessness, the fighting and looting and displays of aggression, he now possessed a self-assurance that had eluded him for most of his life. Were these simply more personality changes due to Mother's grip slackening, or had something occurred at a more fundamental level?

On his back was a new rucksack, the straps tight across his shoulders and digging into his armpits. Inside the bag were his tools, along with the photograph of Sally Nutman. She was his guiding light, his sole aim in all this wonderful chaos. With the city erupting around him, no one would even hear her death rattle; the extinction of her life-force would be lost amid the flowering brutality of this strange new world, a world he felt curiously at home in.

Mother's house was located in a suburb not far from the centre of Leeds. Daryl did not own a car, and he doubted that any taxis would be operating with so much going on, but it was a short walk, really. He'd traced the route many times in the past, and knew every shortcut along the way.

The best way was to follow the canal into the centre. It was usually a dangerous place to be after nightfall, but tonight *everywhere* was dangerous – indeed, the canal was probably safer than the streets and estates right now.

The moon was a faded orb masked by heaving clouds. Starlight was negligible. The pathways were illuminated by the cold light of street lamps, and Daryl picked his way past wrecked cars, overturned bins and piles of shattered glass and rubble. The occasional scream leapt at him from the darkness, garbled words echoed along lightless ginnels and alleyways. Daryl kept moving, trying to blend into the night. He'd always been an unnoticeable figure, and tonight that anonymity was a weapon almost as potent as the ones in his rucksack.

He'd left Mother in her room, staring into the giddy blackness and fearing the sight of her own private Reaper. Perhaps it would have Richard Nixon's face, or maybe it would be dark and featureless, skulking in the shadows of her room. The latter thought pleased Daryl; because of Mother's fear of the dark, it suited that darkness would claim her.

The canal towpath crunched underfoot, pebbles and broken glass scattered across its narrow width. The black waters ran slow and sombre, with not even a duck or waterfowl about to mar its glassy surface. It *felt* like the end of the world.

Daryl hurried along the towpath, his thoughts filled with images of blood and the sound of muted screaming. He had another erection – this was a banner night for his libido. He wondered if Sally Nutman would recognise him, if she had noted his scrutiny at some point over the last few months. Part of him hoped that just before she died, her eyes would blaze with recognition. The other half of him prayed that she would die in utter confusion, not knowing who he was or why he'd decided to use her in such a way.

The waters shone blackly at his side, reflecting his desires. The canal was like a mirror; the images it contained matched those he'd carried around in his head since he was a child. It felt as if the landscape around him was shifting, altering to accommodate his new shape. The sky had lifted, allowing him to breathe, the trees and bushes bordering the path pulled back from his approach, the path itself twisted and undulated to meet his falling feet.

After years of feeling apart, isolated, he at last felt that he had a place in the world. A dark place, filled with demons.

It was only fitting that his first victim be as beautiful as Sally Nutman. He'd adored her features from afar, cementing that face in his mind. The slanted cat-like eyes, the firm jawline, the long, graceful neck. It would not suffice to kill an ugly woman first; a beautiful act must be carried out on a special victim. He began to regret that this long-awaited act might soon be over. He'd spent so long fantasising about it, building the whole thing up inside his head, that he feared the actual kill might be an anticlimax.

But, no. It was stupid to think that way. Here he was, on the cusp of *becoming*, and all he could do was whine! He sensed the disapproval of his heroes, his masters; their long shadows followed him along the towpath, maintaining their distance but never slackening their pace.

He heard a splash as he walked beneath a low concrete footbridge. Graffiti adorned the abutments: crude drawings and obscene slogans meant to express a rage that could never otherwise be demonstrated. The splash came again, softer, as if moving away.

Daryl stopped and looked out at the water, trying to make out what was causing the sounds. His eyes fell upon a discarded shopping trolley tethered to the opposite bank by the knotted fronds of some riverside weed. Nearby, a child's doll floated in a slow circle, pink and naked and deformed. Then, turning his head to face eastward, he finally saw what was making the noise.

A fat white corpse was struggling to climb out of the canal. Water-bloated and covered in black silt, the thing kept gaining a few inches before slipping back down the bank and into the water. Daryl could see it from behind, so was unobserved. He watched it for a while, enjoying its struggling motion. The body was naked, its flesh puffy and discoloured. The fat arms and stubby hands looked as if they were made of dough as they grasped at the mud on the sloped side of the canal.

Daryl edged along the path, watching. It was an amazing sight, when you thought about it, like something from a nightmare. He supposed that the corpse must belong to a drowning victim who'd suddenly risen from the murky depths, heading for shore to return home.

He paused, and wondered why he'd accepted all this so readily. Reanimated corpses. The living dead. Perhaps it took the truly insane to accept a truly insane situation?

The Michelin-man body rolled as it grabbed a handful off moss, its bulk turning in the water. The face was hideous: a mass of jellied flesh and fish-bite wounds. It had no eyes, which went some way to explaining why it found it so difficult to gain the canal bank. The nose was gone, too; all that remained was a clean but ragged hole through which Daryl glimpsed white bone.

The corpse opened its mouth as if trying to scream. Canal water slid from between its fattened lips, spilling down over its flabby breasts and corpulent belly. Its lower portion was obscured by the dark water, so Daryl could not make out if it was male or female. If he was honest, he'd rather not know anyway.

As he drew abreast of the corpse, a fortuitous accident occurred. Still caught in its slow roll, the body's momentum carrying it round in an agonising circle which pivoted at the thing's hand – which was still holding on to the side of the canal – the corpse began to slide towards a steel stanchion that stuck out from the bank.

Daryl watched in quiet awe as the stanchion pierced the side of the thing's head, just above the ear, driving slowly into the sodden skull as if it were paper. The head split, the length of steel tearing it so that the waterlogged contents of the brain pan spilled out into the canal.

The corpse hung there, twisting in the undertow. The split had stretched around the front of the head, connecting with the mouth, so that it resembled a smile. Or a salacious leer.

Daryl laughed, and then continued on his way. For some reason the whole episode felt like a prelude to something bigger.

Knowing how silly it seemed, he felt that the drowned corpse had been sent to him as a sign to show him something he would only understand later, once he was indoctrinated into the league of killers he longed to join.

He passed a burned-out concrete structure, an old storage shed used now for drug taking. Dirty syringes littered the doorway, and something stirred within. Daryl glanced into the darkness and saw a thin figure sitting against the wall. Its white limbs were skinny as pipe-cleaners and pin-cushioned with needles as it searched for a vein.

He hurried on, processing the information in a rush.

Habit. It all boiled down to habit.

These dead things – these hideous revived remains – fell into the same habits they'd suffered in life. The drug addict returned to the needle; the mother came back for her babe; the victim of a drowning once more attempted to climb back on to dry land. Life, he mused, was full of such cycles. The living re-enacted their daily routines, their lives becoming like a film clip stuck on a loop. So when they came back from the dead, what else was there but to *resume* that loop, to climb back into the rut and carry on carrying on?

It made perfect sense to Daryl. The dead tried to copy the living. It was all they knew, all they had within them: primitive urges, tribal acts, a repetition of events tattooed onto their memories by social custom and workaday existence. Strip away the thought process and all we are is habit, routine, learned experience. Like a mouse stuck on an exercise wheel, the dead just kept on running, with no destination in sight.

He crossed the railway line and then doubled back in a loop, the city rising before him. He could see the lights – far fewer than usual at this time of night – and the rooftops of the higher buildings scraped the sky like glass and concrete fingers. He focused on his destination; one of the new docks along this side of the canal, where developers had built apartment blocks and fitness complexes.

Allinson Dock was less than a mile away. He knew the spot by heart, had traced the route both in life and in his dreams too many times to even count. Further along the river, at Clarence Dock, he could make out the blocky structure of the Royal Armouries Museum, with its hexagonal glass and steel tower set amid a clutter of oblongs. The windows reflected the canal water, glittering like huge insectoid eyes. Daryl admired the illusion, enjoying the fantasy while it lasted.

He left the canal and cut across a short bushy verge, stepping over the town planners' idea of an urban green zone. Empty beer cans, bottles and used condoms were scattered between the shrubs.

Heading uphill, he reached a smooth, flat road surface. The road led into the apartment complex where Sally and her husband lived; it terminated in a few parking spaces that flanked the entrance to the underground car park.

Daryl squatted in the bushes and waited, scoping out the site. He watched a dark figure as it scuttled on all-fours, heading for the canal. The figure – it looked like a woman crawling around in the mud – disappeared into the undergrowth, and there followed a single splash as she entered the water. Daryl held his breath; he heard nothing more of the curious figure.

Nearby, the burned remains of a car smouldered, the metal of the bodywork groaning and creaking as it cooled.

He stared at the apartment block, locating Sally's seventh-floor windows with ease. He knew exactly where they were. All the windows were dark, but that did not prevent him from identifying the ones Sally hid behind, thinking that she was safe and secure.

He smiled. The darkness nestled around him, wrapping him in a comforting cloak.

Minutes passed, but Daryl did not keep track of how many. Eventually his legs began to ache from sitting in the same position, his rear end held inches from the ground and all his weight taken on the annoyingly weak muscles of calves that simply would not develop no matter how hard he tried to train them. He stood, stretching, sucking in the night. Sally's windows remained black, silent, and blind to the terror he brought. The temperature dropped around him, the air becoming sharp.

After another few moments he moved on, cutting across the road and entering the landscaped area at the side of the building. A few night birds hopped between the branches of the low trees; something burrowed into the foliage at his feet. There might be rats this close to the canal, but it was probably something as harmless as a hedgehog.

"I'm coming," he whispered. "I'm coming, dollface." It was not the kind of casual language he ever used; the lines were taken from some film he'd seen. All of his best lines came from films, or books. Not that he ever spoke them to anyone other than his own face in the mirror, or perhaps Mother's closed bedroom door...

The main doors operated on an expensive security system, involving a pass code and a CCTV monitor, but there was a man who lived on the ground floor, in apartment Number 03, who habitually neglected certain essentials of home security. He always left his bathroom window ajar. The man worked nights. Daryl knew this from his surveillance exercises; either unaware or uncaring of the dangers inherent in city living, the man never bothered to close the window when he left for his job. Daryl stepped softly along the side of the building, ducking below the eye-line of the windows.

Soon he reached the open window.

He reached up, slid his arm inside, and popped the catch. It was that easy: the fine line between entry and exclusion, life and death, was a scant few inches of air between sill and frame. It was almost absurd the risks some people took without ever acknowledging the possible consequences.

Daryl glanced along the length of the building, carefully inspecting the area for prying eyes. Then, satisfied that no one was around to witness him, he clambered up the wall, finding a foothold on the smart new cladding, and forced his thin body through the window.

Once inside the bathroom he returned the window to its former position, being careful to ensure that it looked exactly as it had before. Once he was satisfied, he walked across to the door and stepped out into a long narrow hallway. The front door was located at one end of this hallway; the living room was at the other.

Daryl didn't bother to have a nose around the apartment. He simply walked to the front door, opened it, and let himself out. He moved swiftly to the fire stairs – the lift might not be working due to the power blackouts – and climbed to the seventh floor, where Sally was waiting for him.

He'd been inside before, sneaking in after another tenant before the main door could close. He'd received a funny look, but was not challenged, even though he had stayed there for two hours, exploring the interior of the building and waiting for Sally's husband to return home from a day shift so he could study any idiosyncratic lifestyle patterns the man exhibited. Even then he was aware that the slightest piece of behavioural data might help him in the future, when finally the time came to put his plan into action.

He was breathing heavily when he reached the seventh floor, and his lungs ached slightly. At home he lifted weights to add strength – but not bulk – to his wiry physique. He had the body of a distance runner: lean, powerful limbs, a hard, skinny torso, but his *lower* legs – specifically his ever-puny calf muscles – remained weak and his stamina was terrible. His upper body strength, however, belied the narrow build he hid beneath his baggy clothing.

He was certain that Sally would admire his physique. He would leave her no choice in the matter.

He approached the door to her apartment and stood outside, running his hands across the surprisingly lightweight wooden door. She sat behind an inch of hollow, low-grade timber, awaiting his ministrations.

"Oh, baby. Baby, baby, baby." He giggled, but made sure that he kept it low, under his breath.

Then, feeling an enormous surge of energy building from the soles of his feet and climbing the length of his body, flowering at the midriff, throat and face, he knocked six times in rapid succession upon the door – exactly the way he knew that Sally's husband, that idiot copper, always knocked.

He repeated the jokey secret knock – again, just like the husband always did – and then stepped back to wait for Sally to open the door and let him in; a shy suitor nervously awaiting his reluctant paramour.

CHAPTER NINE

The crowd's mood was turning nasty. Young men and women were pushing and shoving each other to get through the hastily assembled cordon of officers. Rick took his place in the line, using the riot shield he'd been given moments earlier by a stern-faced Sergeant by the name of Finch. A veteran of the miners' strikes back in the 1980s, Finch was a bull of a man with a broad build, a solid gut and a grey beard. His eyes were steely; they'd looked upon horrors normal men could barely even contemplate. His name was spoken in whispers along the station corridors, and his reputation was immense.

"Hold the line!" Finch's voice boomed above the noise, making him heard despite the rising volume of other voices – shouts and threats and chants. "Make a wall. Be ready!"

Rick shifted backwards and tucked into the wall formed by his colleagues, holding up his reinforced plastic shield to link with those of the men on either side of him. The crowd surged again, forcing a way through. Finch barked more commands, but this time the sound of his voice was drowned out by the rising tumult of obscenities. The crowd would not be held. The mood was building, turning intense and somehow animalistic.

Rick raised his head from the line and looked up at the sky, taking a moment away from the melee. Tiny snowflakes had begun to fall, drifting like confetti thrown onto a wedding crowd. The noise receded; a silent weight flooded in to replace the jeers. He felt calm for a moment, above and apart from the commotion. Bodies slammed against him but he could not take his eyes from those wondrous white specks as they fell to earth in lazy, haphazard patterns. His breath misted before his eyes; he didn't know how long it had been so cold, and had failed to notice the radical drop in temperature before now.

The snowflakes melted on impact with the ground, as if such a pitiless place could not hold on to their purity.

Suddenly the area was flooded with bright white light. The ground became a sort of screen; flat, blank and reflective. Two police helicopters swung low over the scene and hovered, the sound of their rotors deafening. The crowd seemed to pause *en masse* then, as if the mere presence of the 'copters had made each individual aware of what he or she was doing and re-evaluate their stance. Finch took the opportunity to strengthen the line, and the man with the bullhorn shouted instructions.

The crowd still seemed caught between two states of mind; they were all poised on the brink of something catastrophic, yet not one of them was willing to follow through. Then, just before a breaking point was reached, Finch fired his pistol into the air.

Five shots. Rick was so acutely attuned, so *hyper aware*, that he managed to count every one of them. The crowd seemed to take in a single breath, giving up an inch of ground, and at that point every officer present knew that the situation had been salvaged. This was northern England, not downtown LA; when someone started shooting, it was still an unusual enough event to shatter almost any moment of tension.

The life went out of the massed bystanders; they broke up into smaller groups, the mob physically losing its shape. The threat of violence was still there, but now it was subdued and had returned to skulk beneath the surface, peeking out like a naughty child caught in the act of an indiscretion.

"Let's get this shit cleared," said Finch, and Rick was unsure whether he meant the still-present crowd, the bodies, or the whole damn thing.

In Rick's experience, it often happened the same way in battle. One minute the dogs of war were straining at their leashes and the blood ran like lava in the veins of those building for warfare; the next minute, after the initiative had been taken and the pressure relieved, it was as if conflict had never been an option. He had struggled to acclimatise to the wild swings of emotion, the acute stresses, when he first joined the army, but after his initial tour of duty it became like second nature. First nature, if he was honest. Once a man has tasted the potential of battle, he never functions in quite the same way again.

A short time later it was like the standoff had never even happened. Clusters of bystanders still hung around on the fringes of the scene, smoking cigarettes, sipping cans of cheap supermarket beer, even eating burgers and kebabs – unbelievably, some opportunistic local vendor had set up his van a few yards away.

Rick stood watching the vicinity, awaiting further orders. During the lull, his mind returned to Babyface and the way the dead man had bitten clean through the end of the lad's tough leather boot. Surely that was not possible: no human being could bite through that kind of material.

But were these dead things actually human, or in the process of revival did all humanity simply fall away?

He recalled another episode from a few months before, when a training exercise had turned serious. He and a handful of fellow recruits had been practicing manoeuvres on a local football field after dark when a solitary figure had wandered over. The man was pumped full of illegal drugs – PCP, probably, judging by what happened next. The man had gone wild for no reason whatsoever, pulling out a kitchen knife from under his shirt. He stabbed one man and slashed two others, taking several truncheon blows to the head in the process, but kept on coming, swinging that lethal blade through the air.

Finally he'd been felled by a rubber bullet. None other than Finch, the principal officer in charge of the training exercise, had characteristically stepped up to sort things out. The man had gone down only because his body reacted to the shot; his mind was still on the attack, sending signals of aggression to his flailing limbs.

Maybe it was the same with these dead things? Because they were already dead, they felt no pain; their physical responses were not like those of the living. Maybe they would just keep on coming, brushing off all attacks, until somebody destroyed the brain – the engine that drove them.

"How are you holding up?" Finch stood at his side, as if appearing from nowhere. It was because of such feats that he was ranked as a legend among the uniformed officers. He was always there, always watching and waiting for a problem to solve.

"Still here, sir."

Finch smiled. "Cigarette?"

Rick shook his head. "I don't, sir."

"I give you another three months before you do." Finch lit the cigarette, smiling around the short flame. His heavy-browed face looked eerie in the flickering light, like a Japanese demon mask. His iron-grey hair was swept back from his hairline, and his eyes shone. "Listen up Nutman. I know you have a new wife at home, so if you were to have vanished during that little skirmish back there I'd put in my report that the last time I saw you, you were holding the line with the rest of us." Finch raised his eyes, peering out from under his tough-looking forehead. Everyone knew he'd lost his wife to cancer. She had died slowly, and in great pain. After her funeral, the famously hardcore Finch had softened, but in a way that gained him even more respect. Almost overnight, as if it were the result of an epiphany, he'd turned from a hard-edged bastard into someone who genuinely cared about the men under his command.

"I'll hang around a while longer, sir. Just to make sure everything's okay. D.I. Harper's on the warpath. I wouldn't want to upset him again."

Finch smiled again, showing his shockingly white teeth; they looked nothing like the teeth of a heavy smoker. "Listen, your shift ended a couple of hours ago, everything's fine here. Go home, Nutman. Go to your wife. The shit has gone up all over this city – all across the country. Last thing I heard, London was going under. Liverpool is struggling. Fuck knows what's happening in Manchester. We're teetering on the edge here in Leeds. In another hour, you won't even be able to move across the city to get to your missus."

The gravity of what Finch was saying began to sink in. The man was right: if situations like this one were happening city-wide, the main roads would soon be blocked. Gangs and looters were already out in force and whatever units remained on the clock would be struggling to shut down the city, to keep it all under some semblance of control.

Things did not look good, whichever angle you viewed them from.

Finch finished his cigarette and threw the butt on the ground. He stamped on it more times and much harder than was strictly necessary, as if making a point. Giving one final glance at Rick, he winked. Then he was gone, gravitating towards some other part of the night, where men like him were needed, always needed.

The bloodstained desert of Afghanistan, many clicks south of Kabul, was never far from Rick's mind. Even now, back home, the sounds and sights and smells of the hot dunes remained with him, colouring his perception. Back in Helmand Province, when the gunfire had started and a concealed device had blown the tracks off the US military Humvee he and his two best friends were travelling in, he'd made a rushed promise to a God he did not believe in. He'd made a pact with whatever deity might be listening that if he survived this one, he would never abandon Sally again. Surely this was the time to make a return on that promise – if there was a test to be taken, what better time than now, when all the rules had changed and the world had become unbalanced?

Perhaps the God he'd never believed in *did* in fact exist in such an altered world.

He glanced around, noting the positions of all nearby officers, then quietly turned and walked into the darkness towards a low brick wall behind which lay a grotty urban park. He climbed the barrier in a second, hopping over it without making as much as a slight sound. When he dropped down on the other side, he rolled and kept low as he moved towards the small stand of trees at the rear of the paltry half acre of faded greenery.

No one called his name. Nor did anyone come running to drag him back to his post. Acting on the decision had been easier than he'd imagined. Deserting his duty; it felt wrong, against his nature. But if he stayed put and hoped for the best, Sally would be forced to handle events on her own.

No way. That was out of the question.

If a trained killer could not protect his loved ones, then what good was that training? He'd done his duty, even in these extraordinary circumstances – no one could accuse him otherwise. Now it was time to let the populace take care of their own problems and hope that he did not have a serious one of his own.

He glanced back and saw a couple of dark, shadowy figures drifting away from the block of flats, heading off into the side streets and cul-de-sacs of the estate. Had Sergeant Finch whispered into more ears than his, or had those others reached the same decision as Rick on their own?

Good for them, he mused: strange times called for unusual measures, and in a world gone mad, the only thing stronger than death was love.

CHAPTER TEN

The internet server was unstable but still Sally managed to establish a somewhat tenuous connection.

After the lights went out and the TV and radio died, she'd unpacked her laptop and set it up on the dining table in the open plan kitchen. She sat by the window, glancing occasionally over her shoulder to check on the situation outside. She'd seen no one else since the car crash, after which that hideously injured woman had crawled off into the darkness at the side of the canal.

The laptop battery had about an hour's worth of juice and she was linked up to a wireless hub. Scanning news sites and message forums she'd already managed to establish the scale and immediate impact of events. It was massive: an international phenomenon that was even now spreading across the globe, respecting no borders and tearing down all geographical and political demarcations.

London, the capital, was on its last legs. All the major cities were falling. The reason behind this madness was impossible to comprehend; even now, after reading so many first hand accounts online, she refused to accept it as the truth.

The dead, those disembodied cyber personalities – lines of text pretending to be voices – told her, had risen and begun to attack the living. Graveyards, morgues, the cold rooms in hospital basements: all were origins of the attacks. The buried dead, the recently deceased, the murdered, the accidents, the suicides... they were all climbing out of their coffins, off their slabs, up from their death scenes, and walking, attacking, killing. Eating.

It was insane.

Sally was monitoring a BBC message forum, a local chat group dedicated to the Leeds area. It was usually a place where people gathered online to discuss topics of concern or interest – crime rates, council taxes, wheely bins and forthcoming events in and around West Yorkshire. Tonight – or was it morning already; she'd lost track of time – the forum was buzzing with terrified people unable to sleep and sharing information about the situation outside.

mum died half n hr ago

This abrupt message represented the continuation of an ongoing discussion in which Sally was involved from earlier: a thirteen year old girl whose mother had been attacked by a group of teenagers several hours ago as she went out to investigate a ruckus outside their home. The girl did not know how to drive and an ambulance had failed to arrive. The girl's mother had been stabbed. She'd died from her injuries.

stay calm, honey

Sally felt helpless. What else could she do but offer faceless support, floating around like an inarticulate god?

shez moving. just sat up in bed. luks funny. like shez drunk or somethng.

Sally's fingers hovered over the keyboard. What on earth was she meant to do? She didn't even know where the girl was located – just that she was somewhere in Leeds. Even if she did have an address, by the time she got there (*if* she even got there) it would be much too late to make a difference.

get out. get out of the room. lock her in. lock yourself in a cupboard.

Sally held her breath, waiting for the girl's response. She didn't even know her name.

needz me. makng thiz like crying noiz. moaning.
think shez thirsty. or hungry.

"No. Don't!" Sally typed quickly, trying to focus her energy through the keyboard, along the wireless connection, and out towards the girl. She needed help, but none was coming. None was ever coming.

don't go to her. run away. run run run run

The dialogue was over. The girl did not respond.

Sally waited, waited, her heart pressing hard against the bones of her chest, threatening to tear a hole in her breast. She could hardly breathe; this was all too much to handle. Just a girl – a young girl and her dead mother. It wasn't fair, wasn't right. None of this should be happening.

Tears came, with a force that actually stopped her breath, but they were not cathartic. They hurt, burning like a mild acid on her cheeks. Sally's head dropped, her gaze at last leaving the laptop screen. She closed her eyes, wishing that it would all go away, that Rick would arrive and everything would return to normal.

When she looked again at the laptop, the resolution was fading, the screen light dimming. A message popped up in the bottom right hand corner.

Disconnected.

Then someone knocked on the door.

Sally turned to look through the kitchen archway, peering into the swirling darkness and wondering who it could be. Rick. Of course, it had to be Rick. He'd heard her messages and been allowed to return home. She suddenly felt lightheaded, like a love-struck teenager. It was an odd reaction under the circumstances, and the feeling took her by surprise. She'd expected relief, perhaps even a muted form of joy, but not this strange sense of wanton excitement.

Rick knocked again, six times; their secret code, instilled in her as a safety measure for when he was working the late shift. Even when he had his keys, he always knocked first just to let her know it was him.

"I'm coming," she called, struggling to her feet as she pushed the chair away from the dining table. The legs screeched on the hardwood floor. The laptop slid across the tabletop, forgotten for now. She could try to re-establish the connection later, once she and Rick had made the apartment secure.

Rushing along the hallway, she attempted to reign in her emotions. What if it wasn't Rick at the door? Surely he would have responded to her call, putting her at ease with soothing words or a snatch of gentle banter. She approached the door and pressed the palm of one hand against the grainy texture of its surface. The door felt cold to her touch.

"Hello?"

No answer. If it was Rick out there, he must be hurt; otherwise he would be calling her name, telling her to open up.

"Hello. Who's there?"

A short pause, followed by a low, smooth voice: "My name is Daryl. I live downstairs – the next floor down. My wife is hurt and no one else will answer their door. Please... please, I need help. The phone line is dead. I'm afraid."

Yes, she reasoned, the phone lines *were* all down. She'd seen and heard nothing of the other neighbours, assuming they'd all simply gone to ground inside their own homes. This man sounded plausible; he needed help, and because Sally had been unable to rescue the girl she'd communicated with earlier, she felt the need to lend a hand here.

"Daryl? Are *you* hurt? Do you know what's going on?" She pressed her cheek against the door, listening intently to his voice, looking for a flaw in his story. Rick had always taught her to be careful, be sure of herself before trusting anyone.

"No, I'm fine. Just a little shaken. My wife collapsed. I don't know why. I called for an ambulance earlier, but the call was cut off. I'm not sure exactly what's going on out there... but it's bad. Really bad."

The final two words convinced her of his authenticity. His voice had cracked, as if the fear was overwhelming. It must have taken a lot of courage to even step outside of his apartment to go in search of aid. She wondered if she would be up to such a feat if the same thing had happened to her – if she needed to find help because Rick was ill or even (God forbid) dead.

"Okay, Daryl. Please step back from the door, and I'll open up. I want to see you first, in the security spy hole." She moved to the left and put her eye to the tiny glass peephole set in the middle of the door. A short, harried-looking figure stood on the other side, glancing nervously along the landing. He was shorter than Sally by what she guessed was at least a few inches, and his build was slight – even puny. As she studied his smooth bespectacled face, she realised that he did indeed look vaguely familiar. She must have seen him around the building, perhaps had even spoken to him in the lift on her way to work.

"That's fine, Daryl. I can see you. I've seen you before."

The man smiled.

"I'm going to open the door now. Get ready to step inside so I can get it shut again as quickly as possible. I don't want to take any unnecessary risks."

He smiled again. Sally realised that he must be experiencing intense relief that someone had responded to his plea for help. He must be terrified, and worried that his wife might die and... and become one of *them*: the things roaming around out there, in the night, grabbing hold of whatever warm flesh they could find.

Feeling slightly more in control now that she was doing something positive, Sally pulled opened the door and stepped to the side, allowing the man to squeeze past her and enter the apartment. He was a good two inches shorter than her – that must make him something like five foot five. His hair was uncombed and out of condition and he had a mild buzz of razor rash down one side of his throat. Her first impression had almost been correct: he was thin, but not scrawny. Beneath his jacket and shirt she sensed he would be fit and toned. His legs, however, were skinny – particularly the calves – like those of a child.

"Thank you, Sally," he said, moving along the passageway and into the main living area. His feet trod softly; he made very little sound as he walked.

"How do you know my name?" Sally did not follow him into the apartment. She stood by the door, one hand on her thigh and the other held loose, ready to open the door again if she needed to leave in a hurry.

Daryl grinned. "Sorry. I think one of the other tenants told me. I remember when you and your partner – is it Richard – were married. Saw the wedding cars parked outside."

"Rick," she said, shuffling forward, slightly more at ease. "His name's Rick. He's a policeman." She didn't really know why she'd added this information, but it made her feel better that Daryl knew what her husband did for a living. "Armed Response."

Daryl nodded. It was a slow, almost cautious movement. "Yes, I know. I've seen him around. Even spoke to him a few times, down in the lobby."

Sally entered the living room, keeping to the edges of the space. She was unsure of this man but had no concrete reason to distrust his motives. He'd come here for help; surely that made him safe. "Where was it you said you lived? Which apartment?"

"Number three. Ground floor." He was examining a photo frame that contained a picture taken on their wedding day. A grey limo. Rick lounging on the bonnet in his rented suit and she clad in a second-hand wedding dress she'd bought from eBay. Trees stood in the background, soaked by the rain that had never stopped that day and went on well into the following week. A typical summer wedding.

"I thought you said you lived on the floor directly underneath. You did say that, didn't you?" She wracked her brain to remember if he had indeed claimed to live directly beneath her place, but couldn't quite grasp his words.

"No," he said, taking off his rucksack. It was new. He'd even left the price tag dangling from one of the zippers. "I just said that I lived downstairs. Didn't stipulate a floor."

Sally suddenly realised that Daryl had carefully worked his way around the room and now stood between her and the exit. He was taking off his coat. His glasses had steamed up, so he removed them and began to rub them on his sweater. The sweater was like something an unfashionable teenager might wear – some cheap knock-off from a shabby market stall.

"Well. Well, well, well." He laid the jacket across the back of a chair, stroked it with the flat of his hand. His rucksack was resting at his feet, a tame dog; it was still sealed but easily within reach. "I've waited a long time for this, Sally. You wouldn't even believe how long I've wanted to meet you." He put back on his glasses, smiling coyly.

Then she understood. This pathetic little man obviously had the hots for her. He'd spied on her from his apartment, wishing that he could orchestrate a meeting, and tonight had finally summoned the nerve to come calling. The opportunist little bastard. "What about your wife?" she said, glaring at him. "I thought she was hurt?"

"No. Not hurt."

She imagined Daryl's spouse sitting on her own downstairs, probably under the impression he'd gone to find out what was going on, when in reality he was stalking one of the neighbours.

"Not hurt. To be honest, she doesn't even exist. I made her up. I don't have a wife... just a... just a Mother." His empty smile was lopsided, like a morbid scar. It transformed him from a sad little wanker into something far more dangerous and worthy of a lot more caution.

"I... I don't understand. Which apartment do you live in?" The answer was already there, somewhere deep inside her brain, but still she felt that she must ask the question.

He took a step closer. Just the one: a short, nimble movement that took her utterly by surprise with its elegance. "Don't be silly. I don't even live in this building. I've come quite a way to meet you, Sally Nutman. Further than you could ever imagine." He closed his eyes, inhaled deeply, and then opened his eyes again, staring right at her. Through the thick lenses of his glasses, those eyes looked huge and desolate, gaping holes in his vicious skull.

Daryl moved forward again, exercising an impressive economy of movement. He was like a dancer, displacing the air before him rather than actually flexing his body through it. Shock waves shimmered across the room, unseen but felt by them both – a soft draft on the skin of the arms, a disturbance in the atmosphere.

"Don't come any closer..." Her words trailed off, useless.

"Do you even understand how redundant that plea is? Or was it meant as a threat? He bent down from the waist and picked up his rucksack. Unzipping the main pocket, he took out a bundle of rags and discarded the bag. Unfolding the bundle, he first produced a knife. There where other things in there too, but Sally could not see beyond the long serrated blade, the blinking stainless steel smile.

"Oh, God."

"God?" Daryl slashed the blade through the air, practicing. "I don't believe in God. Certainly not Mother's God – and not after the things I've seen tonight. Do you even know what's going on out there, beyond the walls of your fucking ivory tower? The dead are walking about, refusing to lie down. They are no longer at rest."

Sally's gaze flicked around the room, looking for a weapon. Anything would do, but sadly there was nothing that she could use against him, not even a heavy ornament. She had never been a fan of having such things cluttering up the surfaces; she preferred prints on the walls, books and photographs on the shelves. Right now, under the current circumstances, she was beginning to regret her taste in furnishings.

Even the books she owned were lightweight; the thought of throwing a Ben Elton or a Jackie Collins paperback at his head provoked in her a desperate form of laughter that felt absurdly inappropriate.

"Oh, *perfect*." Daryl was grinning now, but still there was nothing beneath the expression – no depth, no real emotion: no humanity. "I've just thought of something. I can't believe that it's only just occurred to me. If the dead are getting up and walking, there's a fair chance that you might rise and attack whoever finds your body. When I'm done with you, of course. After I've finished."

He swayed like a cobra, music she could not hear ululating in his ears. His lips were open; there were twin white dabs of spit at the sides of his mouth. The skin of his cheeks flushed red, as if he was embarrassed. Or aroused.

Sally prayed for a miracle. She wished that Rick would arrive back home, tired and drained from the night's exertions, but still able to save her. Save her from the pain and degradation this abomination of a man must surely have been planning to put her through for such a long time.

As Daryl danced towards her, a silver flash in his hand and dark deeds in his heart, the last thing Sally thought of was her wedding day, and Rick's beautiful face dropping from the sky to engulf her own, lips parted, eyes on fire, teeth as white and as filled with promise as the years she'd always thought would stretch ahead of them.

The night opened before her like a series of gigantic black doorways; the apartment vanished, consumed by limitless darkness. A dull roaring sound filled the universe, and in every nook and cranny, every ditch and hidey-hole, each ancient, forgotten corner of the country, nameless and faceless creatures began to feed...

CHAPTER ELEVEN

...Sunderland, a small terraced cottage. A middle-aged woman named Beth Hardy readies herself for bed. Heavy winter nightdress, thick knee-length socks, a hot mug of cocoa. Climbing into bed, she hears a sound outside her bedroom window. It is late. She suffers from terrible insomnia. Who can be out and about at this hour?

Beth puts her cup down on the cluttered bedside cabinet, beside a James Patterson novel. She slips out from beneath the duvet and crosses the room to the window. Her late husband's watch, key ring and old-fashioned hair brushes rest upon the top of the dresser, a small shrine to the only man she has ever loved.

Smiling sadly, an ache in her chest, she leans across the dresser and opens the curtains.

The face she sees looking in at her is at once familiar and totally alien. It *looks* like her late husband, has the same salt-and-pepper hair, squat American nose (he was born in Texas; his family crossed the pond to England when he was eleven), sad, almost mournful grey eyes, grizzled beard on his blunt chin, but surely it cannot be Norm? The man has been dead for nearly a year, after his heart failed during a midnight visit to the lavatory.

The Norm-thing shifts an inch to the left, the movement enough to break the spell and allow Beth to acknowledge the signs of decay. His cheeks have fallen into his face, those sombre eyes are dried out and sightless, the nose she once loved has been partially eaten away. The salt-and-pepper hair looks more like dust-and-cobwebs.

Beth knows that she should scream; can feel the response building in her throat, travelling up from her gut. But she does not make a sound. Instead she walks through into the living room, and stands before the front door. She listens, her ears alert to the shuffling sound as the Norm-thing traces a familiar route to the doorstep.

For years, her friends had warned her of his gallivanting ways, his dirty stop-out nature, but in the end, like clockwork, he always returned to her bed. No matter which whore he had on the go behind her back, she was always the one he came back to, cap in hand, dick in pants, an apology on his clever tongue.

Beth pauses before opening the door, and then flings it open to greet her dead husband. The Norm-thing, hung in rags and stinking of grave dirt, leans in for one last kiss...

... Birmingham, a run-down sink estate. Danny Blake stands on a street corner, needing a fix. He doesn't care what he ends up with; he just wants something to ease the tension, remove the sights and sounds of the shit hitting the fan. He knows that it isn't exactly safe here, on this lonely corner, but none of his usual contacts can be reached.

He needs to find someone quickly; anyone with a deal to be made.

Becka moaned and griped when he took the food money, but the baby could always suck her tit if it got too hungry. Sure, it was a bit old for that, but when needs must...

A sound startles him. Shuffling footsteps. A can being kicked into the gutter. None of the lights in this grimy street are working; darkness sits heavy across his shoulders like a football scarf, his nerve endings are on fire. He wishes he had enough for crack, but Becka has already been to the shops this week and spent some of the cash. The fucking bitch: always squandering his dole money, using it for shite that means nothing to him. She doesn't even care about his habit. All she wants is his cock twice a week, his fist once a month, and his hard cash whenever he manages to grub enough together to buy the brat a new pair of shoes.

Fuck them. Fuck them both. Shit is going on that he doesn't understand. Back at the house, the baby hasn't moved for over an hour, and all Becka seems to want to do is cry. He heard gunshots earlier, and screams. The mates he rang on his mobile all told him to stay inside and wait for things to cool down.

Fuck them, too. He needs a fix, so a fix is what he is going to have.

Just then a figure weaves around the corner, clutching its head. It's Ally, the dickhead from Sully Street who always has something in his pocket.

He takes a step towards the dealer, raising a hand in greeting. The stumbling figure bounces off the wall, cracking his elbow against the brickwork but not even flinching.

Danny takes an involuntary step back, away from the stinking bastard – God, he smells like dogshit, like a fucking open sewer.

You got anything, like?

His words fall flat; the dealer isn't playing. He twirls in a slow circle, still grabbing at the side of his head. Danny sees that there's blood there, in his hair: it's all matted, like burned candy floss. There's something seriously wrong with the daft cunt.

Shit.

No fix, unless he can take it by force. The tosser must be legless, or stoned on his own gear. Maybe the goings-on tonight have been too much for him, too.

Danny moves in, as swift as he can but not swift enough – clumsy, strung out, reeking of the sweat of withdrawal.

The dealer becomes aware of Danny's presence. Looks up, his

eyes black as liquorice coins, the kind Danny used to eat all the time as a young boy, running through these streets as if they were the whole wide world.

Got any gear?

The dealer pitches forward, towards Danny, his arms outstretched. Too late, Danny sees the knife handle sticking out of the dealer's chest, right where the heart is. Then he remembers the rumours he heard in the pub last night, the story about Ally getting on the wrong side of some twat from Acocks Green and getting himself done over. Danny hadn't believed it at the time; Ally was one of them lucky buggers, the type who never seem to come off too badly, who always seem to avoid disaster.

Danny barely feels it when the teeth sink into his cheek. Only when the hands come up to claw at his face, his throat, his chest, does he realise that this is not a bout of junkie delirium. Cunt! All he wanted was a fucking fix...

... Bedford, a sheltered refuge for homeless girls. Janice Smythe is sick of her job, sick of her life. These ungrateful young girls, the ones she works so hard to keep safe and secure and on the right side of the law, don't ever seem to realise how much she does for them.

Take tonight, for instance. Every twenty minutes or so someone bangs on the front door, making a racket. The police keep saying they are unable to attend because of civil unrest elsewhere in the town centre, but advise her to keep the doors locked, the windows shut. The girls are all in their rooms, listening to their ipods or chatting on their mobile phones, not even bothered that the neighbourhood has gone mad and the sirens outside always seem to be heading in the opposite direction.

So who's left to sort everything out, to ensure that things are kept under control? Muggins here, that's who! Bloody Muggins, the local doormat!

Entering the kitchen, she goes to check the basement door. One of the girls – she thinks it was Sophie – was down there earlier, storing some of her old belongings, and the girls never think to lock the door. The basement is a point of easy access; there's a row of small windows down there located at street level. Anyone could kick them in, bend down, and if they were small enough they might be able to squeeze through one of the gaps.

As expected, the door is wide open. A slight breeze wafts up the stairs, bringing with it the cloying aroma of mould. Janice hates the basement. It has always scared her. The earthy odour, the sense of being buried alive.

She closes the door, her hands shaking as she turns the key in the lock and then transfers the key to her pocket. Stupid girls: always thinking about themselves, or boys – never aware enough to consider the feelings of anyone else. She often wonders why she stays here, why she loves the girls so much.

Shrugging her narrow shoulders, Janice turns away from the basement door, a chill reaching up to caress her spine. She shivers.

The man who was standing behind her – who is now in fact standing right in front of her – doesn't move. He just stands there, expressionless, not even blinking.

Janice is suddenly cold.

She recalls:

The long days spent at Brighton Beach during her early childhood, growing up in Barnet, playing ball with the neighbour's kids; her mother's green housecoat, her dad's old Vespa moped, her sister's forearms, her first pet – a cat called Tony – and the way the wind sings in the eaves during a storm; the sound of rain on glass, a good tenor, cold dry cider, sausage and mash.

In an instantaneous flash of agonising insight, she knows that she will never experience these things, these blissful memories, again.

It has been a good life, of sorts, but also one stained with tragedy:

Her stillborn brother, dad's early death, her mother's stroke; the boyfriend who hung himself when he was eighteen, spoiling her for any other man; the bank robbery in Islington when she was punched in the face; the car crash the following summer, the rape, the abortion; the rotten flowers on her nightstand; the stinging nettles she fell into on holiday last year in Cornwall.

A good life, then – but also a bad one. A little bit of both, to balance things out, to make it like the lives of most other people.

She has nothing to regret; nothing to fear; nothing that important to leave behind. No impact on the world, and not much really to miss, apart from the girls.

The girls.

Who will take care of them after she is gone?

At least the man who will kill her has kind eyes, a nice white smile, nice cool hands...

PART TWO

The Heart Is A Hungry Hunter

"I just can't get an angle
On this twisted love triangle"

-Human Remainders, Nefandor

CHAPTER TWELVE

Rick stood in the middle of the street and watched the flames as they reached towards the sky, his eyes dry from the heat and his face touched by a peculiar sensuous warmth. The kiddies play park lay behind him, hidden by shadow; the light of the fire barely reached the footpath at the base of the high wall, the top of which he'd dropped down from as he left the park.

A small group of people stood watching the church burn. It was a new building, one of those recent houses of worship built to service contemporary housing estates. Redbrick walls and geometric enclaves; a white plaster Saviour stuck to a black plastic cross; tasteful stained glass windows depicting not scenes from the Bible but simple pretty patterns.

Rick approached the conflagration, his hand straying to the holster on his belt. His boots crunched on broken glass. A few cars had been parked, crashed or abandoned at the roadside. The one closest to Rick contained a dead man who was slumped over the steering wheel, his hair a mess of coagulated blood and gore.

It had stopped snowing before it had even had a chance to begin in earnest. The air remained crisp and sharp but was not yet close to freezing.

A tall man in a shabby brown overcoat stood apart from the crowd, his hands in his pockets and a thin dog lead hanging from one wrist. He was about six feet tall but he stood with a slightly slumped posture, as if ashamed of his height. His brown hair was messy. Firelight shone on his intelligent face, creating dark hollows beneath his eyes.

"Quite a fire," said the man as Rick walked up to him. "It's the prettiest thing I've seen in days." His voice was on the verge of breaking.

"Why are they burning the church?" Rick glanced at the side of the man's sombre face, at his round cheeks and his unshaven neck. The man turned to face Rick, and for the first time he saw that there were tears in his eyes. Rick glanced at the dog lead, hanging as loose and pointless as a scarf from the man's clenched hand.

"These people no longer have need for churches. In case you haven't noticed, heaven is now full and closed for business until further notification." He flashed a grim half smile. "The dead are stranded here, with the rest of us." He blinked. His eyes shone with a terrible sick-house brightness.

"I see," said Rick, not really seeing at all. He was utterly unable to understand what was going on and why these things were happening. "So they've turned their back on God?"

The man shook his head, a rueful smile on his thin lips. "Oh, no. I think it's more a case of God turning his back on them. On *us*. All of us." He turned back to watch the capering yellow-gold fingers of the flames, his smile becoming a sad, strained expression, like a grimace of pain.

"What happened to your dog?" Rick wasn't sure why he asked the question. It was just something to say, a few empty words to fill the unearthly silence.

"My girlfriend ate him. She died earlier this evening, from a wound sustained when we were attacked by a dead man." Again that rueful stillborn smile flashed across his weary features. "Then she came back and ate the dog. I had to kill her when she tried to eat me, too."

Once again, Rick was aware of that thin, wavering line between the absurd and the horrific. This entire situation was like a bad cosmic joke, a trick played by bored omnipotent entities making up some kind of awful game for their own eternal amusement.

Rick moved off as the man began to weep. He held the dog lead up to his face, his mouth, kissing it, smelling it. Then he dropped his head and let the battered leather lead fall to the ground, and walked away, shoulders slumped, feet dragging on the cracked asphalt. Rick wished him well, hoped that he found some kind of peace, that he survived.

He paused and watched the fire for a few more moments, and when the other onlookers began to drift away he headed back towards the car he'd seen earlier, the one with the dead man sprawled behind the wheel.

He surveyed the vehicle, noting that – as he'd first suspected – the keys were still lodged in the ignition. The windscreen was cracked, but not to the point that it had shattered completely, and it would still be possible to see perfectly well through the glass. He only hoped that the engine wasn't damaged and there was still enough petrol in the tank to get him on his way.

Behind him, someone screamed. He took out his pistol and dropped into a crouch, scanning the streets and the shadowy, flame-licked houses. The scream did not come again. The people who'd been watching the fire had all gone elsewhere. He wondered if they had been the ones who'd set fire to the church, or if they'd simply turned up to watch it burn.

Holstering the Glock, he turned once more to the car. It was a small four-wheel drive, one of those nippy little Nissan jeeps favoured by hairdressers and young sporty types. He stepped over the rubble and grabbed the dead man by the shoulder, half expecting him to spring to life and attack. The dead man did not budge. As Rick pulled him into an upright position, he noticed the wounds in his skull. The entire top half of the dead man's head had been smashed in, the bone collapsing like egg shell to pierce the exposed brain matter and turn it into what resembled strips of shredded beef.

He tilted the body and hefted it from the car. Straining, he then dragged the corpse a few feet away from the vehicle and shoved it into the gutter. He wiped his hands on his trouser legs, feeling that the blood of this night would never wash off. He was stained forever, destined to walk in a red shadow for the rest of his days – however long or short that might eventually prove to be.

Rick spotted a rag tucked into a map pocket in the driver's door. He took it out and cleaned most of the blood and matter off the steering wheel, dashboard and torn seat cover. Pausing for a moment to ensure that no one was sneaking up on him, perhaps a dead person drawn by the smell of blood, he then climbed into the car. He turned the key in the ignition and was almost overjoyed when it caught first time. The relief he felt did not last long. He had other business to attend to, and could afford no time for a self-indulgent show of emotion.

The engine roared, healthy and eager to go. Looking at the dashboard, he saw that the tank was half full – more than enough to get him home and then a good way out of the city. All he need fear was the roads being blocked. He knew the area well enough to map out a route via the lesser known police rat-runs and backstreets, but when it came to leaving Leeds itself he expected to run into trouble on the motorway.

He pressed his foot down on the pedal, enjoying the sound of the engine as it soared. "Come on, my sweetie," he whispered, allowing a slight smile to twist his lips.

Then, not even bothering to indicate or check his mirrors, he screamed out into the road and set off for home, where he hoped that Sally was waiting for him, cowering behind locked doors and barred windows, or perhaps even hiding in a closet or the cramped section of storage space beneath the kitchen counter.

He knew that he'd taught her well. He had no doubt that Sally would do her best to maintain her own safety, and that she would have faith in him coming to get her as quickly as he could.

The roads were empty of traffic, but he passed the occasional figure as he sped towards the city centre. Some of those he saw were raging, waving their arms in the air in unfocused acts of aggression. Others were running, looking for hiding places. Of these, only the latter caused him to doubt his flight from what he thought was the epicentre of the troubles. His sense of duty screamed at him to stop and help, to act like a police officer and do what he could. But then, with the unbidden intensity of a religious vision, he saw Sally's face: her open lips, her wide, fearful eyes.

Rick drove on, fighting against his training, following instead his instincts towards the one he loved – the one he had always loved, and who had saved him from himself when he'd suffered tremendous physical and mental injuries during a war he had never truly understood or entirely believed in.

He passed the smoking, burned-out carcasses of cars and vans, the blackened spidery-shapes of wrecked motorcycles. Houses burned, too, along with shops and places of business. It seemed that these insane events had inspired within the populace a latent love of fire. Like firebugs, they'd moved across the landscape, lighting things and watching them burn. When the novelty wore off they moved on; or perhaps they fell foul of roaming bands of the hungry dead.

Occasionally he was forced to take a different route, to circumnavigate fiery ruins or impassable pile-ups in the road. Once, while skirting a famously rough estate, he encountered a gang of youths who were, for some reason, in the process of stripping a vehicle down to its chassis. The car's owners sat on the kerb. They were naked and shivering, too terrified to get up and flee as two boys casually urinated on them, laughing and chiding one another into further acts of depravity.

A weeping woman stared at Rick as he passed, her eyes pleading. Her male companion stared at his feet, piss running down his face and neck to pool in the gutter. Resisting the urge to lean out of the window and start shooting, Rick kept moving. The youths hurled bricks and pieces of wood at the speeding Nissan.

He regretted not stopping to help those people for the rest of his life.

Rick witnessed the dead, too, moving like ghosts – or demons – through the strange fire-lit darkness to scavenge scraps of burned meat, plunder abandoned corpses, and chase down ill-hidden victims. A few of them stumbled like drunkards, their movements clumsy and uncoordinated. Others ran at speed, nimble and graceful, and displaying great strength and agility. Most fell between these two extremes, walking stiffly yet unhindered and searching the night for food. He noted the differences in posture, movement and physicality for future study: when he had the chance, he'd try to examine why the dead did not stick to an established set of physical characteristics.

The journey was tricky but not impossible. Vast tracts of the city lay in darkness, while other areas remained brightly lit, possibly by flames. His speed ranged from a slow crawl through debris-lined avenues to a foot-down sprint along wide, empty boulevards. He kept away from the inner ring road, expecting it to be blocked. As long as he remained focused, and kept his mind alert, he would make it home before daylight.

Sally beckoned to him like a needy ghost. He saw her standing on every street corner and crouching in every shadow. Her presence was a constant; her need was like a drug. The only thing on his mind was her safety. If he failed to get to her before anything happened, before their home came under attack from either the living or the dead... then he was lost; lost forever.

"I'm coming," he muttered under his breath, barely aware of doing so. "I'm coming for you. I'll get there. I promise."

The canal sparkled like a ribbon of diseased body fluid, tracing a putrid course from the morgue slab to the drain. He stared straight ahead, his eyes picking out the apartment block against a black slab of sky. The lights were out – like a lot of the lights around the city, other than the constant sparks and flashes from the many fires that washed the skyline like hellish searchlights. His eyes were drawn to these lurid bright smears in the otherwise darkling sky; huge smudged sections of flickering red-gold illumination.

He swung the Nissan into the parking area under the apartments, jumping out and running across the cold concrete surface towards the locked doors. He searched his pocket for his swipe card, and then barged into the building, drawing his gun and heading for the stairs. The doors clicked gently shut behind him.

Something made a soft thudding sound behind a closed door; a voice called out from the floor above; gentle sobs echoed along the hallway to his left, then abruptly ceased.

Due to its isolated location by the mostly ornamental channel that branched off the main canal, the apartment was a relatively safe base. Away from the rough areas, set back from the main roads, it had always been a quiet retreat from the chaos of the city; yet the city began in earnest just opposite, across the canal, where office blocks towered over the narrow stretch of water.

If the apartment block had been situated a mile or so to the east or west, it might have come under attack. As it stood, the place seemed intact. There were no tell-tale signs of forced entry, nor could Rick smell smoke or – worse still – blood.

Rick moved up the stairs, remembering Hutch's messy demise. The memory hurt, just like most of his memories, and he pushed it aside for later. Shadows stirred ahead of him, curling strands and shuddering bulges of blackness. Turning the corner at the top of the stairs, he continued upwards, climbing through the heart of the building.

Finally he stood on his and Sally's floor. The landing was empty, its perspective seeming weirdly telescopic in the darkness, making it look like a constricting throat. Rick blinked, shook his head to dispel the illusion. Then he walked slowly forward, heading for his own door.

His heart dropped like a stone when he saw the open door. His hands began to shake as they clutched the gun. He was suddenly unable to move any farther along the landing; his legs seized, the muscles turning to hardening slabs of concrete. He heard Hutch's dying breath hissing through shattered lips; he felt the blast of an explosive charge in the dry desert heat; he heard the firewatcher's voice as he spoke of God abandoning his people; and once again he watched the twitching corpses in the Dead Rooms as they got up and walked, attacking his unit.

"*Please*," he said, not really knowing who he said it to, just repeating the words, like a mantra. "*Please*."

Finally he was able to move. He forced his feet onward, sliding them across the tiles. They made a horrible whispering-swishing sound, like a knife blade slicing through the air.

Gun held out, he kicked the door all the way open, watching as it slammed against the wall, the handle leaving a dent in the plaster. Darkness forced its way out of the apartment, enveloping him. He smelled the coppery aroma of freshly spilled blood.

A whining sound came to his ears, startling him as it rose in pitch, and it took him several seconds to realise that it was coming from his own lips, his dried-out throat. He swallowed; the spit hurt on its way down his oesophagus.

Let her be okay. Let her be alive and waiting for me.

Clomping along the hall, feeling heavy and lacking in any kind of grace in his movements, he rounded the sharp corner at the end of the entry passage. The living room beckoned like an opening fist. Darkness squatted like beasts in the corners. Reflected fire limned the edges of the window frames, turning them a shade of umber. Shadows inched along the floor towards him.

Sally was stretched out on the floor, face-up, her arms flat and her hands lying limp at her sides, as if she'd been laid out to rest in a peaceful position prior to a dignified funeral. She was wearing a pair of old blue jeans, faded at the knees, one of his ripped gym sweatshirts, and her feet were bare. There was blood on the floor, near her head. It looked black in the dim light, like a puddle of tar, or crude oil.

Rick felt the room tilt; it spun like a fairground fun ride. Nausea built within him, filling his gut with heavy bile. It rose slowly up his throat and edged into his mouth, finally bursting, hot and bitter, between his clenched teeth. The hot puke spattered and rolled down his chin, staining his clothing, but he ignored it. His eyes burned. His hand shook. The gun went off, puncturing the silence. He stared at the gun, at his finger still pressing down on the trigger. It took a substantial amount of mental effort to take his finger away and lower the gun.

There was no one else here: he could see that. The apartment was empty. But for him. But for Sally, sweet dead Sally. Whoever had done this – whatever kind of opportunistic murderer had broken in and destroyed his life – was no longer present; only his or her workmanship remained.

His gun hand dropped to his side, still hanging onto the weapon. He would not let it go; the pistol's work was not yet done.

Moving across the room, he went to her, kneeling down at her feet and caressing the cold skin, rubbing the hard nub of her ankle, his hands travelling slowly upward, towards her thighs, her waist, and her flat belly. He paused there, palm open across her tiny taut stomach, trying to summon some remnants of warmth through the frayed material of the old sweatshirt.

None came. So he moved on, running his fingers along the nape of her neck, gently stroking her chin... then, at last seeing what was left of her face, he stopped, unable to go on any further.

As Rick suspected when he'd first seen her body, Sally's death was not the result of a clumsy attack by the reanimated dead. No, human hands had been at work here, and they had done their worst.

The skin of her face had been inexpertly peeled away from the bone, laying bare swathes of smooth red muscle. Her nose was gone completely, sawn off with careless hands wielding an unsuitable blade. Her hair was bloody, hanging around this horror-mask in tatty crimson ropes. Her skull was flattened into an oval, mashed and elongated by the force of whatever blows had fallen onto her unprotected head; the bones had un-knitted and returned to their separate shards, like the soft, as yet unformed skull of a newborn baby.

No bite marks. These wounds were thought out, orchestrated, despite being messily executed.

"Oh, God. What have they done?" His breast felt like it was filled with a thousand tiny metal balls; he found it difficult to breathe as they rattled around in his chest cavity.

His reluctant hand hovered over Sally's ruined face, her tattered features, a mile of open space concentrated into an inch of air between his sweaty palm and her brutally ravaged flesh. He held it there, shaking, as if trying to counteract an unimaginable weight. Then, soon, he began to realise that the hand was caught fast and he could not shift it. He struggled against whatever held it there, but the dead weight of Sally's passing was simply too much to resist.

So he waited. And eventually the weight lifted, moved on, allowing him to release his hand from the tender trap.

He wailed like an animal, raising his head to the ceiling, reaching out beyond the structure of the building and into the sky and the stars and towards the cold dead light of the white-faced moon. He realised that the moon was death, too: a stark dead planet where nothing stirred, no life existed. He felt like he was sitting deep inside a crater on that moon, ensconced within a hollow formed by his own grief, and if he did not attempt to move he might remain there forever, trapped in this perfect moment of absolute loss.

Sobbing now, Rick dragged Sally's body up onto the sofa. One hand still held the gun, so it was difficult to manoeuvre her lifeless form. He struggled, pushing and tugging and finally shifting her, pulling her on top of him as he collapsed onto the cushions. He sat there with her poor flensed face in his lap, the stripped lips pressing against his crotch. He stroked her matted hair, singing to her in a language no other human lips had ever formed, not once in the entire history of mankind's grieving.

Rick was no longer aware of the passage of time. He had no idea how long he sat there, cradling his wife's torn head. He stared at her candyfloss hair, then at the shiny gun; long moments spent examining each, trying to come to a decision. He put the barrel of the gun in his mouth, feeling it click against his teeth and rest on his tongue. Then he took it out again, setting it down on the cushion but not quite yet ready to let it go.

He raised his hand and put the gun in his mouth again. Took it out. Repeat. Pause. Then repeat.

Again.

He thought of the song that had been playing the night they'd first met, pumping out of the jukebox of a boozy little joint up in Newcastle: *Solitary Man* by Neil Diamond.

Again.

A Solitary Man: that's what he was now, all right. Solitary. Alone. Left behind.

Again.

He tried to recall the words to the song, but all he could think of was the rhythm of the music, the way it had become the smooth, calming heartbeat of the whole wide world as they'd danced to the song in the middle of that half-empty bar, no one else on the dance floor that wasn't even a dance floor at all, just a wide empty space near the back of the room. Dancing, together, for the first time...

Then, achieving some kind of final insight on that ratty two-seater sofa, Sally's dead head resting in his unresponsive lap, he carefully placed the tip of the shaking barrel against his wife's smashed skull, his quivering, bloodless finger resting heavily on the trigger.

The lights came on, shocking him and bathing everything inside the room in an almost unreal level of illumination. The television hissed static. Over on the dining table, Sally's laptop clicked loudly and emitted a single loud bleeping noise before once again falling silent.

Rick stared at the gun.

CHAPTER THIRTEEN

The buzz was fading already, so soon after the kill.

Daryl walked along the garden path, heading back indoors to come down from the emotional high he'd experienced when he'd murdered Sally Nutman. After so long planning the kill, dreaming and fantasising about it, he had finally stepped off the edge and done it.

It had felt good. It had felt strange. It felt... what exactly did he feel now, after the fact? Initially, immediately after the white-heat pleasure of the kill, he'd been energised beyond belief, but now all he felt was a quickly receding warmth and the distant memory of something good.

It was strange how soon the thrill wore off; he could barely remember what it felt like to have her fresh blood on his hands.

He went inside the house and locked the door. Outside, during his journey back, he'd been more afraid than he had been on the outward leg of his little jaunt. Hiding from the slightest sound, edging stealthily through back gardens and along lonely back alleys, he'd felt the tension in the air like an impending scream: yells, gunshots, roaring engines. Police helicopters whirring overhead. Mad – or dead, or both – men and women running through the streets, all baying for blood.

Now, once again behind closed doors, he took a moment to steady himself. His mind was racing; the thoughts inside were vague, blurred and blood-red. Before tonight he'd been a trainee, an *inchoate* murderer, but now he had developed and was almost fully formed. His bloodlust had risen to the surface and he had acted upon it, crossing a line that had vanished as he'd landed the first blow.

The first blow of many.

Thinking back, it had been a clumsy kill. He knew from his reading that most first kills were indeed awkward, graceless affairs. He recalled smashing his fists repeatedly against Sally's surprisingly brittle skull, smashing it against the floor; hitting her so many times that the bone cracked and he felt his knuckles pressing into the soft areas beneath, almost kneading the brain matter like bread dough.

Then, tiring of the effort involved, he'd started in with the knife.

Her face had not come off easily. In fact, it had only come away in chunks. Beforehand, he'd imagined skilfully removing that face like a mask and carrying it off as a ghoulish souvenir – all the best serial killers left the scene with a memento of their deeds; it was *de rigour* in murderous circles.

But things had not worked out as he'd planned.

Instead of peeling away from the bone like some overdone mud-pack beauty treatment, the skin had sliced away in ragged sections. By the time he was finished she looked terrible, and all he was left with was a handful of bloody strips. Still, he'd wrapped them in a rag and put them in his bag, hoping that once he had the chance to examine them the face might look better than he'd first thought.

Entering the kitchen, he placed his bag on the table. He opened it and took out the bloody rag. Then he carefully unwrapped his keepsake and laid out the separate segments of Sally's face on the smooth tabletop. It looked like a badly constructed jigsaw: there was part of a cheek, a jagged flap of nasal cartilage, two thin slivers that could possibly be lips. It was pathetic – embarrassing, really. He'd hoped for so much more than a few bits of tattered meat.

Daryl swept his hand across the table, scattering the remains of Sally's face. The scraps hit the floor, along with a china cup, a crumb-covered plate, and a few pieces of Mother's best cutlery.

"No! Fuck! *Fuck!*"

Anger swallowed him, opening its whale-like maw and taking him down whole. His vision speckled with bright little pinpoints, his lungs inflated, and he could barely even summon a scream. It lasted only a few moments, but the intensity of the episode terrified him. Never in his life had Daryl vented his rage in such a manner; he'd always swallowed it down, just like Mother had taught him. Real men, Mother had always said, never showed their emotions.

He bent down and picked up the separate parts of Sally's face, arranging them on the draining board. He handled each one with care, fingering them, and washed them all with cold water in a plastic colander. Once the blood was cleared away, the pieces of flesh looked unreal, like joke shop artefacts: bits and pieces of a failed monster mask that had fallen away from the dirty mould.

Daryl walked away, promising himself that next time he would do better. His second kill would be more professional, better thought out.

Despite the lengthy planning stage, when he'd finally straddled Sally Nutman, feeling her panic, tasting her terror, he had been carried away by her wonderful reaction and everything had happened much too fast.

Next time, he swore, he would take more time and savour the moment.

In the living room, he tried the television. The TV came on, but there was nothing being broadcast. All the channels were dead, apart from scrolling text informing viewers to keep tuned for further news regarding the 'disaster'. That was what they were calling it, then: a disaster. How prosaic.

He turned on the stereo and tuned it to a local station. The hiss of static almost obscured what was being broadcast, but he managed to make out a few words from the pre-recorded interviews, tapes of repeated advice to stay indoors and banal advice on making oneself safe in an emergency.

No one, it seemed, was ready to admit the tough reality of what was actually happening – that the dead were rising to attack the living. They were still too busy rambling on about terrorism, a possible virus, suspected chemical warfare...

"Christ," he said, rising from his chair. "Do you think we're all stupid? Stick your head out of the window and take a look at what's going on! Hell is walking the streets." He ran his hands through his hair, trying to rub away the tension. Killing Sally had not provoked the required effect. He was still fraught, still frazzled and edgy.

The radio static suddenly cleared enough that he could hear the programme against only a slight background hiss. He sat back down, rocking gently back and forth, and tried to focus on the voices that threatened to enter his head if he let down his guard for even a moment.

"... and some Government sources are reporting a possible terrorist attack. It has even been hinted that the local water supply has been contaminated by a poisonous substance, sending people amok. Other sources have told us that the origin of the violence is chemical. A leading scientist, who refused to be named, told us that a virus has almost definitely infected the populace."

Daryl listened, amazed by the steady, calm voice of the presenter, the way she had managed to detach herself from the story. He wondered if she was still alive, or if she had become food for the marauding dead.

Another voice, this one male, possibly belonging to a politician: part of an interview conducted earlier that evening, when everything had started going crazy.

"The fact remains that people all over the country are turning inexplicably violent, killing their friends, neighbours and loved ones. There have been tentative reports of victims of these attacks getting up to exhibit their own violent behaviour. We will report any new information as we receive it, but in the meantime the police are recommending that everyone stay indoors and take precautions to secure their premises. Do not go outside. Do not answer your door, even to those you believe you know. Repeat: do not go outside; do not answer your door..."

Daryl got up and turned off the radio, feeling like he was floating across the room, suspended mere inches off the carpet. He stared at his hands, at the light pink stains that remained stubbornly on his fingers like an obscure artistic representation of his actions; then he curled those fingers into a tight fist and examined the torn knuckles. Part of him was angry that because of the media breakdown there would be no one to report his antics. Another part – the darkest part of his character – knew that there would be survivors, and they would speak of him as a legend, passing along his story around campfires for decades.

After a short while he climbed the stairs to Mother's room.

The upper storey of the house was in darkness, leaving her drowning in the shadows she loathed – a sea of shadows, all whispering her name. This at least gave Daryl something to smile about.

"Mother?" he entered her room, clutching the door and easing it open.

She was sprawled across the mattress at an angle, having tried to move off the bed. Perhaps the dark had terrified her so much that she had attempted to get away, or had she simply been looking for Daryl to comfort her when she suddenly awoke?

"Come on, Mother. We can't be having you hurting yourself, can we?" he levered her back into position. "That's my job."

Her eyes skittered open, the lids flickering like hummingbird wings, and then she squeezed them shut. Her face was paler than he'd ever seen; its texture was greasy, like cold bacon rind. She was obviously on her way out – even Daryl could see that. He doubted that she would even see morning.

"That's better now. Nice and comfy." He nipped her upper arm, just to gauge the response. Nothing. She was beyond pain, her body no more than a shell for her fading consciousness.

"I finally did it, Mother. After all that planning and dreaming and wondering, I killed her. You would've liked her, too. Such a pretty girl. She was so very lovely, like an old-time film star."

Mother offered no response.

"It was glorious, Mother. *Glorious.* But only for a short time. The rapture soon faded."

Rapture. God, what a perfect word. It described the feeling perfectly: almost religious, verging on the sublime.

"They all say – all the convicted killers and sociopaths – they say that your first time is the best, and then you go on to spend the rest of your life trying to repeat that first-time experience. If only it had lasted longer. I've almost forgotten how good it was. How... *rapturous.*"

A soft gurgling sound, like a plughole draining away a sink full of water, emitted from Mother's throat. It lasted a long time. Constant, never faltering, not even fading. Then, abruptly, the sound stopped.

"Oh, Mother. Can't you just listen for once? That was always your fucking problem. Fuck-fuck-fucking problem. You would never just *listen* to me." His heart rate became intense. It felt like tiny fingers drumming against his ribs. "Too busy with the shouting and the hatred and the hurting. Always the hurting. Never the *listening.* Never the affection I always craved, especially as a child."

Daryl leaned over Mother, sniffing her. She smelled of old shit. He reached down and grabbed the sallow skin of her cheeks, splitting it like paper. Then, his entire body tensing, hardening, he spat in her eyes. Just once; it was enough to vent the poison.

"I blame you for everything, Mother. Everything. The bullying at school, the ill-judged sexual experiences, the lack of any sort of cohesion in my life. The 'morbid interest in death' – isn't that what Mr. Rogers, my English teacher, called it?"

And still Mother said nothing. Did nothing. Was nothing.

"All of it. It's even your fault that I killed poor Sally Nutman. I mean, what had she ever done to me? Or to you? Nothing. She was just a beautiful woman who reminded me that there was no real beauty in my own life."

He stepped back from the bed, disgusted with her, and with

himself for allowing her to affect him even as she lay dying. She couldn't even find it in herself to respond. He wished that she *were* dead; and that she was alive; and that she were both dead *and* alive. He didn't even know what he wished, but surely he must wish something. Wasn't it human to crave, to covet, to hope for things?

But Daryl wasn't human. He was a misfit, an aberration. He had nothing to wish for.

No, that wasn't quite correct; he wished that he could kill Sally Nutman all over again, but this time do it better. Do it *right*. This way didn't make him feel special; it had failed to separate him from the herd. All he had done was copy what others had done before him.

There was nothing unique about simply killing a woman, or a man – even a child. It had all been done before, and better: every depravity had been essayed by another, written in blood upon the pages of terrible history books by those who'd gone before him through this library of despair, treading a path through previously uncharted rows so that others, like him, might follow and read and learn.

Where was the import in being a simple copycat? What horrors remained to be claimed as his own, dragged screaming by his hands from the bloody womb of nightmare?

He thought about what he'd seen that night: the drowned corpse trying to claw its way out of the canal, the dead people hunting for live meat. When he'd watched that bloated river-bound corpse pierced through the head by a short steel bar, he had felt that he was being told something and its meaning would only come to him much later, when least expected.

That obscure message felt at once within touching distance. If he reached out far enough, he could grab it and pull it towards him.

Think, man, think!

Then, in an instant of clarity, it came to him.

Every serial killer in history had done the same thing: acted out subtle variations on the theme of murder. What was the one act none of them had ever carried out – the single trick that only

Daryl might be able to pull off? The one that would guarantee his longevity, despite the fact that society was going to hell.

He smiled, bathing in the lurid light of revelation.

CHAPTER FOURTEEN

dark echoes release falling stopping hungry quiet rising faster light up bright white feelings gone hungry pain gone life none sound fury hungry room motion smell hungry sorrow need memory rick husband meat hungry

CHAPTER FIFTEEN

Rick stared at the gun.

It was beautiful, a marvel of engineering. The barrel was sleek and glossy, the handle a perfect fit in his hand. The trigger felt like a promise of salvation beneath the calloused skin of his finger.

He could barely believe how quickly everything had come apart; the sheer speed at which the world had unravelled like a ball of string toyed with by a giant cat. Rick had never put much stock in God or the Devil, in angels or demons, but current events were causing him to re-evaluate his entire belief system. If the dead could walk, if society could break apart so easily, then what did that say about the delicate balance of the universe?

Tears poured down his face. He had stopped sobbing, but the pain remained, a physical ache clenched deep inside him. His chest was tight, his arms and legs were growing numb, and there was a hollow inside his body where his heart had been torn out by invisible claws.

"Sally," he muttered, realising that even her name was dead. "Don't leave me."

Then, amazingly – like the greatest miracle on this wide, green earth – her head stirred in his lap. Holding his breath, he glanced down at the back of her head. The skull was cracked; sticky brain matter hung out in bloated grey clumps. He'd failed to notice before that one of her ears had been torn off – the left one. He wondered where it was, and had to resist the urge to go looking for it.

Sally's head moved, twitching to the side. Her hands clutched at his thighs, the fingers gripping and releasing the legs of his trousers. Her movements were slow, mechanical. She was like a ruined machine powering up from a major breakdown.

"Sally?"

She twisted her head so that her ruined face was pointing into the room, facing away from him. There was blood in his crotch; his trousers were wet with it. But he didn't care. All that mattered was that Sally was coming back to him, reaching out across a black void to return to his side.

"Oh, baby. I need you."

An awful wet rasping sound began in her throat, like a loud death rattle. He heard blood bubbling at her lips. Carefully, he reached down and began to turn her head towards him; slowly, and with great care he handled her damaged cranium. The flensed cheeks and torn forehead were horrific to see, especially now that her eyes were open. One eyelid was missing; the other hung loose, dangling across the eye like a broken fleshy blind over a tiny window.

"Oh, Sally. Oh, God. Poor, poor baby. Rick'll make it better. I'll protect you this time, and make sure nobody ever hurts you again."

Her mouth ratcheted open, the movement shockingly fast. Blood caught in thin red strings between her jaws. The sound she made was like a yawn, but deeper, more resonant. It was ironic, he thought, because she was in fact coming round from the longest, deepest sleep of all. Her right eye quivered in its socket, the pupil so pale that it was almost white. There was a ragged hole in her skinned cheek and her teeth showed through the moist red tatters.

Rick took her into his arms, wrapping her up in his love.

Sally's head craned round on her neck, moving slightly swifter yet still lacking co-ordination. Her teeth snapped on empty air near his throat. Rick pulled away, pressing his hands into the mush of her face, pushing her teeth back whilst keeping her cold body close.

"No, baby. Don't do that." He felt something snap inside his head; just a fine white pain, like a needle sliding into a gum or a particularly deep paper cut. Lightning flared momentarily behind his eyes. When it cleared he felt changed, altered; the world seemed different, filled with fresh promise.

He held Sally's head away from his throat, watching her teeth continue to clamp down on nothing. She was trying to chew. Her movements were spastic, out of whack. He remembered Hutch, half his head blown away on the concrete staircase, and when he came back from the dead it was as if he'd suffered brain damage. Glancing at Sally's shattered skull, at the grey slugs hanging out of the red-rimmed rents, he realised that she had not returned whole. Pieces of her had been left behind, huge chunks of her consciousness. She was like a child, a damaged and hungry child, and he would have to care for her.

A noise not unlike wordless singing came from her mouth: a fractured tune, the song of the damned.

Rick closed his eyes and tried to clear his head. If he thought too hard about any of this, it would drive him insane. Or perhaps he had already lost his mind, back in the Dead Rooms. Maybe he was still there, lying on the floor with his blood draining out, and these were his final thoughts before death – a weird phantasmagoria of love and loss and longing...

Easing Sally's head onto a cushion, he got up from the sofa. He took the gun and placed it back in its holster, knowing that he no longer required its bleak promise. He'd turned his back on the offer of smoke and darkness.

Sally squirmed on the cushions, unable to stand. She had forgotten even the most basic elements of locomotion. This was good, it would make her easier to control. He could handle her, exercising authority over even her most fundamental functions. He watched her for a short while, wondering if she might fall onto the floor and hurt herself. Then he remembered that she was dead, and the dead can no longer be hurt. Pain was for the living, but even they must put such physical discomfort behind them in this weird new world, this hideous reversed Eden.

There was a new world order forming, and only the strong would survive.

Rick went to the window and looked out at the sky. The promise of dawn hovered at the edge of the horizon, a long, thin band of light shimmering like a mirage in the distance. There was still a long way until daylight, but it was making its presence known. He wished that time would freeze and nothing would ever change again. It was all too much, he needed time and space to sort things through, to get it all straight in his head.

He sat down at the dining table and pressed the power button on Sally's laptop. The screen hovered in darkness, and then reluctantly stuttered into operational mode. Rick connected to the Internet. It took a long time for the connection to be established, and when the window finally opened up a gateway to cyberspace, the graphics had broken up into a clumsy pixellated mess.

Rick attempted to access a few websites: BBC, CNN, Sky News. None of them had been updated for some time. The headlines still comprised of reports of civil unrest, terrorist attacks, rapes and murders and looting in all the major cities of the world. By now things would have moved on. The survivors of the initial outbreaks would be trying to form groups, arming themselves, searching for food and water. Whole streets would be occupied by a civilian militia, areas shut down by gangs. The police would be helpless. There was too much to cope with and their limited resources would be stretched beyond their capabilities. The combined threat of walking corpses and roaming mobs would be too much for the authorities to deal with all at once.

Maybe this uncontrollable free-for-all could work in his favour. If the security forces were busy fighting, then he could move freely. He had his police warrant card, his weapons and riot gear. He even had a sturdy vehicle with which he could tackle potential barriers.

Things were never as hopeless as they seemed. It was a lesson he'd learned in army training and had served him well in all other areas of his life. There is always another plan, an alternative option. Never give up, never surrender. Keep going, keep fighting. Don't stop moving unless you are backed into a corner, and even then make sure you come out shooting.

Sally had slipped half off the sofa. Her arms were trapped beneath her body and her legs were kicking wildly, drumming on the floor. Rick crossed the room and lifted her back onto the cushions, placing her gently across the sofa. She seemed to calm down when he was nearby, but he was unsure if that was simply because she saw him as meat or if there remained a vestige of affection in her vandalised brain.

He'd always been a bit of a romantic but sentiment was something he could ill afford. He decided that Sally was merely responding to the proximity of his flesh rather than demonstrating any tenderness of the heart. The promise of food settled her down, made her rest easy.

He left her there and went through the cupboards, the shelves, the fridge. There were steaks in the freezer and he took them to the sink and ran the hot tap, trying to defrost the meat.

Sally groaned, whined, made other less recognisable sounds.

Rick hammered the frozen steaks on the draining board; he punched them against the walls. The meat began to soften, but only slightly. He carried it over to Sally and sat her up against some cushions, which he laid over the arm of the sofa.

Her mouth opened, the jaw shifting sideways in blind chewing motions. She made nasal grunts, throaty belches, and strange drawn-out wheezing gasps. Rick pressed one of the steaks against her tattered lips. It was bloody, the meat growing softer in his hands. Sally bit down, tried to chew. Her teeth went right through the partially frozen meat, slicing into it with a power and strength that disturbed him. He remembered Babyface and the dead man who'd sheared off the rookie's boot end. Despite their apparent weaknesses, it seemed that these dead cannibals possessed an amazing strength in their jaws, as if all their remaining energy was focused there.

Keeping his fingers away from her mouth, Rick awkwardly pushed the food between her lips. Suddenly, as if realising the meat was no good, Sally began to gag. She regurgitated the still-frozen flesh; shredded strips dropped from her mouth and stuck to her clothes.

"Eat it, Sally. Come on. Eat it up."

She spat out the meat, turning her head to one side. His fingers brushed against her wounds, and he drew his hand away, dropping the rest of the steak onto the floor. Apparently it was no substitute for warm flesh.

He returned to the kitchen and opened a drawer beneath the sink. Dragging things out and scattering them across the floor, he found the first aid box Sally always kept well stocked in case of emergencies. He opened the plastic box and took out all the bandages he could find, and then returned to his dead wife. She sat on sofa and swayed like a drunkard, her neck barely supporting the weight of her head. Her fingers flexed in her lap and her muscles were out of control, tensing and relaxing as if an electrical charge was being passed through her body.

Ensuring that he kept away from her slow-snapping jaws, Rick stuffed wads of cotton wool into Sally's mouth. He packed it tight, forcing her teeth apart and ramming it down her throat. When he was done, she was unable to close her mouth properly over that densely packed throat.

Then he began to wrap the bandages around her bloodied head. He smothered the damage, swaddling her head like that of an Egyptian mummy, ensuring that the bandages covered every inch of exposed, wounded flesh. The first layer absorbed the congealing blood quickly, red stains blooming and spreading and coming together to turn the wrappings into a patchy crimson mask.

Rick applied another layer, continuing to cover her head until the blood stopped appearing on the fresh white dressings. By the time he'd used up all the bandages, the bleeding seemed to have stopped. Sally's features were concealed; her head was a smooth white oval.

He returned to the kitchen and found some tea towels, which he tore into strips. These he wrapped tightly around her hands, giving the illusion that she might be a burns victim. It also served to protect him from her nails, which were long and sharp and could easily rend his skin if she became too excited.

He would need to procure more bandages, but that was something he could control, a normal problem well within his capabilities to solve. He wished for more banal tasks, rather than the outlandish chore of hiding his wife's condition from prying eyes.

This might just work, he thought. *If I'm careful. If I keep a cool head and stay away from trouble.*

Sally was now at rest. Her padded hands rested in her lap and her large white head nodded, as if she had a tune running through her mind. If indeed there was enough of a mind for a tune to pass through. Rick doubted there was; the truth of it was that she was an animal now, a simple thing of hunger and blind instinct. Yet still, despite all this, he loved her. He had always loved her; and he would continue to love her until his own life was over, and possibly even beyond.

Rick sat next to his dead wife, one arm hanging loosely around her shoulders. He stared at the side of her head, at the bandages wound tightly around her skull. There was a perverse beauty to this; she possessed a strange and almost erotic allure. His hand moved across the rough material of the dressings, his fingers tracing the smooth hollows of her eyes, the gentle outlines of her nose and lips. She did not breathe – she was dead, so why should she require oxygen? The chill of her skin made the bandages cold to the touch.

Rick leaned in and softly kissed her cheek. It felt odd, like a kind of blasphemy, but it also felt right. Love, he thought, illuminated even the darkest corners, picking out small pieces of hope amid the most devastating forms of destruction. If love did not exactly conquer all, then it was at least a damn good weapon to have on your side in the ongoing battle for survival.

CHAPTER SIXTEEN

It is busy in the pub. No room to swing a twat, as Hutch might say. He's a charming man, that Hutch, always ready with a witty line to win over the ladies.

"My round, I think," Rick says, moving towards the bar. Bodies sway and press against him, their warmth passing through his shirt and into his already clammy flesh. "I'll get them in – you lot stay where I can see you, so I don't have to come looking!" His words are drowned out in the clamour of music and voices. The combined heat of all those bodies is an animal, ready to pounce.

Rick shoulders his way through the crowds, suddenly thirsty now that the bar is in sight. The black ribbon of the River Tyne twinkles through the huge picture windows, and Rick feels an odd mixture of extreme drunkenness and misty nostalgia. How can you be nostalgic about something you'd never even seen before now?

"Four cans of Red Stripe, please." He shouts the words at the barmaid, unable to take his eyes off her barely-clad torso.

Another thing about Newcastle that has taken him aback: the barmaids all walk around with their flesh showing, without a care in the world.

The heavy-set girl turns to the chiller cabinet without saying a word. She hasn't even acknowledged his order, and Rick isn't completely sure if she is getting his drinks or serving someone else. She bends down, her short black skirt rising up to a level where he can clearly see her buttocks, then straightens up with four cans clasped between her forearms and that wonderful sweet-counter chest.

Rick pays the girl, takes the cans, and moves away from the rugby scrum at the bar area to find his friends.

They are standing by the door, enjoying the cool breeze that wafts off the narrow river. Hutch is chatting up some girl – a tiny blonde with big blue eyes. Micko and Jeffty are watching that afternoon's football highlights on a television screen situated high on the wall, beneath a gold-sprayed bicycle frame meant as some kind of post-modern decoration.

"Cheers, mate!" Hutch smiles as he snatches the drink from Rick's hand. He winks at Rick, then shuffles closer to him, the blonde girl in tow. "This is Kath. She's up from down south for a birthday bash. She seems to have lost her friends."

"Me and Sally," says the girl, swaying to whatever song is serving as background to the raised voices in the pub. Rick doesn't recognise the tune. He isn't very good with current chart music.

It is then that Rick notices the other girl, the one standing on the other side of the door. She is tall, athletic, and has the most amazing eyes he's ever seen. Cat eyes: long and narrow and slanted gently upwards.

He smiles. The girl – Sally, is that her name? – smiles coyly back.

Rick raises a hand; she raises hers in return, mirroring the gesture. Something passes between them, some unspoken truth, and his life is changed forever.

Rick and Hutch ditch the other two men, taking the girls to another, quieter pub. They walk along the bustling Quayside, laughing and joking and feeling like they have all the time in the world. Groups of revellers jostle past; football songs fill the air; women squeal their delight at simply being young and alive and in a place where they can follow their desires.

Rick likes the girl, Sally. They get along just fine. As they move along the bank of the river, they automatically hold hands. The four of them climb the stairs to a bar that overlooks the water. They drink cheap cocktails, sling foul-tasting shots down their necks, and touch each other in that tentative yet eager way potential lovers often do.

Hutch and Kath are soon ensconced in a corner, making a knot of their tongues. Rick shakes his head, knowing that Hutch has a girlfriend back at home and this can never be anything serious, anything that might possibly last longer than a single night and maybe the next morning. He glances at Sally, sensing something more between them than a potential one-night stand. He smells liquor and cigarettes, the heat in this bar presses in on him, making him stumble.

"Let's go outside for some fresh air," she says, taking his hand.

They walk for a while, then come to a pub doorway. She steps inside, beckons to him. He follows. The place is very small, a haunt for real ale drinkers and those who want a respite from the party-frenzy elsewhere along the Quayside. They drink beer that smells of stale farts and eat pretzels from a china bowl. Their hands touch often; Rick wishes it would go on forever.

"I love this song," she says, standing up from the stool at the bar and twirling in a slow circle. Her knee-length dress hovers around her thighs, a beautiful centrifuge. She skims across the bare wooden floor, shoulders shrugging in a comical dance move, mimes pulling him towards her with an invisible rope.

Rick is unable to resist. He likes the song, too, but he likes Sally even more. So they slow-dance to Solitary Man, *watched by drunken strangers. The pub empties before they even realise the evening is almost over. Still they dance, locked into an act that is so sexually charged the bouncer who comes in from outside is afraid to disturb them.*

"Please," whispers an anxious barman, standing at the edge

*of their passion, afraid to intrude upon such a rare moment. "I
need to go home."*

He woke on the floor, stretched out beneath the window. At
first he could not remember where he was or what had happened,
but the memories flooded back in as soon as he opened his eyes.
Sally. Where was she?

He looked over at the sofa. She was still there, where he'd left
her. The washing line he'd used to tie her arms and legs before
he lay down to rest looked vaguely ridiculous; he could never
understand why Sally had bought one coloured day-glo green.
She'd grinned when she'd unpacked it from the shopping bag,
holding it above her head and spinning around on her heels.

"Oh, very nineteen-eighties!" She'd laughed, still spinning. "I
couldn't resist."

She lay there now, her arms pinned to her sides and her
legs laced together, unable to even move. Her head twitched
occasionally, rising from the cushions as she attempted vainly to
bite through the cotton wool and bandages. There was blood on
the side of her head where it had seeped through the dressings.
Not much, but enough to cause him concern. He would have to
get more bandages before leaving the apartment.

Standing, he opened the blinds and peered out of the window.
It was daylight, but drizzle hung in the air, darkening it to a
subtle dusk. A burned out car sat on the bank of the canal. Two
young boys squatted on the ground. They were slowly tearing
pieces off the remains that sat behind the wheel, stuffing the
charred flesh into their mouths and chewing idly, staring across
the canal like bored kids stuffing their faces in a McDonald's
window seat.

Rick felt the proximity of madness. It leaned in towards him
from all corners of the room, throwing its arms around him
and sticking its tongue in his ear. His brain flexed, pulsing in
response. He closed his eyes and turned away from the window,
his hands fumbling with the blinds until they closed.

Bandages. He needed more bandages. Perhaps he'd find some

elsewhere in the building, in a neighbour's place or cleaning cupboard along the landing. It was the first time he'd even considered the other people in the building. He wondered if they had all barricaded themselves inside their apartments, or if any of them had been foolish enough to venture outside.

"I need to get some stuff," he said, walking towards the sofa. "I won't be gone long. No one can get inside when I lock the door, and I'll have the key to let myself back in."

He was talking to a dead woman. The thought wasn't as crazy as it might seem. Yes, Sally was gone, deceased, but her body was still present, still capable of movement. He'd never believed in the soul anyway: that was so much religious bullshit. So what if she wasn't all there. He could pretend that she was simply damaged, a victim of a road accident or a sporting tragedy. If she'd been crippled or brain damaged, he'd still love her just as much and care for her as long as he was physically able. What was so different about this?

She was dead.

Yes, but she still moved and made sounds and tried to do things. Even if those things were frightening and... and *wrong*.

Dead. She's dead.

"Shut the fuck up," he told himself, leaning down to inspect the nylon washing line, checking that the knots would hold while he was away.

"Just a bit of light bondage," he said. Then he giggled. "We always did have an adventurous sex life, didn't we baby?" He giggled again, but this time it was shrill and difficult to control.

Sally wriggled under his hands, her cold limbs tensing. A muffled sound came from her throat; a low, soft gurgling that made him feel nauseous.

What if she's being sick? he thought. *What if she chokes?*

But she couldn't choke, not now. She couldn't choke because she was dead.

Dead.

Dead but here, with him. Always.

"I won't be gone long." He caressed the bandaged side of her head with his open palm, feeling the chill through the bindings.

"I promise."

Okay, sweetheart.

So now she was answering him. Great. Just another small step along the insanity highway, and another voice to add to the growing number already taking up residence inside his head.

I'll miss you.

He stood and went to the door, where he placed his forehead against the frame and tried to clear his mind of all thoughts but the immediate. That was how it had to be now; he could focus only on what lay directly ahead. Everything else would have to be relegated to the back of his mind, where he could smother it in shadow.

If he accepted that his dead wife was sitting upright on the sofa, her head wrapped up in bandages, then he also had to embrace the fact that she was somehow speaking to him. Simple leaps of logic: but not any kind of logic that had even existed in the old world, before these dramatic changes had occurred.

A strange ringing sound filled his ears, building from somewhere deep inside his skull. At first he thought it was a siren, perhaps an ambulance passing by out on the road, but after a few seconds he realised that it was simply the bright-breaking sound of insanity.

"Go away," he muttered. "Leave us in peace."

The sound intensified, building towards a crescendo, and then abruptly ceased. His ears felt numb, as if he'd taken a blow to the head. Was that it? Was he now officially mad?

He reached down and unlocked the door, peering around into the empty corridor. He craned his neck and looked both ways along the landing. There was blood on a closed door further along, on the opposite side of the corridor: a small red handprint near the tarnished brass handle. Rick paused and listened, but he could make out no sounds out there. Whoever had left that bloody print was either long gone or shut up inside the apartment.

His hand was moist as it gripped the door handle. His fingers ached. He pulled the door inwards, moving his body to the side so that he could step around it and onto the landing. Nothing moved out there. One of the ceiling lights began to flicker, casting long shadows near the floor. He held his breath so that he could hear even the slightest sound, but none came to his ears.

Rick took out the Glock and held it with both hands wrapped around the butt. He licked his lips and stepped out into the corridor. Moving slowly, he began to head towards the stairs. He wasn't quite sure where to look for more bandages, but he figured he had to find them somewhere. In one of these rooms, on one of these floors, he was sure that there would be some sort of medical kit.

Just as he drew level with the door with the bloody handprint, he heard a slight sound, like the scuff of a heel or a gentle rapping of knuckles. He stopped, turned slowly, being careful not to make a sound himself. He backed up, the gun pointed at the door, until his back hit the wall behind him. Then he took a single step forward, away from the wall, just to create some space to manoeuvre.

The sound came again, louder this time. It was a footstep; it had to be.

There was someone on the other side of that door, and judging by the smudged blood they'd been injured – which meant that they were probably dead... or worse.

He raised the pistol, levelling it at where he guessed was around head height on an average male. He blew air out through his lips, deflating his lungs, and then held his breath. His finger tightened on the trigger, stroking rather than squeezing it at such close range... *Blam! Blam! Blam!* Three rapid shots, each one a killer.

He listened for the sound of a body slumping to the floor, but wasn't sure if the sound he did hear was anything of the sort. It could have been scuffling feet, or a heavy object being dropped onto the floor.

He put two more shots through the door, the second one blowing away the lock and handle. The door swung open a couple of inches. No light bled through the gap, only darkness, and the promise of horror.

Rick stepped forward, tensed and ready for either fight or flight. His training had kicked in and he was incredibly alert: his senses opened up, taking in every tiny detail. He felt the slight breeze from an air vent above his head, heard the sighing of air through the grille; saw the shadow of a dead moth through the plastic light fitting that encased the flickering bulb; tasted cordite from the gunshots; heard the hushed sound of someone's hand as it brushed against the inside of the door through which he'd just shot.

He was already letting off another round when the door swung open, but it was aimed too high. A small, thin child charged out of the apartment, his face twisted into a mask of rage and hunger and something so alien and ugly that it was completely unreadable.

The short body hit Rick at waist level, shoving him back against the wall. The kid was growling like a wildcat, white froth frosting his teeth and lips. Instinctively, Rick brought the gun down on the boy's head, delivering a glancing blow to the nape of the neck. The boy's feet slipped on the tiled floor and they both went down, with Rick on top. The boy's jaws snapped at Rick's face; cold spittle flecked his cheeks, getting in his eyes.

He groped for the boy's chin, grabbed it, and managed to push his head sideways, into the floor. The boy's flailing hand had grabbed the gun, and Rick wrestled with him to release it. He heard the kid's neck crack, felt his head swing loosely on the smashed vertebrae. The kid's jaws still clamped down, snatching at Rick's fingers as they slid from his chin.

"Fucker!" Rick brought up a knee and slammed it hard into the boy's chest. More bones fractured. There was a sickening crack as Rick's knee sunk down into the yielding torso, breaking right through the ribcage.

"Fucker!"

He wrenched his gun hand free, dropped it and shoved the barrel of the Glock as hard as he could against the kid's eye. It sunk into the aqueous matter up to the trigger guard. Rick pulled the trigger without even pausing to think about what he was doing. The sound was deafening in the enclosed space, and left a ringing sound in his ears.

He was unable to look down at the boy as he climbed off the body. He could barely see through the tears as he turned away, rubbing his hands clean on his already-stained stab vest.

Stumbling, he moved to the apartment door and kicked it open. The hallway beyond was dark, with dust motes slow-dancing in the air. He moved along the hall with the gun held out front, still focused despite the horror he'd just endured. He'd process all that later, when he could afford the luxury of trying to piece together what remained of his mind.

He found two bodies – or what was left of them – in the living room. Thankfully the curtains were closed, so he could see little of what had been done to them. A hand sat in a plant pot on an occasional table; the bloody wrist looked like it had been gnawed. The lower half of a leg was propped up against the television. The upper half of a face had been pressed against the wall, where it had adhered to the wallpaper like a nightmarish example of modern art, something dreamed up by a dead Damien Hirst.

Once again Rick felt laughter building up inside him. He bit down on it, aware that to release it would mark the start of something he did not have the strength to stop.

Rick went through the kitchen cupboards and found a large box filled with professional medical supplies. There were plenty of fresh, clean bandages, and even a couple of hypodermic syringes. He filled a pillow case from the bedroom with canned food and bottled water, and at the back of the fridge he found some glass vials marked as containing Morphine. He knew a doctor lived on this floor, but had never been sure which apartment.

He kept his head turned away from what he guessed must be the nursery – the open door was decorated with childish stickers and a plaque bearing the words: *baby's room.* There was blood on the doorframe, and from the corner of his eye he could see a small red lump on the floor, its edges oddly flattened out across the laminated timber boards.

He put the morphine in his pocket and left the apartment. The kid's body was still there, where he'd left it. He put down the food and the bandages and grabbed hold of the kid's legs, dragging the corpse through the doorway and into the entrance passage. The head flopped freely, almost coming off altogether as he manhandled the body a few yards along the hallway, away from the door.

He gently closed the door, picked up his haul, and returned to his dead wife, blanking it all out, swallowing down the pain and the anguish and the hatred he felt for all of humanity.

Finally they manage to prise themselves apart, blinking like sleepers woken from a wonderful dream. Rick feels that something has been lost forever, but there is also the promise of so much more; a hopeful sense that the future has just opened up before him, and Sally is part of it, an essential element in all the days to come.

Electricity sparks between them. The earth begins to alter its axis and slowly rotate around the point where they stand. The universe halts, making them its centre.

They are standing at the crux of something exquisite, an experience neither of them will ever recover from. The barman turns off the jukebox and they leave the pub, hand in hand, fused forever. That night is their first, and like all first nights it is imperfect – but it is at least the start of something perfect, and even then, at such an early stage, they both know it and cling to it and appreciate its worth.

CHAPTER SEVENTEEN

Daryl stood naked before the mirror, the washed and scrubbed pieces of Sally Nutman's face stuck with glue to his forehead and cheeks. He stared at the absurd partial mask, as yet unmoved. His penis was semi erect, twitching occasionally as he tried to focus his thoughts. He'd tried to masturbate, but could not sustain the energy required for completion. Sally's name was scrawled across his thin, hairless chest in thick black marker pen. His wiry arms were rigid – unlike his dick – and he was straining against something unseen.

It wasn't working. Nothing he tried made him feel any better, or any closer to the truth that he sought. This simply wasn't him, his identity. Perhaps if he tried something else, like a shopper trying on coats in a tailor's shop, he could pick the right direction for his desires.

He flicked and picked the meat from his face and turned away from the mirror, feeling foolish, as if he'd been observed in this undignified act. His skin was sticky with glue, the areas where he'd applied the solution beginning to itch.

The room was gloomy. Not much light could get through the narrow boards he'd hastily nailed across the windows. The back and front doors were protected, too. It had taken him ages to remove some internal doors to nail across the main ones. The back door was blocked permanently, but he'd managed to fashion something over the front door that acted like a medieval bar across a castle entrance. If he needed to get out of the house quickly, he could simply lift it and flee the premises.

Daryl went into the kitchen and glanced towards the cooker. Perhaps if he cooked the remains of Sally's face? Cannibalism might be his thing, if only he tried it. Would it be better pan fried or roasted in the oven like strips of chicken?

But no, the mere thought of such an act repulsed him. The idea of eating someone else's grubby flesh (however much he cleaned and prepared it beforehand) failed to appeal.

Just what kind of serial killer was he, if he lacked the stomach for the more extreme end of the spectrum? It was almost funny: a squeamish killer, put off by the thought of a little recreational anthropophagy...

Looking at the tiny exposed area of the kitchen window, he wondered what was going on out there. Clouds blocked the weak sun, light rain acting as a further filter to restrain the flimsy daylight. The electricity was still out, so he had been unable to receive any news from the outside world. Since last night's revelatory experience, he'd felt trapped inside Mother's house, like a zoo animal shut away from the public, a beast not fit to be seen. There were killers out there now, and they were just like him – or at least very similar. He should fit in perfectly well, if only he could break the final bonds that held him to Mother and step outside these ugly walls.

The long-held illusion that kept normal people from going crazy had been stripped back to reveal the bitter truth: that society was a sham and it was good to do what the fuck you wanted; take stuff, do things, hurt or even kill people. The ones who accepted this truth quickest would reign supreme. Everyone else was just cattle.

He looked up at the ceiling, trying to see beyond the cracked plaster. A spider web caught his eye, strung delicately between the light shade and its fitting. The web contained several dead flies, all balled up to be consumed at a later date. The powerful visual metaphor was not lost in him; he knew that he had to sit down to his own feast. But the Mother spider was holding him back; poised in her web she still had influence over his behaviour.

"Bitch!" he slammed his hand down on the kitchen counter, ignoring the pain when he caught the edge of a knife left out God knew how many days before.

A dull thud came from upstairs, drawing his attention. He glanced once again upwards, narrowing his eyes, his skin tightening across his skinny muscles. A large black spider scuttled across the web, heading for an early dinner. Daryl smiled. "*Bon appetit.*"

The sound was repeated, louder this time, more insistent. Was Mother trying to climb out of bed again? He could not imagine where she might get the energy, or how she had summoned the strength to move even an inch across the sweaty mattress.

Anger flooded his senses, filling him up like steaming water poured into a bathtub. Everything he ever tried to do, every plan he made and each tiny step forward he took, she was there, preventing him from revealing his true self. Keeping him trapped.

He turned and left the room, heading for the stairs. Pausing at the foot of the stairs, he cocked his head and listened. It was now silent up there, as if she knew he was coming. Slowly, he placed his foot on the first stair, feeling yet again like a character in a film. All his life, at every important juncture, he'd felt exactly like a character following a script. The only time he'd felt real, less like a cipher, was when he'd murdered Sally Nutman.

The carpet was almost unbearably soft beneath his feet. He climbed, brushing his hands against the ugly wallpaper – he'd never liked Mother's taste; she made the entire house look like a funeral parlour. There had never been anything young or vital in this house. Even as a baby, she'd dressed him in Victorian style clothing and done his nursery out like a workhouse bunkroom, stifling him before he even developed into a person; cutting off his as yet unformed identity at source.

Shadows gathered at the top of the stairs, shifting across the landing. The curtains were all closed up there, keeping Mother in the dark – just as he'd been kept in the dark regarding his father's identity.

Up the stairs. Up, up, up we go; up the wooden hill to Bedfordshire. The silly children's rhyme repeated in his head, playing like a stuck record or a scratched CD. He could not stop it, and even that small fact began to annoy him.

"Mother," he whispered. "I'm coming, Mother."

He was reminded of times during his childhood when he'd been ill – or when she'd told him so many times he was ill that he began to exhibit symptoms. Stepping out onto the landing, crossing to the stairs, slowly moving down them: afraid of everything and of nothing that he could possibly name. Calling out for Mother, but she was praying in the kitchen, her bare knees on the cold floor, face raised to the ceiling, eyes awash with bitter tears.

She'd always ignored him on these occasions. Or been completely unaware that he was there, out of bed and desperate for contact. So he'd pour himself a glass of milk and return to bed, rejected and forlorn, listening to her fervent chanting as it rose up the stairwell and crawled into every corner of his small room.

"Oh, yes, I'm coming."

Suddenly he became aware of his erection, raising its engorged head when it was least welcome.

Where were you when I needed you?

At the top of the stairs, standing next to the huge vase packed with false flowers, he paused and took a breath. He slapped his disobedient penis, but this only served to make it harder, and sent shivers along its thickened length. The beginnings of an orgasm clutched at his lower abdomen, tightening around his balls like tiny fists.

He could no longer hear Mother. She had either given up

or managed to make it out of bed. Either way, she would be exhausted. Outside, a distant siren wailed, rain began to stroke the windows, a dog barked three times before whining and falling abruptly silent. Another sound, like the roar of some injured animal, cut across all these other sounds, but he blocked it out, unwilling to even imagine its source.

Finally he walked towards the door to Mother's room, his hand reaching out to turn the handle. He pushed open the door, stepped inside, and closed it gently behind him.

"Mother. You've been a bad girl, and I must punish you." He tried to ignore the fluttering at his crotch; it felt like silken wings beating against his pubic bone.

A slow stirring; something hunched, something pained, something slouching out of the shadows at the far side of the room. It moved with a deliberation that at first kept him rooted to the spot, unable to look away.

"Mother?"

And then she was upon him, with no time for retreat and no room for error. Her hands clawed at his face, going for his eyes, and her jaws snap, snap, snapped like a mantrap. Her eyes were all white, no pupil; in death, they had turned back inside her skull. Blind, dead, hungry, she snorted like a pig in search of truffles, snuffling, sniffing for his blood, his fear, his meat.

Reflexively, Daryl threw up an arm and caught her in the face. Her grip relaxed for a moment, just enough for him to make some space for himself and ease backwards, evading her clutches. Her fingernails scraped along his upper arm, drawing white lines on the skin. He still sported an erection; it refused to dwindle, even under threat of being ravaged by a dead mouth.

He ran to the other side of the bed and faced her. She stood between him and the door, shoulders hunched, chest curved and unmoving, hands twisted into bestial talons. "Fuck, Mother." He was breathing heavily, unable to say much more.

His dead Mother began to ease around the bed, moving closer towards him, saliva dripping in a thick ribbon from her mouth. Her nightgown was torn; her withered left breast was showing through the rent in the heavy material. Her scrawny bird-like legs were bowed, incapable of adequately supporting even her slight weight.

The tumours that had grown inside her had wormed their way to the surface. They seemed the only living part of her, and they boiled and popped across the surface of her body, a mass of undead cells creating their own rules, exercising their individual hungers. One of them slid down her arm, across the back of her hand, and slopped onto the floor. It began to inch across the carpet like a fat red worm, still attached to her by thin thread-like veins.

"Oh, Jesus."

Mother seemed to react to the words. Always fanatically religious, the name of the Saviour triggered some kind of instinctive response in her back brain. Her head rolled on her neck; she opened her beak-like mouth and made a strange shrill bleating sound, like a sheep or a goat.

"*Jsssssssssssssssssssssssssssoo,*" she whined.

Daryl edged towards the foot of the bed, his foot coming down on the runaway tumour. It was hard and moist underfoot, and it popped like an egg when he brought all of his weight down upon it. Gagging, he forced himself to remain calm. In this grave new world, all the rules had changed: dead people were killers, cancers became sentient and serial killers were relegated to the bottom of the predatory pile.

"*Eeeh-eeh!*" said Mother, her jaws snapping on air. The sound they made – a hideous *click-snap* – was horrible in its intensity.

"Sweet Baby Jesus. Lord God Almighty. Hail Mary. The Holy Trinity." Daryl chanted the words, believing in them for the first time in his life – their power, the faith they represented, the undeniable beauty they conjured in that gloomy little room on a grubby little street in Leeds.

"*Eeeeeeeeeeeeeeeeeeeeeeeeeeeh!*" Mother moved lightning-fast, click-snapping towards him just as he reached the window and halted. She hit him hard in the side, her sheer momentum carrying him and slamming him against the wall. His upraised arm smashed the window, letting in the cold, harsh night and the ice-cold rain to slap him across the face like an open palm.

"*Moth-*" Daryl scrabbled on the floor, trying to fend her off, but she somehow managed to remain on top, smothering him. Always smothering, even now, when she was dead.

Daryl struggled against her. She wasn't exactly strong, but certainly possessed more strength than when she'd been ill and bedridden, unable to even sit up without his help. Her legs kicked, offering resistance against the floor, and her hands grasped at his face, his eyes. One of her fingers slipped between his lips and into his mouth. Daryl bit down; it was an instinctive reaction over which he had no real control. He felt his teeth sink into her thin flesh, grinding through the gristle and severing the bone. The finger came off in his mouth. He spat it out, vaguely disgusted.

And all the time, during this ridiculous attack, he was able to keep a part of himself at a distance from the action. He watched closely as he fought his dead Mother, noting how her flailing limbs moved without real purpose and her hideous jaws were the only part of her body to pose a genuine threat.

Still slightly detached, he managed to roll her off him, and he slid out from beneath her. He crawled quickly away on his knees, pulling himself to his feet using the bed frame for support. Then, turning, he looked for a weapon – anything would do, just to stop her.

Mother pulled herself across the floor, not even bothering to stand. Her jaws *click-snapped*; her eyes saw only food. Then, like some Chinese martial artist, she somehow flipped her body up so that she was resting on her haunches. She let out a strange strangled cry, like a dying bird, and then leapt towards him.

Daryl shifted to the side, throwing out an arm to grab something, anything, with which to hit her. His hand fell upon a familiar shape, an example of something Mother had kept at her side for most of her life.

Just as she fell upon him, Daryl's hand closed on the crucifix.

Mother's mouth clamped onto his arm, but for some reason – possibly the timing of her lunge – she gained no purchase and her teeth merely grazed the flesh, not even breaking it. Daryl brought the big metal cross between them, as if clutching it to his chest. Then, with a single sharp motion, he twisted his wrist and used the artefact to smash her in the face. Mother's teeth shattered, her body rocked backwards, and once again Daryl forced the crucifix into her face.

The sharp end of the vertical member went straight into her left eye, bursting the china-white eyeball and entering her brain. Mother froze instantly, as if someone had simply thrown a switch to cut off her power. Saliva dribbled from her mouth. Cloudy fluid oozed from the shattered eye socket and down her cheek.

Daryl stepped away from her corpse, fascinated as it toppled forward. Her cheek hit the wooden boards, the fragile bone breaking on impact. The crucifix remained where it was, sticking out of her face like a bad visual joke, an obscene pun he didn't quite get.

Daryl backed up until he hit the door to Mother's room. Then he slid down it, his legs giving way through sheer exhaustion rather than as the result of any recognisable emotion. He stared at Mother's corpse, entranced by the sight of her ruined features. Her clothes seemed to be moving on her body, rippling, as if they were alive. Then, horrified, Daryl realised what was causing the effect.

The tumours that had been growing inside her for so long were attempting to escape their cold host. They burst to the surface of her papery flesh, ripping it and bulging out of the wounds. They looked like raw meat: fist-sized pieces of cheap steak that had gone bad.

Daryl watched as the tumours dropped to the floor, already withering and dying, rolling around as if they were small animals in search of a private place to die. They did not survive long outside of Mother's corpse. Separated from her essence, they became pointless, their parasitic *raison d'etre* now gone.

Daryl, on the other hand, would thrive now that she was gone. The old Daryl did not exist: in the blink of an eye, and the flash of a crucifix, he had been replaced by someone else, a being who would rejoice in the chaos around him and make it his own.

And this brand new being had witnessed such *rapturous* sights, things that the old Daryl could not have imagined, even in his most intense moments of fantasy. Because the old Daryl was dead: he was dead and born again through the destruction of this woman, this monster... this twice-dead Mother.

CHAPTER EIGHTEEN

Rick filled the hypodermic with the morphine he'd scavenged from the doctor's apartment. He wasn't quite sure of the correct technique involved, but was certain that it wouldn't matter if he got it wrong. Sally was dead, so he doubted that a mistake or a slip of the wrist regarding dosage would cause her much pain.

She'd become restless since his return, as if something had disturbed her. *Hungry*, he thought. *She's probably hungry.* He tried not to think of the human remains he'd seen earlier, pretending that Sally wanted a burger, or a pizza from the local takeaway. He recalled the way she'd refused the frozen steaks...

It had taken him quite some time to remove the dirty dressings, clean up the congealing crimson mess of her skinned face, and then apply a layer of kitchen cellophane before putting on the new bandages. But he didn't mind. It was his job; the job of a husband and lover; the job of a true friend.

"This won't hurt," he told her, smiling. "Not really. Just a bit of discomfort, then you'll feel a bit sleepy." He hoped that was true.

During his time in the Paras, and then again in police training, he'd seen the effects of morphine and other painkillers on human beings. But those subjects had been alive; this one was dead. What would the morphine do to dead tissue? Would it even work?

Sleepy? Can we make spoons?

"No. No, we can't." He flicked the syringe, looking for air bubbles. Not that it mattered. He jammed the plastic hypodermic between his teeth, nervous of accidentally pricking himself in the face. Then, slowly but firmly, he braced Sally's arm and rolled up her sleeve. The flesh was already turning pale blue, the tell-tale hue of oxygen starvation. Haematomas had erupted along the length of her arm, discolouring it even further. Under her clothing, she was cold to the touch; her veins stood proud, the blood frozen in her system because the heart had ceased to beat.

Rick took the syringe between finger and thumb, lined up a particularly large vein... and then stopped. If the blood was not being pumped around her circulatory system, then how was the morphine meant to do its job? He knew enough to be aware that it worked by affecting certain receptors, a few of which were distributed in parts of the spinal cord. Most of them, however, were located in the brain.

The brain. It was the only part of these dead things' anatomy that seemed to work, however weirdly. He stared hard at Sally's freshly bandaged head, at the shallow pits where her eyes would be.

"I'm sorry," he said, his voice dropping an octave.

Its okay, baby. I know you're just trying to protect me.

It was incredible how quickly he'd adjusted to her speaking to him in this way. He knew it wasn't real, that Sally could not really communicate and he was imagining her voice, but all the same... it helped, and made it easier to carry out the extreme acts necessary for survival.

I know you would never hurt me.

Without thinking, he diverted the needle to her right eye socket, slamming it in and depressing the plunger. With any luck, the massive dose of opiate would bypass the usual route and go straight to the brain, doing its job and sedating her while also shutting down whatever remained of her central nervous system.

For the first time he wondered why the young doctor across the way had kept morphine in his apartment, especially when he had kids on the premises. He was probably an addict; perhaps he got hooked on the stuff during his training, working impossible hours and surviving on hardly any sleep at all. Rick knew a lot of medics in the army who'd used drugs to get by, particularly when they were posted in high pressure locations – often it was a necessary evil, a way of being able to do your job in impossible situations.

Rick's drug of choice had always been alcohol. He craved a drink now, but forced himself to wait until this unpleasant task was done. Glancing over at the drinks cabinet, he fixated on the whisky bottle. Fifteen year-old Glenmorangie: a nice drop, bought for him as a gift by Sally.

The morphine seemed to be working. Sally was slumped sideways on the sofa, her body loose, and the tension had gone from her limbs.

Sleepy... so sleeeeeepy... time for beddy-bye.

She was docile, easily manoeuvred. Rick put away the drug kit and transferred it to his rucksack, which he'd taken out of the wardrobe earlier. Inside the bag were also the neighbour's medical kit (including the rest of the fresh bandages), toiletries, some ammo for the Glock, a map and compass, some Kendal mint cake and a few essential items from the cutlery drawer – a can opener, a spoon and a cork bottle-stopper he'd grabbed purely because it reminded him of their holiday in Greece the year before.

Rick left Sally on the sofa and retreated to the bedroom. He took off his clothes and laid them out on the bed, then went to the bathroom and took a shower. There was still enough hot water for him to remain under the jet until he felt at least partially cleansed.

After showering, he cleaned his teeth with Sally's toothbrush until his gums bled. The bristles were worn, but he imagined that they tasted of Sally. Tears ran down his cheeks. He refused to wipe them away. In the mirror, his face had become harder, leaner; the face of the killer he was trained to be. That face had always lurked beneath the face he wore every day, waiting for the slightest opportunity to surface and show itself to the world. It was a face that had felt the desert sun, the hot shower of blood, the grit of explosions and nearby gunshots. It was the ancient face of warfare, a dark countenance worn by so many before him and countless more warriors who would come marching after, battling their way through whatever kind of world was left behind.

In the bedroom, he opened the secret door at the back of the wardrobe. He was forced to remove all the clothes on hangers to gain access, but Sally would not need her blouses and dresses any more. He picked up a long overcoat she hardly ever wore and put it to one side. He would put it on her before they left the apartment.

Inside the hatch was an M16 assault rifle he'd managed to smuggle back from Afghanistan. There was also a second-hand gun, another Glock like the one he had in the holster on his belt. Boxes of ammunition for these two guns sat on a couple of shelves he'd screwed to the wall. Hanging on a hook was a large hunting knife, one edge serrated and the other smooth and scalpel-sharp. Fresh riot gear hung on a peg. He put on the clothing, enjoying the clean feel of it against his skin.

Rick took the guns, knife and ammo and returned to the living room. He wrapped the M16 in an old black dress Sally used as a dust sheet whenever she decorated, and put the other stuff in his rucksack. The bag was full now, but he still managed to squeeze in the whisky bottle and an old photograph of Sally, taken by a mutual friend, name now forgotten, when she and Rick had first become a couple.

Sitting on the floor, the rucksack between his knees, Rick sipped the whisky. It burned a path down his throat and heat bloomed in his stomach, making him feel that somewhere at the end of all this there was hope. He finished his drink and set the glass on the floor. Then, standing, he prepared to move Sally.

First he inspected the landing. It was clear; nothing had disturbed the silence since he'd shot the kid. He traced a route along the landing to the stairs, then descended the stairwell with his gun at the ready. He propped open the doors along his route, mindful that if he was carrying Sally's by now largely unresponsive body it might prove difficult to open them as he went.

Outside, he pulled the Nissan up to the front entrance, scanning the entire area for movement. He left the car doors open and made for the cover of the lobby. Pausing before re-entering the apartment block, he stared around him, taking in the seemingly tranquil atmosphere. Nothing moved, and there were no sounds other than that caused by the light sing-song motion of the canal. Even the birds had stopped singing.

Overhead, the sky was a vast dark canopy, covering the hell below. There were no planes up there, not even a light aircraft. The extent of the situation must be huge: it was impossible to prepare, to set out plans, for something as insane as this. He wondered again if, as had been intimated on the few news reports he'd managed to glimpse, terrorists were responsible, or if this was some kind of cosmic accident. Perhaps God had judged humanity as unfit to carry on, and instead of another cataclysmic rainfall he had simply decided to flood the earth with the dead.

It was clear now that anyone who died would return to attack the living, and that all they wanted was to eat. Humanity stripped down to an awful basic drive to consume. Take away the trappings and progress of evolution, the intellectual ground man has made up over the millennia, and all that remains is a brutish appetite. Beneath all that emotion, beyond love, hate and even fear, all you have left is hunger.

For years now, he thought, *we've been trained to become the ideal consumer. Now that's all we are. Mindless consumers, just not in the way they intended...*

Rick turned his back on the thought and entered the building. His finger was light on the trigger of the gun, but the triggers at his nerve-endings – the ones that really mattered – were all-too-ready to react and make him spring into action.

He made his way back up the gloomy, windowless stairwell, keeping an ear out for the telltale signs of anyone creeping around on any of the floors. All was silent; the other tenants were either dead, had hit the road in an attempt to escape the city, or were hiding indoors, afraid to even move.

Then: laughter. A soft, echoing chuckle that rose up the concrete throat of the stairwell. Rick stopped, turned around, and dropped to his knees, peering back down the way he'd come. The laughter did not come again, and after several agonising minutes he stood and climbed to his floor.

Sally looked as if she were asleep when he entered the apartment, her head on the cushions, arms lying straight down at her sides. Her white-covered hands were clenched, the fingers stiff as windblown twigs against her thighs.

Earlier, when he'd cleaned her up he had slipped some running shoes on her feet and managed to get her to slide her arms into a heavy woollen cardigan. Now, he eased her upright so that her back was against the rear of the sofa, then clumsily manhandled her into the long overcoat he'd retrieved from the wardrobe along with his portable arsenal.

Sally moaned once, almost a word... a real word, not one that existed only inside his mind. Then, like a blissed-out crack-head, she lapsed into a deep silence. He slung her up and over his shoulder, into a fireman's lift. She was heartbreakingly light, not much more than a bag of bones. Her muscles were already beginning to waste away, hanging slack on the bone beneath. Rigor mortis would set in soon – maybe that was why some of the dead things moved so stiffly, their limbs seizing up hours after death. The state, he knew did not last long; and after it wore off, the arms and legs would move easier, but still they lacked co-ordination. Sally, her brain only partially functioning, would probably be incapable of independent movement: even without the morphine, her body would be as floppy and unresponsive as a rag doll. The drug was more for his peace of mind, a safety precaution in case the hunger that drove these things broke through and gave her away.

Rick could barely believe that he was about to try and pass off his dead wife as the victim of an accident. She certainly looked the part – no problem there; the disguise was realistic to a fault. But the psychological ramification of his idea, the damage already being done to his sanity, was surely immeasurable.

He carried Sally downstairs without incident. By the time he'd buckled her into the passenger seat of the little four-wheel-drive vehicle, the washed-out sun was already on the wane. Night was dominant in these dark days, as if what was happening to people was somehow reflected in the very cycle of the earth as it shuddered through a mockery of its usual routines.

Rick started the engine but did not drive away from the apartment block. He stared through the windscreen, at the sketchy twilight, and wondered if his slowly emerging plan could ever work. He had a vague idea that rural areas might be the safest places to hide, and he and Sally had rented a cottage up in North Yorkshire two summers before. He still knew the way, and they had always planned to return to the cottage. They had spent a two-week period there which had, in retrospect, been one of the happiest times of their lives.

The cottage was miles away from the nearest town, and hidden from the road by acres of fields and woodlands. It had taken them hours to find it that first time, and only once they'd actually done so where they able to find it again. Every trip out to the shop, or to some local point of interest, held the fear that they'd get lost upon their return to the small stone cottage.

It was the best he could do, the only option he could think of. He hoped that no one else had gone there, and that the roads were passable. If they couldn't make it there, to that isolated potential refuge, then he was fresh out of ideas.

He glanced at Sally. She was still out cold, her head tilted against the headrest. A scrap of hair had crept through a fold in the bandages, and the sight of it almost killed him. Even now, like this, he loved her – but was it really her that he felt compassion towards, or some other woman who had taken her place? His wife was dead, and this slow-witted impostor was all he had.

Rick closed his eyes and turned away. He could not let himself dwell too long on such thoughts: that way lay madness, and probable destruction. He let his foot fall onto the accelerator and pulled away, the rear wheels skidding on a patch of gravel. Their old home shrank in the rearview mirror, turning into a small-scale replica of the place where they had lived. Like the rest of the world, it was becoming even smaller, dissolving into nothing more than a wan memory of what had once been and could never be again.

"I know exactly where we're going," he said, still not looking directly at Sally, "but I'm not sure if we'll ever get there." He watched her reflection in the darkening glass of the windscreen. She did not stir.

CHAPTER NINETEEN

Two-Time Killer.
No, too cheap and pulpy, like an old 1950s film noir.
The Man Who Killed Her Twice.
Ditto.
Daryl smiled as he packed his bag, amusing himself by imagining alternative titles for the TV-Movie-of-the-week that would never be made about his exploits. He knew that he should be shaken by what had happened with Mother; but, as usual, human emotions were beyond him, as if separated from his body by a plate glass window. He could see them capering around in the outside world, and even believe that others experienced them, but to him they belonged to an unknown culture he did not understand.

Instead, all he felt was... well, a bit *tired.*

He finished packing and went to the bedroom window, looking down into the drizzle-damp street. Only a few people had passed by since he'd despatched Mother, and they were either racing along in bashed-up vehicles or running on foot. Most of these latter were carrying weapons – garden tools, table legs, cricket or baseballs bats: anything they could get their hands on.

For now, the street was once again quiet and empty. The embers of dying fires were reflected in the sky but there were no more sirens tearing through the evening air. Daryl remembered reading somewhere that society was always no more than four days away from absolute chaos. This was at least the second day; perhaps that estimate had been off by about forty-eight hours.

Daryl passed Mother's room on his way to the stairs. He paused outside the door, trying to feel something. His body felt like an empty canister; nothing stirred in there but the blood pumping through his veins. His mind, however, was a nest of vipers, a coiling mass of madness.

"Goodbye, Mother." He continued to the stairs and descended to the ground floor, where he headed straight for the front door. There was nothing left here – not a single thing to keep him or even to delay his journey. The only thing that mattered lay somewhere out there, in the gathering darkness: Sally, his first, his one true victim.

The absolute love of his life.

He had a rough plan to retrace his steps along the canal and see if the Nutmans were still at their apartment. He imagined that the husband might have committed suicide when he came home to find his new wife slain. That would make things so much easier. If, when he got back there, she had risen and was occupied feasting upon her husband's corpse, he could move in for a swift second kill. Or, better still, he could somehow incapacitate her and enjoy himself, making the second time last longer than his first stab at killing.

First stab. That was almost funny. And the perfect title for his imaginary biopic!

He reached the garden gate without incident, then heard a strange sound. He paused, listened, and identified it as the sound of eating. Standing beside the high line of privet bushes that separated Mother's property from next door, he remembered the neighbours and their earlier battle. They must have ordered out for food, and were now enjoying an open-air meal.

He smiled. Then crept softly to the end of the garden and turned right out of the gate, heading for the end of the street where he could access the canal.

At first he thought that someone was coughing, or more likely struggling to breathe. Then, as the sound became louder, whatever was making it drawing closer, he realised what it was. The noise was too muted and belching to be coming from a motorcycle, so he suspected that there was a moped heading his way, like the ones used by pizza delivery men.

Daryl ducked into some bushes and waited as the vehicle sputtered towards him, its rider bent over the handlebars and not wearing a helmet. Comically, there was a large white plastic container attached to the front of the moped, the words PIZZA YOU, PIZZA ME, stencilled across it in bright red letters.

"You've got to be kidding. End of the world take-out food?" This whole situation just got funnier and funnier, as if the movie of Daryl's life were morphing from a low-budget horror movie into a knock-about farce.

He took a short crowbar from his bag and waited until the farting, belching machine drew level with him. Then he threw the crowbar as hard as he could, aiming for the front wheel. The projectile fell short of its target, hitting the asphalt road. But, absurdly, the ten-inch long piece of machined metal bounced when it made contact and then flipped up and caught the rider on his knee. The bike swerved, the rider shocked and hurting, and then it went down, skidding into the gutter a few yards along the road.

Daryl ran out and reclaimed the crowbar. Then he jogged to where the young man was sprawled in the road, clutching his knee and trying not to scream yet still making an awful din. Glancing around, Daryl was all too aware that dead things might arrive at any moment. Bushes rustled. Someone – or some *thing* – began to wail. A metal gate screeched not far from where he was standing.

Acting quickly, Daryl headed immediately for the moped. He righted the small, unwieldy machine and climbed on. The engine was still running, so he simply slipped the clutch, revved the handle, and set off in the direction of the canal. He glanced once in the rearview mirror and saw the dazed young man sitting in the street, still holding onto his knee. Behind him, advancing at varying speeds, there approached three dead people. One of them was a small child; the lower part of its face was crimson with whatever it had been feeding on prior to the idiot moped rider announcing himself with his pitiful cries.

"Pizza you, pizza me," said Daryl, unable to resist. It was a shame that such high humour was wasted without an audience.

When the man finally began to scream Daryl could not help but stop the moped. He kept the engine running and climbed off, turning to watch. The three dead people had already set upon the young man. He was flailing beneath their combined attentions. Two women – one fat, the other slender as a rake with either clothing or flesh hanging from her in strips – were busy disembowelling him, while the small child buried its face in his crotch.

Daryl watched for as long as he felt safe, then climbed back on the moped and set off. The last thing he'd seen was the dead child playing with the young man's head and the two women fighting lazily over a length of grey intestine. The fat one was winning by weight advantage alone.

This was going to be easy. Things had reached such a stage that Daryl could move unnoticed through the world, killing whoever he pleased. Like a virus moving through the bloodstream of a butchered body, the greater damage would mask his presence. It was every killer's dream come true: an avenue of hurt opening up before him, stretching ahead towards a distant blood-red horizon.

He pushed the little moped as hard as it would go, passing the occasional mutilated corpse in the road. Often he encountered dead people. They reached out for him as he passed them by, but no contact was ever made. Daryl was now untouchable. He had travelled so far away from humanity, and had become such a different beast, that he moved among them like a chill wind, slipping through their fingers and barely even registering in their vision.

A police car was parked on the corner of Whittington Road and Commonwealth Avenue, its doors flung open. The body of one officer hung out of the driver's side, his belly opened, ribs sticking out like accusatory fingers. He was stirring, trying to move, but the lower half of his body had been so ravaged that it would no longer respond to whatever was driving his brain. His mouth gaped, the jaws clicking from side to side like a feeding cow. His eyes were white, turned back in his head, and his useless hands grabbed at his ruptured abdomen, dragging out chunks of bloody meat and stuffing them between his teeth in a horrific act of auto-cannibalism.

The other officer was on the ground, not much left of him but bones. The flesh had been chewed away, and the ruin that was now trying to crawl across the road and join his partner in the nightmarish feast could barely move without more of it falling away.

Daryl rode on, feeling like he was journeying through a Hieronymus Bosch painting: scenarios of damnation plucked directly from Mother's Old Testament picture books unfolded around him. But whatever god walked here was one of blood and brimstone, a vengeful maniac, a self-unaware psychotic.

"You would have loved all this, Mother." Daryl threw back his head, the wind in his hair; the stench of death was in his nostrils. "It's all your warnings come true, your dreams become reality."

He dropped down onto the familiar canal towpath, guiding the moped along the rutted route much used by weekend walkers and mountain bikers. He heard splashing sounds in the water but did not glance away from the track. He had to be careful. If he fell and was injured, he might die alone here... and to die meant that he would rise again, hungry for human flesh and with no memories of how to do anything but search for food.

When he reached the apartment block he had a gut feeling that he'd already missed them. His initial thought was that Sally had killed her husband, but then another idea struck him. What if the man had not even found her, and she was roaming the area for prey?

He parked the moped and ran into the building through the unlocked main entrance, ready to bolt if anyone approached from behind the closed apartment doors. He heard somebody weeping, saw a discarded child's doll in a corner, smelled the bland aroma of gas – the result of some poor bastard putting their head in the oven or gassing their children as they slept. He wondered, if he kicked down a few of these doors, would he find behind one of them a family curled up together like sleeping animals, their faces blue and elongated, their knuckles white as they'd clutched each other in their death throes?

To Daryl, the whole idea of suicide had always seemed like an easy way out, an escape route that offered nothing but brief pain followed by infinite darkness. *And besides*, he thought, *if you topped yourself you might miss all the fun when all the idiots who claimed to care but never really did found you dead.*

The door to Sally's apartment was open. He knew the place was empty even before he stepped inside. The floor beside the sofa was littered with bloody bandages: they lay in a coiled heap, like the shed skin of an ugly snake. A lot of the kitchen drawers and cupboards were open, their contents spilled out onto the floor. Someone had packed in a hurry.

In the bedroom, behind the main door, a wardrobe hung open. The back wall of the wardrobe contained a wooden hatch, which was also ajar. Daryl reached out and pulled it fully open. He saw a couple of leather gun holsters and some empty ammunition boxes on a shelf, but nothing more.

"So," he said, impressed. "You think you can save her?" Shaking his head in the mirror on the dresser. "And I thought I was fucked up."

Daryl went through a chest of drawers, upending each drawer until he came to one containing women's undergarments. He ran his hands through her underwear, bringing up to his face sports briefs, thongs, lacy dress-up panties with see-through gussets: a cornucopia of knickers that sent him reeling back on his heels.

Raking with his fingers to the back of the drawer, he discovered an old threadbare pair of granny knickers with a stained crotch. *These*, he thought, *must be the pair she wears when she's on her period. Oh, God...* he held them up to his nose, inhaled, and took in the coppery scent that still clung stubbornly to the worn material.

Grabbing a second pair – blue, frilly, scanty – he retreated to the bed, where he lay down on his back and loosened his trousers. He was already hard, so began to stroke himself, wrapping the blue panties around his fist. The other pair – the stained, dark-gusseted period pants – he pressed against his nose, pushing his finger against them and into one nostril.

He tried hard enough, but was unable to climax. Even the scent of her blood didn't do it. He came close when he recalled cutting off her face, but the memory remained at a distance, too far away to engage with.

Disgusted with himself, Daryl stood and pulled up his trousers. He tossed the underwear into a corner, pretending that it did not exist.

He heard Mother's voice in his ear, her awful brittle laughter; then he felt her warm breath on his neck as she whispered to him that she was the only girl he would ever need and hers was the only true love he could know...

"No!" His voice hung in the air, a mockery of negation, a sad, wasted energy that even now seemed weak and inconsequential.

Blocking out the ancient memory, he left the room and surveyed the living area. The laptop was dead, the TV lifeless. The lights were out. The local electricity supply must have been interrupted, either by the dead or by vandals. If he was honest, the only difference between these two groups was the hunger... they were identical in every other way: mindless, moronic creatures with no real purpose to their existence. Only the *form* of their hunger differed.

He spotted on the coffee table, by the window, a pair of leather gloves. Slim, brown, obviously belonging to a woman: Sally's gloves. He strode over and picked them up, forced them onto his small hands. The fit was tight, but they were not uncomfortable. He stroked his cheek with her fingers, licked the end of her thumb. The old, faded leather smelled wonderful.

Daryl left the apartment and descended the hollow staircase. Outside, he climbed back on the moped and thought about where they might be heading. He glanced away from the city, along the new blacktop road that led towards the motorway. Lights flickered in the distance, beyond the trees. He glanced at his hands, wrapped up tight in Sally's gloves. He imagined that they were still warm from her flesh.

Revving the small engine, he set off, certain that he had not seen Sally Nutman for the last time, and that their paths would eventually cross again. He did not know where this certainty originated, but he trusted it implicitly. If he was honest, there was little else to do now but follow such hunches. Who knew where they might lead, and what blood-filled adventures he might experience?

Once again, just to occupy his racing mind, he imagined the titles of the popular paperback volumes that would never be written about him: *Kill Me Again, Death in Double Doses, Murderer of the Living Dead...*

If anyone living had been around to hear it, the high, whooping sound of his laughter would certainly have chilled them to the core. This thought, when it came to him, just made him laugh all the more.

CHAPTER TWENTY

motion empty dull voice engine what how hunger hunger taste dry empty live not dead not something sweet dark inside forever hungry forever hungry pain release rage hunger hungry

CHAPTER TWENTY-ONE

"I'll find a way to get you to safety." Rick barely believed his own words, and wondered if he was speaking them to soothe his fears or those he imagined for Sally. She sat beside him, her hands limp, the seatbelt forming a tight diagonal band across her stomach and chest, saying nothing.

"I promise you, honey. We'll get to safety somehow."

Darkness fell from the dusky sky, wide drapes being lowered over the top of an open coffin, hiding from sight whatever had been laid to rest inside.

I know. I know you will.

He screwed shut his eyes, fighting against a force he didn't want to confront, and when he opened them again he saw lights in the distance. About a mile along the road, off the main route, tall lampposts were still shining. When he passed the signpost he realised what the lights represented: a service station. He glanced at the petrol indicator on the dashboard: still almost half full. *Or half empty*, he thought, *depending on your point of view.*

These days Rick was definitely a half empty kind of guy.

His hands gripped the steering wheel, his knuckles white, and he kept his eyes locked dead ahead. He'd seen no sign of life (or death, or any other state of existence) since leaving the apartment block behind, but he couldn't be sure that there wasn't some danger lurking at the side of the road, just waiting to pounce.

Anything that strayed into the road – be it human or otherwise – he was simply planning to mow down. There was a specialised impact bumper on the front end of the Nissan, and he fully intended to test it.

The clouds smothered the sky, breaking apart into rough-edged stains. The stars were nowhere to be seen, as if even they had given up the hope of illuminating mankind. Everything felt fragile, temporary, as if something was rapidly approaching an end.

Rick tensed when he heard gunshots. They didn't sound too close, but if he could hear them it was close enough to cause concern. Considering his passenger, he needed to be wary of everyone – especially some gun-toting broth-head who thought the best way to sort out this situation was by shooting anything and everything in sight.

The stark service station lights loomed closer. One of them flickered, but the rest remained constant, bathing the concrete forecourt in a harsh white glow that hurt Rick's eyes when he looked directly at it. He eased the Nissan off the main road and guided it onto the forecourt, checking the immediate area for signs of potential danger.

He drew level with the first petrol pump and switched off the engine. As he listened to the mechanism cooling, he strained to hear anything beyond the faint clicking. There was nothing, not even the song of night birds or the thrum of an overhead police helicopter. The world felt empty, a huge open space waiting to be filled with death.

"I won't be long," he said, opening the car door.

I won't go far.

He smiled, but the expression felt horrible as it spread across his face, like a badly healed scar opening up to infection.

Rick unlocked the petrol cap and slipped the nozzle into the slot. He pressed the lever, hoping for the best, and felt like cheering when he felt the hose tug against his grip as fuel poured into the tank. He remained stationary, scared to move his hand even a millimetre in case it stifled the flow of fuel – a silly, superstitious action, but nonetheless one to which he clung until the tank was full.

He gazed at the back of Sally's head through the window, inspecting the wrappings for signs of leakage. They looked fine, and when he pulled the fuel hose out of the tank he managed to drag his eyes away from her.

He was just about to climb back into the car when he was halted by the sight of the small shop attached to the service station. It was the kind of thing he saw every day, a small grocery store stocked with everyday provisions, ready-made sandwiches, vehicle maintenance accessories, and hot and cold beverages.

Rick shut the door and walked across the forecourt, Glock in hand, eyes skinned and expecting an assault. He reached the main entrance unmolested, and gently pushed open the glass door. A buzzer sounded somewhere deep inside the bright one-storey building, and he clenched his teeth in anticipation of sound and fury and bloodlust. None came. So he stepped into the shop.

Overhead fluorescent lights droned like insects; his feet slapped on the smooth tiled floor; the door whispered shut behind him, once again setting off that damned buzzer.

Rick paused, dropped down below eye level, and waited.

Be ready for anything, he thought. *Any-fucking-thing.* It was something Hutch had often said during their army training; a lesson they'd both learned together but that only Rick was still alive to follow.

He could hear the low, maudlin murmuring of a refrigerator unit, and moved slowly towards it. He could do with stocking up on bottled water. In a few days the stuff would be worth more than gold. Unless someone had been here first and cleared the shelves, he could fill up any large bag he found with bottles and then get the hell out of there and back on the road. A few sandwiches would be good, too; maybe some chocolate bars.

Rick's mouth began to moisten at the thought. When had he last eaten?

The shelves around him were fully stocked: bread, a few canned goods, biscuits and family-packs of kettle chips. It looked like this place was so out of the way that it had been missed, or perhaps there were simply no looters in the area. At least not yet.

Places like this held a strange atmosphere when they were emptied of people. It was like the entire building was holding its breath, waiting for something to happen or someone to arrive. The effect was unnerving; it made Rick feel a strange mélange of paranoia and vertigo, as if he were falling through miles of empty sky into a giant, silently waiting mouth.

Rick tried to recall if he'd noticed the service station before, but had no memory of it. He'd lived here for two years, so must have passed the station countless times without ever really noticing it. Like most of the commercial trappings of modern life, he'd simply taken it for granted, not seeing it until he actually needed it, as if his desire had summoned it from the greyness of non-being and brought it forward to supply him with whatever he required. And wasn't that just the purest metaphor for a consumer society? The common magic of need.

Rick didn't even realise he'd heard the tiny sound until his gun hand twitched, drawn in its direction as if magnetised. It was followed by a low whisper, hushed words of warning to whoever had made the initial sound.

He moved along the narrow aisle, crouching, with both hands on the handle of the Glock.

The shuffling of feet on the polished floor; followed by a small voice, almost a stifled cry. Then silence, but not enough of it, and what little there was seemed haunted by the words already spoken, however quietly.

He saw them before he even reached the end of the aisle, folded into a corner next to the coffee machine. An old man and a young girl, reflected in the convex security mirror on the wall next to the lavatory door. Rick relaxed when he saw them, allowing the tension to leave his arm and the gun to drop a fraction.

"Listen to me," he said, trying to infuse his voice with authority. "I'm a police officer. I mean you no harm, but I *am* armed, so I'd strongly advise against any sudden or threatening moves."

In the mirror, the stunted image of the man wrapped his arms around the girl, who looked up into his face, her eyes wide and wet. Small freckled face; a question mark-shaped cluster of those freckles on her right cheek.

"I promise you that I do not want to hurt you. I repeat: I mean you no harm." He paused, allowing them time for the information to sink in.

"Okay. We're coming out. We're unarmed, and I have a little girl here – my granddaughter. She's... she's very scared."

Rick felt his body relax; he let out the breath he'd been holding. "I assure you, sir, I don't want to hurt anyone. Just step out where I can see you and we can talk."

The reflection nodded, and then stood awkwardly, as if the man's aging limbs were stiff. The two of them walked out from the end of the aisle, hand in hand. Their steps were small, tentative, and Rick lowered the gun to assure them once again that he was not an enemy.

The man raised a hand, a nervous half-smile on his lips.

"Hi," said Rick, standing and returning the Glock to its holster. "My name's Rick Nutman, and I'm just here to get some supplies."

The man shuffled forward, keeping himself between Rick and the girl. Rick admired that. It was a simple gesture, but one that told him a lot about the man's character.

"Is there anyone else here?" Rick nodded towards the back of the shop.

"No," said the old man. "I suspect the cashier legged it when things started to get weird. We found the door unlocked, so we came in for a while. Just getting supplies, the same as you."

His grin was a desperate lunge for approval.

"I'm Stan Rohmer, and this is my granddaughter Tabitha... Tabby." He walked forward with that same hand now outstretched in an awkward greeting.

"Good to meet you," said Rick shaking the hand and smiling at the girl. She peered out from behind her grandfather's leg, yet to be convinced that it was safe to come out.

"We've been hiding out from... well; I assume you've seen them for yourself." Rohmer was a tall man. His limbs were rangy, almost gangly and his back was bowed, giving him the appearance of being much shorter than he actually was.

"The dead people," said the girl, stepping out from behind Rohmer. "We're hiding from the dead folks."

"I've seen them," said Rick, once more crouching down, but this time to meet the girl at her own level. "Hello, Tabby. I'm glad you found somewhere safe to hide."

"Oh, it was Granddad's idea. He's very clever."

Rick smiled. Rohmer laughed, ruffling the girl's reddish-brown hair with the palm of a long-fingered hand. His face was small, and he wore black-framed glasses that were so large they made his eyes look like those of a koala bear. They blinked almost comically as he spoke again: "I'm not that clever. If I was, we'd be far away from here."

"Where are you headed?" Rick moved to the drinks cabinet as he spoke, filling a sports bag he casually picked up from a display with bottles of water.

Rohmer began to fill a second bag without being asked. "Down to the canal. We... I have a boat."

Rick paused, turned to stare at the old man. His long grey hair was pulled back into a ponytail, and strands had come loose from the rubber band he'd used. Those huge eyes blinked. "Why are you telling me this? You don't even know me. I could be lying about not wanting to hurt anybody."

Rohmer placed a hand on Rick's arm. He did not pull away. His long fingers twitched like pale stick insects. "Listen," said the old man. "You have a car and I have a boat. We could help each other. You're armed, and presumably know how to look after yourself. I'm an old fuck trying to look after the only thing of worth left in his life." His eyes became larger, more desperate behind the comically thick lenses of his spectacles. He licked his lips.

Rick nodded. He glanced at the girl and nodded again. He and Sally had often discussed having children, and although neither of them had ever voiced an opinion, he knew for a fact that they both wanted a girl. "I'll help you," he said. "You and the child."

Tabby looked at him, her gaze bold and unflinching. "Thank you, mister."

They filled their bags and set them down by the door. Then they filled two more, and scoured the place for weapons. Rohmer found a baseball bat under the counter, and hefted it as he walked down the aisle towards the doors.

"Why can't anyone have a cricket bat these days? Have we all become so Americanised that the good old willow is no longer the home security implement of choice?"

Rick grinned. He was beginning to like this old man.

They stood at the entrance and stared out at the forecourt, checking the shadows for movement. The long grass at the side of the service station undulated in a breeze, the trees shivered, the overhead telephone wires seemed to spin.

"Who's that in the car?" Tabby tugged at his sleeve, her mouth dark with chocolate from the bar she'd opened as the two men filled the bags.

Shit. He'd neglected to tell them about Sally. "That's my wife." He spoke steadily, keeping his nerves under wraps. "She was injured earlier this evening – had her face burned in a fire when everything started going crazy. I'm trying to get her to safety."

Rohmer put down the bag he'd been holding and turned to face Rick. His face was solemn, unreadable. Did he know that Rick was lying? Had he seen through the deceit? "I'm sorry to ask you this, but... well, was she bitten?"

Rick frowned. "What do you mean, bitten?"

"By one of those things. The dead people." Tabby took a step back, moving away from him.

"No. No, she wasn't bitten."

"You sure?" Rohmer's grip tightened around the bat's handle. His arms were rigid.

"I'm absolutely positive." Rick's hand rested on the butt of the Glock.

"I'm sorry. I really am, but I've seen a grown man get bitten on the hand and die within half an hour. Then he came back... came back and killed his wife. Killed my daughter." His comedy eyes swelled, almost pressing against the thick lenses of his spectacles.

Suddenly Rick understood the depth of what these people had been through, and felt sorry for their loss, for everyone's loss.

"Anyone who dies comes back. If you're bitten you die – why wouldn't you? They're dead, and dead things carry infections. So, you get bitten, you die, you come back. Everybody comes back."

"Unless you chop off their head," said Tabby, at his side, once more feeling safe enough to stand close to him. Her hand slipped gently into his. Her mouth worked on another chocolate bar.

Rick nodded. "I know. I'm sorry. I..." he didn't know what else to say.

"I've seen so much over the last couple of days... so much horror. Dead bodies dragging themselves out of graves, murdered neighbours in turn murdering their own children, men and women I have known and loved eating the ones they knew and loved. We've entered dark times, son. Dark and insane times. Those of us left, the ones who survive... we're gonna have to rebuild it all, from the bottom up."

Rick reached out and laid a hand on Rohmer's shoulder. The old man looked at it as if it were something he no longer recognised. Then, slowly, with great affection and dignity, he placed his own hand over the top of it and nodded.

"My wife's hurt very badly. I'm keeping her on morphine, just to ease her pain. She isn't dying, but the burns were bad. I have them under control, but eventually she'll need proper medical care."

Rohmer squeezed Rick's hand. "Don't worry, son. I know of a place, somewhere we can get all the help we need. It's where we're heading."

Tabby wandered to the rear of the shop, picking sweets off the shelves. She was singing a simple child's tune, something Rick remembered from school but couldn't name.

"There's an island," said Rohmer, his eyes staring beyond Rick. "I know someone who works there. It's a mile or two off the northeast coast, not too far from the Scottish border – Northumberland. You know: Hadrian's Wall and all that? Off the coast between two little villages called Bamburgh and Seahouses, a place called the Farne Islands. The whole mass of islands is a bird sanctuary, with the inner islands and a few other, smaller islets scattered around them."

He paused, swallowed, and then continued.

"They're doing all kinds of experiments there, on one of the smaller land masses. The last I heard from my friend was to warn me that something was happening, and if I could make my way to the island he'd take good care of me. Told me to bring along my family, my friends... the next day, all this happened. I realise now that he was warning me, but I was too slow to act."

Rick stared at the old man, hypnotised by his words.

"There's help there. I know there is. He even told me to try and bring along the bodies of anyone who died. I thought that was a crazy thing to say... at the time. But now I know better. Now I realise that they must be working on a cure, that they probably need test subjects to develop an antidote or something."

Rick could barely believe what he was being told. If this old man's friend had known about all this before it even happened, and then contacted Rohmer to warn him, what did that really mean? That this whole thing was man-made, or at least someone had prior knowledge?

"What are you saying? What exactly are you telling me here?"

Rohmer's head swayed, as if he were about to faint, but he managed to pull it together. "I'm saying that I think my friend knew that this was about to happen, and that he tried to warn me. I even suspect that he and his colleagues might be responsible for at least part of it. Maybe they were working on some kind of chemical weapon – that happened during the war, you know: scientists working in isolation to produce new methods of winning the damn thing. Nerve gas. Poisons. Weird neurotoxins and compounds. It wasn't just the Germans who carried out unethical tests. I know because my friend was part of it."

Rick grabbed Rohmer's shoulders, shaking him. "How do you know? Who are you?"

Rohmer's trapped eyes glazed over; they shrunk behind the chunky lenses. "Me, I'm nobody. But my friend – he and I were lovers once, a long time ago. He worked for the government, on all kinds of things. It's why I left him and married my wife, trying to lead a 'normal' life. I couldn't live with some of the things he told me he'd done in the name of progress. But we always kept in touch, all through these years, and finally he came through for me, only I was too fucking stupid to listen." Then he fell silent, his head drooping, hair coming loose from the ponytail.

"Granddad?" Tabby was back at their side, her face pale and terrified.

"It's okay, baby." Rick leaned down and picked her up, hugging her to his chest, stealing her warmth. "He'll be fine. We'll all be fine, when we get to this island of yours."

Tabby wrapped her arms around his neck, almost choking him. It was the closest thing to affection he'd experienced in days, and the shock of it sent him reeling.

Seahouses. The Farne Islands. He'd never heard of these places, but by God he'd find them. Even if it was the last thing he did. Even the slightest hope of a cure was enough to make him change his plans. He'd keep these people safe so that they could all travel there together, and when they reached Rohmer's unnamed island, everything would be better. It would be fine.

It was all going to work out okay.

Rick dropped Tabby to the floor, where she stood between him and Rohmer, holding one of their hands in each of hers. And as they watched, something truly magical happened: flowers of colour lit up the heavens, exploding in the darkness like a thousand tiny sparks of crystallised hope. Distant detonations peppered the night; the sky bled spots of fire.

Yes, thought Rick, *it really is going to work out okay.*

CHAPTER TWENTY-TWO

eyes open see nothing dark smell not hope food hunger promise stirring bang pretty sky bang imagine flowers loud colour memory opening heart soon gone bad head bang live smell hunger moving past present gone now end hunger

PART THREE

True Love Ways

But I do love thee! And when I love thee not,
Chaos is come again

William Shakespeare
Othello. Act iii. Sc. 3

CHAPTER TWENTY-THREE

Daryl felt their gaze upon him as soon as he entered the bar, crawling across his face and body like swarms of insects, picking at his clothing and trying to get underneath, under his skin.

"This is Daryl," said the girl... what was her name again?

"Who is he, Claire?"

Ah, yes, that was it: the lovely Claire.

"I just told you, he's called Daryl."

"I don't care about his name, I just wanna know who the fuck he is." An old woman stepped forward, away from the wall, where she'd been sitting on a pile of blankets.

"I'm no one," he said, at last. "Just another survivor, like you people."

A low murmur passed through the group of nine or ten people; most of them were nodding, and Daryl knew he'd said the right thing. After a lifetime of being verbally challenged, at last he seemed capable of saying the right thing, and at the right time.

"I said we'd help him, Rose" said Claire. She looked a lot like

Sally, which was why Daryl had stopped to help her when he'd spotted her running along the road in her bare feet. She'd been trying to escape a group of youths, who'd decided it would be fun to rape her, and when she clambered onto the back of the moped Daryl had enjoyed the way her arms went around his waist and her chin pressed into his back.

"If you vouch for him, then I suppose I can't argue with that," said the old woman, retreating to her nest of blankets. "Just keep out of my way – both of ye!"

Claire grabbed his hand, her grip warm and tight. She possessed Sally's build, and had similar cat-like eyes. But her hair was short, and the wrong colour. Instead of Sally's ash-blonde bobbed style, this girl had a dull brown mop-top cut far too close to her skull and above her small ears. She wore clothes that Sally would never buy, too. Trendy rags Daryl wasn't exactly taken with.

But she would do for now, until he could have the real thing. Then he would dispose of her, and enjoy doing so, but right now she was merely an adequate substitute.

"This way," said Claire, pulling him away from the others. They turned away, he had ceased to be of interest. "My stuff's over here." There were no lights on in the pub, but he could still see well enough to make his way behind her.

Just as they approached a booth near the back of the bar, there was the sound of gunfire outside, distant yet close enough to be heard clearly.

"Somebody's shooting," said a male voice. "Is it the police?"

"Will you look at this?" This was spoken by a woman, her voice rising with excitement. "Come here, Penny. Come and look at the loud colours in the sky."

A short, stocky Downs girl with her hair tied in bunches moved forward and approached the window. Her face reflected the fireworks outside and her eyes were filled with tears. "Beautiful," she said. "The loud colours are beautiful."

That phrase... it triggered something in Daryl's memory. When he was ten years old Mother had taken him to the dentist to have a tooth removed. He'd been eating too many sweets, drinking too much fizzy pop. This was back in the days when dentists still used gas to knock out their patients, and Daryl recalled the stale rubbery smell of the mask as it was lowered onto his face, the way it had smothered the world with its cruel odour. Then, the gas: it smelled of rubber too, because, of course, it was odourless.

While he was under Daryl had a vivid dream, so real that it was really a hallucination. He'd been sitting in a small wooden rowing boat, looking up at a bearded man dressed in a long white robe. The robed man was using a long paddle to push the boat through what looked like quite shallow water. But the water was black, and it was impossible to see what lay beneath it.

The man, Daryl had known instinctively, was Christ. But he was the Christ as pictured in Mother's picture books: tall, robust, serene, and very white. A picture-perfect Anglo-Saxon messiah, with clear blue eyes and a big white smile.

Daryl had looked around him, peering into the darkness that surrounded the boat. He noticed that they were sailing through an arched chamber, and before long he realised that the low, vaulted roof and ribbed walls were in fact the ribcage and vertebrae of a huge fish, or possibly a whale.

This strong caucasian Christ was steering them through the belly of a whale.

"Why am I here?" the question had seemed perfectly natural at the time; the right thing to ask.

Christ looked down at him, smiling that toothpaste ad smile, and spoke softly: "The loud colours will smell of the universe."

The phrase troubled him, and just as he was about to ask for clarification, he'd woken up in the dentist's chair, minus one back tooth. Daryl had experienced nightmares about the dream for weeks, and had wept in confusion, wondering what Christ had meant. He had not thought about it for years, but now he felt as if one of life's mysteries had been answered.

He moved to the window, with Claire at his side, and watched the impromptu firework display. At the edges of the city, in all the estates and suburban communities, people were letting off fireworks. They appeared in small pockets, ripping up the sky. Other areas answered with their own brief displays, like small signs of life amid all this marching death. Who knew where it had started, but it continued for quite some time, mystical and magnificent, a crude form of magic.

"Oh, God. Do you realise what day it is tomorrow?" Claire held his hand; her fingers were warm.

Everyone gathered around the windows, opening the shutters and staring out at the display.

"No," he said. "What day is it tomorrow?"

"It's November fifth: Bonfire Night."

Daryl smiled. "And that, of course, makes this Mischief Night." The irony was almost painful, and he saw it as yet another example of how comedy and tragedy were intrinsically linked, like two chords tied into an impossible knot.

Mischief Night.

Twenty-four hours before bonfire night, or Guy Fawkes, as it was more commonly known when Daryl was a boy; the evening when the youth of Yorkshire were expected to play pranks in the streets, egging cars and houses, letting down tyres, playing all manner of practical jokes and causing low-grade problems for their neighbours. It was a tradition, something he'd even feared as a boy.

"Oh," he said. "How fucking perfect."

All too soon the fireworks ended. People shuttered the windows, pulled the heavy drapes, and drifted back to their positions, none of them willing to speak and break the momentary spell.

A man was drinking at the bar; he was the only member of the group who had not watched the fireworks. His face was set into an expression of determination, as if he were insistent upon getting drunk. His hand rose and fell like a metronome, its rhythm compelling. Daryl watched the man for a while as Claire made up a bed on the long velvet-lined seat. The man's chin was covered in a thick layer of dark stubble and his eyes were darker still. He narrowed those eyes and glared at Daryl, then nodded once. Daryl nodded back before turning away.

"We can rest here," said Claire, settling down onto the cushions she'd piled up on the seat. She had on a short skirt which showed off her bare legs. Her feet were bare, too, and dirty from the road.

"Thanks," Daryl lay down next to her, unsure of how to act. He'd never had a girlfriend, had never even had a girl as a platonic friend. Females were strange to him; all he knew was Mother, and he knew just enough to gather that she was not typical of her gender.

Claire cuddled up close, her arm going around his waist; the other hand crept into his lap, where it rested like a contented house pet. "Where were you going when you saved me?"

Her use of the word 'saved' was weighted with significance, but he failed to understand what that meant. He was wary, yet at the same time her body was warm and soft, and he felt a new sensation stirring within him, a sense of closeness; a sort of heat that he had never before experienced.

"Mmm..." she murmured, burying her face in his side.

"I was just driving, looking for somewhere safe." He could barely form the words; his lips felt like rolls of rubber and his teeth had grown suddenly too big for his mouth. "What about you? How long have you been here, in this place?"

"We all sort of gathered here last night, when everything went wild. Tonight, I got caught out looking for supplies – we're running low on food – and I got separated from the others." Her hand spread out across his lap, teasing him erect.

Daryl shifted his body, trying to protect himself from her touch. This was all too much; it was way beyond his narrow understanding of human relationships. He felt more comfortable thinking about murder than he did sex. "I need to pee," he said, getting up and crossing the room, eyes searching for the bathroom.

"Over there," said the man at the bar, the heavy drinker, as Daryl passed his position.

Daryl headed for the bathroom, barged through the door, and leaned his back against it. He closed his eyes and counted to ten, willing his erection to go away. He thought about Sally's battered body, but that only aroused him more, so instead he thought about Mother and the prayers she had muttered every day of his life. The darkness in the bathroom pressed in on him, faces lunging out of its depths: Mother, Sally, Richard Nixon (of all people!)... Daryl gritted his teeth and wished them all away.

When he re-entered the main room, the drinker at the bar motioned him over. "Drink?" he raised a spare shot glass.

Daryl approached him, not yet willing to return to Claire. "Thanks," he said, reaching for the glass. The man grinned. His eyes shone, spit glistened on his brown-stained teeth. He was pissed.

Daryl sipped the clear fluid – was it vodka? The taste was awful, like strong medicine, but he enjoyed the way it burned his throat, cleansing it. "Cheers," he croaked.

"She's had them all," said the drinker, motioning his head towards Claire. "All the young blokes. She used to be a regular in here. I'd watch her chat 'em up, take 'em home, and then ignore 'em the next night in favour of some other stud." His eyes rolled in their sockets, dull and unfocused. "She'll show you a good time, mate. Give her one for me." He raised his glass, belched.

Daryl staggered away, back to the girl, her flat, lifeless eyes, her base lust, her small soft, breasts and the unknown wetness between her legs. She reached for him, her fingers like claws, and he could do nothing but succumb to her hunger. Her lips, when she pressed them against his mouth, were bland and moist and puffy; her hand grabbed at his cock, pawing him like a piece of meat. He thought of the dead things out there, the way they pulled bodies apart, and only then did his erection return.

She fucked him right there, under the thick blankets, with everyone ignoring the sounds they made in the musty darkness. Daryl allowed her to control it all, watching from afar, inspecting how she pushed him inside and rode him, her mouth open, eyes closed; the way she no doubt imagined that he was someone else – someone better – as she bucked against him and brought herself to a shuddering climax. Daryl had little to do with the act. It was all about Claire, *her* need, *her* desperation. He could have been a tree stump, or a fence post.

He rolled away from her, his cock still sticky. He wiped himself on the blanket and stared up at the ceiling. Someone laughed nearby, and when he glanced over at the bar, the drinker was watching, always watching, and he raised his glass in another of his mysterious silent toasts.

Give her one for me.

Daryl did not even know what that meant.

If this was what it took to be a man, to be human, then he did not want to know. He was better off remaining free of emotions, staying away from social and sexual intercourse, and killing those he felt drawn to. This girl, this cheap barroom slut, was nothing compared to Sally. She might possess a slight passing resemblance, but that was where it ended. Sally would never act this way. She was pure and graceful; even dead, she was better than this filth he'd rutted with on a low bench among strangers.

His mission was firm in his mind now; at least he could thank Claire for that. The initial repulsion he'd felt gave way to something akin to pity. He felt sorry that she was forced to live this way, and that she had never been given a direction in life. Bar to bar, stranger to stranger, she had been passed along like a shared cigarette. She had no idea what she was worth, yet in his eyes she was truly worthless.

Daryl watched her as she snored beside him. He snaked his arm around her neck, feeling her warmth. She snuggled up against him, turning her body slightly and raising one leg to slide it across his belly. He lay on his back and thanked her for showing him the true face of human relations, the grubby reality that skulked beneath the surface glitter he'd seen in films and on television.

Better to be a killer than a lover, he thought. *At least killers wake up alone in the morning.*

A solitary firework detonated far away, on the other side of the city, as if punctuating the thought.

CHAPTER TWENTY-FOUR

They stood looking at the Nissan, each waiting for one of the others to speak. Tabby still held the two men's hands; she was the glue between them. Rick watched the dead man stumble out of the bushes, amazed that such a decayed corpse was still capable of motion. Bones showed through rents in clothing and flesh, and the hairless skull moved jerkily on the wasted muscles of the withered neck, as if it were a shoddy computer animation.

"It's a shambler," said Rohmer, taking a step towards the doors.

"What's that?" Rick stared at the man, thinking he'd probably lost his mind.

"Haven't you noticed there are different types? This one's a shambler. It's probably been dead for ages, and clawed its way out of the grave."

The barely mobile corpse continued its slow advance, shuffling in jittery half-steps towards the petrol pumps, and the jeep where Sally was still knocked out on morphine. She would be due another dose very soon, and Rick would rather not leave it until she began to stir.

"There are also two other main groups, or types." Rohmer was warming to his theme. "Runners are the freshly dead. They can move fast, almost as fast as us, but they are uncoordinated and easily confused."

Rick was impressed with the man's powers of observation. He'd noticed these things too, but had not given much thought to what they actually signified.

"Then," continued Rohmer, "we have the partials. These are the ones who return with some kind of brain damage. Either they've taken a knock to the skull, and the brain matter has suffered serious trauma, or they have actually had part of their brain destroyed. They move slowly, if at all, and act like severely retarded mental patients, the kind you see in old stills and movie reels from Victorian asylums. They remind me of lobotomy victims, all weak and clumsy and incapable of autonomous motion."

Rick glanced at Tabby, but the girl was occupied tying her shoelace. She'd apparently heard her granddad's theories before. "You've put a lot of thought into this, haven't you?"

Rohmer turned and looked into his eyes, not smiling; not now. "It wasn't by choice. I've see a lot of these things over the last twenty-four hours, and if you watch closely enough certain behavioural patterns become apparent."

Rick swallowed; his throat was dry. He uncapped a bottle of water and took a sip. "What are you... what *were* you, before all this happened. You know, back in the real world." And wasn't that exactly how it felt? Like they'd left their own world behind and entered another realm, one filled with the dead?

"Oh, I used to be a lab technician, but I've always had an interest in anthropology. I read a lot, you know. Well, I used to read a lot. Hopefully I can do so again."

Rick didn't have an adequate response, so he left it at that. He glanced back over at the shambler, which had not got far. Its left leg was twisted around so that the foot faced almost backwards, and its right arm was not much more than bare bone.

Slowly, he opened the left hand door with his foot. Then he raised the Glock and waited until the thing gained a few more feet. The shot took off the top of its head, sending up a cloud of dried-out decayed matter. The shambler began to weave on the spot, like a comedy drunk in an old film, and then simply tipped backwards, hitting the floor with a barely audible *whump*.

"Shall we?" Rick used his body to open the other door, and stepped aside for the others to follow him out of the building. The fireworks had stopped a little while ago and the sky was dark and silent. A few birds had returned to the trees, but their song was cautious, as if they were testing the air before committing fully to the nightly chorus. "The Farne Islands, you say?"

Rohmer smiled uneasily, as if he still wasn't quite sure he should be doing so. "Yes. It's a bird sanctuary. The island we need is more of a land mass. It doesn't even have a name."

"Okay," said Rick, leading the way back to the jeep. "Let's get going." Tabby once again took his hand. For a moment, he felt like crying. Reality quivered at the edges, threatening to tear away and give him a glimpse of things as they really were, but then his gaze fell upon Sally, propped up in the front seat, and those edges repaired, the illusion holding. He squeezed the girl's hand, and they all made for the jeep.

Rick opened the back door and helped the girl inside, nodding at Rohmer, who glanced at Sally. "My wife," he said. "I'll have to give her more painkiller soon."

He eased behind the wheel and started the engine. He gave one last look around the service station, and then pulled away, the rear wheels spitting up loose stones in a tiny round of applause.

"Which way?" He kept his eyes on the road, conscious that if there was one dead person wandering around there could easily be more. From what he'd seen, they tended not to act in groups, yet seemed to mass together out of some vestige of racial instinct.

"Down to the canal," said Rohmer, from the back. His voice had changed, becoming slightly anxious. "I'll direct you, but we're going to a little place called Crow's Beak Corner. That's where my barge is tethered."

They continued for a while in silence, then Rohmer began to call out "left" or "right here." Rick concentrated on the road, his attention occasionally drawn by Sally, who stirred very little in the seat next to him. Once she moaned softly, but she didn't call out again.

"Here. Take this gravel road. It's a bit bumpy, but the vehicle should be able to handle it." Rohmer's hand rested on Rick's shoulder, and gave it a little squeeze.

Rick took the vehicle off the road, under some straggly trees, and followed the path the old man had indicated. The road itself was an unmade track, covered with loose gravel that became dirt after a few hundred yards. It led downwards, to the canal, and when they emerged from the undergrowth Rick's breath was taken away by the sight of the moonlight on black water.

He pulled up beside a short concrete jetty. The edges had long ago crumbled into the canal, exposing rusted steel reinforcement bars, but Rohmer's barge was exactly where he'd promised it would be.

"There she is. The *Queen Anne*. Named after my wife, God rest her soul." Rohmer's voice cracked on the last few words, as if it still caused him pain to speak of her. "It looks quiet. No one ever uses this place – they go to the better sites further along the water. But we always liked it here, under the trees, in the shade..."

"Okay," said Rick, trying to bring the man out of the past and into the potentially dangerous present. "You go and sort out the barge, and I'll dose up Sally with some more morphine."

"Is she all right? Your wife. She seems bad." Tabby's concern touched him more than he thought possible. He turned and faced the girl in the darkness of the car, hoping that she could at least see his smile.

"She'll be fine, thank you. Just needs some medicine. She's not quite given up yet." He blinked back tears, his eyes burning. His hand rested on the seat back. He wished someone – anyone – would hold it.

"Are you sure about this?" Rohmer leaned forward out of the shadows now gathered on the back seat like uninvited passengers.

His face was rigid, his bug-eyes hard. "She doesn't seem too well."

Rick sighed. Everything felt so heavy – the weight of his responsibility to Sally, the expectations of these people, the night itself. "I promise you," he said. "If it comes to that, I'll do her myself. I have plenty of ammunition, and I'm not about to allow anything to put you and Tabby in danger." The lies tripped off his tongue, smooth as honey, cold as ice. He felt nothing but justified in his actions. She was his wife, and he loved her. Everything else was just dressing; ultimately pointless.

"Here," he said, handing Rohmer the second Glock, the one he'd picked up back at the apartment. "Just in case."

The old man stared at the gun before taking it.

"Just point it and squeeze the trigger." Rick nodded.

The old man held the gun away from his body, as if he were afraid of everything it represented. Then, glancing at Tabby, he slipped his fingers around the butt of the gun and swallowed hard.

Rick watched the old man and his granddaughter as they climbed slowly out of the car. He kept his window down, the barrel of his pistol pointed out into the darkness. The moon had emerged from behind the wispy clouds, and it lit their way, but anything could be hiding in the trees and the shadows.

Once the two of them were untying the boat from its moorings, and when he was sure that Rohmer was ready with the gun, he took the morphine from a pocket in his rucksack. He administered the dose once again through her eyeball. Even if he ruined her eyes, she would have no further use for them. What did it matter if she were blind and dead or just dead? As far as he was concerned, it mattered not one bit.

Sally's hands flapped in her lap, bandaged birds shifting in their uneasy dreams. He held them, clasping both, and waited for her to quieten down. "It's okay, baby. I've found somewhere to take you – a place where we might be able to make you better."

I know.

He stared at her covered face, imaging how it had looked before any of this happened. The more time moved on the less he could remember the finer details.

Just promise that you'll always love me.

He shut his eyes, lowered his head. For the briefest moment, there in the darkness of the car, he felt that he would never be able to raise it again. The weight of the world was pressing down on the back of his skull, threatening to break it.

Then, after what seemed like a thousand years contained within the blink of an eye, he opened his eyes and looked up and out of the open side window. The old man and the girl were standing there, watching him. Rohmer's hand was resting on Tabby's head, his fingers curled over her scalp. They both looked sad, tired, and afraid. Rohmer held the gun loosely in his free hand. He kept his fingers well away from the trigger.

"Tabby, come and help me unload the stuff. Your granddad can keep watch while we load the boat." He widened his eyes, asking a question.

Rohmer nodded and took his hand away from the child's tousle-haired head.

The water chortled as they worked, amused in its own mysterious way. Birds moved in the trees, but remained relatively silent: just the occasional chirp of song, the sudden flapping of wings. The canal was wide where Rohmer kept his barge, and the water was deep. Rick saw the black glint of a fish turning in the water, but only heard the splash it made a split-second later.

Nature, it seemed, went on, even when the men who had tried to master it were suffering. The world kept turning, the tides came and went, all the creatures of the night continued their usual rituals, if a little more subdued than usual.

Only man was changed; the rest of the animals simply watched on, possibly even amused by the failings of the bipeds who had always sought to master them.

Once the guns, ammunition and other supplies were firmly tied into the barge and covered by tarpaulins, Rohmer climbed aboard and started the small engine. It was initially too loud for such a low-key craft, but Rick soon became accustomed to its throaty growls.

"All aboard who's coming aboard," said Rohmer, a feeble

attempt at a joke that nonetheless had Rick laughing.

Rick returned to the car and picked up Sally's unresponsive body, hauling her across his shoulder. He carried her back to the jetty and placed her gently into the craft, wedging her in so that she would not slip or fall overboard.

Tabby watched in silence, her tiny pale face a bright spot in the darkness, the question mark on her cheek seeming to demand an answer to all the questions in the world. Rohmer stared at the canal, his focus on the dark waters that might just lead them out of this, keeping them safe from the madness occurring along the shore.

The engine guttered; thick, acrid smoke poured from somewhere at the back of the craft. Rick held on to the sides of the barge, feeling as if he was sitting too high above the surface of the water. When the barge began to move, slowly, with no sense of panic or haste, he felt a little calmer. The more distance he put between Sally and dry land, the better he felt. The little Nissan moved away from them, twisting slowly on an unseen axis as they made for the middle of the river.

"She may be slow," said Rohmer from his perch at the head of the barge. "But she's reliable. Never let me down yet!" He almost sounded happy. If it were not for the knowledge of his wife's cold, dead hand resting not far from his own, Rick might have closed his eyes and pretended that they were on a relaxing boating holiday, and Rohmer was the captain of the craft. But the illusion would not hold: bloody reality crept in from the edges, turning everything red.

Have some rest. We'll be safe out on the water.

He turned to face her. She sat near him, her head turned as if she were looking out at the canal. The bandages looked too bright under the eager moon, and he wished that none of this had ever happened – then he wished that this moment would never end.

"We need to head for the Selby area," said Rohmer, raising his voice to compete with the sound of the engine. "We can hole up for a while in a cottage I have there before setting off again on the roads to Northumberland. I have transport there, and plenty of supplies. It's been my little bolthole for years now."

When Rick turned back to face the front of the barge, Tabby was watching him. Her face was unreadable, and the smile she finally offered was stunted, a thing not quite fully formed.

Rick wasn't sure how long he could keep up this charade, but when the truth broke he hoped that he would not have to hurt these people. Especially the girl. Maybe he could make her see that this wasn't wrong, that he was acting out of love. He thought that she might be young enough and innocent enough to appreciate the sentiment.

The water rolled out beneath them, a black carpet leading to the promise of salvation... or a rippling, blackened tongue leading down into an infernal throat. Either way, they were safe for the time being.

Something flopped heavily in the water. Rick couldn't bring himself to look and identify what it was.

CHAPTER TWENTY-FIVE

Daryl didn't trust the lone drinker.

The man was still awake while everyone else slept – or tried to grab some sleep – and had, by now, consumed so much alcohol that his head was tipping slowly forward towards the damp length of wooden bar top. He kept mumbling: incoherent words, snappy little phrases that meant nothing to anyone but him. They could have been the words to his favourite song, the names of his wife and dog: anything.

Claire was snoring lightly at Daryl's side, lying flat on her back with her mouth open wide. Her breath smelled of slightly degraded eggs.

"In the boxes," she muttered, tossing her head on the cushion. "I put 'em in the boxes."

Daryl had no idea what she was babbling about. He leaned in close so that his face was directly over hers, blocking his nasal passages so that he didn't catch a whiff of her breath, and carefully dribbled a long line of saliva out of his mouth. The thick string of spit dropped slowly, stretching, and finally broke, hitting her cheek just below the left eye before it oozed down and across her temple.

"*Bull's-eye*," he whispered, grinning. A child's game, but it was something to do. He remembered being pinned down years before in the school toilets at break time and having the same thing done to him... and with worse substances than spit. Much worse.

The thick drapes and wooden shutters at the windows kept the interior of the pub dark. Sleeping people were simply twisted shapes scattered in all that blackness, some grouped together and others yet further apart.

The drinker sat alone, twitching, still muttering darkly.

Daryl wasn't sure how long these people had been here, but it seemed that the beer was yet to run out. There were still plenty of bar snacks on hand – crisps, pork scratchings, salted peanuts – and the water supply had not yet been cut off. If they were careful, this lot might just be able to ride out the worst of it in here, rationing their supplies and going out on reconnaissance missions like the one Claire had been running when he encountered her. If they were organised, and did not make any silly mistakes, they were onto a good thing here.

He inspected the bar, taking note of the solid oak doors, the old-fashioned leaded windows, most of them with wire mesh security barriers attached to the outside, set a few inches back from the glass. Yes, he could see the appeal of staying here... but it was not for him. The old Daryl would have been happy to cower in the shadows, finding protection in numbers and allowing himself to be one of the sheep. But the new Daryl... oh, he was a lone wolf, a man on a mission. The new Daryl would hear nothing of crouching in the darkness, waiting for the storm to pass. The new Daryl *was* the storm – at least part of it, a significant element within the overall terror.

Daryl eased himself from beneath the thin blankets Claire had provided and slowly picked his way across the room. He was not quite sure why, but he felt drawn to the solitary drinker at the bar. The man had a presence about him; he stood out from the crowd, and not just because of his actions (or lack of them). He possessed the air of a minor celebrity now gone to seed, someone who might once have been important but was now just another nobody in a grimy parade of nobodies.

Daryl slid sideways onto a worn barstool beside the man, watching him as his head dipped forward once again, and then jerked abruptly upwards. "I think you might have had enough." He reached out to take the glass from the man's hand.

"Fuck off," said the man, surprisingly lucid for his apparent state. "I'll have had enough when all this *shit* goes away." He made an expansive gesture with his free hand, and then gulped at the glass, emptying it completely, before pouring himself another. It looked like whisky, but the label was peeled off the bottle, so Daryl could not be sure. The result of idle hands; a nervous drinking habit, like the way some people tore up beer mats.

"Sorry. I thought you were about to black out." He kept his voice low, unwilling to disturb anyone else in the large room, but the acoustics made the words seem louder than they actually were.

"That's what I'm aiming for: total fucking oblivion. Unfortunately, the void is yet to swallow me up."

Daryl examined the man properly for the first time. He had shoulder-length brown hair, which had turned greasy. His dark eyes were intelligent yet dulled by alcohol. His narrow face was shadowed by stubble and there was a faint air of nobility to his features. The dark shirt he wore was stained with dried blood and one of the sleeves was torn. Visible on the wedding finger of his drinking hand was a pale, untanned band of skin.

"Cheers," said the man, sipping slower this time, savouring the drink.

"What you said earlier. About Claire. What did you mean by that?" Daryl felt at once defensive, slightly on edge, but could not understand why. She was nothing to him, this girl, just something to cling to for a while. Yet still, he felt the need to stick up for her, to protect her honour – if indeed she had any, which seemed doubtful.

The man smiled. His teeth were coated brown; his tongue resembled a slug coiling in the wet cave of his mouth. "She was a regular here, came in all the time. In the few years I've been coming here, I must've seen her dance with every man in the place." He raised his eyebrows: fat slow-worms wriggling across his brow.

"Dancing?" Daryl felt dumb, as if he were a child struggling to decipher the codes and ambiguities of an adult's conversation.

"Come on, you know what I mean. The dance. The horizontal mambo. She fucked them all, sometimes more than one at a time." He swayed on his seat but managed to correct his balance by grabbing the edge of the bar. The ends of his fingers were yellowed with nicotine, but Daryl had not yet seen him smoke. "She's nothing but a filthy whore."

"She fucked everyone," said Daryl. "But she didn't fuck you." Finally, understanding dawned upon him. He had cut to the quick of the man's hurt. He smiled, pleased at gaining the upper hand. "You sad old bastard. You've been letching after her forever, just wishing she would look your way, give you more than a drunken smile. But she never did. She took on all comers... *apart from you*." He laughed softly, enjoying the man's silent rage and the way he was now asserting his will upon the sorry old sop.

"That's where you're wrong," said the man, his voice dropping. "I did have her *once*. Just once."

He stared at Daryl, his red-rimmed eyes moist.

"Outside in the alley, up against the wall. She kept calling me by another name, but I didn't care. Not while I was inside her." He paused, regaled by the power of the memory. Then his face took on a pained expression, as if the recollection was not in fact everything that he had wished. "She called me all kinds of names, before, during and afterwards. But she never called me by the right name. The one that would hurt the most." He winced, clutched at his side with a beefy hand. "She never called me *Daddy*."

Daryl at first thought he'd misheard the man, but there could be no mistake. He stood up and backed away, terrible memories of his own threatening to burst through the mental dam he had spent so many years constructing. Mother's bare thigh, the feel of her hands on the bones of his hips, the slow journey her tongue had made over his face, down across his chest and lower, lower, until she had him right where she wanted...

"No!" he lashed out and grabbed the bottle with the peeled label, striking instinctively. The bottle caught the man on the backswing, making contact with the side of his head and knocking him sideways off the stool. The sound it made was almost surreally loud.

The man hit the floor heavily, a sack of meat; as if there was already no life left in his body.

Then Daryl was upon him, gloved hands going for his soft, exposed throat, fingers closing around the frail trachea and crushing it as easily as he might bend a plastic pipe, feeling little resistance to his grip.

"Not again. Never again, Mother!" He squeezed as tightly as he could, a sense of power surging through him. Mother's face overlaid that of the man, her mouth open, a thin white trail of fluid snaking from between her lips to stain her chin. Blood flowed from the wounded temple, pouring onto the grubby boards. The man made an odd croaking sound; it seemed to go on forever.

At last the man's hands came up in weak defence, but it was much too late to matter. They batted lamely at Daryl's forearms, bouncing off like small birds flying into a brick wall. His face was already swelling, the skin turning a bright shade of crimson, and his blue-black tongue pushed between his ugly teeth to loll horribly across his lower lip, like a sodden flap of untreated leather.

Hands grabbed at him, clutching his shoulders and tugging uselessly; pointless voices screamed in his ears. But Daryl would not, *could* not release the man until he was dead. It really was that simple.

Finally, the body beneath him went limp, and the stench of fresh shit drifted into his nostrils. The yelling continued around him, and when he blinked his eyes and turned around everyone had taken a single, almost choreographed, step back, as if put off by the terrible faecal odour.

"It wasn't me," said Daryl, needlessly. "He crapped himself. They sometimes do that as they die." Again he felt on the verge of hysteria, as if crazed laughter was building up inside him and demanding release. He was giving these people data from the books he had read, offering up snippets of information like an eager student.

"What have you done? He wasn't doing anything." The old woman from earlier had once again assumed the role of mouthpiece for the small band of survivors. "He was just drunk. Not causing any harm." She made the sign of the cross, her eyes flashing wide. "You're evil. A *devil*. No better than those things outside."

Feet shuffled on the boards. Someone shoved Daryl back onto his knees.

Sighing theatrically, Daryl righted himself and got slowly to his feet, well aware that these people were frightened of him. The reality of the situation flared before him, bright lights at the frayed edges of his vision. This was the power he had always felt that he deserved, the awe to which he was surely entitled.

"Oh, I'm a lot worse than them." He chuckled, adding to the effect, bringing yet another dimension to the character he was still in the process of creating.

"Please." Claire approached him. "Leave him alone," she said to the onlookers, her hands held out before her, palms open. "I know why he did this. He did it for me." She eased to Daryl's side, one arm snaking around his waist and the other held outwards as if she were stopping traffic. "That rotten bastard had it coming."

This turn of events confused Daryl even more. He would never get the hang of human emotions. Every time he felt that he'd made up some ground, grasped something of vital importance, the rug was deftly pulled from under him by someone acting completely the opposite to the way he'd come to expect. It was fascinating, really; a profound learning process.

He stared at Claire, saw something cold and terrible flick like a snake's tail behind her eyes, and was suddenly drawn to it.

"Get out," said a man Daryl could not identify in the gloom.

"Get out now."

"Leave," said the old woman, moving sideways and setting off a chain reaction so that the others followed suit and an opening appeared in the small, agitated group. "Make your own way. You're more suited to this world than us."

"Go."

"Get out!"

"Fuck off!"

The chorus was raised; they sung their little hearts out. Even those not part of this immediate group joined in, shouting from their cosy hidey-holes.

Claire gripped Daryl's leather-clad hand as he began to walk towards the main door, trudging like an ancient warrior leaving the battlefield. He paused so that Claire could grab her things, and then turned to face his audience. "Don't think you've seen the last of us," he said, making it up as he went along. "It's a small world and it's about to get even smaller." Then, with Claire at his side, he concluded his dramatic exit, silently congratulating himself on improvising such a good last line.

A short man with muscular arms unlocked the main door, and the two of them strode out of the building, arm in arm, like a nice modern young couple.

The street was empty, but that state of affairs might not last for long. Daryl went to the alley where he'd hidden the moped when they'd arrived, kick-started the machine, and waited for Claire to hop on behind him.

He thought that he might keep her for a while; at least until she got boring. He'd originally intended to either leave her in the morning or kill her when he got the chance, but her strong performance in the pub had changed his mind. There was more to this girl than met the eye, and the more she appealed to him the more her resemblance to Sally Nutman grew.

Every star needs a leading lady, even if she is the understudy.

Then, feeling like he'd just given a triumphant performance, Daryl resumed his epic journey to nowhere.

CHAPTER TWENTY-SIX

The *Queen Anne* moved at a sedate pace, but sitting on its cramped deck Rick felt safer than he had for some time. He'd moved Sally down into the rear cabin, out of sight of the shore, but could still hear her occasional soothing communications.

I love you.

We'll be safe.

He hoped that she was right about the latter, and that it wasn't just wishful thinking – *dead* wishful thinking.

Can you still hear me, lover?

Hear? Was that the right term to describe how he picked up her thoughts? He didn't really *hear* her voice, just caught an echo of it in his mind, like a series of vibrations on the surface of his brain. Yet as their journey continued, that voice became increasingly real – more solid and meaningful than anything else going on around him.

"Do you believe in God?"

Rohmer's question pulled him out of himself, dragging him

back into the immediacy of their situation. "Sorry?"

"God," said the old man, still facing forward, his eyes on the water. "Are you a believer?"

Tabby was in the main front galley, trying to find a broadcast on the portable television or the old transistor radio Rohmer kept onboard, so the two men were alone up there on deck. The sound of the diesel engine was now a gentle rumble, and the sound of the water lapping at the sides of the vessel was strangely soothing. Rick had never been on a canal barge until now, but he could certainly see the appeal. There was a strange beauty here, a sense of being apart from the crowd.

"I never used to believe in God," he said, flexing his hand, trying to relax his fingers where they were stiff from clutching the gun for so long. "But now I'm not so sure."

"I've been a believer for ten years, since my Anne died." Rohmer still stared ahead. The darkness before them was lifting, making way for faint glimmers of early daylight. "Faith helped me through some dark times after her death. It got me off alcohol and made me start to engage with people again."

There was a pause then, during which both men simply listened to the throbbing of the engine and watched the black and undulating surface of the canal.

"It's like this whole thing has changed me in ways I never thought possible," said Rick, glancing at the wooden floor and imagining Sally down there on a bunk, her bandaged head resting on a soft white cushion. "My wife and I drifted apart, but this thing brought us together. It's made me realise that my entire worldview was naïve. I've come to appreciate that there *must* be something else to the world than what we can see and feel."

Rohmer grunted and nodded his head. His ponytail swung like a pendulum.

Rick continued: "When I was in the army I saw a lot of men die. Some of them were my friends and the others were enemies that I killed."

The lapping of the water against the boat. The soft fuzz of pre-dawn light spreading like a film across the canal.

"The first man I shot was a Taliban soldier in Afghanistan. I was in the Parachute Regiment, third battalion. It was during Operation Mountain Thrust, July 2006. I can remember it like it was yesterday. The Yanks were leading us into the hills to oust Taliban insurgents. We were ambushed. Snipers pinned us down. Eventually we got the upper hand, and I shot a man in the head. I cradled him in my arms as he died, and as I watched him something went out of his eyes – a light dimming, going out. Call it what you will: his soul, his life-force, his essence. I just call it his presence in the world. Once it had gone, there was nothing left of him. Just meat."

Rohmer turned around then, and there were tears in his eyes. "What about these things? The dead. Are they just motorised meat, or is there something – that presence you mention – trapped inside them? Are they more like walking ghosts, with a sliver of their soul stuck inside their bodies, or is it a case of the soul being partially reactivated like a damaged computer hard drive?"

Rick glanced behind and over to his left, out over the water. Two people stood on the canal bank, waving and shouting as they jogged along the towpath, but they were too far away to hear. He raised his hand; shards of brightness were visible through the gaps between his fingers, but when he let the hand fall the light had all but vanished.

"There has to be something human left inside them, powering them." Rohmer's attention was focused elsewhere. He did not even notice the couple on the bank. "I mean, they look like us, move like us, were once exactly like us. Just because they're dead it doesn't mean they're monsters.

The couple continued to wave, their movements frantic. They were running now, clearly in distress, trying to catch up with the barge.

"Why are there no dead animals running around attacking us?" said Rohmer. "It's only humans who are coming back. That *must* mean something"

Rick stared at the couple. The woman was still waving, but the man was now bent over and rummaging inside a bag. Was she trying to summon help? Did she want them to guide the barge ashore so that they could come aboard? There wasn't enough room on the boat for passengers, and Rick wasn't sure if he liked the idea of exposing Sally to the scrutiny of yet more strangers.

"I think God is responsible. Perhaps he's had enough of what we've become – violent, warlike, empty of everything but the hunger to accrue and amass more and more money and useless items. Maybe He wants to punish us, make us pay for forgetting about Him."

The man on the canal bank stood upright and brought up his arms in a rigid yet amateurish shooting posture. Before Rick could move, the man had opened fire.

"Get down!" he yelled. "Shooter! Get down in the boat!"

But the sound of gunfire was distant and the handgun was too small a calibre for the bullets to reach them. Rick peered up from behind the faded wooden rail that ran around the craft, then when he was certain that he was in no danger, he raised his head into the open. The woman looked like she might be weeping; the man kept firing the empty gun, long after the ammunition was used up.

Rohmer resumed his station at the wheel. The couple retreated into the tree line, moving away from the canal and out of sight. The man had his arms around the woman, comforting her.

The barge kept moving, sticking to its own steady pace. Tabby popped up her head from below deck and asked if anyone else was hungry. Both men shook their heads, and she went back down into the galley to prepare herself something to sustain her until the next meal time.

Dawn broke slowly, as if the day were reluctant to emerge. Once again the sun was weak and the clouds were heavy. It grew colder as the light bled across the land and the water. Rick thought it might try again to snow, and the thought depressed him more than he could express.

Rohmer remained stoically behind the wheel of his vessel. He had not said much since mentioning God, and Rick thought that the man was sinking into his own inner landscape, searching for that very God to send him a sign. Perhaps he was even thinking about his wife, or his former lover – the man on the island. Now there, thought Rick, was a strange and tangled situation...

Then, as they approached a lock, Rohmer broke the silence: "I'm starting to think that it might not be such a bad thing to die. I mean, to die properly, not come back as one of those things. The world is dying, and what's left behind will be unbearable." He slowed the boat to a crawl, and then turned to face Rick. "You know what I'm saying, don't you, son? What I'm asking."

Rick swallowed. His throat felt constricted. "Don't worry. If it comes to that, I have more than enough ammo to make sure the three of us don't come back."

Satisfied, Rohmer nodded once, and then returned his attention to the looming lock. "You stay on board and I'll see to getting us through. You're better with the gun, and I can turn one of these things quicker than you ever could." He grinned, winked, and eased the boat towards the waiting gate, his hands firm on the wheel.

"Come on, grab the wheel."

Rick went to the front and took up his position, one hand steering the barge and the other releasing the Glock from its holster. The gun felt more natural than the wheel.

Rohmer leaped from the barge and opened the lock gates, then walked quickly up the incline to the lock gear. Rick watched him closely, ready to start shooting at the slightest provocation.

The two stone walls encompassed the craft as it entered the tunnel, and Rick began to feel on edge. It was fine when they were in motion, but this close to dry land they could be asking for trouble.

Rohmer worked the rack and pinion and released the gears, allowing water to be forced into the area where the barge now sat. The vessel rose slowly, buoyed on the surging waters. It took five long minutes for the lock to be filled, and finally Rohmer released the top gate so that Rick could guide the barge to the upper level of the canal.

It all went smoothly until Rick saw the pike.

The fish was trapped in the lock, and had risen to the surface because of the water level being disturbed. It nudged the side of the barge, blindly looking for a way around the vessel. Rick watched it, slightly puzzled. He was anxious, but had nothing upon which to focus his bad feelings.

"Nearly done," Rohmer shouted from above. The water level was almost right; Rick's hands tensed on the wheel.

As if in a dream, a fat white hand broke the surface and grabbed the angry pike from below, pulling its long sleek form swiftly beneath the restless waters of the lock.

Rick aimed the pistol at the spot where the fish had been, trying to keep his breathing shallow. Concentric circles painted the surface. His hands shook with tension. Something clattered gently, gently, three times so gently, on the underside of the hull.

Rick tensed, watching and listening. The sound was not repeated.

"Guide her through!" Rohmer was oblivious to what had just happened.

Slowly, Rick returned his attention to the lock and eased the boat through the gate. The balance beam across the top of the metal gate clanked loudly, the sound dull and somehow even more frightening than what he'd just glimpsed in the water.

Rick watched closely as Rohmer closed the gates and made his way back to the barge. He saw nothing this time – certainly nothing that resembled white, pulpy flesh – emerging from the water inside the lock. Whatever was resting there, rested for now still and easy. But the incident had changed the entire complexion of the journey for Rick. Now he realised that he'd been foolish to drop his guard and relax, even for a moment.

Even when danger was out of sight, it remained a constant reminder of the fragility of human existence. One false move, a single moment of distraction from any one of them, might cost them all their lives.

He stepped back and allowed Rohmer to take control of the *Queen Anne*. Only when it was back in the middle of the canal did he begin to feel less anxious. The memory of the white hand claiming the pike felt like a brief warning of worse things to come.

CHAPTER TWENTY-SEVEN

slow rhythm sounds motion hungry dark throb muted pain lurch hungry voice language girl child smell food hungry lapping swell hungry hungry hungry hungry hungry girl hungry hungry hungry hungry child hungry hungry hungry hungry hungry hungryhungryhungryhungryhungryhungryhungryhungry

CHAPTER TWENTY-EIGHT

Daryl had no idea what they were doing down by the canal. After leaving the temporary shelter provided by the public house, he'd simply allowed the moped to carry him wherever it may. Rattling along empty streets, turning a corner at any junction where he suspected that trouble might lurk up ahead, he had enjoyed the sensation of the vehicle under his body. Claire's arms around his waist had been a novelty, and for a wonderful moment he felt halfway normal.

Whatever that word 'normal' actually meant.

He heard the gunshots first: short little barks from what sounded like a toy gun. They went on for a little while, and then stopped abruptly.

"What is it?" Claire rested her chin on his shoulder, her cheek pressed against the side of his neck.

"What does it sound like?" He was rapidly losing patience with her idiot questions.

"Gun."

"Clever girl. Now let's see if you can spell that."

"Fuck off." She pulled back from him, her arms unloosening the knot they'd made around his middle. A sigh escaped her lips; the air against his face felt stale and odorous. He held his breath.

"I vote that we head away from the gunshots. We don't want to run into any of those things."

He sensed rather than saw her nod in agreement. Her hands returned – lightly – to his waist, the touch almost cautious. Daryl released the throttle quickly, causing the moped to jerk forward slightly. Claire's grip tightened abruptly, and he grinned, feeling the liquor of his power over her as it coursed through his system.

He guided the moped along the track through the trees, keeping his speed down so as not to upend them and damage the machine. The last thing he needed now was damage that he did not possess the knowledge to repair.

The sun was rising slowly; its light was feeble, a mere flicker of brightness against the charcoal sky. Again he felt like he was stuck in a monochrome movie, and as usual the thought pleased him.

"Look." Claire pressed against him, drawing close in a sudden burst of terror.

He slowed the moped, placing one foot down on the stony track and dragging it along to cut a swathe through the dusty, uneven surface.

Two figures ran out of the trees a few hundred yards up ahead. They did not look Daryl's way, and in fact failed to even notice the moped and its gawping riders. The couple ran, hand in hand, into the bushes on the other side of the track. The woman was repeating something over and over, but Daryl could not quite hear what it was. A word? A name? Perhaps it was even a number. Just one more thing he would never know...

Turning his head to the left, Daryl caught sight of the canal glinting darkly through the trees. He stared, trying to make out what he thought he saw... an object on the water, heading along on the tide. A long barge, with a couple of figures standing on deck, both of them staring in the direction of the bank, probably at the retreating figures who'd passed only moments before.

Daryl experienced a temporal shift: reality seemed to bend, curling in on itself and meeting at both ends like a Möbius strip. He had the sensation of watching himself watch himself, as if he stood in an endless hall of mirrors. Then, just as quickly as it had occurred, the weird sensation passed, leaving his head spinning with a combination of vertigo and a strange giddy nostalgia for something he could not name.

"Are you okay?"

God, he wished that stupid bitch would just shut the fuck up and allow him to enjoy his little epiphany, whatever the hell it meant. The closeness he'd felt towards her back at the bar, when he had been afforded a glimpse into the darkness at her core, was now forgotten. He could barely believe that he'd felt anything other than disdain for this ridiculous puppet.

"No." He eased the moped forward, sending it rolling onto the rough ground at the side of the track. Then, parking it up, he climbed off and began to walk down the embankment towards the towpath that ran below.

"Wait. Daryl, wait for me!"

He kept on going, hoping that she'd trip and fall, maybe break her leg so that he could leave her there to become food for passing dead folk.

The thought made him smile, easing the frustration.

"Wait. I'm coming, too." Her rapid motion sent small, loose stones tumbling down the incline. It was lucky for her that the barge was too far away for the crew to hear the commotion; otherwise he might be forced to silence her.

A distant gunshot, or perhaps the sound of a car backfiring, drew his attention away from the canal. He stared back, over Claire's shoulder, but could see no one in the vicinity. Listening intently, he picked up no incongruous sounds other than the ones made by the silly girl as she clumsily descended the embankment. A dog began to bark and howl, but it was not close by; after a few seconds the anxious baying ceased.

Daryl turned back towards the canal, his attention drawn to

the boat like iron filings to a magnet. He was not sure what the pull was, but he was unable to ignore it. Something about the figures on deck – at least one of them – seemed familiar and important. The way he stood, moved; the shape of his body. Like an echo from a dream he'd once had but could no longer fully recall.

He trod carefully the rest of the way down the cluttered embankment, his feet sinking into the debris, dead leaves and fallen branches at the base of the incline. Litter was everywhere; a tawdry second skin over the earth.

He stopped behind the last line of trees, their November branches already shedding to adopt winter's skeletal nudity. Pressing himself against one of the wider trunks, he watched as the barge chuntered lazily towards a distant stone footbridge.

Finally he realised why he'd been so drawn to the vessel. The old man piloting the craft he did not recognise, but there was no doubt in Daryl's mind that other man – the younger of the two – was the policeman: Sally Nutman's husband. Daryl watched as the man stood and stretched, scanning the towpath with a pistol in his hand.

"Well, well, well..."

Claire finally reached his side. She was panting, struggling for breath, and Daryl manhandled her as he grabbed the torn pink rucksack she wore on her back. He pulled the flap open and removed the binoculars from inside. Putting them to his eyes, he focused on the policeman. Oh, it was him all right; there could be no mistake. He zoomed in on the man's face. His mouth was a tight line; his eyes were narrowed; his cheeks were dark and sunken, shaded by thick stubble. He looked... *hard*. Hard as nails.

Daryl would have to be careful with this one.

He watched the barge until the policeman's face was out of eyesight. Then he took away the binoculars and watched it still, hoping that Sally, sweet dead Sally, would emerge from the space below deck – what was it called, the galley, the hold? Something like that.

She did not appear.

The two men chatted while Rick checked his pistol, running his hands over the weapon in a way that seemed almost loving. Then, eventually, Daryl decided that he had seen enough.

Was this luck or fate? He had known all along that he would run into Sally again; it was a certainty. He had not once questioned this eventuality, simply accepted it as a fact of this strange new life. But for it to happen so soon, and when he least expected it, was wonderful; a gift; a favour. It was almost enough to make him believe in Mother's God. Almost... but not quite.

"I need to go," said Claire, shuffling her feet in the loamy earth.

"Go where?"

"*Go*. You know. The toilet." She rolled her eyes, and he imagined popping them out of their sockets and rolling them across a flat surface – a tabletop, or perhaps a smooth stretch of footpath.

"Oh. Yes. I suppose you'd better go over there, in the bushes. I'll make sure no one sees." He smiled.

"Very funny," she said, drifting off toward a dense little stand of trees that were surrounded by waist-high foliage.

Daryl watched as she pulled down her jeans and knickers in a single swift movement (oh, she was used to that manoeuvre, if her father was to be believed), and squatted, her pale backside swamped by the almost leafless yet still thick undergrowth. She stared at him, and when he did not look away she averted her gaze, cheeks and throat flushing red.

Daryl watched her straining to urinate. It was the first time he'd ever seen anyone but Mother do their toilet, and he was fascinated at the way her thighs tensed and her hands gripped the belt-band of her trousers.

"Holy fuck!" She tried to run while still in a crouch, her legs tangled with her clothing. Her feet slipped on the knotty ground, and she went tumbling forward, rolling a little way down the incline. Her buttocks were dirty and as she rolled he saw that her pubic hair glistened, like the pelt of an unwashed dog. He felt suddenly nauseous.

"Get the fuck away. Fuck, fuck!" She struggled to get to her feet, all the while tugging up her garments, and as she buckled her belt and zippered the front of her jeans, Daryl stepped towards the spot where she'd been urinating.

"What is it?" he said, gaze fixed on the ground, then flicking upward and taking in the damp, dense foliage.

"In there," she said, breathless. She was pointing directly into the undergrowth, right behind where she had squatted only seconds before. "It's in there..."

Daryl inched forward, his hand straying to the kitchen knife he now kept tucked into the back of his pants, wrapped in a ragged square of chamois leather to prevent the blade from slicing his flesh. Then, when he saw what Claire was making so much fuss about, he had to restrain himself from laughing out loud. He doubted that she – or anyone else for that matter – would see the humour in such a gruesome sight.

The remains – for that was surely what they were – consisted of male body parts. The torso had been pummelled and stripped clean, the offal removed. Ribs were broken, sticking out of the compressed mass like white spiderlegs from a mutated arachnid. Various innards had been left behind, but Daryl was unable to identify them: a gristly chunk of what might have once been part of a heart; bloodless strings of arteries; a few sausage-like sections of intestine attached to a rubberised section of bowel. The rest was just so much red gunge.

He stared at the thing, truly amazed at the baffling sight.

Its head was relatively intact; the throat had been peeled back, exposing its inner workings, cheeks stripped away like wads of paper, half a nose with one wide nostril left to gape.

But the eyes... they were a lovely shade of cornflower blue, heavy-lidded, and blinking.

Blinking.

Somehow, against nature, what was left of the corpse had returned to a travesty of life, and even now its shattered jaw snapped shut on a flap of its own shredded flesh. The limbs were bent and folded; the whole stunted cadaver was collapsed in on itself, forming a tight knot of living-dead matter. And it was steadily eating what little meat remained on its own bones.

Daryl watched in silence as the jagged teeth tore free a large slab of flesh, chewing it; as the meat was swallowed; as it journeyed down into the exposed stomach cavity to plop onto the long grass, completely undigested.

The thing did not even know what it was doing. Brute instinct had taken over, the desire to feed... no, not feed: the desire to *eat*. There was no sustenance being gained here. This was simply eating for the sake of it, like a morbidly obese patient hiding cold burgers under his hospital bed, or a greedy child forcing down sugared donuts even as he vomits them back up.

"Fascinating," he said, unmoved yet interested on an academic level. Even if there was nothing left in which to store food, these things ate. If you dissected one of them, vivisecting it to the bone, reducing it to nothing but a mouth attached to a brain, would it still try to consume?

It was an interesting theory, and one that he would love to test if ever he had the necessary time and privacy.

Maybe it was even something he could try out on Sally, a way of discovering exactly how much he loved her.

Instead of putting an end to her living death (or should that be her dead life?), perhaps he could kidnap her and use her as a test subject. If the policeman had her with him, on the boat with others, she was obviously under some kind of strict control – he must have used medication, rendering her placid.

The possibilities of love, he was beginning to realise, were endless.

CHAPTER TWENTY-NINE

It seemed like months had passed since they'd been on the canal, and yet Rick didn't want the journey to end.

"It's just over here," said Rohmer, easing the barge towards a short bank overgrown with ferns and hanging flora. Their leaves kissed the water, causing tiny ripples to disturb the stillness beneath the gravel towpath.

Rotting timber boards made up most of the old jetty. It looked unsafe, but Rohmer promised them that it was fit to walk on. "It never gets used," he'd said. "Except by me. There's nothing near here but my cottage."

The barge drifted inward, cutting a calm line through the water. Rick had brought up the M16 from below. Rohmer kept the second Glock pistol close to hand.

The heavily thatched roof of a thick-walled stone cottage rose suddenly into his eye line. It sat on a rise, which made it easier to defend if it came to that, and Rick guessed that the cottage probably lay a few hundred yards from the bank.

"I think your wife is trying to get up." Tabby's head popped up from below. Her eyes were startled, too wide, like those of a shocked cartoon character.

"Thanks," he said, ducking down and passing her on the tiny set of wooden steps. He headed towards the rear of the barge, noting a nasty smell that hadn't been there before. Was Sally the source? He thought of her decaying flesh, the hideous dry wounds beneath the dressings.

He approached the bunk and lowered the rifle. She was sitting up, her hands twitching on the thin mattress. She was making a low sighing sound, air escaping through dead lungs, slashed lips.

"Hush, baby. It's me. It's Rick." He sat on the edge of the bed, no longer quite knowing how to touch her. She was like a stranger, another woman whose quirks and habits he was forced to learn.

Are we there yet?

"No. Not yet. But almost." He already had the syringe in his hand. He introduced the morphine by the other eye, taking turns so that he didn't ruin whatever matter was left in the sockets. He knew he'd have to change her dressings again before long, and his mind withdrew from the thought of what she might now look like under there.

That's better.

Her body slumped; the tension went out of her limbs. Could a dead person even become tense? Did their bodies react in the same way, even though there was no blood being pumped, no oxygen fuelling them? Perhaps they could explain everything on Rohmer's island. When they got there it would all be put in some kind of order.

But did he really believe that, or was he simply clinging to an old man's second-hand hope of salvation?

It'll be all right. We can be together like we used to be. Once we get there, you can undress me and love me again.

Undress... did she mean the bandages, or was there something sexual to the invitation? He felt like an adulterer: his wife was dead, and this was his lover, his easy, queasy lover.

He giggled, and then quickly cut off the reaction. A shudder passed through his body, not of fear but of loneliness; a deep, almost supernatural loneliness which knew no bounds, not even death.

Sleepy. So sleepy.

He watched as her body slumped even further down onto the bunk. Her hands relaxed; her skin was white as new, unmarked paper. He bent down and hoisted her across his shoulder. Her body was as light as a sack of bones dumped in a bin outside a fried chicken joint. It scared him to feel her fragile body under his fingers, her delicate skin against his shoulder.

Back on deck, Rohmer was slowly pulling in towards the jetty. Rick's breath misted white in front of his face. In a few days, if the temperature drop continued, the water at the sides of the canal would begin to ice over. He picked up his bag, held the M16 at the ready. Sally was still draped around his shoulders like a human stole. He could barely even feel her weight.

The barge nudged the bank, scraping against the loose dirt and stones.

"Keep an eye out." Rohmer gritted his teeth as he brought the *Queen Anne* around to berth, her nose pushing into the long grass that grew in the shallows. Then, nimble as a man half his age, he leaped ashore and tethered the barge to the moorings – a series of short wooden uprights, each lopsided and not looking even capable of the task for which they'd been driven into the ground.

"Come on, now. Let's be quick."

The cottage was no longer visible from the jetty, but Rick was heartened that they didn't have far to run. Despite Sally's negligible weight on his back, he didn't feel safe enough to make a long trek inland.

"We ready for this?" he glanced at Rohmer, then into Tabby's wide eyes. They both nodded, silent and watchful.

Rohmer looked back at the *Queen Anne*, his right hand drifting unconsciously to rest above his heart, and closed his eyes briefly. When he opened them again there was steel in his gaze. "Let's go."

Rick took the lead, tapping like he was back in basic training. His legs adjusted quickly to the familiar pace, the muscles flexing as if in recognition of the labour ahead. He climbed the slight incline and stood on the gravel path. Now the cottage was visible again: its rough-crafted roof poked up teasingly above a thin line of trees.

Rohmer and Tabby came up behind; they were both breathing heavily. Rick made a mental note to remember that his travelling companions were an old man and a small child. He would have to restrict his pace if he wanted to keep them with him. And he did, he admitted to himself at last, want them with him. He wanted that more than anything else.

This was his family now: a ragtag pair of strangers and a dead wife hanging like a hideous neck scarf across his battle-broad shoulders. A family unit forged in the fires of hell.

Rohmer held the gun like a pro. The man obviously adapted quickly, and this trait made Rick respect him even more. Tabby was in good hands here; even if Rick hadn't stumbled across them, he suspected that her beloved grandfather would be doing a sterling job of keeping her alive.

"Okay," he told them, ducking down out of sight. "This is how we do it. I'll run ahead and check the area for strays. You two stay here and watch my back. Let's not mess this up."

"I hear you loud and clear, son." Rohmer tensed his jaw. He was serious, ready to do what was necessary. If anyone else had called Rick *son* in the easy manner of this old codger, he'd have put them on their arse. But it felt natural coming from Rohmer; he was the father Rick had never known.

The realisation shocked him. Was it really this easy to accept someone?

"Be careful," said Tabby. "All of us, just be careful."

Rick straightened with tears in his eyes. Pretending to adjust Sally's position on his back, he winced to clear his vision. "She keeps wriggling." The lie burned his tongue. He wished that he could be honest with these people above all others, yet knew that it simply wasn't possible.

He turned and jogged along the towpath, gravel crunching

underfoot. The rifle kept him company, and he knew it would never fail him. This rifle had blown off the heads of enemies, punctured holes through doors behind which dwelled those who meant him harm. It was a good friend, a valued servant.

Don't drop me.

"I won't. I'll carry you forever." He knew it was true. This burden would remain his and his alone until their journey was done, wherever the darkened road might lead.

There was a dark blue Volvo estate parked beside a small outbuilding near the cottage. The car's headlights had been left on, but the light was weak, the battery running low but not quite dead.

He recalled that Rohmer had mentioned a family who sometimes rented out the cottage. They must have come here seeking refuge.

Shit. He didn't think he could carry any more baggage. He gripped the rifle, wondering...

When the gun went off he knew exactly what had happened, and his heart sank through his body and deep into the earth. *Nothing lasts*, he thought. *It all goes away in the end.* Then he dropped Sally onto the ground and ran back along the towpath, not even pausing to assess the situation.

Don't leave me.

He took it all in as he ran, looking for a shot.

Unfortunately, there was no shot available.

Tabby was moving in a low crouch, trying to gain her feet as she hurried away from what was happening immediately behind her. Because of Rick's position in relation to her and Rohmer, she was blocking his direct line of vision, making it impossible to squeeze off a few rounds while he was running.

So he dropped to his knees, the gravel grazing his kneecaps, and carefully took aim along the length of the assault rifle.

Rohmer was panicking and grabbing at the gun; because of his unfamiliarity with firearms, he was unable to act quickly in a crisis. Rick suspected that the gun had jammed – something he'd be able to resolve in an instant but a novice would struggle to deal with. Again, the shot was blocked because of the old man's position.

It was another of Rohmer's shamblers. In all honesty, it wasn't fit to be much else: there wasn't enough left of it to do anything *but* shamble. And eat.

The thing moving slowly towards the old man had at one time been human, but now it looked to Rick bizarrely like a tree. That was the image his racing mind grabbed onto: a fucked-up mobile sapling; bonsai of the living dead.

Below the beltline, the thing was intact, with thick legs clad in bloodstained jeans. It tottered on those sturdy legs, understandably unable to find a centre of balance.

Above the waist was the spine, a long, white segmented tube that had been picked clean of flesh. The naked spinal column moved like a serpent, swaying from side to side in a hypnotic fashion. The splintered ribcage retained a covering of meat, but it had been shredded and mostly flayed. The odd red mass looked like the branches of a tree, spindly appendages stuck out at odd angles and festooned with dangling leaves of shredded skin.

The neck, like the lower torso, had been stripped of flesh; the shocking white bone glinted in the weak daylight. The bottom jaw was missing completely – perhaps torn off when the thing had been created. A top row of teeth lined the area above this, and the tongue lolled insanely long from the crimson cavity.

The top of the head, from a line level with the eyebrows, had been scalped. Runnels and tears in the pate; vague tufts of fuzzy hair left to cover the area like random bristles.

It was the most bizarre sight Rick had yet seen, and again the image of a tree snagged in his mind. That burst ribcage was the foliage, balanced atop a skinny trunk of spinal chord.

"Move!" he yelled, trying to get the thing in his sights. "Get out of the way!"

Tabby finally got to her feet, but instead of running towards Rick she turned to help her grandfather.

Rick jumped to his feet and thundered towards them, screaming sounds no one would have recognised as words.

The tree-thing reached Rohmer in what seemed like slow-motion. It reached out its grasping hands, took hold of his shoulders, and drew him into a weird embrace, that juddering upper mandible gearing up to scoop out his throat.

Rick, acting on instinct, shot the old man through the meat of his upper shoulder, hoping that the exit wound would be in the right place. The dead thing twitched backwards, and thankfully Rohmer stepped back, giving Rick a single clear shot at the gaping jaw.

He took off its head whilst running at speed. It was the best shot he had ever pulled off, and there was nobody there to admire his skill.

"I'm okay," Rohmer was saying, trying to calm down Tabby, who was almost strangling him as she wrapped her arms around his neck.

"Did it bite you?" There was no time for niceties. Rick still held the M16 at waist level, not yet ready to lower it fully.

"No bite. It was a close thing, though." Rohmer's face was drained of blood; it was a paper mask, a child's sketch of an incredibly ancient man.

"You sure?" Rick lowered the rifle.

"That was good shooting, son. A one in a million shot. Gave me a nice flesh wound."

"What happened?" Rick nodded at the gun, still gripped in Rohmer's hand. His other hand clutched at his wounded shoulder.

"I dunno. It just seized up in my hand."

He stepped inside, reaching past the still sobbing Tabby, and took the pistol. Aiming it up, he pulled the trigger, letting off two shots. "It's fine now." He handed Rohmer the gun.

Rohmer's face was whiter still; as if he'd only just realised how close to death, or something worse, he'd been.

"If it happens again," said Rick, "remain calm. Here." He took the hunting knife from his belt and handed it to Rohmer, who took it gratefully. "A back-up plan."

Rick turned away and headed back along the towpath, towards Sally. His hands were shaking but he didn't want anyone to see. "Follow me," he ordered. "And for Christ's sake, keep close. We don't want any more accidents."

They reached Sally together, and Rick picked her up like she was a bundle of dirty rags. "Who are they?" he said, motioning towards the Volvo.

"The Kendalls," said Rohmer, one hand resting on top of Tabby's head. She seemed unwilling to let him go. "The family who come here when I'm not. They must've fled town and thought they could hide out here, until all this is over."

Rick resisted the urge to comment on that final remark. "We tread carefully." He glanced at Rohmer, saw the new fear in the man's old, old eyes. "I don't want to lose either of you, not when we've only just become friends." He smiled.

Rohmer nodded, unable to speak. He gripped his wound, blood squeezing through his fingers.

"I'll sort that out once we're safe," said Rick.

Rohmer nodded. His lips were tight and bloodless.

Rick walked towards the cottage, making sure that they stayed close. He didn't know what he was going to find in there, but for the first time in over a day the terrible Dead Rooms of Leeds crossed his mind, and he prayed that after his scare Rohmer would be quicker to react.

What remained of their future might depend on it.

CHAPTER THIRTY

Daryl had finally grown tired of the stupid bitch.

"Will you please just shut up for a moment? I'm trying to think."

Claire sat on the moped, her bare feet dragging in the grass. She was pouting, putting on a ridiculous show to stir his emotions. If only she knew that Daryl did not possess emotions; that would be a laugh. Oh, how he'd laugh... right before he cut off her head and used it as a hat.

"I just want a little attention," she said, folding her arms across her perky breasts. She pouted again, a pathetic council-estate Monroe. It probably worked on most of the men she'd ever been with – but Daryl was not like most men.

Daryl tried his best to ignore her and watched the cottage through the binoculars. It was located on the other side of the canal, and the old barge was moored at a shitty little jetty right near it. They must be inside the cottage, hiding out for a while, taking a breath. All of them. The policeman, the old man, the little girl. And Sally, his one true love.

He looked again at Claire, and wondered why he'd thought she even slightly resembled Sally. She didn't. She was crude and cheap... and stupid. That last was the most unforgivable thing of all. It made her just like everyone else, one of the mindless swarm of humanity Daryl had always felt separate from.

At first he'd thought that her hurt had singled her out and formed a connection between them. Now he realised that it made her the same as the rest of them – everyone has their own private parlour of pain, the place into which they like to retreat and act like a martyr.

"Silly bitch," he said, almost snarling the words.

"What was that?" She stood, hands on hips, and tried to act like she was strong. Her legs were shaking and her face was pallid. She looked about as strong as a child's doll.

"I said," he advanced towards her. "Silly. Fucking. Bitch." He slapped her across the face before she could respond, taking her by surprise. Her feet went out from under her, and she fell on her scrawny arse, a look of pure shock on her face.

Daryl's hand stung from the contact, even inside Sally's increasingly tattered gloves. He began to laugh, flexing his fingers and staring at them as if they'd suddenly taken on a life of their own.

The look of shock on Claire's face turned quickly to one of fear, and she tried to shuffle backwards, retreating from him. "What's wrong? Why are you doing this? I thought we were... friends. You know – a couple."

"A couple of cunts," Daryl snapped, between bouts of girlish giggling. His mind was strung between high wires, stretched so thin that it just might snap. He could picture it spread out above his head like a fleshy sheet.

Once the bout of uncontrollable hilarity had passed, he grabbed Claire by the hair and dragged her to her feet, gritting his teeth against the death lust that rose up his throat and into his mouth like bile. He could almost taste her extinction, and it was wonderful, growing within him like the shivery stirrings of an orgasm.

"Get on the bike," he said, pushing her towards the machine. "We're going."

"Where?" she whined.

"Just going." He nipped her arm, prodded her left breast, kicked her up the backside.

"Ow," she said, rubbing at the spots he was casually abusing. "That hurts."

"Good. It's meant to. Much more of this nonsense and it'll hurt a lot more than that."

Their relationship had entered a new phase. Now that the thrill of sexual conquest was over and done with, Daryl felt nothing but disdain for this snivelling little bint. She was an annoyance; a mere sub plot in the ongoing script of his life. The sooner he wrote her out of the story the better he would feel about the whole thing.

Carefully he steered the bike along the track, dodging large stones and heading for the footbridge he had spotted some time ago. He didn't want to enter the cottage and spook them. All he required was a safe vantage point, a place from which he could continue to watch the show. They were doing fine, this shabby band of survivors, and watching them was like viewing a film running in conjunction with his own wonderful cinematic adventures.

Daryl was not yet ready to switch the channel.

The gunshot was close. He heard it as he pulled up the moped at a fallen tree trunk, bringing the rear end around in a looping skid in the loose earth. It sounded to his untrained ears like an old blunderbuss, or something, so he guessed that it must be someone's inherited shotgun. He'd never been educated in firearms, so all big guns sounded the same.

He sat on the bike and listened, waiting for the sound to come again. Claire's hands pressed into his sides, hurting him because of her unnecessarily tight grip. He shifted on the seat; her grip tightened. The sound of laughter was carried on the breeze, putting him on edge.

"Bloody hell," he said.

"What is it? Are we in danger?" Her voice was quiet, fear-soft.

He liked it that way.

"I don't know. It could be the police or maybe some yokels messing about with a gun. We need to be careful."

She whimpered like a hurt dog. Daryl was not even sure that she was aware of making the sound. It made him dislike her even more. Jesus, what had he ever been attracted to? Ah, yes... he remembered now: her *ease*, the way she had given herself up to him in a flash.

He got off the moped and pushed it over to the grounded tree trunk. Claire got her leg stuck as she swung it over the seat, but managed to dismount before he forced her off the vehicle. She scowled at him, arms crossed and feet splayed outward. Her forearms were folded across her chest, as if barring the way.

"I'll check this out," he said, not even looking at her. What on earth had possessed him to let her tag along with him in the first place? Could the unaccustomed attention of a female have given him such a buzz that he was blinded to her obvious flaws?

Yes, he admitted to himself. *That's exactly what it was.*

"Don't leave me here..." She took a few steps towards him and then stopped, torn between maintaining her pained demeanour and following him into the trees. The undergrowth rustled, and somewhere above them a bird took to the air, rattling the dry branches like castanets.

"I won't be long. Just hang around here, and yell if anyone comes along. Yell and I'll come for you." He pushed through the undergrowth and headed towards the approximate area where he thought the gunshots had originated. There was no more commotion, but the air felt pressurised, as if a thunderstorm were approaching. There was a sense of unresolved anxiety, of violence waiting to happen.

Small animals scurried before him, following unseen trails and fleeing from his approach. Daryl enjoyed the sense of power. It was an echo of how he felt when he ordered Claire about, and he realised that this was also part of the reason he had allowed her to hang around for so long. But the novelty was wearing off; her questionable allure had become stale. She did not have long left as his side-kick: it had always been a temporary position, a mere cameo role in the film he was creating.

Up ahead there appeared, out of the limp greenery, the grey bulk of a single-storey structure. It looked like a disused power station, an old reinforced concrete shell once used to contain electrical apparatus that had long ago been abandoned and left to rot. Parts of the structure were missing – rusted steel rods stuck out of the crumbling concrete like lethal booby traps. Daryl recalled the public information films he'd seen in school, vicious shorts made in the 1970s and featuring bowl-cut teenagers coming to dire ends in such derelict properties. There was a famous one about the 'spirit of lonely water' that had fuelled his fantasies for years... a hooded figure that hung around isolated ponds and lured kids to a death by drowning.

The young Daryl had masturbated over that commercial, filling his mind with images of dead boys and girls floating face-down in shallow water.

He smiled at the memories. This type of recollection was rare from his school days – most of the time he'd been bullied and pestered – so when good thoughts came to mind he felt that he should always take the time to enjoy them.

"Fuckin' hell!" The voice came from just up ahead. It was dull, uneducated, lacking any favourable qualities as far as Daryl was concerned. It reminded him of the voices of kids he'd attended school with and the moronic adults they had developed into. Ugly boys usually brought up in single parent families, who would rather hit someone than discuss any potential differences in a calm, sensible manner.

"Took its bastard leg right off!"

Daryl crouched down and moved slowly, not wishing to be seen by the owner of the voice. He suspected that despite the changes currently reshaping the world, his presence was still something a certain kind of person might not exactly cherish. It had always been this way, and Daryl never expected it to change. Some things would remain the same forever; some people were incapable of transforming themselves into different personalities.

Thankfully Daryl was not one of these people. He was changing all the time, with a regularity that made him feel frightened and thrilled in equal measures. A few days ago he would never have treated a woman how he was treating Claire; today he could just as easily slit her throat as offer her a kiss. Tomorrow... well, who knew? Daryl the ever-changing was an unreadable entity, and he was quickly learning to live life day by day instead of as one long, unbearable sequence of hours (as it had been with Mother).

He watched the two men as they drank beer from cans and giggled. They were wearing winter clothes, some of which still had the price tags attached – gear they had obviously looted from a store. Their faces were ruddy from drink and their postures were loose and unpredictable. They laughed like madmen, slapping each other on the back and dancing in little circles, shuffling their booted feet on the hard dirt.

Daryl was more afraid of these men than he was of the walking dead.

There was a doorway in the side of the concrete power station: a rectangular opening made irregular by vandalism. The door itself was long gone, leaving just a dark hole. The concrete slab floor at the centre of the doorway had been broken away by the ravages of time and the elements to reveal a shallow basement, and suspended above this dark space, tied into a makeshift harness, was a severely mutilated body.

Daryl realised immediately what was going on here and the knowledge sickened him, despite his own recent activities.

The two men were using the woman's reanimated corpse as a target for shooting practice. Both of her legs had been blown off, leaving rough-edged stumps, one of her arms was missing below the elbow, and there were several huge wounds in her naked torso. Her head remained intact, but her face had been slashed to ribbons.

The dead woman made tiny moaning noises as she swayed on the harness. Loops of rope had been wrapped around her shoulders and under her armpits, the other end looped over the steel lintel above the broken door opening. Some of the rope coils were red, and it took Daryl a little while to realise that her stomach had been opened and her intestines looped around her body along with the hemp.

"Get her in the head," said the smaller of the two men, lighting up a hand-rolled cigarette. "Get the bitch in the fuckin' mush! She's asking for it."

His friend laughed, and then tried to aim, but his hands were unsteady – probably due to his alcohol intake. Cans and bottles littered the ground at the men's feet, and there were a couple of crates of beer leaning against a rotten tree stump. "Can barely see the twat," he said, swaying slightly from side to side.

The small man laughed; a manic chuckle that chilled Daryl more than the cold and the sight of the guns.

A selection of weapons were laid out a few short yards away from Daryl – guns, knives, a machete, even a bow and arrows.

He eased forward, keeping his eyes on the two men. They were too drunk to even notice as he inched through the undergrowth, heading towards the makeshift armoury.

"Your turn... I can't even see, I'm so pissed." More laughter.

Daryl reached out carefully. His fingers grasped the handle of an old-fashioned shotgun and he lifted it, glancing at it briefly to register that the barrel had been sawn off half way down its length. He knew enough from movies to realise how much damage such a weapon was capable of doing to the human form at close range.

He brought the shotgun into his hiding place, cocked the hammers, and then stepped into the open, hoping that he'd done enough to arm the thing – and that it was loaded.

It took several seconds for the men to notice him, and Daryl waited until they had turned to face him before opening fire. He wanted to see their faces as their bodies were torn to shreds by the wide spray of pellets.

After he had let rip with both barrels, Daryl stood shrouded in smoke and the stench of cordite burned his nostrils. The two men lay on the ground, one of them still twitching. His torn clothes were bright red from the blood and as he raised his head, his eyes rolled in their sockets. His screaming was loud and wordless, like a siren. Daryl listened to it for a while, amazed that the throat could contort enough to make such inhuman sounds.

Then he stepped over to the man and brought the stock of the shotgun down on his skull with all the force he could muster, the bone cracking in a straight line down the centre of his brow. He repeated the process until the man was still and his head was reduced to a red mush, and then moved on to the second motionless moron: he did not want these two to come back. Even the dead had standards, and these two scumbags would bring down the entire group.

Daryl was sweating, his arms ached. He had an erection.

"Fuckers," he whispered, all-too aware that by killing them he had been venting his hatred of the people who had made his life so empty. For all his days he had been harassed by men like these; his every move mocked, each word he'd spoken turned into a joke. Manual workers, office drones, every so-called 'real man' he had ever encountered: stupid muscle-headed fuckwits with more machismo than common sense.

But now it was Daryl's turn to assume the role of the alpha male, and if he could reduce a few of these idiots to shredded meat along the way, then that was fine by him.

"*Gnnnnnnn...*" The dead woman moaned again, her bloodless torso thrashing. Daryl had forgotten that she was even there, and her movements dragged him back to reality. She was twisting on the rope, her shattered body moving like a bizarre mobile or weather vane.

Daryl bent down, retrieved a small handgun from one of the men's cold hands, and shot the rope that held her. She fell into the hole that led to the basement, cracking her head on the rim as she vanished into the darkness. The accuracy of the shot had been a result of pure luck, but it made him feel once again that certain scenes had already been written for him to enact.

Daryl heard shuffling sounds, and then other moans emerged from down there in the black basement. He realised that there must be more dead people beneath the ground, perhaps deliberately trapped by these two men to provide more savage sport to amuse them. He actually appreciated their methods, and thought that if they had not been such arseholes he might even have joined in their fun. Unfortunately, men like these were not worth the trouble. They were better off out of the picture.

Daryl walked over to the hole and leaned over it, staring down into the basement. The floor was formed of compacted earth and there was just enough light that he could see the space was relatively small and sealed off by further underground walls. It was more like a pit than an actual room, and as far as he could see there were at least three or four other dead people in there beside the twisting torso he had released from the harness. He caught a glimpse of pale limbs, dirty clothing, and thin, shadowy faces with gaping mouths.

Daryl smiled. An idea had begun to form, and it seemed to him that he could have a little fun while ridding himself of a problem.

"Claire!" He doubled back and pushed his way into the bushes. "Claire, get over here."

He glanced at the men's bags and his eyes widened when they fell upon a small digital video camera. He picked it up and located the power button. The compact hand-held machine whined and then the lens cap slid back and the tiny screen flared into life.

Daryl pointed the camera at the power station and watched it on the screen, one remove from reality. It was the way he had always felt before these events: separated from everything by a camera lens, as if his life were being projected onto a vast screen for the amusement of others. Only this time *he* was the one being amused; the film was turning into something of his own devising, and whoever had scripted the first act was long gone.

He listened, heard the clatter of Claire's clumsy approach through the undergrowth, and stepped back, smiling.

"What is it?" She was breathless when she broke through the trees.

"It's okay. I've taken care of these jokers, so we can have a look around and see if they had any supplies." He watched her through the camera, sizing her up for the next scene.

Claire was already rooting through their bags, her face lighting up at the sight of the beer. "Well, they have this." She lifted a whisky bottle from the pack, grinning and smacking her lips.

The little camera whirred. There must be something broken

inside, but it still worked well enough to allow Daryl to view the events around him. Even if the playback function had been disabled, it was enough that he could experience this all through a viewfinder. It felt more real this way.

Claire was standing so close to the pit that Daryl was amazed she did not hear the sounds coming from down below. It just went to show how unobservant she was, how up herself. If it wasn't directly beneath her nose, then the bitch remained unaware, utterly absorbed in her own activity.

Daryl raised the pistol he had taken from the dead men's stash.

"Claire?"

She looked up, her eyes shining, cheeks full of rose petals as she drank deeply from the whisky bottle. .

Daryl shot her once in the left leg, knocking her sufficiently off balance that she fell right into the pit. For the second time that day he was pleased with his aim, considering that he was a total novice, and was holding the camera to one eye as he pulled the trigger. A second shot went astray, missing her completely. Claire screamed his name, her hands grasping at the uneven edge of the pit as her body weight pulled her down. She stared right at Daryl, a look of dawning horror on her face, and then she slipped beneath the surface of the earth. Screaming.

"I'm so sorry, dear," said Daryl, walking softly towards the pit, filming it all. "But you were getting right on my fucking nerves." The sounds of her screaming were already dying out; they were soon replaced by those of feasting.

Daryl peered into the pit but could only make out a large shape being torn apart by other shapes. Even the camera's screen showed only a hazy image. The best was kept from him by darkness: he barely even caught sight of the blood as Claire was stripped to the bone. However long the dead people had been down there, it was long enough to make their hunger insatiable. The sound of their feeding frenzy was repellent, and Daryl had soon heard enough. He turned off the camera, the scene at its end.

Slowly, he walked back to the moped. There was a tin of corned beef in Claire's rucksack. He fished it out, opened it, and began to eat. By the time he had finished the meat, Claire was a distant memory. Her name, her face, the echo of her words no longer made an impact on the surface of his life; not even the slightest ripple.

He packed up his stuff, slid the camera into his bag, climbed onto the moped, and set off towards whatever future he chose to create.

CHAPTER THIRTY-ONE

The front door of the cottage was locked but Rohmer already had his key out as they approached, clutching it like a talisman in shaking hands.

Rick quickly scanned the area, seeing nothing to be afraid of, while the old man unlocked the heavy wooden door. It swung open soundlessly, with not even the hint of creaking hinges. Rick was almost disappointed; his senses were unnaturally keen at this point, and a jokey horror movie sound effect might have served to break the tension and relax them all.

"Wait," he said, moving inside the building and pressing his back against the wall. He moved along the short hallway and entered the first door on his right, adjacent to the stairs.

The room he surveyed was long, with a low ceiling, and not an item seemed out of place. The neat furniture was clean and undamaged; the shelves and writing desk had not been interfered with; the floor held no bloodstains. Rick's keen battle senses did not even detect the telltale atmosphere of recent violence.

Judging by the presence of the car parked outside, the visitors – the Kendall family – must still be somewhere on the premises. Rohmer had said that the family consisted of a middle aged couple and a thirteen year-old boy. They'd probably fled here when the city erupted in violence, and had no doubt been planning to hole up for as long they could, existing on whatever supplies they'd managed to bring along and those already in the place. According to Rohmer the cottage was well stocked, with a large fruit and wine cellar, and even had its own independent source of power – a small emergency generator located in one of the outbuildings at the rear of the property.

"Hello!"

Rick waited for a response, but none came. The place *felt* empty... it was a sensation he had encountered before, during training missions. When a building is occupied it holds a sense of life between its walls, a certain tautness in the air, but when there is no one living in the vicinity, that too becomes obvious by the invisible vibrations it is possible to pick up on.

He moved back out of the room and into the hall, where he dropped to his knees and aimed the M16 up the narrow staircase. Nothing moved, but the darkness seemed to swirl before his eyes: a slow snake-curling motion that unnerved him.

Then Rick heard a single sound: a soft knocking, as if of a fist rapping lightly on a door, or the tip of a boot making brief contact with the base of a skirting board. It wasn't much, but it was enough to set his well-honed instincts popping, especially after what had happened outside, when Rohmer had almost been killed by what amounted to a walking skeleton.

He waited. And, as expected, the sound came again. It continued, building a rhythm and gaining in volume, like someone slamming their hand against a wall up there.

Thud... thud... thud...

Slowly, cautiously, Rick began to ascend the stairs, using the difficult tactic of keeping his feet light by taking up as much of the tension as possible in his calves as he gently lowered the soles of his boots onto the timber treads. His nerves tensed with each footfall, expecting the squeal of old boards and the crick-cracking of support timbers.

The thumping noise continued. It was a regular beat, with a few seconds of silence separating each strike of whatever it was that was making the sound.

Thud... thud... thud...

Like a drumbeat, the sound continued, guiding him up the stairs towards the landing.

The stairs began to creak slightly as Rick climbed them, but he managed to adjust his centre of balance just enough to minimise the noise. He glanced back, over his shoulder, but could no longer see the front door. He hoped that Rohmer and Tabby were okay standing out there on the doorstep. The old man had proved more of a hindrance than a help during their last encounter with the dead, and he hoped that a lesson had been learned. Rick hated the thought of anything happening to his recently adopted family.

The thought disturbed him, yet he was overwhelmed by the fondness he felt towards these people after such a relatively short amount of time in their company. He had allowed himself to grow close to the man and the girl, and keeping them alive came second in importance only to the safety of Sally.

He dropped to his knees when he reached the upper landing, keeping the rifle at the ready. He wished he'd swapped it for the pistol in such a confined space, but it was too late now to regret thoughtless decisions. The secret of success was to work with what you had, to focus on the moment and nothing more.

The thumping sound continued.

Thud... thud... thud...

It was coming from behind the closed door that lay directly at the top of the stairs.

Rick peered along the landing in both directions, noting that all the other doors were also closed. If anyone was hiding up there, he would be signalled of their intention to attack by the opening of a door. It might just give him enough time to gain the upper hand: the difference between life and death, survival and extinction, often hung on such minor details.

Thud... thud... thud...

He shuffled forward in a low crouch, keeping his head down below the level of a stray gunshot. The rug shifted beneath him, inching across varnished boards, but he had faith enough in his sense of balance to overcome the matter.

When he reached the door he stood and quickly slipped to one side, taking a deep breath. He waited. Listened. The timbre of the sound had not altered, nor had its rhythm changed in any way. Either whoever was making the sound was locked into some Zen-like state, or it was simply the sound of a loose pipe knocking against the wall or a faulty window latch shifting in the breeze.

Thud... thud... thud...

Rick moved smoothly and quickly. He faced the door and kicked it open, ready to fire.

The room beyond was small – more of a storeroom than a bed chamber – and sparsely furnished. There was a single bed pushed against the rear wall, a low cabinet piled with papers and magazines to his left, a narrow wardrobe to his right... and at the centre of the room the reanimated body of a young boy hung from his neck by a noose.

Thud... thud... thud...

It was the sound of one of the body's feet clattering against the back of the wooden chair which he had clearly used to climb up to the noose. He must have kicked the chair away as he stepped off it, his body plummeting, and the chair had fallen not quite far enough away from the body to leave the floor beneath clear. Then he'd come back and found himself still hanging there.

So as he swung in place, clawing at his throat and trying to escape the noose, his foot came into regular contact with the chair back.

Thud... thud... thud...

Rick's vision blurred, and only when he blinked to clear it did he realise that he was crying. He adjusted his aim and fired a single round, taking one side of the boy's head off and sending part of the skull spinning across the room. It came to rest like a little bowl near the wardrobe.

The thumping sound came no more and Rick had never been

happier to hear the end of something. He knew that he would hear that sound in his dreams, probably for the rest of his life. It would sound behind the voices he carried within him, a low-tempo backbeat to their unending screams.

"Rick?" Tabby's voice drifted up the stairs, soft and tentative, yet with an edge he could not identify. Was it terror? He realised that so far he'd not seen the girl truly afraid. It was as if she had the utmost faith in her grandfather, and now in Rick. As long as they were by her side, she would never be completely afraid.

But now she sounded lost and alone in the dark, just like everyone else.

"I'm coming." He ran down the stairs, making sure that the door to the small bedroom was closed firmly behind him. "What is it?"

Her face was wet; fine red veins stood out in her eyes, a tracery of pain. "It's Granddad."

"Where is he? I told him to stay outside with you and keep watch." Rick moved to the door, the hot barrel of the M16 nosing before him, sniffing out danger. The front door was closed.

"There were sounds... something was moving out there. He pushed me inside and said that he'd get them away from here."

"Where's Sally?"

The girl shook her head, her eyes growing even wider. "With Granddad. She sort of stumbled off... and he followed her. He told me to come and get you."

The old fool. He was planning to take on the dead in numbers in order to keep them away from his granddaughter... and from Rick.

"Stay with me. Don't leave my side." He grabbed the girl roughly by the shoulder and opened the door. "I don't know if it's safe in here, so we need to stay together."

Tabby nodded just as the gunshots began.

Rick headed for the back of the cottage, the girl keeping pace. He could hear her breathing, sense her panic as it rose within her tiny frame, but she moved with the speed and grace of a gazelle. He wanted to cry; he refused to let the tears come but they came anyway, washing down his cheeks like warm rain.

"Where's Sally?" Panic was rising in him, too. It made his limbs shudder and his resolve harden. Like always, he used a typically negative reaction in his favour, drawing strength from it and using it as raw fuel.

I'm here, darling. Don't worry.

Sally was wandering around in the open, a few yards away from a low barn. She looked like a lost sheep, turning in slow circles, unable to locate herself and pick a direction. The morphine must still be working.

"Stupid old man! I told him to stay put. I *told* him..."

When he reached Sally he gently guided her away from the barn and sat her down on a tuft of grass at the base of a slight rise. He kept one eye on the open barn doorway, and both ears open for anything that might signify trouble. Rohmer must be in there: it was the only logical place he could have gone. Perhaps he'd chased one of his runners in there, and that was the source of the gunshots.

"Rohmer! I'm coming, mate. Just keep cool!"

Sally flopped onto her back, the morphine still doing its job and dulling her senses. Her hunger.

I'm okay. I just went for a little walk. Tired now...

Rick stroked her bandaged head, feeling the rough contours of whatever was left of her face. The wrappings were grubby, but he had not been able to bring himself to remove them again, not yet. Maybe later, when all this was over and done with and they could rest for a while.

Standing, he walked straight towards the barn, not even pausing on his way through the doorway. Whatever was in there, it was going down.

Tabby was behind him, her view blocked by his body, so thankfully she did not see what had happened to the old man.

Rick turned, angling his torso so that she would not catch sight of what now lay behind him, almost unseen in the dim interior. "Go and stand outside. I need you to do this – you have to do what I say. Stand over there and look the other way. Keep an eye on Sally and scream like fuck if you see anything."

Tabby's eyes widened... then she knew; she was not a stupid

girl, and she knew immediately that something had gone badly wrong. She pressed her lips together, being a brave little girl, and Rick's heart tensed as she took a few steps away from the barn's entrance.

Rick made sure that she was still in plain sight yet unable to see deep inside the barn. Then he turned his attention back to Rohmer, poor, poor Rohmer.

The old man was on his back and holding his throat. Blood had sprayed the front of his jacket and even now continued to seep out of the ruptured artery in his neck. His eyes were almost fully closed, but he nodded once, signalling his approval at Rick's actions regarding the girl.

Two bodies lay nearby, each of them sporting gunshot wounds to the head. A woman in a long skirt and a short coat was missing the front of her face; a man was sprawled face down, most of the back of his head splayed outward in a white flower of bone.

The pistol was still in Rohmer's hand. He lifted it and pulled the trigger. The hammer clicked onto an empty chamber. His eyes were wide and tearful. If a man could apologise without words, then this was it.

Rohmer closed his eyes and removed his hand from the side of his throat. Blood gushed at an alarming rate, there was so much of it that it looked black in the dimness.

"Oh, fuck." Rick shot Rohmer in the face and turned quickly away. He did not want to see this man die. He could not bring himself to witness what he had been forced to do. As he stepped outside he heard the distant groaning of a small engine – perhaps a little motorcycle hammering away in the distance. He went to Tabby, fell to his knees, and held her. Her grip was slack at first, but soon she clung to him with a force and an immediacy that was terrifying in its intensity. Rick waited for her sobs, but they did not come, and when finally he pulled away her face was vacant, her eyes staring into the middle distance.

It was a look he'd seen before in the desert: the face of pure clinical shock.

When he turned back to look at Sally, the place where she had been was empty. His gaze returned to the barn doors, and what lay beyond.

Rick stood and walked back inside the barn, gun loose at his side.

She must have crawled in there on all fours, like an animal, perhaps smelling Rohmer's blood through the bandages. She was kneeling before him, both hands on his leg, and attempting to take a bite out of his thigh. Because of the double layer of bindings, and the fact that her mouth and throat had been stuffed with cotton wool, she was unable to do much else than scrape her mouth against his trousers. Rick could see her jaw muscles working; the motion beneath the bandages was strong and deliberate, despite the fact that her body was still floppy because of the drugs.

Even doped up to high heaven, his wife was trying to eat.

Rick walked towards her, grabbed her by the neck, and dragged her away. There were no tears now, nor was there any room for rage. He felt numb, empty, bereft of human feelings. Even the love he felt towards Sally was mutated, a shapeless thing twisting away into an inner darkness.

Tabby had not moved, so he grabbed her with his other hand and guided both his girls back to the cottage, his face slack, eyes seeing nothing but what was directly ahead of him. He felt like he was crossing some imaginary border and entering a place where few men had ever been: a blasted zone where the dead walked and he loved a hungry corpse with all the compassion that remained in his withered heart.

Back at the cottage he barricaded them in. Sally was on the sofa, dosed up with yet more morphine; Tabby stood in a corner, refusing to sit, just staring at the wall.

Thank you, darling. That feels good... safe.

He tried to ignore Sally's voice, but was unable to shut it out. Each time she spoke in his head, he felt that dark love pulsing like a cancer.

He checked every inch of the house and proved to himself there were no other bodies present. He cut down the boy and disposed of him in a ditch out the back, where he found the tattered remains of three more cadavers. There was not enough left of these to get up and walk, but he stamped on their skulls anyway, reducing them to flattened pulp. As little as a few hours ago his actions might still have disgusted him, but now he saw these remains only as meat.

He surmised that the boy's parents must have died and come back for their son, and that they had perhaps fed on a couple of passing strangers – maybe people hiking to safety, or a wounded man and wife who had stopped by for help. The boy had probably hidden from his dead parents, and taken the only way out he could think of when he realised that no one was coming to his aid and his mother and father wanted to devour him.

Rick admired the boy's single-mindedness. It took a lot of courage to leave behind all that you loved, however much they had changed.

What a fucking mess. And not just this situation: the whole world was a calamity, an ongoing mindfuck.

He found a bottle of wine in a kitchen cupboard, then some medical supplies in another. There were plenty of bandages.

It took him quite some time to coerce Tabby up the stairs and into the bed in the main bedroom. She was stiff and unresponsive; her eyes remained open but she was asleep on her feet. He left her clothes on and covered her with fresh blankets from a drawer. He stroked her forehead and sang to her – not a real song, just a strange tune that occurred to him, possibly a jingle from some advert he'd seen back when the world was still in one piece.

Once he was sure that she was finally resting, he left the room and went back downstairs.

He positioned Sally at the dining table, propping her up in a high-backed chair. Then, acting out of impulse, he loosely tied her legs and arms to the chair. Her head rolled on her neck and she was making tiny grunting noises.

Hungry.

Rick closed his eyes, resisting the urge to answer.

He cut off the bandages with a pair of medical scissors he had found in the kitchen, being careful not to cause any more damage to Sally's face. The cellophane-wrapped wounds were completely bloodless by now. Because her heart was no longer pumping, any blood remaining in her system would probably have pooled in the lower cavities, congealing there and forming bruises on the dead flesh of her back, abdomen and upper legs.

He averted his gaze as he applied the fresh dressings, preferring not to examine too closely what her features had become. He was reminded of the aftermath of atrocities he'd seen during his tours of duty in war-torn trouble spots: the shredded corpses of bomb blast victims; dry dead flaps of skin; slashes of yellowing bone.

As he was working, the neck of Sally's top slipped sideways and down, baring the upper part of one still-perfect breast. He wasn't disturbed to find that he had an erection, merely surprised that he still had the energy to be aroused.

"There, there... soon be safe. Once we get to Rohmer's island everything will be different." He no longer even believed it; for all he knew, the island itself was little more than an urban myth, a hopeful dream concocted by a desperate old man to calm his terrified daughter and provide meaning in the madness the world had become.

I know, baby. I trust you. Always have, always will.

He finished up with the dressings and emptied the wine bottle. Standing, he crossed the room and grabbed another from a shelf just inside the kitchen doorway. He downed half this second bottle in a single mouthful, and only when he closed his eyes did he feel the buzz of the alcohol.

Not too much, baby. You never could stomach a lot of red wine.

It was dark now, so he secured the shutters and closed the curtains across the small cottage windows. Nothing moved outside; even the air was calm and still.

He inspected the bookcase along one wall, finding mostly text books, and then stumbled upon a record collection. No CDs here: just an array of old vinyl albums. It felt like fate when the third one he slid off the shelf was a double-album collection of Neil Diamond's greatest hits... and, yes, *Solitary Man* was on there. Side one, track four.

Perfect. What could be better on a night like this? The kid's in bed and we have the whole night ahead of us...

Rick felt the magnet-pull of attraction, and with it came a strange guilt. This was his wife, the woman he loved, yet she was also *another* woman, someone with which he was having some twisted kind of affair. Was it even possible to be unfaithful to the dead?

He'd noticed some candles in a kitchen drawer – the kind he thought might be called tea lights. He fetched them and brought them into the main living room, then dotted them around the vicinity, lighting each one with matches from a box he found in the same drawer.

On one level he knew exactly what he was doing, but on another he watched the whole thing play out like a stage performance, a sad, melancholy drama.

Romantic light caressed Sally's white-masked features, soft shadows creating new dips and hollows across the clean padded surface of her face. It was like seeing another woman – or seeing Sally for the first time, stripped of all artifice and illusion. She had become the meat behind the mask, the reality beneath the torn veil.

He approached the table and poured her some wine. She was still tied into the chair, and he decided to leave her that way. Back in the day, they'd both enjoyed a little light S&M as foreplay.

"Merlot... it's your favourite." He smiled, touched her cold arm. There was nothing inside him but a screaming wind, and at the heart of the storm rested a kernel of desire.

Thank you, baby. You always knew how to take care of me.

He put on the record, and the sound of Neil Diamond's husky voice sent shivers across the exposed flesh of his arms and neck, making the small hairs there stand up to attention in the same way as his dick now stood proud.

Our song.

"It always will be. No matter what happens, we'll always have that night... and I'll never stop loving you. I love you more every second of each day we're together. I know things are different now, and you're a different person..." the wind within howled and then dipped, leaving behind a void "...a different... being.

But still I love you."

I love you more.

He sensed her smile beneath the bandages, even imagined that he saw the faint twitch of movement at the lower part of her face.

Slowly, he moved towards her, the world dimming and the edges of the room fading to a soft-focus blur. He felt exactly like he had on that first night, when they'd entered the bar and danced like no one else was there. He and Sally became the focal point of the universe, the pivot on which the heavens tilted.

"I never stopped loving you and I never will. Nothing can separate us... *nothing.* Not even this."

His hand gently traced the line of her shoulder, feeling the still ice of her skin. The flesh rippled, slipped, folded... lacking its former elasticity, it remained that way, curled up like crepe paper. It was new and interesting; he thought he might even like it.

Leaning in close, he placed his lips against the spot where he knew her mouth would be. She had no breath. Coldness seeped through the wrappings; it made his lips harden and his cheeks prickle. He kissed her softly, carefully, not wanting to cause further damage to her frame. His tongue lapped at the dim curve of her bandaged mouth.

The fact that she did not respond to his advances seemed like a come-on; she was simply playing hard-to-get.

He caressed her cold, hard breasts, the nipples like tiny stones beneath her clothes. Running one hand down her body and across her thigh, he eased in towards her, bending her back on the dining chair. The legs creaked under their combined weight, but he slid into her lap and wrapped his legs around her waist, straddling her like he used to do. It was all so natural, like things had never changed between them.

His hand found the place between her legs that represented a kind of heaven, but it was cold, desolate... a barren region that now shunned life. He ploughed on, refusing to accept that this wasn't working, that it was impossible to make love to the dead. His hips bucking wildly against her lower abdomen, he attempted to transfer the heat of his erection into her stalled system, as if the very energy of his passion might rouse her enough to couple with him.

Darling... it feels so good.

He lifted his feet off the floor and pushed his chest against her, feeling her eager stiffness and trying to break through the barrier death had placed in his way. He felt her striving towards him, straining to make contact...

When the chair leg broke, tipping them both onto the floor, he continued his seduction as if nothing had happened, fumbling at the buttons on her pants and pulling them down to her ankles. He forced her unresisting legs apart with one knee; while at the same time he dragged his own trousers down to release his throbbing erection.

Don't, baby. Not here. Not now. It isn't right.

He wept into her throat, thrusting his dwindling cock against her. Its softening tip entered her ice-cold navel, and then slid down against the roughened skin to probe her knotted pubic thatch. He reached down to guide himself inside, almost snapping her spine with his ardour. Rubbing at her to sustain the moment, he suddenly felt something writhe wetly against his fingers... he pulled them away and lifted his hand to his face, amazed that he'd encountered moisture.

Maggots curled around his fingers, fattened on the corruption at his wife's core, their lazy white bodies falling from his knuckles and landing on her chest, where they coiled sleepily.

Sally's covered mouth nuzzled at his chest, her ineffectual jaws trying to clamp down on his flesh.

"Nooooo!" he lurched to his feet, pulling up his trousers, and lashed out at the table behind him. The wine bottle shattered, slashing the skin of the world, and suddenly he became aware of what he had been in the process of becoming – a rapist of the dead.

"Aaaaargh!" The sounds he made were barely even human, just empty noises.

He fell to his knees, pounding his fists on the floor, and heard sharply and clearly the final strand of his sanity as it snapped with a loud thunderclap. That internal wind returned, this time haunted by the moans of the deceased.

Then he was still. The earth spun beneath him, continuing its rapid journey towards oblivion, but Rick was a statue, a man frozen in one moment forever – however long that might be.

Sally was motionless, her bare legs bruised and blackened, the skin ruptured in several places and white maggots boiling forth. Her white-wrapped head seemed incongruous, like some kind of allegory for a reality that was now far beyond Rick's grasping hands.

Her head moved from side to side. He could see the shape of her mouth under the wrappings, and yet again she was attempting to clamp them down onto something... to feed.

Hungry.

He stood, stared at her damaged body. "You want something to eat?" He was snarling now, leaving his old self far behind at the side of a road, a track which could only lead deep inside the darkness that sat at his centre. "You want some fucking *food*?"

He shrugged on his jacket and stalked outside, heading towards the barn. The moon hung suspended, like a cheap prop in a bad movie, and beneath its chill light he passed into the dense shadow cast by the barn.

Rohmer would have wanted to be of use; he would have hated his body to have gone to waste, rotting in a quiet corner of an empty barn.

Rick crossed the space and grabbed an axe from its place near a pile of chopped timbers. Its weight was a comfort in his hands, promising the nullifying emptiness of manual labour. He turned, walked towards Rohmer's cooling corpse.

The body was already stiff, but there was plenty of meat on it.

CHAPTER THIRTY-TWO

*hungryhungryhungryhungryhungryhungryhungryhungry
hungryhungryhungryhungryhungryhungryhungryhungryhungry
hungryhungryhungryhungryhungryhungryhungryhungryhungry
hungryhungryhungryhungryhungryhungryhungryhungryhungry
hungryhungryhungryhungryhungryhungryhungryhungryhungry
hungryhungryhungryhungryhungryhungryhungryhungryhungry
hungryhungry*

CHAPTER THIRTY-THREE

After what seemed like hours but was in reality a much shorter span of time, Rick left the barn and returned to the dismal moonlight.

He felt exposed.

His hands were bloody and he was carrying an old sack he had found hanging from a nail on the wall. The sack had originally contained a few pieces of rusted engine – random machine parts perhaps meant for the scrap yard – which he'd emptied out onto the ground. Now it contained only meat.

Faceless, nameless meat.

Back in the cottage he sat Sally on the sofa and once again removed the bandages from her tattered head, then placed the resultant white snake on the floor at her feet.

So much had changed between them but he and Sally had never been closer. He recalled the man he used to be with fondness, and truly waved goodbye to the past. Those were different people, the ones who had lived in a nice apartment and went to normal jobs.

The people they were now would not even recognise themselves in the shabby meat puppets who had gone before.

The ghost of himself passed quietly from view, head down, hands open... he stared at Sally with fondness; her slashed features, the maggots that writhed in her bloodless wounds, the alien hunger that drove her.

Things were different. *They* were different. He loved his new wife in a way that he would not have been able to imagine as little as a few days before.

Very carefully he took the wadded cotton wool from her mouth, pulling it out of her throat like some huge mutated eel or giant maggot – the larger brother or sister of the ones he'd found between her thighs.

The cotton wool was now densely compacted, and it had absorbed whatever moisture had remained in Sally's throat after her death. When it was removed, the throat closed up over the absence; it made a faint sucking sound, like a vacuum.

Rick got a knife from the kitchen – the sharpest he could find – and cut Rohmer's meat into strips. He also found a tool box in there, so he brought it through, a rough plan forming in the fractured landscape of his mind.

Then, carefully, and without tears, he dropped the strips into Sally's open mouth, forcing it down the unnaturally tightened cavity of her throat with the handle of the knife. After a few scraps had passed along her throat and the swollen, dead muscles relaxed a little, he was able to simply scoop the meat into her mouth.

It reminded him of a nature programme he'd once seen, where a mother bird dropped bits of food into the upturned beaks of her brood.

Despite the morphine, Sally's jaws worked well enough to snatch at the slivers of flesh.

Rick kept his hands well out of the way, mindful that she did not snap off the end of a finger or thumb. Hideously, her yellow teeth began to crack when they came together, the force of her jaws too strong for the thin pieces of meat to fully absorb, and the jagged shards which remained looked lethal as tiny daggers.

After Sally had taken her fill he smashed out the rest of her teeth with a hammer.

CHAPTER THIRTY-FOUR

heat meat hurts good light dawn sparkling full ease good good mine good god good red wet meat god content

PART FOUR

And All Is Meat

Is not the life more than meat, and the body than raiment?

Luke 12:23

CHAPTER THIRTY-FIVE

It was the fire that woke Daryl, or at least the reflection of it behind his closed eyelids. He stirred, bringing up his arms and feeling like he was restrained somehow, as if someone had tied him up while he dozed.

His limbs ached. The air was freezing; the chill had slipped between his layers of clothing to caress his skin and cool his blood. It was dark, daylight was still a couple of hours away.

He was sitting within the desiccated branches of a stout bush, half-hidden by the grasping twigs and the thickened roots showing above the soil. For some reason he'd felt the spot was a good vantage point – like a hide used by birdwatchers – and had positioned himself there hours ago.

The fire flickered in the distance, catching his attention from behind the trees on the other size of the canal. Because of his elevated position, he could clearly see the cottage and the two vehicles parked outside. One, he knew, was the ex-army jeep that had been stored in one of the outbuildings. He'd watched

Nutman drive it into the open during the night, scrutinising him through the binoculars. The man had looked intense as he worked; his face a mask of concentration, his hands steady as he manoeuvred the jeep across the uneven ground.

Nutman had spent a few moments looking up at the dark sky before returning inside, and the look on his face had been unreadable. Daryl had been unable to work out if it was fear or longing or both...

Not long after that, Daryl must have fallen asleep.

He watched the flames as they licked at the side of the barn, clasping the structure from beneath like a giant demonic hand. Nutman stood nearby, staring at the conflagration. Daryl raised the binoculars and examined him close-up; his eyes were like stones in his unmoving face.

Daryl wondered if the man had finally lost his mind.

"Join the fucking club," he said, easing his arse off a particularly tough root.

He used the binoculars to glance along the edge of the canal, a few miles east of where Nutman was setting fire to the outbuildings. Off in the distance, a group of dead people wandered in a field. He watched, fascinated, as they pulled apart an old scarecrow, as if thinking it might contain some meat. One of the group was not much more than a skeleton with drapes of flesh hanging from its bones; the rest were in good condition, apart from the usual bloodless bite marks, death-wounds and missing bits and pieces. One of them sported gunshots; large holes peppered its torso and half the biceps on its right arm had been vaporised.

It was fascinating. No matter how they died, they came back... unless, of course, that death involved destruction of the brain. Otherwise they returned, picking themselves up and running, shambling, even crawling across the landscape in search of prey. Daryl mused about their hunger for human flesh. Just why did they need to consume human meat? Was there something in the warm flesh, or maybe in the fresh blood, that eased the pain of being dead – or was it simply a natural desire, repressed by eons of evolution, which awoke after these things were revived?

So many questions... and Daryl doubted that anyone had an answer. Not the absent media, the surviving dregs of the government, or whatever doctors and scientists had managed to escape to secret think-tanks buried under the streets of the major cities.

All we have is faith. That was something Mother had always believed in, even near the end. She swore that society was constantly on the brink of coming apart, and rather than rely upon politicians or scientists we should all be putting our faith in God.

Daryl thought she might have had a point. Not about God – no, he could never believe in that bullshit. But perhaps her ideas regarding faith were pretty much correct. When everything else slips away, and the world becomes a battleground of the dead, faith is all that remains: faith in oneself, faith that good will triumph, and enough faith that before your end arrives you'll have one bullet left to put in your brain.

Faith.

The fire had almost consumed the barn when he swung the binoculars back in the direction of the cottage. Nutman was nowhere in sight.

Daryl struggled to his feet and crossed the dirt to the moped. He could barely believe that such a ridiculous vehicle had served him so well. He'd had ample opportunities to trade it for something bigger and better – a real motorcycle, or a fast car – but for some reason he'd kept the moped. It seemed fitting somehow that the world's greatest serial killer, the only man ever to kill the same woman twice, should possess such an idiosyncratic chariot.

"Hello?"

Daryl tensed at the sound of the voice behind him. Then, taking a breath, he continued fastening his bag to the moped.

"Oh, God. I'm so glad to see you..."

He slowly turned, pasting a smile onto his face, and confronted the owner of the voice.

A tall man stood there, framed by the distant flames and the black smoke. He was slim, narrow of build, and was leaning on a thick branch to support his weight. Daryl glanced at the man's leg and saw that it was strapped up with rags, probably broken by the look if it.

"I never thought I'd see another... well, living person again. Everyone's gone, out of the city and into the countryside. I haven't seen a live one for at least two days." The man was smiling. He seemed on the verge of genuine joy.

"Where have you come from?" Daryl took a step forward, keeping his hands behind his back.

"Leeds," said the man, stumbling forward a few steps. "The whole place has crumbled. Buildings on fire, looters running wild, what few police left on the streets killing people on sight. By the time I got out of there, there was hardly anyone normal left. Just dead people and crazy coppers. It's carnage." His eyes were wide and wild; his teeth were black and his lips split and swollen.

"I'm Daryl."

"Alan. Alan Harley. It really is good to meet you, Daryl. I had some trouble about a mile back, came off my bike when I ran into some of those dead bastards in the road. They nearly got me..." he glanced at his leg. "It smashed when I hit the deck. Hurt like hell, but still I managed to get up and run."

Daryl nodded, pretending that he was interested. Then, swiftly, he brought out the camera from behind his back.

"I'm making a sort of documentary, Alan. Filming people I meet; capturing their stories in digital media. It might be useful once everything goes back to normal. A kind of document of events from ground level."

"Uh-huh." Alan did not look convinced. He was too tired to even attempt to hide his frown.

"Care to participate?" Daryl switched on the camera and began to circle Alan, viewing him through the lens. Everything looked different through the lens: it looked better than reality.

"I... I'm not sure, Daryl. I mean, isn't this a little crazy? I kind of need some help here, you know."

"Oh," said Daryl, lowering the camera. "I see. You don't want to play."

Alan's confused smile hung on his lips; his eyes were wet.

Daryl took the gun from the waistband of his trousers, bringing it around to point the barrel at Alan. The other man did not at first register the weapon, and then when he finally saw it he sighed heavily. That was all: just a sigh.

"Goodbye, Alan." Daryl pulled the trigger. The first shot missed its target, pinging off into the air somewhere to Alan's left. Alan stupidly turned his head to follow the round, as if trying to catch sight of it in mid flight.

Daryl pulled the trigger again.

This time blood spattered from Alan's left arm, high up near the shoulder. The man pitched backwards, his balance lost.

The third shot caught him in the face, smashing his nose and cheekbones and turning the grey air around his head a bright powdery red.

Daryl did not even watch him fall.

He returned his attention to the burning barn, filming it with the camera. Soon Nutman came out of the cottage, carrying the young girl in his arms. He held her close to his chest, like a baby, and stared into her upturned face. It took him several minutes to lay her down in the rear of the jeep and cover her with blankets. Then, after reaching down to muss her hair, he turned back and once again entered the cottage.

This time he was carrying Sally. Her bandaged head looked bright white in the darkness and her limbs hung stiffly as he carried her to the vehicle. He placed her in the passenger seat, pressing her legs into the foot well.

Daryl alternated between camera and binoculars, caught between viewing and filming.

Nutman watched the blaze for a little while longer and then climbed into the jeep. The rear tyres spat up dust as he drove away.

Daryl turned around to climb aboard the moped, and was mildly shocked to see Alan standing behind him, his shattered nose not much more than a hole in the centre of his face.

"Oh, my," he said, aware how stupid that sounded. "My, oh my. What do we have here, then?"

Alan opened his mouth and bared his blackened teeth. He

hissed like a cat; spittle erupted into the air. His eyeballs were red, filled with blood from the damage, and Daryl was fascinated by the aura of menace the corpse wore.

"Come on, then. Let's be having you." He felt no fear. All that was well behind him now, back in his old life; fear had died with Mother, and any lingering traces which may have been left behind had gone with Claire into that pit under the dilapidated power station.

Daryl was now a man without fear, a breed apart from other men.

Alan sidestepped, then lumbered forward. If it were not for the broken leg, he would have moved a lot faster: freshly dead, with no damage to his brain, he should have been quick and nimble. The shattered limb meant that Daryl had time to watch.

He lifted the camera to his eye and did just that, grinning at the silly dead bastard. "Action!" he said, trying not to laugh.

Alan pushed off his back leg, lurching towards Daryl. His hands were quick, and his jaws snapped at the air. Daryl jumped to the side and jogged around his attacker, entertained by the developing scenario.

He continued this mad dance for a few minutes, but soon grew bored. Alan slashed at the air with his hands, moaned and made other decidedly inhuman sounds, and continued to fail at every attempt to capture Daryl.

The dead man was teaching Daryl nothing; all he demonstrated was that once a human being was dead whatever intelligence he or she had possessed simply left the scene. These things were like idiot animals, absurd creatures existing only to feed. They had no reasoning, no sense of the world around them. They were simply eating machines.

"God, you dead people are dumb. It's all very disappointing." He pointed the gun and pulled the trigger. There was no boom or recoil; either the gun was jammed or it had run out of ammunition. Daryl knew absolutely nothing about firearms, so made no attempt to examine the weapon. Instead he threw it to the ground, annoyed and impatient.

"Fucking hell! You are bothersome, aren't you, Alan?"

He moved in close, dodging Alan's clutching hands, and kicked the broken leg out from under the corpse. Alan fell to the ground, his red eyes wide and panicked. He clawed at the earth, grabbed at bushes and the bases of trees.

Daryl looked around, and when his gaze fell upon a long stick with a pointed end, he smiled.

"This shouldn't take long," he said, and moved in for the kill.

He stabbed Alan through the right eye and twisted the branch as it went in, grinding it thorough the gristle and deep into the brain. Alan's hands stopped clutching; his jaw dropped open; his eyes sunk into their sockets. The pointed end of the stick penetrated Alan's skull, emerging out of the back to sink into the soil. Daryl leaned on it, pressing it down until he was bent over at the waist. Alan's mouth snapped open and closed like the beak of a demented turtle.

Daryl left the corpse and climbed onto the moped, lamenting the loss of the handgun. He had not had anywhere near enough fun with it. Perhaps he'd get lucky and come across another; next time he might even stumble across something bigger. If he'd been thinking straight back at the power station, he could have taken the rest of the guns. But it was too late now to regret the omission. He could never go back, only keep moving forward and into the third act of the motion picture of his life.

He patted the bag, feeling the bulge of the camera through a side pocket.

Then he started the moped and headed east, towards the coast. He had worked out by now that must be where Nutman was heading. It was a good idea: most other people seemed to be going in-country, trying for the woods and the open fields. The coast was a sensible option; it presented opportunities for crossing the ocean, if suitable passage could be found.

He thought of Alan as he rode towards the rising sun. What a pathetic excuse for a being. Even the dead, it seemed, were useless. Daryl had briefly hoped for more – that they might exhibit more potential than the living. But that was not to be. Meat was meat and dead was dead boring.

His story was the only interesting one left; all it lacked was an appreciative audience.

He hit the road and kept an eye out for danger, expecting attackers from all sides. Empty cars littered the roads, bodies were scattered here and there, a lot of them partially eaten. Smears of red marked the blacktop.

Daryl stopped at a petrol station and filled the moped's tank to the brim. He also filled two plastic containers and strapped them to the side of the vehicle. This was one reason he should have upgraded to a bigger machine: the moped hardly held much fuel, and if he failed to keep an eye on the level he risked being stranded.

He passed a family laid out neatly in the road – mother, father, son, daughter, their bellies opened and cleaned out, their faces gnawed off, their limbs stripped clean. It struck him as odd that their positioning was so tidy. Rather than sprawling like broken dolls, their corpses were set in a row, each facing the same way.

Beyond the disturbing familial frieze, a small roadside house was in flames. Daryl stopped the moped to watch it burn, and he was perversely pleased to hear the windows shatter and pop from the intensity of the heat. The fire must not have been going for long.

A naked woman ran out of the front door, her hair aflame. Her hands were raised above her kindling head, clutching at the heavens, and as she ran by him she did not even notice Daryl. She passed by so close that he could feel the heat of the flames and smell her burning hair. Her screams were thrilling, a polymorphous perversion.

The woman made it a few hundred yards along the road before she went down, thrashing at the asphalt with her fists. Eventually she grew still. Then, after something like five minutes, she calmly stood up and kept walking in the same direction, hair smouldering, the skin of her neck and back blackened from the flames.

The time between life and death was but a fraction, a sliver; a journey so brief that it was barely consequential. Daryl wondered if she had remained sentient as she had passed between states, or if the transformation had been like a switch first flicking off and then turning on again, but with something missing.

"What are you?" he whispered, awed by the sight. He watched the woman as she padded into the distance, vanishing over the brow of a hill. The molten flesh on her shoulders had looked like a shawl.

Was she still alive in some way or truly dead? What powered these corpses when they returned? He refused to believe in the fairytale of the soul, but could think of no alternative theory.

Mind. Body. Soul. Surely they were all the same thing; and the living brain was a filter for the body's interaction with the world in which it existed. The human machine, as Daryl had come to understand it, was a combination of all these elements, and they were merely a function of the body reacting in and to the world.

But what did that theory mean when you applied it to the walking dead?

"What are we?"

Nothing answered. So he rode on, perplexed by his own inadequacies and his inability to understand the subtleties of this damned entertaining apocalypse.

Daryl journeyed through a landscape that Mother might have referred to as hell: small villages and towns either taken over completely by the dead or populated by only a handful of survivors, the rest having fled to the imagined safety of the countryside. He passed wan faces at boarded windows, peering out through narrow gaps and pleading for aid.

If this *were* a movie, he thought these images might be part of some lengthy slow-motion montage. Classical music playing on the soundtrack. The dead plodding through empty streets, looking up as he motored by, reaching out for him...

He saw the occasional police or army vehicle, usually parked at the kerb or pulled up on the verge. None of the officials he caught sight of looked sane; each of them had a look in their eyes that was a glimpse of madness. He passed through unmolested. The atrocities being committed – people dragged out of burning houses, the dead used as target practice, women and children raped on the front lawns of country houses – were enough to keep these bastions of a dying civilisation busy for now.

Daryl knew that if he ever stopped at one of these places he would become a victim, just like all those others he saw kneeling before uniformed madmen, screaming at the sky, or staring blankly at the moped as he roared through the epicentre of their agony.

Often he raised the camera to one eye as he rode, logging countless images of bloodshed: a pack of dead men and women bringing down and tearing apart a small boy; two men in uniform raping a teenage girl while a uniformed woman leaned across the bonnet of a police car smoking a joint; a dead schoolgirl, still dressed in her pleated skirt and blazer, walking along the footpath holding onto a severed head by its hair.

None of this stirred him; it did not move him at all. Daryl remained intrigued yet distant. It was all background to his story, secondary characters crossing the scene. He was the focus.

Then, after what seemed like years of travel, he began to near the coast. Seagulls flew overhead, the salty air stung his nostrils, the horizon flattened out and turned a shade of grey which held a sullen dash of blue.

Figures moved in the fields to his left and right, their ragged silhouettes giving away nothing about their state. Alive or dead, it didn't really matter, not to Daryl. He had begun to realise that everyone was dead; it was simply a question of how far along the process each individual was. A line from an old song crossed his mind: born to die. Yes, that was exactly the truth of the human condition.

Humanity was a dead species, a race born into instant obsolescence. Only those who stepped to one side and abandoned the herd were ever truly alive. Men like the killers Daryl had once idolised and now only looked upon with a form of pity, as even they had not completely realised the essence of what it is to live, to be alive, to exist.

Daryl was the first of a new breed. Once he had killed Sally Nutman for the second time, he could accept his crown and rule as king of the dead. His entire life had been but a preamble to that moment, every step along the way bringing him closer to what he had always been meant to do.

The sun glimmered behind a sheet of grey. The flat fields stretched into forever. Daryl roared ahead into a world he was busy recreating with every mile he travelled, every piece of black road that unfurled before him.

It was a world of infinite possibilities.

CHAPTER THIRTY-SIX

Rick no longer felt like himself. It was a strange sensation, but not an unpleasant one. People spent small fortunes on drugs, alcohol and new age religions to achieve the same thing. All it had cost him was the world.

He'd driven all day, across and up, always parallel with the sea, keeping a few miles away from the coast as they headed in a north-easterly direction, towards Northumberland.

Rohmer's directions, given during the memorable boat trip along the canal, had proven sound. Rick had kept away from the larger towns and cities, hugging the jagged coastline as they skirted places he'd never before heard of, and soon began to notice road signs for Sea Houses, the place Rohmer had told him to head for.

A lot of the small towns and villages they passed through were deserted. Burning buildings, broken windows, abandoned dreams. Relics of a now dead age littered the streets and footpaths: images like snapshots; of a child's bike, a school blackboard, scrawled with obscenities, a burned and blackened sofa, a row of stuffed toys lined up outside a house with shattered windows.

The dead roamed in the ashes of this dying way of life, feeding off scraps and hunting down stragglers. Rick had not stopped to help anyone; his focus remained on the road ahead, and the promise of a perhaps fictitious sanctuary.

Now it was dark again, and Rick was exhausted. He had not slept well last night. After the failed seduction, he had lain awake staring at the ceiling, listening to Sally's subtle movements in the dark. He had not dared sleep next to her and had instead lain on the floor beside the sofa. She was always within touching distance; he had reached out several times in the dark just to feel her cold skin against the back of his hand.

Rick couldn't remember the last time he'd eaten. He was surviving on a combination of whisky and adrenalin.

Not long now, he thought. *Then I can finally rest.*

He was surprised at how easy it was to continue the myth, to keep believing that Rohmer's island was the answer to everything. He supposed that when the alternatives are unthinkable, any scrap of faith is worth clinging to. He had never believed it in the past, but now he was certain that faith was the only thing that could save whatever was left of humanity.

He prodded the camp fire with a stick, turning the embers and sparking fresh flames. It was a smaller version of the blaze he'd started back at the cottage, the one which had served as Rohmer's funeral pyre. He was sure the old man would have appreciated it.

The camp was in the middle of a small grassed roundabout. Rick had lain out blankets and built the fire. He was more comfortable out here in the open as it would allow him to see anyone who wandered by, both the living and the dead. After the cottage and what had happened there, he wasn't quite ready to be crowded in, blocked on all sides. Open air was better, it felt freer, less restrictive.

Tabby sat at his side, unmoving, and stared at a point beyond the fire. She had said nothing since her grandfather's death; nor had she moved very much, apart from when Rick had coerced her into some kind of action. She was limp and unresponsive: it was a classic symptom of shock fatigue. Rick had seen this all before, out in the field, but still it unnerved him.

They weren't very different right now, his dead wife and his surrogate daughter. Neither of them spoke, and each had their own strange hunger.

The sky was black and starless, with thin clouds hovering overhead. The transition between day and night had been almost seamless. The only significant alteration was that the shadows had become longer before vanishing, and the moon was a segment of the pale circle the sun had been.

We'll be fine when we get there.

Rick smiled. "I know we will. It will all be different then."

They'll cure me. We can start again.

They. It was always *They*. Whenever things went wrong, or when people needed someone to blame, they called out to the mythical They: *They* put a hole in the ozone layer; *They* started the War on Terror; *They* put the chemicals in our food; *They* destroyed the environment; *They* brought the dead back to kill us.

"We did it," he whispered, once more stoking the fire. "*We* fucking did it all."

He looked up at the sky, peering into the blackness. He couldn't remember the last time he'd seen a plane, or a police helicopter. Back on the road he'd passed various groups of refugees, both large and small, and none of them seemed to have any idea what the powers-that-be were doing to solve things. For all anyone knew, there were no powers left; the government were all dead and roaming around Westminster looking for people to devour. Just as they'd done all along, but in a less literal manner.

Among the people he had seen on the road, one or two of them had even mentioned the island. He hadn't stopped to talk to anyone for long, but had felt compelled to pass a few words with the occasional stranger, if only to pretend he still had a link to the remains of a crumbling society.

One man had spoken of a small island in the Outer Hebrides.

An old woman had told him of a land mass located off the

coast of Ireland.

Two children – a boy and a girl – had passed on the story of a supposed sanctuary on the Isle of Dogs, in London.

It was like the old game, Chinese Whispers, where the truth was mauled in the passing of information. Each time the tale was told, it was altered: parts were added or taken away, even changed completely to fit the world view of the teller.

The island was an urban legend, a story that might be told forever, by dirty survivors huddled around dwindling campfires; a modern myth sent down the generations to comfort those as yet unborn. Santa Claus. Jesus Christ. Rohmer's Island.

Rick smiled, and the expression felt funny, like it didn't belong. He was no longer used to smiling...

"I know she's dead."

Rick twitched in shock when the girl spoke. It had been so long since he'd heard her voice that he had almost forgotten what it sounded like.

"What do you mean, love?" He was afraid to turn and look at her in case it made her lapse back into silence, so he stared ahead at the flames, making mental pictures in their midst.

"Your wife. She's dead. I've known all along."

Rick closed his eyes. When he opened them again his vision was blurred, as if he was crying... but there were no more tears left in his body. "Why didn't you say?"

"Because I liked you. We liked you, Granddad and me. We both knew that she was dead, but we just let you get on with it. We had no right to judge you."

"Well, I'll be damned." His amazement was not directed at what the girl had said, but at the tears now rolling down his cheeks. It seemed that there were some left after all, and they had arrived in abundance.

"I'm sorry." Only now did he turn to face her.

The side of her face was bathed in firelight; her eyes were wide, expressive, but he could not decipher what secrets they held. "It's okay."

"No it isn't. I should never have lied to you. Not to you..."

But she said no more, and it was dark and it was cold and the heavens were empty of everything but the suggestion of a deeper darkness, an empty void that even now was curling around the edges of the sky, threatening to swallow it all.

She's lovely. Our daughter. The one we can never have. I'm glad I haven't been able to get to her. To eat her.

Rick felt like screaming, but he bit down on his tongue, keeping it all inside. The darkness he'd been aware of only moments before hovered, poised on the brink of complete destruction, and then slowly receded, going away for now, yet more than capable of returning at any time. His illusion was so fragile; none of this was ever meant to last.

He stood and crossed the roundabout, the M16 in his hand. The roundabout was located at the top of a rise, which was why he'd chosen it. An elevated position was always easier to defend: you could see whoever was approaching a long time before they announced themselves, and taking the high ground was difficult when it was already occupied.

He thought again of missions in Iraq and Afghanistan. Old friends screamed inside his head, their long-dead voices struggling to be heard amid the uproar. No words made it through, it was just so much mental white noise.

"I'm going to secure the perimeter." He marched across the road and into the trees, heading towards the open land beyond. Sounds were muted; the air was thick and pregnant with expectation. Rick's senses became attuned and he heard the struggling of night creatures through the landscape: their constant endeavours for survival never ceased, despite the state of the humans who thought that they ruled over the earth.

But that imagined rule was about to end.

Beyond the grove of trees he came to a clearing that allowed him to look down into a valley. There was a shopping centre located at the base of the valley – large prefabricated sheds containing rows and aisles of foodstuffs and clothing and every other kind of knick-knack everyone had thought they needed; the separate components that together were meant to construct a happy life.

The mall was surrounded by scores of the dead. They stood in unmoving rows, circling the buildings, following some instinct that had brought them here to the places they once haunted when they were alive. The place was far enough away that Rick had no fear he would be seen, yet still he stayed back in the shadows, cupping his hands to his eyes to examine the pathetic scene.

The dead had returned to their old stomping grounds: shops, supermarkets, city centres. That explained why huge swathes of the countryside remained clear of their presence. They had begun to mass in the only places they could remember, the churches of capitalism, the prayer grounds of a lost world.

He heard the sound of distant gunshots. Someone must be hiding out in the shopping centre, thinking it a good place to sit out a siege. There would be plenty of food there, and all the things they had ever wanted before the world went tits-up. It was what Rick's generation had been taught all along: there is comfort in stuff, safety in the pursuit of objects. This was the living end of that empty philosophy, and Rick pitied the fools who had believed it right up until the last cash register had rung up its final sale.

He watched the dead as they swayed in place, moving to some unheard rhythm. They stood facing the shopping centre, most of them simply standing and staring. When Rick concentrated, he could hear the sound of their moaning: it was a sad song, a lament for everything that had been lost.

He turned away, feeling emptier than before.

Trudging back to the camp, he wrestled with the thoughts he had experienced when he'd watched them, grouping together for the World's-end Sale, the Last Great Shopping Spree of the Century.

Sally had not moved when he got back to the camp, but Tabby was now lying down, perhaps even sleeping. He hoped that she was at least getting some rest. All of this had been so hard on the girl – first she had lost her parents, and then the old man. Rick was all she had left, and even he was uncertain how much he could do for her or how long he might be around.

He heard the sound through his babble of thoughts: a low

stuttering roar, like bees swarming around a hive.

Rick turned quickly and dropped to his knees, shouldering the rifle and looking along its sight.

A small moped struggled up the hill, heading towards the roundabout. A scrawny man sat astride the machine, leaning into the climb. The bike was festooned with bags and plastic containers, which probably contained food and fuel. Rick could make out no heavy artillery either on the bike's frame or strapped to the man.

He stood, but did not lower the rifle.

The moped halted a hundred yards away. The rider sat staring at Rick, and at this distance he could not make out the stranger's face. The man raised a hand in greeting, then he turned off the little engine. The silence filled the space between them, pouring in like flood water into an open grave.

Rick kept his sights on the man.

The figure climbed off the bike and started to walk towards the roundabout, his hands held out from his body. He had a rather feminine-looking bag on his back, the straps hanging loose at his shoulders, and unless he was mistaken the kid was wearing an ill-fitting pair of women's leather gloves. As the visitor drew closer, Rick could see that he was smiling, but the expression didn't seem to fit his face. It was sickly, like something painted on in haste.

"Hello. I'm unarmed." His voice was slightly high; he sounded like a small boy rather than a fully-grown man.

Rick kept the rifle on him, not ready to trust anyone, even a seemingly harmless young man with a girl's rucksack on his back.

"I'm alive... not one of those dead things. I've travelled a long way. I could do with some company, if that's okay by you."

There was something off about the kid, a certain insincerity that niggled at Rick's keen combat senses. None the less, he lowered the rifle slightly, nodded.

"Thank you. I'm saddle-sore from that thing. If I could just rest for a while by your fire, I'd be grateful."

"Come on up," said Rick, finally dropping the gun. He took his finger off the trigger and let the weapon hang at his side. "I have some hot tea if you'd like. A few biscuits."

The kid clambered up the side of the raised roundabout, his thin arms and legs scurrying for purchase on the soft ground. "Thanks. That would be wonderful."

They stood not quite face-to-face; Rick was at least three or four inches taller than the younger man and so much broader at the shoulders. If the little fucker meant trouble, he figured that he could overcome him in seconds.

"My name's Daryl," said the kid, sticking out a small hand.

Rick shook the hand, feeling briefly like he was missing something, some vital element that he needed to complete the picture. "Rick. You're welcome here, in our camp."

"What happened to them?" Daryl tiled his head towards Sally and Tabby. His eyes shone, but Rick thought it was just the reflection of the camp fire flames.

"My wife was badly burned. Our daughter is in shock. We were attacked yesterday and her grandfather was killed. I had to deal with him; make sure he didn't come back." Rick walked towards the fire and made sure that he positioned himself between Daryl and the girls.

Daryl nodded. He obviously had his own story, and Rick thought that everyone's tale would be much the same: dead friends and relatives, lost loves, abandoned homes and lives.

"You look like you've been through some stuff yourself, Daryl." He lifted the tin pot from the fire and poured some tea into battered mugs.

"Yes. I used to live with someone. She died and came back. Just like you, I was forced to deal with her." He stared into the flames, his eyes empty and reflecting only the brightness from the fire.

Rick felt that the kid was leaving something out of his brief account. It wasn't a problem, but the whole thing rung false somehow. He was sure that what he was being told was the truth, but with certain elements excised, or perhaps altered for public consumption. There was something about this Daryl... something unpleasant. He didn't come across as a complete person; for some reason, the kid seemed more like an actor playing a part. He said all the right things, paused in all the right places, but it was all too studied, as if he were striving for an effect rather than being open and natural.

They sipped their tea in silence. It was too hot and too weak; there was no milk or sugar. The sky felt like a vast canyon yawning above them, as if everything had been turned on its head and somewhere up there was the earth. The effect was disorientating, and Rick tried not to dwell on it.

A breeze moved through the foliage at the side of the road, ruffling the tops of trees and disturbing the night birds. Something cried, far off and moving away from them; from somewhere inland came the muted sound of a single scream. Rick looked in the direction of the sound, but he knew that the awful cry was being carried on the wind, and whoever had made it was perhaps miles away.

Daryl did not even glance away from the fire.

Send him away, baby. I don't like him. He isn't right.

Rick tried to ignore Sally, but as usual her voice cut right through his brain and into his very core.

He wants to hurt us.

How could she know that? On the surface, the kid was harmless: a skinny little runt in search of some company. But underneath the performance, at the heart of the matter, he might be very dangerous indeed. Long ago Rick had learned never to trust the image a person was attempting to portray. Initial instincts were usually correct; whatever you felt about a person within the first five minutes of meeting them was all too often close to the mark. In the field you learned to read people fast or you died... it really was that simple.

What he read in Daryl was an empty page, a space waiting to be filled. There was no real person here, just the reflection of how he thought a real person should act. In the silence that hung between them there was an absence; rather than a companionable lull, this was a shocking emptiness, a lack of contact at a fundamental level.

"I think you should go now." Rick grasped the rifle. He did not raise it, but he did enough to inform Daryl that he was ready to use it if necessary.

"But why? What have I done? Or is it something I failed to do?" The kid's eyes were stones, pieces of mineral stuck into a hunk of flesh. There was nothing behind them; no personality to tie everything together into a whole human being.

"Cut the fucking act and leave. Move or I'll take off your head." Rick stood, slipping his finger beneath the trigger guard.

Daryl finished his tea. It was still hot, but he took it in one large swallow. Then he stood and turned away without speaking, heading back towards his silly little moped. He climbed onto the bike, scratched the side of his face, and cocked his head like a dog. "I'll be seeing you," he said, and then before Rick could answer he fired up the engine and *put-putted* away, his back held straight this time and presenting the perfect target.

Rick raised the rifle and took a bead on that slim back. His finger tensed on the trigger.

Do it.

One round. That was all he needed. It was an easy shot.

Kill him, baby.

He blinked hard, aware of that white noise behind his eyes again. Then he lowered the rifle and went back to the fire, where he took some more of the weak tea and wondered what had held him in check. It would have meant nothing to have killed the kid; just another dead man among the many who now inhabited the world. Maybe that was why he hadn't done it. Perhaps the lack of meaning in the act had stayed his hand.

CHAPTER THIRTY-SEVEN

Daryl was experiencing a rush like he imagined a sky diver must feel. Adrenalin powered through his body, making his extremities tingle. His vision possessed a clarity which he could not quite believe and the moped bucked beneath him like a stallion as he roared towards the coast.

After returning down the hill he had doubled back, just to ensure that Nutman didn't realise he was being followed. But Daryl was no follower now; he was the leader.

He still could not believe that the policeman had left the maps in full view. Granted, that wasn't the reason why Daryl had approached him – it had been more of a personal dare, a test to see exactly how far he had come on his journey and how much he had changed from the fearful runt he had been before Mother's death had freed him.

No, the maps were an added bonus. All laid out at the fireside, with red pen marking the route. He'd probably seemed rather suspicious as he pretended to stare into the fire, all the while trying to peer at the maps, but that did not concern him. He did not plan to be face-to-face with Nutman again – not until he killed him, of course, prior to reclaiming the lovely Sally.

Sally. She had been so close – near enough to touch. To cut. To bludgeon.

God, how his mind raced. He went through a hundred different methods of killing her, each one more extreme than the last. He could kill her again and again, as long as he protected her brain.

He could even have killed her then, in front of the bastard she had married, his love rival.

But then had not been the right time. He must wait until he could take her with the minimum resistance from her dangerous husband; perhaps their destination would offer up the perfect opportunity.

The Farne Islands.

Daryl had even been there before, on a school trip years ago. As far he could recall the place was a bird sanctuary; the only people who stayed there were ornithologists who dedicated their lives to the study of certain breeds of wildfowl. He remembered a lot of terns, guillemots and puffins. Back then, the puffins had made him laugh, even when the school bullies had forced him out onto a rock ledge and left him stranded there.

He wondered what was there, why Nutman was heading for the sanctuary. Was it something to do with the old man – the girl's grandfather? It amused him that Nutman had referred to the girl as his daughter: he was either delusional or spinning a yarn to cover his tracks. But why would he even need to fabricate a cover story? He had no idea that he – or, more precisely, his wife – was being stalked.

The salt air grazed his nostrils as he approached the coast. The stench of rotting fish and seaweed accosted him as he swung into a tight curve and the sea finally lurched into view. The sky was huge and wide above the flat line of the sea; sea birds hovered far out, dipping towards the waves to pick at whatever scraps they could find floating on the surface.

Daryl grinned. He actually hated the sea, but it was worth

putting up with if it meant that he could spend time with Sally. If he could get to the island first and identify where they were going, he could prepare an ambush. Then it would be plain sailing – and he'd certainly intended the weak pun.

The air was harsh; the temperature was even lower here than it had been inland. There were no vessels out to sea; the expanse of faded blue water was empty, bereft of the boats or yachts or working ships which usually cluttered the horizon.

A few dead people roamed on the dull yellow sand, stumbling around like wind-up toys. One of them had wandered into the surf and fallen to his knees. He was unable to get back up because of the waves, which kept tugging him off balance as he attempted to right himself.

"Stupid," said Daryl, appalled at the sight. "Fucking stupid corpse."

He pushed the moped along the empty coast road, heading towards what appeared to be some kind of small private dock. There were boats anchored at a jetty – expensive looking crafts and smaller, cheaper working boats. He did not have the first idea how to sail, but it would come to him. He was capable of anything lately, even things he'd been afraid of in the past.

He stopped at a huge weather-worn National Trust sign that offered local information, climbing off the moped to inspect it close up. The sign gave brief details of all twenty-three separate Farne Islands, and listed all the endangered species – sea birds and seals – which made their homes there.

Daryl remembered walking across guano-spattered rocks as a child, afraid of the birds yet fascinated by their natural beauty. When he returned home and told Mother all about the trip, she'd claimed that God was present in places like these – His work evident in the birds and animals, even the tiny rocky islands themselves.

She had never missed an excuse to invoke the name of her lord. It was habitual, her way of coping with the world and of codifying everything within it.

According to Mother, everything was God's will, even the bad stuff. *Especially* the bad stuff. It was meant to test us, or so she said.

"God moves in mysterious ways, all right." He smiled, placed a hand on the large wooden sign, feeling a thrum of latent energy. Or did he just imagine that? He could no longer be sure.

Birds called out far above, their screeching voices a constant backdrop to the sound of the surf. White bird shit covered everything like spilled correction fluid: evidence of God's typist correcting the errors in the ongoing script of creation.

Daryl brandished the digital camera, taking a shot of the information sign, the unruly sea, the ugly beach... the scattered dead who walked there, unable to leave the sand, like machines stuck in grooves. Maybe they'd keep going until they ran out of steam, and then simply keel over and stop. Didn't sharks do that? Just keep on going until they stopped swimming, and when they did cease moving through the deeps, they just died on the spot.

Or was that another myth, a piece of misinformation?

Nothing was certain these days. Everything was in flux.

The idea of sharks seemed somehow fitting. The dead were like land sharks: eating machines, roaming across the earth and consuming anyone they encountered.

He got back on the moped and headed towards the jetty. There were a lot of spaces between vessels, probably caused by people frantically taking to the sea to find somewhere to wait out the apocalypse. Daryl imagined hundreds of them, sitting on small land masses, running out of supplies, trying to summon a voice on a failing radio set.

The damn fools. Did they not realise that it was all here for the taking?

Daryl strode along the timber boards, looking down past his feet at the gaps and the water beneath. The sound of water lapping at the rotting timber pilings was hypnotic. He glimpsed movement down there: darting shapes, sharp little waves caused by something shifting in the water...

So caught up was he in the water's weird movement that he failed to see the dead woman as she lunged at him from behind a boat. Just at the last minute, Daryl glanced up and managed to back away so that she caught hold of his jacket rather than his skin. She was quick, strong. The skin of her face hung in tattered strips from the bone of her skull and her tongue lolled snake-like from the black cavern of a mouth.

The woman's skin was waterlogged; it sagged on her bones. Her eyes had been mostly eaten by fish or seagulls and her reaching fingers flashed bone-white as they tightened around his collar. Her clothes were sodden, hanging heavily around her.

Daryl lashed out and caught her on the side of the head. She barely moved, just tightened her grip and shuffled towards him. He kept backing away, trying to keep his balance so that they did not pitch over into the water.

The dead woman made a hideous gurgling sound deep in her throat. That tongue flapped at her chin, far too long, the colour of raw liver.

"Get off!" He back-peddled furiously, terrified of losing his footing, yet desperate to be away from this ravenous creature. Her jaws snapped shut like steel pincers, severing the tongue. It slid down the woman's flattened chest and dropped to the timbers, where it slid off the edge and into the restless water like an eel returning to its natural habitat.

Then Daryl slipped. His feet got tangled up in a thick rope line, and he teetered backwards, grabbing the dead woman's forearms. He dragged her down with him, trying to turn so that she did not fall on top of him and pin him down. Timbers creaked; water lapped; the woman hissed again.

He saw the anchor as he fell, and acting quickly he somehow managed to twist so that the woman fell towards it. He pushed out, forcing her to the side, and was relieved when he felt her body shudder as it made contact with the metal anchor.

The top of the anchor pushed out of the centre of her chest, forcing apart ribs and sending a rush of stagnant water gurgling out of the wound. The stink was horrendous: dead fish, decayed matter.

The woman was pinned like a butterfly in an exhibit. She struggled madly, arms and legs pounding against the wooden jetty, but was held fast by the anchor.

Daryl got to his feet and shambled over to her, keeping his

distance. Her blind eyes turned upon him, and for a moment he was convinced that she could smell him – live meat.

He grabbed a boathook from a stand and held it poised above her. Then he brought the end of the hook down and drove it through her skull, just above the brow. The top of her head peeled back like an opened can, the skull cap splashing into the water below. Small crustaceans and silvery fish wriggled out of her head, the drowned remains of her brain following them down into the grubby waves lapping at the jetty supports.

He heard running footsteps, and when he glanced behind him he saw more dead people moving towards him. There were four of them, with a further group running up the beach to join the fun. Those closing in on him were in better condition that the woman he had despatched, but still they were repulsive. Missing limbs. Black, rotten flesh. Holes where faces should be.

Daryl turned away and jogged towards the nearest boat.

He moderated his breathing and controlled his heart rate; he felt like an athlete, in supreme control of his body and able to bend his physicality to his will. In the past a manoeuvre like the one he'd used on the dead woman – twisting and turning to slam her onto the anchor – would have been utterly beyond him, but now it was like second nature. A paradigm shift had occurred; Daryl had finally *become*. But what was it he had turned into? What exactly had hatched from the shell of his old life?

Finding out would be such fun...

The old Daryl would never have dreamed of even attempting to sail a craft, but the new Daryl carried it off with ease. Granted, it was a basic vessel, with only a small outboard motor to power it, but his body adjusted to the demands of the boat with an alarming speed. Daryl had the feel of the craft, became attuned to its gait in the water, within the first few moments of it cutting through the waves.

The dead stood at the edge of the jetty, bellowing as he left them behind. One of them dived into the water but did not resurface. He remembered a probably spurious statement he'd once read that stated dead things would not immediately float when dropped into fluid; instead they sank, their trapped internal gases dragging them to the bottom until they rose only much later.

He headed for the islands, which he could just about see in the rising gloom. They stood proud against the sky – a large group of dark silhouettes, their angles and edges sharp and inhospitable. They seemed huge. Daryl knew that each was actually a small limestone crag jutting like broken teeth out of the grey North Sea.

Daylight was now shuffling onto the scene, and within thirty minutes he expected to be able to see the ring of islands in all their glory. He could already make out the slashes of dark birds as they flew around the rocks, and the sound of their cries was carried to him across the surface of the water. Watching them, he could almost believe that nothing external had changed, that the only transformation was his and the rest of the world carried on as usual.

He guided the craft towards the group of islands, being careful not to fall foul of hidden rocks beneath the choppy waters. Soon he could make out the white shit-coated outcroppings, the many tiny hides dotted along the humped backs of the islands, and the occasional stone ruin, wooden shack or simple dwelling. He knew from the school trip that scientists conducted studies of the indigenous flora and fauna, and kept records of the birds, but was unsure if they actually stayed overnight on the islands or lived on shore and travelled out on the morning tide.

The sign back at the jetty had said something about Inner Farne – the central island of the group – having a lighthouse, a historic ruined chapel and some kind of visitor centre. There had been no mention of proper accommodation, but he would have bet that there was some kind of National Trust presence based on at least one of the more hospitable islands – a couple of wardens who passed their time diving and fishing.

Some of the islets apparently hid underwater at high tide; others were simply inaccessible, or so it looked. A red and white candy striped lighthouse caught his eye; stone dwellings perched on precarious ledges; the islands seemed to shift as he approached them, as if moving away from his gaze.

Daryl was just beginning to worry which island Nutman might be headed for when he saw the sign. Splashed across a thrusting pinnacle of rock face in bright red paint was a single word: *SANCTUARY.*

He knew that it meant more than the birds and the rare grey seals; this was an invitation, a message to inform all-comers that here was safety, and perhaps even answers to all the questions of the past few days. There were people here and they were trying to put things right, perhaps even seeking a cure to whatever had caused the mass reanimation of the dead. Maybe they had already found it.

Daryl would take great pleasure in destroying it all, burning it to the ground and pissing on the smouldering ashes.

He slowly turned the boat – amazed at his own rapidly developing skills – and brought the craft into a natural bay carved out of the bald rock face. The boat drifted in when he cut the engine, aiming straight for the area where the land fell to provide a low platform ideal for disembarking from a small craft.

A small flag fluttered in the breeze. It was attached to a pole wedged into the rock face.

The faded words printed on the tattered flag proclaimed: *Staple Island, Outer Farne. Population Zero.*

If it was some kind of joke, the humour was lost on Daryl.

Far above him, perched on the topmost edge of one of the frightening stacks of rock, he could see a ramshackle single-storey prefabricated hut. Its windows were boarded, but there were lights fixed under the eaves. Some of the lights – those which had not been shattered – were on; they bled sickly illumination down across the crap-stained crags to light his way to the heights.

The words on the flag must be lies.

It was almost as if he were expected.

"Somebody up there likes me," said Daryl, staring up at the sky, at the struggling sun and the threatening clouds. He imaged that he saw faces up there: long, gaunt, undead faces; leering grins and laughing mouths. They spoke to him, those hungry mouths, but he was unable to hear what they were saying... or perhaps they were simply chewing, consuming the lost souls from the sky, the ones that never quite made it to Mother's picture-book heaven.

The boat edged into shore and Daryl threw a line at the platform. He climbed from the boat and tied it up, making sure that it was unable to drift away, even if the wind got up and stormy weather tugged at it. He thought that he might stay here for a while, but he also wanted the option of escape. The new Daryl always had a back-up, a Plan B to utilise if everything else went wrong.

He trudged across the rocky ground, moving ever upwards, dodging wide slits and gullies as he climbed towards the bare, grassy plateau above.

Birds wheeled overhead but kept their distance. Even they knew not to annoy him. In his new incarnation, Daryl felt sure that if he wished he could simply pluck them from the sky and break them like so many miniature versions of Icarus having flown too close to his blazing radiance.

CHAPTER THIRTY-EIGHT

Rick watched the dead as they moved through the town, brushing up against the quaint stone buildings and bumping into each other as they paraded along the narrow cobbled streets. Sea Houses was the type of place tourists loved, sitting in a pretty bay and packed with B&B establishments and bric-a-brac shops. The dead looked incongruous against its quaint backdrop, like a turd in a flower bed.

Rick stared along the sight of the M16, wondering how the hell he was going to get a shell-shocked young girl and his dead morphine-addled wife to the sea front and into a boat without being brought down and torn apart. It was a conundrum he didn't really want to think about.

He let off a shot and a head exploded; another shot and a thin, pale face turned into a large red flower, blossoming quickly over a bone-white skull.

Picking off a number of walking corpses, he weighed up the odds.

The only plan that seemed like it might work was the most direct: he would simply drive through the bastards, mowing down however many stepped into his path. The jeep was long and low and compact, but it was a heavy vehicle with a big engine. As long as he kept his nerve, he could carve a path through the dead and make it to the bay ahead of them. They were like cows; not very bright, and one tended to blindly follow the other.

He was currently lying on the roof of the jeep, and when he stood he felt faint for a moment. The roof creaked beneath him, his boots dimpling the thin steel capsule. His head swam, the visions barely kept within it.

He leapt down and opened the passenger door. Sally was sitting in the seat, a seatbelt wrapped around her torso and her hands tied in front of her with a length of rope. The morphine had run out and he was afraid that she might get frisky, so had taken the extra precaution to ensure that if she broke free of the grip of the drug she couldn't get to him without first warning him of her intentions.

I promise I'll be good.

He shook his head. "I'm sorry, Sally. I can't take that chance. If it was just you and me, things would be different. But we have Tabby to think about now. We have responsibilities as adoptive parents."

She said nothing more.

Rick glanced at Tabby, who was lying on her side across the back seat. Her face was blank, devoid of anything approaching a readable expression; her wide eyes stared at nothing. There was no way he could manhandle these two down to a boat; his initial plan would have to suffice.

He stowed the rifle on the back seat, next to Tabby, and grabbed the Glock from the glove compartment, where he'd stashed it earlier. It was fully loaded. He was expecting a lot of resistance.

"Here we go." He climbed behind the wheel and gunned the engine. It sounded healthy, as if Rohmer had maintained it regularly. Every car Rick had ever owned had been falling to pieces, so it was nice to drive something someone had taken real care of – their pride and joy, something they appreciated. It was also a pity that he would have to wreck it by driving into dead people.

He pressed the accelerator, and then let out the clutch. The jeep darted forward, and Rick steered it along the picture-postcard streets of the small town, feeling not for the first time like this was all some weird dream, a surreal sleep episode from which he might soon awake.

He hit the first column sooner than he'd expected: a small group of them came stumbling around a corner and headed directly into the road.

The loose-limbed bodies made loud noises of impact; their dead weight slamming against the front bumper and bonnet caused shock waves to course along the length of the vehicle, which were then absorbed into the well-designed bodywork.

A woman stood and watched his rapid approach, her mouth hanging open in a perfect circle, eyes peering, hands grasping at empty air... her head left a red smudge as it slammed into the windscreen and her body skidded cleanly across the bonnet and into the gutter. He felt the bumpy motion of the rear wheels rolling over her flailing limbs.

Rick began to pretend that it was all an elaborate video game, a major new prototype he'd been asked to test. If he thought of it this way, he could almost have fun. The very fact that he did so reinforced his sense of losing his grip on reality. His mind had broken long ago, and the remnants of his sanity were now being blown away like dust in the wind.

"Fuckers." He spoke harshly, through gritted teeth. Another body rolled beneath the jeep, causing him to tighten his grip on the steering wheel as the vehicle lurched sideways.

Calm down, honey. Nearly there.

He resisted the urge to turn and gaze at Sally. She did not look at her best: the bandages had come loose near the bottom of her face, exposing a part of her chin. He caught movement out of his peripheral vision, and swallowed hard. The drug was wearing off now; she was flexing her dead muscles and limbering up to execute a sequence of stiff, awkward movements which might just culminate in her attacking him as he steered the jeep.

He had to get her on a boat quickly, if only to ensure that he could properly restrain her.

Tabby stirred on the back seat, mumbling something under her breath. It sounded like she said the word "love," but he couldn't be sure.

The rear wheels slid away from him as he turned sharply, the jeep drifting round to face the dead. More of them had now emerged from shop doorways, the broken windows of terraced houses, overgrown gardens and upturned trash containers outside deserted fish and chip shops. Some of them ran, others shuffled, and yet more half-jogged-half-fell in a pathetic facsimile of movement as they chased the car towards the sea.

He felt like a sardine in a can.

Rick pressed his foot down on the brake and fought to control the skid. Finally the vehicle stopped, and he wasted no time in jumping out, opening all the doors, and grabbing his bag and the M16 from the back seat. He already had his eye on a boat, and prayed to the God he now curiously believed in that it was fuelled and ready to go. He ran towards the small vessel, bent down and untied it from its moorings. It was a white schooner – tiny but with plenty of room on deck and a small hold – and Rick believed that he knew enough to at least sail it out to sea. After that, he would simply put his trust in God... and in love, true love, which had already guided him here.

He ran back to the jeep and lifted Tabby from the back seat. She was limp and unresisting, almost like a corpse herself. He slung her over a shoulder, alarmed by how light she was, and then released the seatbelt from around Sally. He grabbed hold of her arm and dragged her unceremoniously from the seat, not caring when she fell to the ground. She was dead anyway; further injury mattered not one bit.

He made his way to the boat, a young girl over one shoulder and hauling his dead wife along the ground like a caveman with his mate.

He threw Sally onto the deck of the boat, wincing only slightly at the loud, loose sound she made as she fell. Tabby he lowered gently, taking care not to hurt her.

He took one final glance at the pursuing dead, and then leapt aboard, pushing the boat away from the side with his feet. He was a car's length away from the concrete moorings before the first of the dead halted at the edge, roaring and waving their arms.

He turned away, no longer interested in them.

Sally was crumpled like an abused shop window mannequin. Tabby lay curled in a foetal position near his feet. His heart broke, just as his mind had, and he wished that there were tears left to shed. The poor girl... his surrogate daughter... she should not have to suffer this. It wasn't fair; none of it was fair at all.

He looked around for God, and then looked within, finding the holy spirit cowering in a dark part of himself that he'd left on a distant battlefield. It was now time to let that part out of the darkness and force it into the grey light, where it could take over for a while and allow him to rest.

Rick sat at the bow and stared at the islands, frightened by their appearance. They resembled splinters of rock which had shattered and thrust out of the sea, grasping at the sky. Hundreds of sea birds circled these jagged pinnacles, soaring and landing, then taking flight again. The birds acted as if nothing was unusual. It was nature's cycle continuing even as the earth's dominant species surrendered to nightmare.

Rick sailed by instinct, feeling as if he were channelling Rohmer, and the old man's restless ghost guided his hand. He threw a blanket over Tabby but let her rest. For the first time since the cottage, her eyes were closed and he thought that she might even be sleeping.

You'd have made a great dad. The best.

He closed his eyes and wished that Sally wouldn't talk like that. It reminded him of all the things they would never do, never have. The empty years that now stretched ahead.

"I love you. But I also hate you."

She went quiet, pondering that one. He felt bad for saying it, but he could no longer understand his emotions. It felt like his sense of humanity was dripping away, leaking from the wounds in his psyche, and the closer they got to Rohmer's island the less human he felt.

Fingers of rock stretched upwards, piercing the grey gloom and striving toward something better. Rick guided the boat around the island, and when he saw the red-painted sign he knew instantly that it was the symbol Rohmer had intimated. "You'll know it when you see it," he'd said, not even certain himself how they would identify the island his ex-lover had summoned him to.

But here it was: the island. Sanctuary. The old man had been right; it wasn't a lie or a myth. It was real, and they were here, at last.

A small wooden boat was already tied up at the makeshift landing station, a large rent in its hull; it looked like the vessel had either hit the rocks or someone had deliberately sabotaged it. Rick pulled up alongside the boat, fighting the currents so that he did not hit the rocks. Something told him he might still need the boat, and that the island might not represent the sanctuary Rohmer had claimed it to be. It was too quiet. There was no welcoming party or waiting committee. The whole place felt as dead as the cold, lifeless husks of people he'd left on the shore, raging for his flesh.

Sally was moving. Her legs twitched, the soles of her feet drumming on the deck, and she was writhing against her bonds. The bandages had unravelled and he could now see most of her butchered features. As he watched, she somehow managed to get one hand free. She began to claw at her face, pulling away the bandages, and then tugged at the wadded remains of the cotton wool he had forced back into her throat.

She was awake.

And she was hungry. Oh so very hungry.

He moved over to where she flailed on the deck and grabbed a long rope. He lassoed her, and then carefully wrapped the rope around her body, working it like the coils of a spring and lashing her arms to her sides.

Sally seemed to realise, dimly, what he was doing, and she began to fight against him. But it was too late: she could barely move her arms. The bandages had fallen off completely, and lay at her feet like party favours. Her face was puckered, unrecognisable, and the deep cuts opened and closed, sending him gruesome air kisses. Her mouth, now bereft of teeth, gaped like that of a landed fish. The gums were raw, and they snapped together like a beak.

Once he was satisfied that she was properly restrained, Rick tugged the rope and encouraged her to walk ashore. She stumbled, her co-ordination long gone, and he had to be patient as she limped after him. It would make a comical sight, he thought, if anyone were to see: a man walking his dead wife like an oversized and disobedient dog.

He tied the rope to a sturdy rock and went back for Tabby, lifting her gently and carrying her off the craft. She stirred, her eyes flickering open. "Granddad..." Her eyes held a panicked look, and it took the girl a few moments to get her bearings and recognise Rick. She said nothing more, but at least she was awake and partially focused.

Rick set her down on the ground and grabbed his bag and the rifle from the boat. When he returned ashore, Tabby had moved away from Sally, who was walking in small circles around the rock to which he had tethered her like an unruly beast.

"I'm sorry," he said, not knowing what else to say, or how to say it.

It's okay. We'll be home soon. A new home, where we can be happy. The three of us.

He had finally emerged from the grand illusion that Sally was communicating with him, and realised (or admitted) now that he was putting the words in her torn and twisted mouth. But just because the words were his, and he was making her say what he wanted to hear, didn't mean that they were untrue.

If Sally was in fact capable of speech she *would* be saying all this, and all he was doing was providing her with a voice.

"Are you okay to walk? It's bit of a hike." He stared at Tabby, thinking for a second that she might answer. The girl said nothing, but she did glance up at the craggy rocks they were about to climb.

Rick untied the end of the rope from the boulder and took the lead, heading up. "Stay close to me, but I'll go up first. If there's any trouble, I want to be the one to tackle it." He held the Glock in one hand and the loose end of the rope in the other. Tabby followed in silence, her feet firm on the uneven rock.

A group of small boats had been dumped behind a large granite shelf, their hulls punctured. Whoever had been staying on this island had not intended to leave. Now he knew what had happened to the other boat, the one they'd passed earlier.

He peered over his shoulder at Tabby. The girl was doing okay, keeping up the pace.

If he and Sally had at any point been blessed with a daughter, he would have wished that she were exactly like this girl. Tough, resilient, and filled with so much love that she almost glowed.

It was a steep climb but not a long one. Rick managed it without letting go of the pistol or the rope, but Tabby often had to bend over and drag herself along with her hands, grabbing onto small, dry shrubs and spiky boulders.

Along the way Rick saw several instances of a shape carved into the rock. It was clearly not a natural occurrence; the carvings where too regular, too deliberate. Soon he recognised it as the Egyptian ankh; the symbol of eternal life.

He smiled at the irony.

At the top of the crag sat two small prefabricated sheds, one on the edge and the other set slightly back. A hillock linked the two structures, which signified to Rick that there was some sort of underground compound beneath the sheds. It reminded him of the places they'd used during army training: temporary barracks hastily assembled in far-flung locations. For more than one reason, the end of this journey felt increasingly like he was coming home.

A few signs were attached the sides of the sheds, and there were yet more ankh symbols embossed onto the external walls. One of the signs read *Hummingbird Inc.* Another was a hazard warning announcement detailing what looked like a list of emergency procedures, but it was so weather-beaten that Rick could hardly make out any of the text. Words like 'danger' and the phrase 'ultimate precautions' stood out, but the rest was a faded blur across a disfigured grey board.

The doors of both of the sheds stood open. The far one was charred, as if a fire had been set inside. There was no smoke, no heat, so Rick assumed that the blaze had gone out days ago. The closer shed, the one he now stood beside, showed no signs of destruction, but there was a lot of litter in the entrance. Boxes and cans of food, various torn textbooks, broken medical equipment and computer terminals... someone had really gone to town here and smashed the place up.

Rick at first thought that a dead body was lying half concealed inside the shed. It had no head. The body was badly mutilated, as if it had been flattened somehow; the hands and feet were missing. Rick could not even tell if it were a man or a woman: a body, just another body.

As his eyes became accustomed to the murk inside the shed, he realised that the body was in fact a pile of clothing – a uniform of sorts, consisting of a rumpled grey boiler suit. Other clothing was piled next to it, overflowing from several receptacles and spilling onto the wooden floor. He could now see that the breast pocket had been torn from each suit, as if someone had removed the name tag of these missing workers.

"Wherever we go, we see death. We can't escape it. It's everywhere, in every little thing, at every junction. I can even taste death."

At the sound of her voice, Rick turned towards Tabby, but her face was once again blank, as if she had not uttered a word. Was he simply imagining that she was speaking now, just as he'd been doing all along with Sally?

Madness was now a comfort, a warm bed, a perfect home. He never wanted to be sane again.

The wind was wonderful up here; a sharp, cool phantom that coiled around his head, clearing his mind of the clutter it had accumulated over the past few days – the past few years, if he was honest. He imagined that wind entering his ears, nose, mouth, and cutting through the matter of his brain, scouring his soul.

"Come on," he said, squeezing the Glock. "We have to get to the end of this, if only for your grandfather's sake."

Then he stepped across the threshold and moved inside the shed, and was swallowed by an unearthly darkness.

"Welcome to Sanctuary," said a voice.

CHAPTER THIRTY-NINE

The cell was six by ten paces; Daryl had walked it repeatedly to measure the dimensions of the room. The man who had brought him here seemed reasonable enough, but there was the whiff of madness and neglect about him. He wore a dirty grey boiler suit with the name 'Tim' etched onto the breast and his beard was long and straggly.

Tim had been waiting for Daryl at the top of the bleak rock finger he had climbed, sitting on the stubbly grass and drinking water from a plastic bottle. He'd guided Daryl into the shed and then down into the low tunnels beneath, saying little. Daryl had followed because he could not think what else to do.

They had eventually come out into a wide passage with a series of doors on either side. Each of the doors had windows set into them at head height, but Tim had artfully diverted Daryl's attention so that he could not look inside.

He'd been brought to this cell to 'wash and brush up' in the tiny bathroom, and Tim had quietly disappeared, mumbling something about preparing some food.

Daryl realised immediately that this was some kind of military or government compound, but it was all so basic that it felt like a forgotten relic from the Cold War. With its low ceilings, steel doors, stone walls and floors, there was very little that was even remotely high-tech about the whole set up, and Daryl was even more confused as to what Nutman actually wanted here.

He walked to the door and tried the handle. The fact that it was unlocked startled him; he'd expected to be locked inside like a criminal.

He opened the door.

The corridor outside was cold and bare, and curved away at each end so that he could not see where it led. He went back into the room and picked up the digital camera from the bed. The red warning light was flashing to inform him that the battery was just about flat. He felt sad that the movie was almost over... but perhaps there would be a sequel.

He returned to the door, examined the corridor through the camera lens, and picked a direction at random. Left: the way of all things evil.

The rock platform upon which the compound was seated was tall and narrow, so Daryl estimated that the corridor must curve around in a circle, possibly forming a perimeter to the central rooms. He guessed that Tim had brought him right through the middle, and then led him part of the way around the outer ring.

Soon enough he came to the junction with another corridor, this one straight and lined with grey doors. It was the tunnel he'd walked down earlier. Now he would get his chance to see what was inside those rooms.

He heard the sound of water dripping, the groaning of hidden pipes, and the fractured wheezing of a cheap air conditioning unit. Behind all these were voices; soft, flat, monotonous, they seemed to be chanting. Was this, in fact, the home of some kind of religious cult, hermetic monks hiding out from the end of the world?

"Shit," he muttered. "That old man. He must have been like Mother, clinging to some stupid religion."

Cool air buzzed through poorly installed vents, the sound like a chorus of whispers.

The chanting remained constant, the volume neither increasing nor decreasing; it was eerie, particularly in this banal setting. If he closed his eyes, Daryl could imagine that he was deep within the catacombs of some Italian church vault and not crawling around inside a hollowed out, bird-shit-covered rock.

He came to the first door.

Slowly he approached it, reaching out to touch it with the palm of one hand. The steel was cold, impersonal, a barricade meant to keep something in as well as deny prying eyes. He had to stand on tiptoe to see through the glass; the weirdoes who made their home here must all be taller than him. Everyone was taller than him, it had always bothered him.

The glass was grubby but he was able to see into the room. It was sparsely furnished with a bank of old fashioned computers, the free-standing kind like those in early James Bond films. They looked ridiculous: ceiling-height towers of flashing lights and tape decks, with tickertape print-outs piled in wire-mesh baskets on the floor.

Against the far wall there was a gurney, and on it was a painfully thin, naked woman. She lay flat on her back. There was a sheet draped across her lower torso, but her bony upper body was bare. The low temperature had made her nipples hard; gooseflesh striated her pale skin. Daryl gaped at the woman, unsure what to think of the scene. There were wires taped to her temples and between her breasts; they trailed back to the absurd computers, where they were connected to black plastic terminals.

Daryl moved on without trying the door. He did not like the look of the woman, and was damned if he wanted to be on the other side of the door if she woke up.

The next door was more promising. Through the small glass window he viewed more modern equipment: desks and chairs, laptop computers, flat screen monitors, slim-line terminals. The walls were covered with computer printouts – graphs and bar charts; 3D graphic models and photographs – and religious iconography. There were wooden crucifixes, paintings of the Madonna and child, even a Day-Glo Jesus standing on a crowded bookshelf, arms held aloft to welcome the righteous.

Daryl pushed open the door.

He liked unlocked doors; they were welcoming.

The room was very cold; the air conditioning was obviously set at a level to cool the computer apparatus. He walked around, examining the posters and pictures and cheesy religious artefacts. Mother's room had contained similar items, and over the years he had grown to loathe them. His vision shimmered, blurring, so he raised the camera and took it all in through the lens. That was better: things were clearer when viewed as a sequence of isolated images.

A central desk was flanked by two main filing cabinets, and on the shelves were hundreds of box files marked with dates. From the files he examined, the contents went back to the mid nineteen-sixties, and those were just the ones left out in the open.

He picked a file at random. It was dated a few years before.

Opening the file, Daryl saw that it was filled with reports and memos. They outlined some kind of medical tests, pertaining to a major breakthrough. Something called 'The Ankh Derivative' was referenced throughout. From what he could make out, the experiments involved some kind of toxic plant from the Amazon, something discovered in the late '50s by a German anthropologist named Hoffman. The plant had been synthesised and a drug produced.

He went through more files. One of them outlined US army test subjects in Vietnam: they had been given the drug and went on a killing spree, mutilating the bodies of VC collaborators in a small village called Tai-Mah.

There was a memo from an American government official, which essentially presented the plan for covering up the massacre.

Daryl put down the file and picked up another. Here he read about a political uprising in Italy. 1976. Bodies from a morgue in central Rome that got up and walked, attacking the general public, causing a minor riot. Another major cover-up was orchestrated, blaming the Cosa Nostra for everything.

There were too many to count. The governments of the world had been hiding this information for decades, conducting their immoral tests and burning the evidence of their failures.

Daryl was impressed by the ruthlessness of what had been going on.

"It all started so well."

Daryl spun around, dropping the file on the floor, where it clattered like a gunshot. Another man – not Tim, but someone equally as spaced-out – stood in the open doorway. His face was etched with black cruciform tattoos; holy wounds that ironically contorted his features into something devilish.

"We meant well at the start... at the beginning of all this.

"Hoffman's plant was first used by a lost tribe to make their enemies into *zombis*: not the type you see in films, but shuffling, somnambulistic echoes of people who were used as slaves.

"When we first brought the plant into the civilised world, it was meant to be used to synthesise a new drug, an anaesthetic inherent in its sap. It took patients so far under during surgery that they were almost dead. They became very cooperative, and open to suggestion. Life signs were minimal. The heart rate dropped alarmingly. By the end of the '60s the drug was almost ready – we called it 'The Ankh Derivative' because it represented a step towards extended life. If we could put people that far under, then who knew what medical miracles could be performed..."

The man's eyes were blazing above his inked cheeks.

Daryl backed up, his hands scrabbling across the desk at his side. He fingered a staple gun, pens, pencils, a pencil sharpener, Post-it notes.

A letter opener.

"Like all things that start off being about the greater good, it was hijacked by those seeking power. There was an accident... a mistake. A team working with the plant somehow managed to extract a further toxin from the root. This one was much more powerful. They were all deeply religious, this team, and they worked in an atmosphere more like a cathedral than a lab. They brought in members of the clergy at gunpoint and had enforced prayer breaks, they read their bibles... and *something* happened. It was like a synthesis of science and the supernatural, and what they created was a fusion of the two ideals. All kinds of holy relics were ground down to powder and synthesised – the finger bones of Saints and martyrs, a supposed drop of Christ's blood from a church shrine in Bruges, even what was meant to be a cutting from the Turin Shroud. It was crazy."

Daryl clutched the sharp little blade, wrapping his fingers around the cold shaft.

The man lowered his head. "They blurred the limits between life and death and tore a hole into the eternal. What leaked out of that hole then combined with the Ankh Derivative to produce something – well, something *terrible*."

Daryl took a step forward. He noticed then that the man was weeping: a holy fool shedding tears for what he had done – what they had *all* done.

"I'm sorry. We've brought many people here and used them. Used them as guinea pigs, test subjects to help us go further; deeper, darker. Then we used them as meat for the ones we keep in the corral. The dead ones we examine, chart, and vivisect, trying to find some kind of meaning in their condition."

Just as Daryl raised the blade, the man looked up. His eyes were beatific, as if he had seen the face of something wonderful; the face of God or the Devil or something between the two.

"Why are you telling me this?" said Daryl, ready to strike the man down.

"Because there's nobody else *to* tell. We're finished here. A joke. A handful of broken men looking to God for an answer... but we don't even know what the question is." He paused, catching his breath before the big finish.

"Two weeks ago the transformed and mutated Ankh Derivative was released into the atmosphere. I thought it was another accident, but it wasn't. There are no accidents. They did it on purpose, as part of some larger, top secret test. Once it was let out, there was no turning back." He fell to his knees and exposed his throat. "There can never be a way back, not now. This is just the beginning, the curtain raiser: what follows it through will be so much worse. "

Daryl stepped forward and slashed at the man's throat. Blood spattered in a thin arc, spotting the desks and the computer screens and the filing cabinets.

With his other hand Daryl raised the camera and watched the man die.

Then he stabbed the man through the eye and into the brain, just to make sure that he could not come back for revenge.

Moving away from the bloody corpse, he swung the camera in an arc around the cramped room, taking in the shelves and the drawers and the crazy décor.

There can never be a way back, not now. This is just the beginning, the curtain raiser: what follows it through will be so much worse.

The man's words echoed around Daryl's skull, like the backing track to his movie-in-the-mind. He remembered the faces he thought he'd seen forming in the clouds, the sense that something greater than himself was peering down from far above.

Then he pointed the camera at the motionless corpse, following a trail of blood as it snaked from the sliced neck and across the uneven stone floor.

"Fucking maniac," he muttered.

CHAPTER FORTY

"We used to have funding. This was once a major site dedicated to medical advancement."

Rick kept the Glock pointed at the bearded man as he spoke, but the man did not seem to notice. He just kept talking as he led them down a narrow staircase, along a low hallway, and into a wider area that was filled with medical supplies and boxes of canned foods.

"We were working on something big, a project that would change everything about the way we live... and the way we die."

Rick was barely listening.

Tabby gripped his hand and stared into space; Sally followed close behind, her mutilated head twitching. She was still attached to the rope. The man had not even mentioned her condition, just thanked Rick for bringing her. "We need fresh subjects," he said. "To find a cure." The last few words had seemed like an afterthought, something tacked on to garner his trust.

Rick didn't trust the man as far as he could spit – which wasn't very far as his throat had dried up hours ago.

"This is all we have left, now." The man kept walking, his long strides putting distance between him and his guests. "The rest of the world is tearing itself apart at the seams, so we simply continue our work. It's all we know. We run the tests and tabulate the results, then we run them all again and look for discrepancies. God is in the minutiae, the tiny, seemingly inconsequential details. But they *are* of consequence, believe me. That's how this all started: with someone forgetting to monitor the minor details."

He quickly genuflected, making the sign of the cross.

"Where is everyone? Your bosses? The military?" Rick felt like shooting the man just to shut him up, but he needed answers more than silence.

"There's no one else left. Just me and a handful of lab technicians. Even the project supervisors are gone. We used them as subjects for a while. Some of them are still in the corral, waiting to be fed."

If Rick was crazy, then he also recognised the madness in this man. He was long gone, his mind was blown. There was nothing here that Rohmer had promised: not sanctuary or salvation, not friends and saviours. Nothing. Just like out there, back in the world.

"So you can't help us? You can do nothing for my wife?" He already knew the answer, but needed to hear it spoken aloud, as if that would make it real and give him the encouragement he needed to put his final plan into action.

"I'm sorry," said the man, without even breaking his stride.

Rick's body clicked into combat mode, the remnants of his mind flapped like a sheet in the wind.

"Where's this corral you mentioned?"

The man stumbled once, and then resumed his regular rhythm. "It's at the end of this tunnel. A doorway marked with a red symbol. You'll know it when you see it."

"Thank you."

Rick shot him once in the back of the head. The sound of the gunshot echoed loudly, reverberating through the stone rooms and hallways before finally giving up the ghost.

No one came to investigate.

Rick was alone, with his dead wife and his comatose daughter. *The family that slays together stays together,* he thought, recalling the tagline from some old horror movie. He pulled Sally's rope; Tabby simply followed, a lame dog trailing behind its master.

He kept going, glancing into the rooms along the tunnel. Behind one door was another man in a grey boiler suit. He was staring at a TV screen, watching a video recording of some old game show. Rick kicked open the door and shot him in the face, not even pausing for breath. He shot the television, too, not really understanding why but feeling better for the act of destruction. Television and the media were part of the old ways, the time before.

When he arrived at the door that was marked with the bright red ankh, he stopped and stared at it, his thoughts empty.

Sally moaned.

Don't do this. I love you.

"I have to." He opened the door next to the one which led to the corral, and stepped into the room. One wall was covered with TV screens, each one displaying a different series of images. There were news clips, clearly filmed before and during the madness outside; amateur footage filmed on mobile phones and handheld cameras played on a continuous loop; the panicked faces of officials and world leaders filled the room, their dead eyes and slack mouths reciting the prayers of a lost world.

The soundtrack was muted on all these televisions, and in their place was being played a strange soundtrack. Religious chanting: low, reverberant male voices repeating a Latin lament over and over, their separate voices blending into a single dirge. If this was a prayer, it was a dirty one, something about the underlying cadence made him feel unclean.

The sound was maddening. Rick began to fire the pistol blindly, hoping to hit the hidden speakers and silence those terrible tones forever. The other voices – his voices; the ones he carried within him – joined in the chant, taking up the refrain and filling his head with the profound sadness of its litany.

"Shut up!"

He let off round after round, reloaded with his last clip, and then kept firing until finally he hit the target and the chanting ceased. Tears painted his cheeks; his eyes were burning. A static hiss filled the room, coming from a speaker he still could not see.

"*Nnnnnngeeeee!*"

It was Sally, but this time her voice was not trapped inside his head. This time it was out in the world, straining at the tawdry remains of reality.

"*Nngyeee!*"

He dropped the pistol, fell to his knees, and raised his head to the low ceiling, and cried out her name, again and again and again...

And someone stepped through the open doorway, entering the room with slow, deliberate steps.

CHAPTER FORTY-ONE

hungry

CHAPTER FORTY-TWO

"And so we meet again." Daryl stepped forward, his eyes focused on Sally's beautiful torn face. Had he really done that? Was such gorgeous carnage the result of his own fair hand?

If time did not heal, then it certainly made the wounds prettier.

"I'm glad you managed to turn off that racket. Fucking awful, wasn't it?" he took in the sight of Nutman on his knees, unarmed and begging for destruction. It was a fitting final image, really, and he slowly raised the camera to record it for posterity.

The battery light flashed madly, and then it went out. The automatic lens cap closed over the aperture, prematurely ending the film.

"Shit. I was hoping that wouldn't happen." He shoved the tiny camera into his jacket pocket and adjusted his grip on the letter opener. He had already proved that it was a thoroughly lethal weapon, and Nutman seemed too far gone to fight back.

He stared at Sally: her artistically starved carcass, the way the already decaying skin clung tightly to her face, taut across the cheekbones like plastic sheeting. The wounds were wonderful; extra little mouths ready to swallow his seed.

He ignored the little girl. She was not important; a mere bit player, a non-speaking extra. When the audience departed, they would forget she had even been involved.

Sally turned her attention on him, her lower jaw hinging open. She had no teeth, just blackening swollen gums. Her lips were torn, frayed, and the skin around her mouth was paper-thin. He imagined that he could see her tongue through the almost translucent sheet of her cheek, wriggling like a fat black snake in its den.

He giggled, and then fought to regain control.

Control was important now. He had come too far to give himself over to hysteria.

"I'm afraid this is the final scene, the one where the anti-hero kills the protagonist and gets the girl. It was always going to end this way. The best films always do." He smiled, enjoying the direction the scene was taking.

Nutman did not respond; instead he stared at the floor, his eyes narrowed, his hands folded loosely in his lap. He was a wasted man, a shadow, a wisp. There was barely anything of him left to kill. Daryl almost felt sorry for him – at least he might have done if he were still human.

He circled the policeman, examining his torn uniform, his loose arms, the lack of expression on his defeated face. He had come so far, gone through so many horrors, only to end his time on his knees. It was almost poetic, in a twisted kind of way. Daryl savoured the moment, tasting it, touching it, experiencing an almost sexual satisfaction from prolonging it. Time stretched, broke, and then reformed again, lifting him up, spinning him around, and then setting him down in the exact same place where he'd started.

"Oh, my." His words were not enough, but they pleased him. "My, my, my. What to say? What to do? Isn't this almost an anticlimax? I've rehearsed the moment so many times in my head, but it never played out like this. Usually we fought. You were stronger, of course, but I was always your intellectual superior. Eventually my brains always outdid your brawn, and I waltzed off into the sunset with Sally, my Sally, where I could enjoy killing her for all eternity."

Nutman shuffled on his knees. He placed the palms of his hands flat on the ground. He then began to make a low whining noise at the back of his throat, which increased steadily in pitch and volume. It was slightly irritating, and Daryl raised the blade, ready to silence him with a delicate flick of the wrist.

"Please," he said. "Let's not be undignified about this. Leave that to me, later, when I'm alone with your wife."

He was giggling uncontrollably now, unable to stop. But it did not matter; why not have a little fun now the game was just about over?

The television sets around the room were smashed, apart from a single screen in the corner. Religious imagery played out silently on the screen: static images of the crucifixion, crowd scenes featuring men and women in white robes, shots of Roman soldiers constructing huge wooden crosses. Then there came a scene portraying a white, bearded Christ on the cross, his hands and feet nailed to the timber axis. It was the same figure from Daryl's childhood vision in the dentist's chair – the one who had passed on the cryptic message about the smell of colours. Christ hung there, in that famous pose, and watched as people gathered beneath him. One by one these followers looked up, and each of them was a rotting corpse, a reanimated cadaver.

Christ wrenched one hand from the crossbeam, the thick iron nail tearing his palm. Then he reached down into his loincloth, took out his holy penis, and began to urinate on the watching masses, anointing them. Daryl saw that Mother was part of the crowd. She stood there with a look of adoration on her shrivelled face as blessed piss poured down into her open mouth...

Daryl blinked and the images scattered like insects. The screen was blank, a large crack bisecting it from top to bottom.

He knelt down beside Nutman placing an arm around the man's shoulders. He ran the blade across his cheek, down along the side of his neck, and finally across his throat. Nutman tilted his head, looking up and exposing the underside of his chin, baring the soft, yielding meat.

He wanted to die.

"*Ungyee!*"

Daryl looked up, startled. His grip slackened.

Sally was swaying on the balls of her feet. She had gathered up the end of the rope that was bound around her and was toying with it in her small hands. She stared at Daryl, nothing but a depthless hunger in her ruined eyes. Then, slowly, she began to stagger towards him, dropping the end of the rope and taking awkward little steps across the cold stone floor. Her feet made a scraping sound; her jaw clicked as she opened and closed her mouth lightning fast, the speed of her response belying the fact that she was moving so slowly.

Daryl was hypnotised. The woman he loved was finally coming for him, ready to fall into his arms and be swept away into a brand new form of horror.

"I love you," he whispered, his arm slipping from around Nutman's neck.

"*Ungyee!*"

"I know you are. I know you're hungry. So am I, but I think we both hunger for different things. Maybe when I'm done with you, we can get you some food. I could keep you fed as long as you keep dying for me. It's a deal, yes?"

He stood, feeling all-powerful, like a god. Indeed, he was about to commence upon a godly act, to carry out godly things: life and death, love and hate, beginnings and endings. A heady cocktail of creation, all mixed up and with a cherry on top...

Everything after that moment happened far too quickly for Daryl to properly assimilate.

The policeman suddenly grabbed him by the arm, pulling him round and hitting him in the face with a clenched fist that felt like solid rock. Sally toppled forward, uncertain on her feet and falling face-down on the floor. The little girl (who he'd already forgotten) appeared in the doorway. She was grinning. Freckles formed a question mark on her pale cheek. Her dark red hair was lank and greasy.

"I've let them out," she said, her face calm, white and shining, like that of an angel. "I've let them out of the corral." A *vengeful* angel.

Then the girl was gone, as if she had never really been there and was just a mad vision, an angelic avatar summoned by his freewheeling imagination. He glanced again at the television screen; the girl was there, too, and he watched as she ran along the tunnel and out into the main area. Then she went through the outer door and was gone, lost to his dimming sight.

When he looked back at the doorway where the girl had stood, he saw a nude man with deep diagonal gashes across his belly and chest, hands grasping the door frame, bald head pivoting like that of a strange giant bird as he heaved himself into the room.

"Fuck off!" Daryl snarled and lunged for the policeman's gun, grabbing it and hoping that it would work. He went down on his side, turned, and aimed the gun at Nutman's wide, avid face.

Nutman seemed to stir again from his stupor. Before Daryl had the chance to pull the trigger, he grabbed the gun and tried to wrestle it from Daryl's grip. The two men rolled on the floor, kicking and punching and biting. Daryl thought for a moment that he might even gain the upper hand, but then he was flat on his back and Nutman was straddling him, beating him around the face and neck with his fists.

This scene was so very different to the one he'd described.

The gun was lost, perhaps dropped in the confusion.

Daryl closed his eyes, barely even feeling the pain.

Behind the closed lids he met Sally, who was there waiting for him. She opened her arms and he fell into them, his cheek on her soft breast, her blood warming his face.

When he heard something crack he did not even realise that it was his cheekbone. The sensation of his neck breaking was nothing, a mere trifle. He was at last with his love, his one and only love, and they were floating above it all, bathed in a deep red glow that could only be blood

blood

red light

dark echoes release falling stopping hungry quiet rising faster light up bright white feelings gone hungry pain gone life none sound fury hungry room motion smell hungry sorrow need memory sally love meat hungry

Rick had broken the bastard's neck with his bare hands, twisting, twisting, until the bones ground together with a sound like boots crunching on gravel.

The kid had gone still; all struggles had ceased. He was dead.

He was dead for a moment.

And then he came back.

Rick scrabbled on all fours for the Glock, scurrying across the floor to locate the weapon, wherever it had fallen during the scuffle. Finally his hand fell upon it, and he almost raised it to lips and kissed it. Instead he turned, aimed, and fired, all in one quick, fluid motion.

The kid's forehead creased, and then broke apart, a huge flap of bone unhinging and hanging by a thread of skin. Blood poured down over his battered face and his body crumpled, deflating, dying again.

Dead. Really dead.

Sally was rolling on the floor, trapped by the rope he'd used to restrain her. Behind her, a horde of the dead were stumbling through the open doorway and into the room. They were in different stages of decay, and all of them were naked. He remembered the discarded grey boiler suits with the name tags removed, the untidy stacks of clothing left upstairs in the dark of the empty shed.

He scuttled over to Sally, held her, fought to calm her.

"I'm here, baby. I'm here."

She made baby-sounds: small moans and groans and belching noises. Ever since she had attempted to speak, to form words in her dead throat, the voice he'd supplied her with had faded. He doubted that he would ever hear that voice again.

"Come on, Sally. That's it, my love."

He dragged her backwards, moving across the stone floor on his backside. The dead people were crowding the doorway, jamming themselves into the narrow gap. Luckily this meant that they were stuck fast, and could not make headway into the room. It was a slight delay, but all he really needed.

He knew what he was going to do, and he required very little time to finalise things.

His madness had come full circle and become instead a new form of sanity: for the first time in his life he saw things clearly, as they really were, and he was almost happy.

"I hope you're okay, Tabby. My daughter. I hope you got out alive."

He backed up against the far wall, expertly untying the rope from around Sally's waist and midriff. He released her with ease, and then pushed away from her, taking a deep breath to prepare himself for what came next.

The corpses in the doorway were struggling free, as if fighting against their own decay. Eventually one of them collapsed inside the room, his momentum carrying him over the threshold. He stood and stared, inspecting his new surroundings. A woman joined him, one arm missing, and half her face in crimson ruin. Together they began to advance upon Rick, smelling the meat of him, dancing the dead dance and eager to satiate their hunger.

"Sally. I love you, and I have always loved you. I give you everything. I offer you my heart and my soul... and my flesh."

He tore off his stab vest and the shirt beneath, baring his heaving chest, exposing the wounded heart that beat beneath his aching ribs.

"*I give you my heart.*"

Sally struggled to her knees, suddenly keen and alert.

The dead moved ever closer, groaning and hissing.

Sally leaned in close, her jaw dropping, the tortured gums bared. Her dead breath chilled him, penetrating the muscle and going in deep, straight for the innards.

"Eat me," said Rick, closing his eyes and giving himself over to true love.

"Eat. Me."

As long as she left enough of him to return afterward, they could still be together again, undead and happy and existing on this rugged island, hungry for all eternity.

She fell upon him, her gums barely penetrating the flesh despite the strength of her jaws as they worked at his chest. He felt them nipping at his arm, his shoulder, his throat. He threw back his head to aid her, opened his arms in a wide embrace. Sally's hands raked at the soft flesh of his throat, finally breaking the skin. She tore at the flesh, tugging the slit wider, pushing deeper, and then she hauled her arms down, ripping off his skin like a thin layer of clothing.

Rick ignored the agony and felt the love... so much aching love.

Surely it was meant to hurt this way; the blood-bright agony was the price you paid for feeling so deeply, loving so truly.

He bled for her, for his darling wife, and thought that he could not imagine a more fitting end, a better way to die; and when at last she tore the fluttering heart from his shattered chest, he opened his eyes and stared into her lovely wreck of a face, watching her consume the very best part of him – the part which had belonged to her all along.

CHAPTER FORTY-THREE

dark echoes release falling stopping hungry quiet rising faster light up bright white feelings gone hungry pain gone life none sound fury hungry room motion smell hungry meat husband rick

rick?

EPILOGUE

The young girl lay on her back in the wooden boat and looked up at the sky. It was pale blue, almost grey. Wispy white clouds hung motionless, strung across the faded expanse like fine cobwebs in an attic.

Enormous faces seemed to form above that cosmic ceiling, peering down at her with vague interest. A group of birds wheeled overhead – seagulls foraging for carrion – but they remained at a height, afraid to fly any lower. Their cries were muted by the distance, the tiny screams of lost souls.

The sun was weak and insubstantial; a light slowly going out in that huge attic, perhaps forever.

The faces receded, disinterested for now in her lowly existence.

The girl could not remember her name.

She had no memory of how she had got here, in the little rowboat.

Her arms and legs were aching and there were cuts on her

knees and shins. The skin of her hands was lacerated. Fresh blood stained her clothing.

She sat up and stared at the distant shoreline, blinking as she examined the lines of the dead who stood calmly looking out to sea, as if waiting for something. They stood in neat rows, stiff and unmoving; their white faces were a series of smudges atop their ragged shoulders. One or two of them raised their arms and pointed out to sea, towards her; others followed suit, setting off a chain reaction. Before she turned away, most of them were pointing at her, singling her out. For an instant the girl thought that she recognised one of them, but could not be certain.

The girl's boat was moving away from the dead, drifting gradually out to sea, buoyed on the strong current. She was glad: they looked scary and threatening.

They seemed ravenous.

The girl hoped that she would be lucky enough to run into a ship and be rescued. Otherwise she might simply drift until she starved to death. And then she would return, weighed down with a hungry heart that could never be satisfied.

THE END

GARY MCMAHON's fiction has appeared in magazines and anthologies in the UK and US and has been reprinted in both *The Mammoth Book of Best New Horror* and *The Year's Best Fantasy and Horror.* He is the British-Fantasy-Award-nominated author of *Rough Cut, All Your Gods Are Dead, Dirty Prayers, How to Make Monsters, Rain Dogs,* and has edited an anthology of original novellas titled *We Fade to Grey.* Forthcoming are the collections *Different Skins, Pieces of Midnight* and *To Usher, the Dead.* You can visit Gary's website at www.garymcmahon.com

TOMES OF THE DEAD

EMPIRE OF SALT

WESTON OCHSE

Now read the first chapter from the next
exciting *Tomes of The Dead* novel

ISBN: 978-1-906735-32-6

UK RELEASE: January 2010
US RELEASE: April 2010

£6.99/$7.99

WWW.ABADDONBOOKS.COM

CHAPTER ONE

"Sorry, Frank. No more fish."

Frank stared over his empty beer glass at Lazlo Oliver, the bartender and owner of the Space Station Restaurant. Frank's used car salesman expression melted. His eyes narrowed. His grin receded, exposing a mouthful of broken and grimy teeth. "What do you mean, no more fish?"

"No more. Sorry, Frank." Lazlo squared his shoulders. At six foot three, he was a big man for all of his seventy years and still in pretty good shape. He hoped there'd be no trouble, but with Frank you never knew. Sometimes the drunk would teeter off into the night, and sometimes he'd go off like a roadside bomb.

"But it's fresh fish. It's real fresh, Laz." Frank reached down and jerked a string of tilapia from a battered Styrofoam cooler and held them over the bar. Somewhere between the hard-drinking age of thirty and sixty, the years slipped away as he grinned like a teenage boy, proud of a day's catch.

Lazlo looked at the milk white eyes of the three tilapia, mouths gaping around the waxed yellow stringer. The scales were still a mosaic of bright greens. Sometimes Frank would get red tide fish he found rotting on the beach and try and pass them off as freshly caught. Not this time. These had been caught this afternoon, probably between Frank waking up after passing out last night and this evening's dinner and beer. Such was Frank's drunken cycle: drink, sleep, fish, drink, sleep, fish.

"Listen, Frank. I'd love to take your fish, I really would, but I have three freezers full of the damned things and, if I were to bet, half of them would be from you. Honestly, Frank, I have fish coming out my eyeballs."

Frank looked back and forth from his fish to the bartender. For a moment he seemed as if he was going to cry.

Lazlo stepped away and wiped down the bar. Gertie was in the kitchen. By the looks of it, she was almost finished closing it down for the night. Business had been brisk until dark, then had fallen off like usual, leaving only locals and the occasional tourist too stunned by the reality of the Salton Sea to know that they never should have stopped here.

He refilled beer for Andy, their local daft. The man claimed to be a rocket scientist but looked more like a mad scientist. The only thing more guaranteed than Frank trying to trade fish for beer was Andy sitting in his usual spot, mumbling to himself, doodling in his little notebook as he sat, with his ever-present tortoise shell glasses and clothes so wrinkled it was as if he'd bought them that way.

José sat by the door. Laz didn't know if the man was illegal or not, but he was the all around handyman no one could do without. He didn't talk much and had a haunted look in his eyes. Whatever the reason for the expression, the rail-thin Mexican took his own counsel.

The Cain and Ables, their real surname was Beachy, were sitting at their own table. They'd come in for fish and now sat and talked low amongst themselves. The Space Station was the area bar, restaurant, and general store, which is why the Amish family of five more often than not found themselves in for a night's dinner.

Then there was the tourist from Maine, who'd stopped on his way to Los Angeles, and ended up sitting down next to Frank. Laz never caught his name, but it didn't matter. In the morning he'd never see the man again. He could tell by the look in his eyes and the eyes of the other seven tourists who sat at tables, that none of them would ever return.

Laz had seen it a thousand times. A tourist family tired of the long trip through Texas, New Mexico and Arizona, riding along Interstate 10 or 8 towards the Pacific Coast, too blitzed to drive any farther, saw the old signs pointing to the Salton Sea promising resorts and fun in the sun. Instead of driving another four or five hours to their destination, they'd convince themselves that staying the night in an 'Ultra-Cheap' Seaside Resort would be a reward for long hours in the car. Their intent would be to wake up the next morning, and maybe after a morning swim at the resort, drive the rest of the way at a leisurely pace. But when they finally saw the dark, beer-colored Salton Sea and rolled down the windows to breathe the ever-present bouquet of rotting fish, they probably hadn't known what hit them. Most of the time they turned their cars around and continued on their way, eager to be free of the awful stench and horrific sight, but there were always a few who decided to tough it out.

How bad could it be? they thought.

The smell will go away, they told themselves.

But it never did, the smell of dead and rotting fish working its way into everything – their clothes, the fabric of the seats, the carpet, their hair, their skin, even into the depths of their luggage.

"Get away from me!"

Lazlo grabbed his bat from beneath the bar and rushed over to where Frank was manhandling the man from Maine.

"Come on, one beer," Frank begged. "Three fish for one beer. My God, man. Can't you people do math in Maine?"

"Let him go," Laz commanded in his characteristic deep voice.

Frank had one hand on the man's collar and his other holding the fish up between them. The tourist's nose seemed to touch the middle fish, while the lowest on the string rested against the man's T-shirt.

"But Laz, he wants to trade."

"Frank, if I have to tell you again, I'm going to knock that head of yours right out the door." Laz brandished the bat. "Do the math, Frank. One bat! One head!"

Frank glared at Laz like a cornered rat.

"Go sleep it off, Frank."

Frank hesitated another moment, then let the tourist go and backed away. His eyes narrowed as tears converged. With a sob, he grabbed his Styrofoam cooler, cradled it like a child, then ran out the door. Everyone was silent for a few moments, then resumed their conversations.

Laz hated when Frank got this way. He wouldn't remember what he'd done the next day, but damned if Laz was going to let him come back in as if nothing happened.

He replaced the bat and hollered at Maude.

"Watch the register, sugar. I'll be back in a few."

His fifty-five year old ex-girlfriend, who still worked as a waitress, glared at him. He grinned in return. Their relationship, along with Gertie's, his other ex-girlfriend who was the cook, was one predicated upon stoked anger.

Laz walked past the walk-in freezer and continued out the back. He grabbed the trash Gertie had bagged by the door and hauled it to the cans across the sand-covered alley. He tossed the bags in, returned to the back door, reached inside, and brought back his cigarettes and a notebook.

Laz took a short walk to a retaining wall and sat on it. He lit a cigarette and deeply inhaled the welcome smoke. One thing that could be said about the smell of cigarettes was that it hid the stench of rotting fish.

From his vantage point on the wall, it was ten meters to the edge of the water. In the moonlight, he could make out a dozen small shadows. Fish. More dead fish. Would it never end?

In the light of the bar's sign, he opened his notebook and turned to the first unused page. He pulled a pen from his pocket and wrote today's date and, after checking his watch, added the time beneath. He wrote a few sentences in what appeared to be a nonsensical code, then sat back and began to watch the sea.

He'd been keeping track since he first noticed the lights. It hadn't taken long for him to find a pattern to them, so on nights when he knew they were going to occur, he made sure to bear witness and record the events as he saw them. He wasn't a scientist, nor was he very smart in a bookish sort of way, but he knew that if he watched and listened long enough, he might understand what was going on.

He didn't have long to wait.

First it came as a gentle lightening of the water. From a black to gray, the water brightened as if it were powered by an invisible source. He inhaled the last of the smoke, held his breath and tossed the cigarette into the sand. The pressure began to build in his chest, but he kept the smoke trapped. He knew it wouldn't be long. As the pressure built and built, he *hoped* it wouldn't be long.

Then it happened.

The water flashed a brilliant green, then returned to gray.

He exhaled slowly, relishing the taste of the menthol cigarette. He grinned as he watched another flash. Lasting less than a second, if he blinked at the wrong time, he'd miss it.

Then a third time, it flashed.

Then darkness.

Then nothing.

Whatever it was, it was over.

Laz looked at the time and began to scribble down his observations and thoughts. It took longer than plain writing, because of the code he used.

A faraway scream made him look up for a second. He waited to see if the sound would come again, but he didn't hear anything except the gentle lapping of the almost dead sea. As Laz thought about the sound be became certain that it had sounded like Frank. Laz shook his head. There, but by the grace of God, goes a drunk. Laz knew that it could have just as easily been him had he not been able to conquer his own demons.

He heard the sound of the back door opening and closing, probably Maude or Gertie looking for him, wanting to rehash some old slight or beer-soaked memory. He'd let them have at him once he finished. The sound of feet shuffling through the sand was accompanied by the horrible stench of rot.

"Frank, is that you? I told you to go sleep it off."

The sound came closer.

"Frank, you really need to get –"

Lazlo was jerked from his perch.

"What the *fuck*?"

He was hurled to the ground so hard his ribs cracked. The air left him and he gasped, desperate to breathe. Framed by the neon sign of a space station, that served as the restaurant's logo, stood something man-sized, green skin a match to the green on the sign.

"Who–?"

Instead of answering, the strange man fell upon him. Lazlow fought to keep him away, but the other's strength was unbelievable. Laz gagged at the smell of decay. His attacker's glowing yellow eyes stared through him. Part of his brain registered the glow and wondered how.

Laz kneed the thing in the side, sending it off balance and into the sand. Rolling the other way, Laz struggled to his feet, then began to run. But instead of back inside, he headed off down the beach because the thing blocked his way.

After a dozen meters, Laz turned to look, hoping the thing had been a figment of his imagination, or perhaps his body's opening salvo of dementia. But he wasn't to be so lucky. It was after him.

Laz kept running, but felt his strength already beginning to wane. He was seventy years old and not made for flight. He could take care of himself with the likes of Frank, but against... against... what was he against? A black and white image came to his mind of black water and a lagoon and a creature rising to the surface to carry away a vivacious blonde. The Creature from the Black Lagoon?

He was breathing heavy now and his legs were on fire. He felt himself slowing against his protestations. Try as he might, he couldn't keep going. So with a cry of desperation, he stopped, turned and brought his hands up like a professional boxer.

And still the thing came on. Laz couldn't make out its features in the darkness, but the eyes glowed an unearthly yellow.

When it came near, Laz swung and hit it in the side of the head. It was like hitting rotting fish. He swung again and hit, with the same result. He tried to dance out of the creature's way, but tripped on the sand and went down in a sprawl.

The creature landed on top of him. Like before, Laz held it at arm's reach. Now he could hear teeth gnashing, but curiously no breaths. In fact, he couldn't feel the chest move at all. The skin radiated a deep sea cold.

Jesus-Mary-Christ in a basket! It's not alive!

Laz felt his arms weaken and the creature took advantage, pushing through until it was within Lazlo's embrace. Rotting lips kissed his cheek, then pain exploded as broken teeth came away with flesh. The creature swallowed, lifting its head to the sky, then fell upon Laz again. The speed and ferocity of the attack increased until its head and hands were a blur.

Lazlow tried to scream, but the intensity of the bites kept him from taking a breath. The second before he died, Lazlow understood what was being done to him.

He was being eaten.

Eaten!

And then death claimed him.

For information on this and other titles,
visit www.abaddonbooks.com